Passion Song

"Damn you, damn your black soul!" she spat at him.

"Aye, damn me to hell, Lucy! Hate me and damn me!" But even above the wild, angry wrath of the storm, she heard the desperation in his voice, remembered the countess's words that night: *There are some people in whom the darkness lies very deep* . . . She stopped fighting him, but still he held her, his grip like iron.

"Hate me, Lucy," he said again, only this time the words sounded like a prayer. His hands slid up over her throat, catching in her hair. "Oh, Christ, Lucy," he whispered brokenly. "I want you so much that I think it will tear me apart."

And then he kissed her, drank in the taste of her like a man who'd been dying of thirst for a thousand years.

PASSION SONG

CATHERINE FITZGERALD

AVON BOOKS ◆ NEW YORK

For Nancy,
logically and lovingly

AVON BOOKS
A division of
The Hearst Corporation
105 Madison Avenue
New York, New York 10016

First Avon Books Printing: May 1989

AVON TRADEMARK REG. U.S. PAT. OFF. AND IN OTHER COUNTRIES, MARCA REGISTRADA, HECHO EN U.S.A.

Printed in the U.S.A.

K-R 10 9 8 7 6 5 4 3 2 1

Let the world slide, let the world go;
A fig for care, and a fig for woe!
If I can't pay, why I can owe,
And death makes equal the high and low.

—John Heywood, *Be Merry Friends*

Part I

Chapter 1

In the light of a brass oil lamp that a widow from March Street had left with her and then died without redeeming, Lucy Jones counted up the coins in the till. After she subtracted the half-pence and farthings she'd put there at the start of the day, she jotted down both numbers in the open book lying beside the coins.

As she did, she glanced at the squiggles and numbers printed across the top of the page. July, 1585. She could read the numbers, but she only knew the month because the page was the seventh in the account book she'd bought from the stationer at the start of the new year. How anyone could actually reason out "July" from that sequence of curves and loops was beyond her grasp.

Lucy much preferred numbers. She leafed through the book, admiring the neat columns she'd inscribed there, lined up tall and true as Queen Elizabeth's soldiers when they marched on parade. Her satisfied smile faded as she eyed the totals at the foot of each page "One 'ell of a way to make a livin', that's wot this is," she muttered, scooping the coins into her purse and pushing back her mane of thick black curls.

She sorted through the slim pile of numbered tickets she'd issued that day, punching them with her awl and slipping in a string so she could tie them to the assortment of objects atop her counter. A man's bronze belt buckle engraved with the head of a boar—Lucy had given Bart Turkle five pence for it, though she could resell it for ten. He'd just spend the money gambling at cards. If he won, he'd only have to pay five again to get the belt back. And

3

if he lost, which was a good deal more likely, he'd only
have lost half as much.

She slipped another ticket onto the handle of the pierced
pewter spoon ten-year-old Georgie Chapman had dropped
off that morning. Any other boy that age and she'd suspect
the spoon had been stolen. But in the months since Georgie's father died, Mistress Chapman had been sending one
or another of her shy, pale children round to Lucy's shop
with bits and pieces of the household furnishings. Lucy
nibbled her lip, thinking of Georgie's sad smile, wondering how much of the furnishings might still be left.

Then she tagged the next item, the huge iron kettle Nell
Harper had dragged in just before the shop closed.
"Reckon ye 'eard me comin' a mile off, eh?" the old
woman had asked, grinning toothlessly. "Well, 'ere 'tis,
such as 'tis, for wotever ye think 'tis worth. With Ethan
off soldierin' 'n' Em'ly married 'n' Chet gone to sea,
there's only me 'n' the old man left. I could make our slop
in a thimble nowadays."

Lucy saw the way Nell's crabbed fingers rubbed the old
pocked iron. " 'Ow much soup 'n' stew d'ye reckon ye've
made in this 'ere kettle over the years?" she'd asked gently.

"Faith, luv, I ain't got yer 'ead for figures!" The old
woman laughed. "Still, enough to fill the whole bloody
Thames, I'd wager." In the midst of her laughter she
brushed a tear away impatiently. "The old 'ouse seems
mighty empty these days."

Lucy gave her three shillings and a hug. "Don't fret,
Nell. I'll keep this right 'ere in the shop till ye needs it to
stir up soup for yer grandchildren."

Nell's lined face brightened. "Grandchildren, eh? Well,
maybe ye ain't seen the last of me yet, ye old black monster!" She'd given the kettle a pat and gone on her way.

Lucy hesitated over the last item on the counter, a shiny
golden ring set with a huge red stone. She remembered so
clearly the day Jeannie Paget first got that ring from the
"young gentleman" she'd taken up with, the way she'd
flashed it all around Barkers Lane and the square. "Son
of a lord 'e is," she'd proudly proclaimed, "a real one!
'N' 'e's goin' to marry me, 'e is!" All the neighbors had
jeered her, but she paid them no mind. She was fresh-

faced and lovely then, no more than sixteen years old, and her eyes had sparkled brighter than her shiny ring.

When she'd come into the pawnshop that morning the freshness was gone. Though it had been less than twelve months since she paraded her new ring around the square, she might have aged twelve years. She held her tiny squalling baby low on her hip, pushed slack hair from her face, and slapped the ring down on the counter. " 'Ow much?" she demanded, her blue eyes hard as stone.

"Oh, Jeannie." Lucy had pushed the ring back toward her. "Ye doesn't want to be sellin' that. And anyway, I can't afford it. Take it to one of the jewelsmiths out on the Long Road; they'll give ye—"

"I already did," Jeannie said shortly. "They told me, 'twas glass. Worth five shillin's tops." Lucy stared at her, stricken, as she yanked the baby higher on her hip. "Well, why should it be real? Nothin' else that bastard ever gave me was—'cept for this 'ere baby," the girl—woman now— went on impatiently. " 'Aven't even seen 'im in more'n six months. Not since I told 'im 'e'd got me in the family way."

"Well, did ye go round to see 'im?" Lucy demanded. " 'E owes ye, ye know. 'E's got responsibilities!"

"Aye, I went round." Jeannie's brittle hardness cracked. "The gateman threatened to run me off. I sneaked about to the kitchens. One of the scullion maids told me 'e 'ad got married, three months past. To the daughter of an earl."

"I'm sorry," Lucy said softly, knowing the words were hopelessly inadequate.

Jeannie shrugged. "I'm the one's sorry. Wouldn't listen to nobody, I wouldn't, not me friends nor me mum nor dad. Wasn't I just so much smarter 'n them, 'n' didn't I know best?" She blinked back tears. "I knows better now, don't I. 'Ow much can ye give me for the ring?"

Lucy gave her six shillings; she and the baby both looked so wan and frail. Jeannie kissed the coins and tucked them into her pocket. "For luck," she said grimly, and was on her way.

Luck. Lucy frowned and found a place for the ring on the shelves. Everyone in Shoreditch, London, was down on his luck these days. And running the pawnshop meant she saw the worst of it. Why the hell couldn't her father have left her something cheery, like a flower stall?

A brisk knock sounded at the shutters. Lucy wedged Nell Harper's pot up on a shelf between a spindled chair and a cradle and sang out, "It's open! Well, Joseph Jacob Reilly," she told the short, stout man who came into the shop, "ye're late tonight."

"Wait'll I tell ye why!" he said excitedly. "I saw the queen!"

"No!" Lucy leaned both her elbows on the counter, her green eyes wide. "Where?"

"Comin' over the river in 'er gold barge, big 'n' bold as life."

"Well, 'ow did she look?"

"Beautiful as ever. Mind ye, I wasn't real close, now; I couldn't see much more'n 'er crown 'n' 'er 'air. But she looked grand all the same."

" 'Ave ye ever seen Queen Bess when ye didn't think she looked grand, Joe?" Lucy asked slyly.

"No, I ain't," the little bald man said emphatically, " 'n' I'll tell ye why. She's the best damned ruler, king or queen, this country's ever 'ad."

" 'N' why is that, Joe?" Lucy asked, biting her cheek, knowing perfectly well what the answer would be.

"Because 'er mother was a commoner, just like ye 'n' me, Lucy Jones, 'n' that's God's truth. She ain't like them mucky-muck noblemen always 'angs about 'er like a pack of leeches wot looks down on folk like us. God save 'er, I hope she lives forever. She's got the love of 'er people right enough, 'n' do ye know why?"

"Because she loves us," Lucy finished in chorus with him.

"Well, laugh if ye likes," Joe said, sounding disgruntled. "But it's true."

"Oh, Joe, I wasn't laughin'. I loves Good Queen Bess every bit as much as ye do."

"All right, then." He held out a scanty purse to her. "Count this up for us, would ye, Lucy pet? I tried to do it just like ye tells me, but I keeps gettin' the numbers all jiggled."

Lucy poured the purse's contents onto her countertop. "Countin' is simple, Joe."

"Simple for ye. Ye've got yer father's 'ead for money."

"If Pop 'ad such a bloody 'ead for money," Lucy said absently, "then why didn't 'e get rich 'n' leave me somethin' more'n this ragtag shop? 'Ow much did ye count 'ere, Joe?"

"Ah—thirty farthin's?"

She pushed the coins toward him. "Try again. Count 'em in twos."

"Two," said Joe. "Four. Six. Eight. Ten. Twelve." He paused, scowling at the silver.

"Fourteen," Lucy prodded. "Sixteen. Eighteen—"

"Right, right, eighteen. Then—twenty?" Lucy nodded; slowly, patiently, she helped him count all the way up to fifty-three.

"Good! Fifty-three farthin's, four farthin's to the penny. So 'ow many pennies?" she demanded.

Joe scratched his bald head, mumbling to himself. "Four, that's four, 'n' another, that's eight—" Lucy bit off a smile as she saw him waggling his fingers. "Three fours, 'n' four of them . . ." He peeked at Lucy tentatively. "Would it maybe be—thirteen?"

"Very good!" He beamed in triumph. " 'N' 'ow many left over?"

"Left over?" He blinked.

Lucy pushed the farthings into piles of four. "Left over. Thirteen piles of four, that's fifty-two. 'N' then there's still one more. Honestly, Joe, wot d'ye do if a customer pays ye a shillin' for tuppence of apples?"

The fruitseller gave her a disarming grin. "Asks don't 'e 'ave tuppence instead. Anyway, who in Shoreditch 'as got any shillin's?"

"Ye've got one, as a matter of fact."

"Really? Ye don't say."

"I do. 'N' one pence one farthin' left over besides."

"Gor, that was a good week, weren't it?" Joe marveled.

"Glad it was good for somebody." Lucy opened the till and took out the account book beneath hers, the one she'd kept for Joe for the past three years; she'd inherited that job, too, from her father. Dipping her pen into the inkwell, she noted down the amount. " 'Ow much d'ye need for market on Monday?''

Joe pondered the question. "Eight pence. I saw some of them sour yellow things—lemons, they calls 'em—there today. Reckon anybody in Shoreditch would want to buy lemons?''

"Nah. Life 'ere's sour enough already." Grinning, Lucy counted out eight pence. "Put that in yer pocket, then, 'n' I'll 'old the rest.''

" 'Ow much is the rest?''

"Why don't ye tell me? A shilling five farthin's less eight pence.''

Joe groaned. " 'Ave an 'eart, girl!'' He was spared for the moment by another rap at the shutters. "Now who might that be at this time of night?''

"Ain't ye never met me midnight visitor before?'' Lucy went to open the door, her green eyes sparkling with mischief. Joe gaped at the tall young man who came into the shop. He was clad in a fine black velvet hooded cape lined in white fur and clasped at the throat with a gold-set jewel; the scabbard of the sword hanging from his belt was studded with pearls. He had a thin, bony face that ended in a blond beard waxed to a sharp point; the hood of the cape was pulled so low that his eyes were nearly hidden by the fluff of fur. He drew a brown sack from beneath the voluminous folds of the luxurious cloak as Lucy stood aside to let him in.

" 'Ello, guvnor, wot can I do for ye today?'' Lucy asked, with a sidelong glance at gaping Joe. The young man unwrapped his bundle to reveal a shining applewood lute, the body inlaid with ivory and gold. He handed it to Lucy, and she brought it close to the lamp. "Oh, this is right lovely,'' she told him briskly. " 'Ow about five pounds?''

Joe's gasp was audible. The gentleman in the fancy cape glanced at him before nodding to Lucy. "That seems fair,'' he told her, with a slight hiss to the beginning and end of the second word. Everyone in Shoreditch knew what that little lisp meant; it was the way the queen's courtiers talked, affected and sweet.

"Right, then, guvnor." Lucy counted out crownpieces and shillings and gave them to the stranger with a ticket. Without even counting his bounty he slipped it into a rich brocade purse. "Good night to ye, sir."

"Good night, miss." He spun on the heel of his brightly polished boot and, with the fur-trimmed cloak swirling around him, strode back out to the street. Giggling at Joe's astonished expression, Lucy locked the door in his wake.

"Who in 'ell was that?" the fruitmonger demanded.

Lucy dropped him a curtsy. "Sure 'n' 'e ain't never introduced 'imself proper to me, milord, so I couldn't say."

Joe's round face was stamped with suspicion. " 'N' wot's a la-di-da swell like 'im doin' in Shoreditch, pray tell?"

"Pawnin' the family 'eirlooms, wot else?" Lucy searched the shelves for a spot in which to set the lute. " 'E gambles. 'N' swell or no, 'e's got Shoreditch luck. Been comin' in late every Saturday night for the past month or so."

"Ye don't say. Wot else 'as 'e brought besides that thing?"

"Let me see. A book once, with a gorgeous leather cover. 'N' a portrait of some lady, 'n' a saddle—oh, 'n' a jewel case, all made of silver with a little lock. Right cunnin' it were." Failing to find any empty space, she set the lute inside Nell Harper's soup pot.

"Well, let's see 'em!" Joe said eagerly.

"I ain't got 'em. The day after 'e comes in, Sundays when I'm closed, another fellow comes by 'n' redeems wot this fellow leaves 'ere. That's 'ow I know 'e's a gambler. 'Twas the other fellow told me. 'E pays me wot I give 'is friend, 'n' then a shillin' more."

"Don't that seem a mite strange to ye, Lucy, luv, wot they're doin'?"

"Everybody knows that the gentry's queer. I've got no problem with wot they're doin'. Way I figure is, they've got plenty of gold, so why shouldn't I get a piece?" She shook her head, looking up at the lute. "I'll tell ye, Joe, I ain't never seen nobody with such rotten luck at cards. I damned near feel sorry for 'im."

Joe Reilly snorted. " 'And me over five quid, why don't ye, 'n' I'll let ye feel sorry for me, too! But why come to Shoreditch, d'ye reckon?''

"I guess 'e's embarrassed to go where somebody might know 'im. I'd be, too," she said with a giggle, "if I lost as bad as 'e does!''

"Ye shouldn't ought to get mixed up with that kind," Joe said worriedly.

"Why not? I needs money, 'n' they've got it to spare."

"Aye, but rich folk 'n' poor, they're—''

"I know," Lucy said with a sigh. "Like fire 'n' water. Don't ye think Pop drummed that into my 'ead all my life? But they takes from us all the time, don't they, with their bloody excises 'n' taxes 'n' wot-not. I'm just lookin' after my own, I is. Just gettin' a bit of it back while I tries to make a go of this bleedin' shop."

"Ye wouldn't need to make a go of it if ye'd do the logical thing 'n' get married."

"Joe, please don't pester. I'll wed when I'm ready. When I find the right man."

"All right, pet." He leaned across the counter and kissed her forehead. "Ye knows I only wants to see ye 'appy. I did promise yer Pop I'd do my best by ye." He saw her clear green eyes shade dark with sadness at his mention of her father and quickly changed the subject. " 'Ow much did we say I'd got left after ye took out eight pence?''

"Five pence 'n' a farthin'," she told him absently, and then, realizing he'd duped her into doing the subtraction for him, gave him a swat. "Get on with ye, then; I'm starved for me supper."

Joe grinned, scooping up his coins, then presented her with a pear. "Nearly as sweet as ye are, luv. Enjoy it!''

Lucy saw him out. "Don't go spendin' all yer coins at the Mermaid!" she called as he hauled a sack of unsold fruit across the darkened street to his house. He laughed, waving over his shoulder, and Lucy came back inside and locked the door.

Upstairs, in the single cramped room above the shop that was her home, she cleared a table of overflow from the shelves below and took bread and cheese from her cupboard. Then she sat and ate, biting into the ripe mellow pear. Through the open windows poured the sounds of the city in summer: children wailing, mothers scolding, men shouting greetings, all against the low rumble of horses and carts clattering over cobblestones. With the sounds came the smells, a melange of dung and peat, slop and hot sweat and ordure that was riper even than the pear.

Lucy hooked her boots over the rung of her stool and tried to eat without breathing. Summer in the city. She remembered the long tangled skeins of dreams her father used to spin out on sweltering nights such as this. Dreams of escaping from the noise and stink to some faraway spot where the only sound was the hum of honeybees, where the scents of lilac and hawthorn perfumed the air.

"There's places like that, pet," he'd tell her, leaning back in his seat, staring over the rooftops. "Places where the grass grows long 'n' sweet 'n' green, stretchin' for miles 'n' miles. Where the streams run clear 'n' bright as jewels, 'n' wildflowers pop up right between yer toes! We'll go there someday. Ye'll see."

He'd been a great one for dreaming, had Willie Jones, for all the good it had done him. If there were such places, he never got there. The city finally took him, just as it took his wife before him, just as, Lucy knew, it would surely take her one day. Still, as Pop used to tell her, dreaming didn't cost a farthing. A London shopgirl could dream just the same as the queen.

She missed him on these nights. If he'd still been alive, he'd have taken her down to the Mermaid Tavern tonight for his weekly treat. She'd have sat wide-eyed at his side while he and his cronies downed pints of ale and traded tidbits of gossip. Who was the favorite at court? Was that French prince still courting Queen Bess? Were Raleigh and Essex squabbling? What was Mary, queen of Scots, up to in her castle prison in the Northcountry? Lucy still heard the latest rumors from neighbors and friends, but it wasn't the same as on those endless evenings at the Mermaid, when she'd listened till she dropped off to sleep at her father's side.

She always woke up, though, when the players came in, rowdy and loud, after their last show at The Theatre James

Burbage had built in Shoreditch ten years past. Lucy had
had a terrible crush on the players when she was younger;
what girl in the parish didn't? They were so different from
the Shoreditch menfolk; they were dashing and mysterious, magical. Her father would take her to The Theatre
every fortnight, when he could afford it. She would stand
on her tiptoes in the hard press of bodies in the groundlings' pit and stare up at the stage, at the glittering costumes, the gorgeous men and beautiful women parading
by above her, hating and loving, killing and rescuing one
another in a grand panoply.

And the language they spoke! It wasn't clipped and
harsh and ugly the way the Shoreditch tongue sounded; it
flowed like a song, rolled like the mighty Thames. Lucy
would listen with all her might and then come home and
whisper, in secret, that gilded accent of rich gentility.

She flushed and giggled thinking of the night at the
Mermaid when she'd finally screwed up her courage and
approached James Burbage to tell him she wanted to join
his company of players. The man had been remarkably
kind. He'd withered his jeering companions with a glare,
fondled Lucy's black curls, told her she was lovely—and
then shattered her dreams by confiding that all the grand,
elegant ladies she'd seen on his stage were boys.

Lucy didn't want to believe it, couldn't believe it, but
he finally convinced her by bringing forth two grinning
lads who were his queens and princesses to speak their
lines. "But that's not fair!" Lucy cried, bursting into tears.
"I could do better! I want to be on the stage!"

"It's too hard for a girl," one of the cocky lads sneered.
"You have to be strong; you have to jump and tumble—"

"I am strong!" Lucy said. "D'ye want to wrestle?"

The other boy eyed her blandly. "You have to be smart,
too. You have to know how to read."

That silenced her, for of course she didn't know how.

It hadn't been long after that night, when she was fourteen, that her father took sick. After he died there hadn't
been any money to go to the Mermaid, much less The
Theatre. She still saw James Burbage from time to time,
though, when he came into her shop to search for properties for his plays. He never failed to tease her about

wanting to join his company. Once he caught her singing to herself, some old lullaby that her mother used to rock her to sleep with. She'd blushed furiously when she turned and saw him listening. But he made her sing it through for him again and said she had the voice of a nightingale. "More's the pity," he added ruefully, "that you weren't born male. I'd wager a voice like that would bring folk to The Theatre from miles around."

"Well, why can't ye 'ave girls on the stage?" she demanded.

He shrugged. "That's the law."

Even though Lucy knew now she'd never be on stage, she still dreamed about it sometimes. She'd pretend she was there at The Theatre in a fabulous gown, not like the plain gray serge she always wore now because it didn't show dirt, standing up in front of everyone she knew, all her neighbors and friends, singing like a nightingale. And they would all shout "Hooray!" and applaud for her until their hands were sore.

On impulse she darted downstairs to the darkened shop and pulled the lute out from inside Nell's kettle. Playing an instrument couldn't be all that hard, she reckoned as she hurried back to her room. She stood in the middle of the floor, striking a dramatic pose. Here she was on the stage. High in the gallery was a tall, dark, handsome man in a plumed hat who could not take his eyes off her. She drew in her breath, then strummed the lute as loud as she could.

It made a dull, muffled sound, not at all like the glorious chords of The Theatre's musicians. Perturbed, Lucy turned it upright. It had four strings; there was nothing wrong with them that she could see. She shook the instrument gently and heard something slide about inside the body. Working two fingers down into the soundholes, she pulled out a sheet of parchment covered with squiggles. "Now wot in 'ell," she said crossly. "Who'd ruin a lute by stuffin' papers inside?" She tossed the sheet onto the pile of scraps she kept to start her fire, then resumed her pose and struck the lute strings again.

There was nothing wrong with the chord this time, but suddenly she felt silly. Who was she fooling? She'd never be up on the stage; no man, plumed hat or no, would ever admire her from the gallery. She was plain old Lucy Jones, Shoreditch shopkeeper, seventeen years old and unable to read or write. And the way her life was going, nothing would change in the next forty years except that she'd be forty years older. If she lived that long.

Still, she reminded herself, dreams didn't cost a farthing.

She put down the lute and went to bed, to sleep and dream.

Lucy answered the knock at the door the next evening at dusk, expecting to find the lute owner's friend; she was surprised to see Joe Reilly instead. "Wot's up with ye?" she asked.

"Is that any way to greet a friend?" He handed her a greengage plum. "For yer supper. 'N then I thought I'd just wait about a bit to see this 'ere gentleman wot's comin' by."

"Oh, Joe." Lucy rolled her green eyes.

"It just strikes me strange, these 'ere comin's 'n' goin's," he said stubbornly. "They ain't our kind of folk."

"No. They pays me better." Lucy laughed at his suspicious expression. "Of course they're strange, Joe! They're gentry, ain't they?" Someone knocked at the shutters. "Now, there, ye've got yer wish. 'Ere 'e comes. Mind yer tongue, if ye please, 'n' don't say anythin' to upset 'im. I needs the cash." She kissed his nose, then smiled at the lute owner's friend as she let him in. " 'Ello, guvnor. 'Ot night again, ain't it? 'Old on just one second; I've left the goods upstairs."

She popped up to fetch the lute, returning to find Joe glaring at the well-dressed stranger, who asked, "How much did you pay my friend?" as he accepted the instrument.

"Five pounds, guvnor." He pulled out a purse, the weight of which made Joe blink, and gave her back that and a shilling. "Right, then," said Lucy. "Thanks ever so much. See ye next week, eh? 'Ere's wishin' yer friend better luck at 'is cards."

"This friend of yers," Joe broke in, " 'as he got a name? Or 'ave ye, fer that matter?"

"Joe!" Lucy said sharply. "Leave the gentleman to 'is own business, why don't ye?"

" 'Tis a simple—"

"Joe!" Lucy looked at the gentleman apologetically. "Sorry, sir, 'e's just a bit protective, that's all. Good night."

"Good night," said the man, and went out with the lute tucked under his arm.

"Wot're ye tryin' to do, Joe, take money out of my pocket?" Lucy demanded when he'd gone.

"I don't like 'is looks."

"Well, I reckon 'e don't like yers, neither, from the way 'e scowled at ye when ye asked 'is mate's name." She laughed. "Still, I know wot ye mean. 'Tis that nose of 'is, all long 'n' crooked. I calls 'im 'Awk-Nose, I do. Though not to 'is face."

" 'E's up to somethin'," Joe said darkly.

"I know 'e is; 'e's 'elpin' out 'is friend. Come on, Joe, 'tis too 'ot to quarrel. All I wants is to eat my supper 'n' go to bed."

"I'd watch my step if I was ye, pet," he warned.

Lucy sighed. " 'N' I wish I'd never told ye about it. They're rich folk, that's all, 'n' rich folk is queer." She pushed him toward the door. "See ye tomorrow, then, eh, luv?"

"Lucy—"

"Good night, Joe."

She watched bemusedly as he crossed the street and went into his house. She'd just put the key to the lock when the door burst open so violently that she went stumbling back halfway across the shop.

"Where is it?" a harsh voice demanded. Lucy blinked, looking up from the counter edge she'd caught to break her fall. The rich fellow she'd nicknamed Hawk-Nose was standing before her, the lute still clasped under his arm.

"Where's wot?" she asked in astonishment. His face was red with rage; the knuckles on his hand were white as he brought the beautiful lute crashing down on the counter, smashing it to bits. "Look 'ere, now, why'd ye do that?"

He brought his florid face very close to hers. "Don't toy with me, bitch," he snarled, giving her arm a swift wrench as she tried to back away.

" 'Ey!" Her own temper flaring, Lucy aimed a kick at his finely hosed shin. "Ye've no cause to be callin' me names!"

"Where's what was in the lute, you stupid Shoreditch slut?" he roared, and struck her, hard, right across the cheek.

"Ye bleedin' bastard!" Reeling from the blow, Lucy fell against a shelf and sent a load of Mistress Chapman's best plates crashing to the floor. "See wot ye've done, broken all that good woman's crockery—"

"I'll break your neck, bitch! Where's what was in the lute?"

Lucy circled the counter, keeping its bulk between them. "Take yer dirty bleedin' mouth," she said bravely, " 'n' get out of 'ere!"

He put his fist to his sword, making Lucy's heart drop suddenly into her stomach. "I'll kill you if you don't hand it over. Don't think I won't. No one would ever miss a cheap Shoreditch shopgirl like you."

" 'And wot over?" Lucy countered.

"The letter, whore."

It was the way he was acting, bursting in this way, cursing her, threatening her, that raised Lucy's hackles. If he'd just asked her nicely in the first place, she would have given him the paper she'd found in the lute, and that would be that. But just because he is a nobleman and rich, she thought furiously, he thinks he can push me about any way he pleases. "I don't know anythin' about any letter," she told him, her green eyes flashing with defiance.

"Liar." He flourished the sword. "Suppose I carve it out of you?"

"Suppose ye tries!"

In the lamplight she saw his pale eyes shift, refocus. "You read it, didn't you? That fat little bald man put you up to this. You read the damned thing, and you think you can get something out of me!"

Lucy wasn't about to admit to this haughty, high-blown fellow that she couldn't read. "Wot if I did?"

The cold stare clicked down over his eyes again like a knight's steel visor. "Then I'll have to kill you," he said evenly.

" 'Ave to catch me first, won't ye?" Lucy feinted toward the door and, as he lunged that way, made for the stairs.

She scrambled up them on hands and knees, hearing him curse and reverse direction, coming after her. She reached her room and slammed the door shut right in his big hawk's nose, jamming home the bolt. He pounded on the wood, throwing his weight against it. Lucy swallowed as it threatened to give way. Damn, she'd been meaning to ask Joe to fix that weak hinge!

But there wasn't any time for such regrets. Lucy snatched the page she'd taken from the lute off the scrap heap and thrust it into the bodice of her gray gown. She'd be damned if she'd hand it over to him now, after he'd made such a mess in the shop! Her cheek still stinging where he'd struck her, she clambered through the window and dropped down onto the roof next door, just as she heard a splintering of wood and a resounding crash.

From the rooftop she looked back and saw him glaring out the window. "So there, son of a bitch!" she cried, shaking her fist at him, then gulped as he started to climb down after her. Drat! Across the slanting tiles she scrambled, skirts tangling around her legs, until she reached the clay gutter overhanging the street. Her neighbors, she saw, had very thoughtfully collected a huge pile of rubbish just beneath the drainpipe. Holding tight to the gutter, she swung out over the edge of the roof and hung down.

Her boot tips were still six feet from the top of the pile. She looked up between her stretched arms and saw Hawk-Nose coming toward her. Praying the rubbish would be soft, Lucy let go.

She landed with a thump, scattering bits of straw and cloth and wood. Above her head the man with the hawk's nose was muttering curses as he made his way across the roof. Lucy hied herself out of the junk pile, catching up her skirts, and darted off into the night, wondering what could possibly be written on the paper in her bodice that her pursuer should want it so much.

Where Barkers Lane led onto March Street she turned, searching the shadows behind her, and caught a glimpse of flashing fire as lamplight from Joe Reilly's window glinted on the edge of Hawk-Nose's sword. Jesus, he's fast for such an old coot, Lucy thought briefly before grabbing up her skirts again. Down the street she fled, hearing footsteps behind her, loud against the cobblestones.

As she passed the hostler's shop and ducked down Green's Alley, it occurred to her that she really ought to have some sort of plan. She could take refuge at the Chapmans, but she didn't relish telling Georgie's mum what had become of her good dishes. How about the Mermaid Tavern? Sunday—it would be closed. Everything was closed. "Oof!" She screamed as a hand grabbed her from behind, yanking her about by the shoulder so hard that her teeth snapped. The hawk nose loomed above her; the man's eyes glittered, pale as the moon.

He shoved her against the side of a house, jabbing his fist into her mouth as she started to scream. Lucy squirmed and tried to bite his fingers; when that failed she grabbed his thinning hair and pulled it as hard as she could. His lips drew back over his teeth; his narrow, bony face reminded her suddenly of a death's-head, gapemouthed and staring. "So," he muttered, yanking her arm away, fist splaying her to the wall, "you thought you could escape me, my little Shoreditch slut. Bid farewell to your miserable life."

As Lucy saw him draw back his sword, ready to run her through, she suddenly remembered a trick she'd seen played in a comedy at The Theatre. She forced her eyes away from the weapon, focusing on a point beyond his shoulder, and started in mock surprise. "Constable Duffy!" she cried, relief flooding her features. "Just in the nick of time!"

Her captor loosed his grip on her abruptly, whirling around. Lucy kicked him as hard as she could, right in the kidneys, and watched in satisfaction as he sprawled across the cobblestones. "Filthy bitch!" he snarled, twisting to grab for her ankles. But Lucy was already off and running again.

She was more shaken than her brave feint showed, though. Up to the moment when he'd pulled back that sword, Lucy hadn't actually believed he would kill her. But that horrid, grinning death's mask, the nonchalance with which he'd been prepared to send her to her doom, convinced her. This was dead serious. He'd meant what he said. And even if she gave him the letter now and told him she couldn't read, he'd never believe her. He would only think she was lying to save her skin.

She could hear him again, coming after her. As she ran, Lucy scanned the dark streets, trying to see where she might be. She'd crossed Kingsland Road; that meant she was out of Shoreditch. Foreign territory, that's where she was now—in Stepney or Bethnal Green. She started to double back toward home, but Hawk-Nose was too close behind her. With a gulp, she plunged on.

How could the streets be so damnably empty? Had every soul in London disappeared? Where was the bloody constable when you needed him, or even a bleeding beggar with good strong arms? But this wasn't the sort of neighborhood that would have beggars, she noted as she flew past rows of huge, handsome houses. She was the stranger here; old Hawk-Nose, with his silk hose and velvet doublet, would be right at home.

She knew what sort of people lived in these houses. They walked right past poor, shivering children in Shoreditch in winter in their fancy fur coats; they had a way of looking through you as if you didn't exist, talked as if you couldn't hear. If Hawk-Nose caught her here he would get away with murdering her; none of the swells in these houses would come to the aid of a pawnshop girl from Shoreditch.

She had to get back to her own kind. Darting a glance over her shoulder, she saw she had a lead of only a dozen yards. In a wild burst of energy she lengthened it to twenty, then to thirty; the old coot's age was catching up with him at last. But then she tripped turning a corner, and her pursuer reappeared behind her, his eyes still gleaming ghost-cold.

She ducked around another corner, raced down an alley, and came to a sudden stop. She was in a close, a courtyard lined on all sides by houses, with no escape except the alley she had just run through. Christ, what now? Already she could hear Hawk-Nose's footsteps as he chased after her. She was going to die right here in wherever the hell she was, and nobody in all these grand houses would so much as come to his door to find out why she screamed.

But one of the doors was standing open, just a crack; she could see a thin stream of light pouring from it. She glanced back at the alley, then dashed up the stairs toward that beckoning beam. She lifted the heavy brass knocker, but before she could let it fall the door opened wide, pulling her with it so suddenly that Lucy very nearly went flat on her nose. She caught herself on the lintel and looked up to see who had come to her rescue so unexpectedly.

The man who stood before her was the biggest human being she had ever seen, and that included Gerald the Giant, who'd come to Shoreditch once in a traveling show that you had to pay a whole penny for. He must have been six and a half feet tall, with shoulders broad as a church door and legs as long as battering rams. He had long black hair and black eyebrows that were, at the moment, knitted together in a ferocious scowl as he looked at Lucy. Then he stood aside to let her in and slammed shut the door.

Unable to believe her good fortune, Lucy started to stammer an explanation. But the huge man's scowl deepened, silencing her before she could say more than "I—"

"Mistress Moncrief," he said, and though from the looks of his elegant black doublet and hose he must have been rich, there wasn't any courtier's lisp in his deep voice. "I was under the impression you would not arrive until tomorrow."

Lucy stared at him, dumbstruck. Still scowling, he raked her gray serge gown with eyes that were clear blue ringed with gray, like a summer sky that hinted of forthcoming storms. "Not exactly what I expected you to wear," he went on. "Not that it matters. I am riding up myself tonight, and the children will follow in the coach with you in the morning. Where are your bags?"

In the space of this speech, Lucy's mind had been working like lightning. By some unimaginable stroke of luck, this man had mistaken her for someone else, someone he was prepared to accept into his home. If she confessed who she really was, she had no doubt he would kick her straight back onto the street, where old Hawk-Nose was surely still waiting. If, on the other hand, she could play for time . . .

"My bags will be sent on later," she told him cautiously, coaxing her short Shoreditch accent into an approximation of the rich, glossy tones Burbage's men used up on the stage. He scowled even more savagely, and for an instant she was certain he'd seen through her act.

"On time for your departure, I trust," was all he said, though, and Lucy realized the scowl was perpetual. Rather a pity, she thought fleetingly, for without it he'd be as handsome a man as ever she'd seen. His thick, jet-black hair swept back from his forehead in a gleaming wave, his chin was square and strong, his nose straight and elegant. The sheer size of him was what one noted first, of course; that was overwhelming. But after that, Lucy found herself staring at his eyes, so clear at the center before they shaded to stormy gray. She had never seen eyes like his before.

"I beg your pardon, milord." Lucy peeked beyond him into the richly furnished entranceway and saw that someone else had appeared: a fellow dressed all in black, neither young nor old, with a plain face and colorless, thinning hair. "I've had Bellerophon brought around," the newcomer went on, "if you—" He stopped, catching sight of Lucy. "Forgive me, Lord Carlyle. I did not realize you had a guest."

"Jeeves." The blue-eyed man nodded toward him. "Mistress Moncrief has arrived precipitously. Mistress Moncrief, the butler. Jeeves."

Jeeves bowed. "Mistress Moncrief."

Lucy nodded to him, even as she wondered what *precipitously* meant, and who Mistress Moncrief was, and how she ought to address a butler. She settled on saying nothing. It seemed to be the right decision, for the man the butler called Lord Carlyle went on: "Mistress Moncrief's baggage will be coming later, Jeeves."

"Very good, milord. Shall I take her up to meet the children?"

The man's scowl turned so fierce that Lucy's knees quaked. "No, dammit all, I suppose I had better. Have Johnny hold Bellerophon, Jeeves. This won't take but a minute."

"Very good, milord." Jeeves bowed again and backed away. His master held out an arm to Lucy.

"This way, Mistress Moncrief."

Lucy laid her arm on his the way she'd seen Burbage's boys do on stage, and though her fingers barely touched him she could feel the raw strength of the muscles in his forearm beneath their covering of fine black cloth. His steps as he led her through the grand entranceway to an enormous flight of marble stairs were so long that she had to take two to each of his; she had the impression he might have taken the stairs five at a time had he chosen to. But he climbed them one by one while she gathered her skirts and ascended beside him, not certain whether she was out of breath from her run through the streets of London or from sheer awe at his imposing presence and the way he moved, as though a force as powerful as the Thames surged below the surface of his civilized skin.

"How is your father?" he asked as they neared the top of the stairs.

"My—my father?" Lucy gulped. "Quite well, thank you," she guessed, hoping Mistress Moncrief's was.

He made a sort of snorting sound. "I am glad to hear it. Are you disappointed, Mistress Moncrief, to be coming to Derbyshire instead of joining him at court now you're of marrying age?"

"I—" Lucy hadn't the slightest idea what to say to that.

He snorted again. From behind the door at the top of the stairs Lucy heard muffled laughter. "The nursery," he said briefly, throwing open the portal. Lucy stepped through cautiously, blinking in a sudden blaze of candle-light. "Eustace. Minerva," said the man beside her. "Mistress Claudia Moncrief. Your new governess."

Out of the brightness emerged the two most beautiful children that Lucy had ever seen. Their golden hair hung in perfect ringlets around angelic, pink-cheeked faces; their blue eyes sparkled; their smiles were warm and gay. The boy came forward and bowed smartly; he was dressed in a cunning little white velvet suit trimmed with gold braid. "Mistress Moncrief! How do you do!" he exclaimed.

" 'Ow—" said Lucy, and swallowed the false start in a cough. "I beg your pardon, Eustace. *H*ow do you do?"

"Very well, thank you." He nudged the cherub beside him. "Minerva, say 'How do you do' to Mistress Moncrief. Tell her how happy we are that she is come to be our governess."

The tiny exquisite girl—she could have been no more than six, Lucy thought, and the boy perhaps eight—dropped a delightful curtsy. "How do you do, Mistress Moncrief?" she piped. "It is true; we are terribly happy to have you here."

"Thank ye-ou very much, Minerva," Lucy said, with a growing sense that she must be dreaming. This magnificent house, these unspeakably lovely children—she wasn't just in a different neighborhood from Shoreditch; she was in another world. "I am *h*appy to be *h*ere."

The little girl sidled shyly closer. "And are you going to teach us all sorts of clever things, Mistress Moncrief, so that Father will be proud of us?"

Lucy swallowed, looking into the angel's bright eyes. "I certainly *h*ope so, Minerva." Dammit, everything she said had that bloody damned sound no one ever pronounced in Shoreditch. She patted the girl's shining curls. Well, she wouldn't have to keep this farce up for long—just until she could be sure old Hawk-Nose was gone from the close.

The children's father shifted his weight, clearing his throat. His daughter made a motion as if to take his hand, and he moved it away. "It is past your bedtime," he said shortly. "I am riding to Derbyshire tonight; you and Mistress Moncrief will follow tomorrow in the coach. Jem will put you to bed. Mistress Moncrief, Jeeves will show you to your rooms. Say good night to Mistress Moncrief, children."

"Good night, Mistress Moncrief," they chanted dutifully in unison. Lucy waited for their father to hug and kiss them, but instead he turned his back and left the nursery.

In the hallway he shouted down the stairs for Jeeves and Jem. They hurried up to him, Jeeves carrying a black cloak and hat. "Put the children to bed, Jem," their master directed a little dark-eyed woman in a crisp white smock. "Jeeves, show Mistress Moncrief to her rooms." Jem scurried into the nursery while Jeeves reached up to help his master into the cloak and handed him the hat. He turned toward Lucy briefly; she looked into those strange, stormy eyes and suppressed a shiver. He would crush you like an ant, Lucy Jones, she told herself, if he knew what you've done . . . "Enjoy your journey, Mistress Moncrief," he told her, and strode down the stairs.

"This way, Mistress Moncrief," said Jeeves, preceding Lucy along the corridor away from the nursery. He opened a door, stood aside to let her enter, and lit the candles on a wide marble mantel with the same deft efficiency Lucy had already remarked in him. Her mouth dropped open when she saw the room, all done up in rose chintz and white wood, with a bed the size of her whole room at home. She snapped her mouth shut quickly as the butler turned toward her. "May I bring you a cold supper, Mistress Moncrief, or some wine?"

"N-no, thank you," Lucy stammered.

"As you wish. Should there be anything further that you require, you have merely to ring." He nodded toward a braided velvet rope that hung from the ceiling by the bed. "Good night."

"Good night," Lucy said faintly as he bowed out and closed the door with a crisp click.

Lucy stared in wonder at her opulent surroundings, at the dainty chairs and mirrored dressing table, the enormous fireplace, the wood floor so polished that it gleamed. She crossed to the bed and ran a hand over the soft, cool coverlets, wondering what it might feel like to sleep in such grandeur. "Gor, girl, ye'll never know," she said aloud. " 'Tis 'igh time ye got the 'ell out of 'ere, before someone finds out wot ye've done!" She went to the windows, pulled aside the rosy drapes, and found herself peering down into the close.

The moon had risen. She turned the handle of the window, winding the pane out as wide as she could, leaning over the sill. There was no sign of Hawk-Nose anywhere among the housefronts and stairways. Relieved, she wound the window shut and started toward the door. She bent her ear to it, listening, but could hear nothing. As quietly as she could she pulled it open and tiptoed out into the hall.

At the far end of the corridor, right at the top of the stairs, another door opened, and two curly golden heads appeared. "If you need anything, Mistress Moncrief," Eustace called to her, "you've only to ring the bell. That will fetch Jeeves or Jem."

"Thank you, Eustace." Lucy ducked back into her room and ran through her six and eight times tables in her head, then the nines, too, just for good measure. Then she opened the door with careful, silent stealth.

Just as stealthily the door at the end of the hallway opened, and those two yellow heads popped out. "Didn't they hear you ring?" little Minerva lisped prettily, her eyes like blue cornflowers.

"No," said Lucy, "I'm afraid they did not."

"They must still be packing then, for the morning," said Eustace, pointing toward the corridor downstairs.

"Aye," said Minerva, "everything's been in a tizzy all day."

"Don't say *tizzy,* Minerva," her brother scolded. "That's a servant's word. Say *upheaval.* Or *state of chaos.*"

"Yes, Eustace." The girl's smile was sweetly adorable. "Is there something we could do for you, Mistress Moncrief?"

Lucy peered over the banister into the entranceway. Jeeves and the maid called Jem were stacking bundles and boxes against the front door; they reached almost to the ceiling. Christ, she thought, I'll never get out that way!

"No, thank you," she told Minerva faintly. "Good night."

"Good night, Mistress Moncrief," they chorused as Lucy shrank back into her room again.

She plopped down on the bed, then jumped up hastily, fearful that her skirts might leave a mark on the pristine cloth. Christ, what a bleeding mess she'd got herself into! She paced back and forth across the gleaming floorboards, nibbling a fingernail. Then she went to the window and stared down into the moonlit court.

There was a little wrought-iron ledge just below the casement, she noticed this time. Quiet as a cat, she wound out the pane and leaned over as far as she could. Off to her left a clay drain ran down from the eaves overhead to the street. Lucy eyed it for a moment, then shrugged. ''Climbed out one window today, ye 'as,'' she said bravely. ''Won't kill ye to do it again.'' She gathered up her skirts, hung one leg over the sill—then froze as she heard a soft rap at the door.

''Mistress Moncrief?'' a small voice sang out.

Lucy jerked her leg back inside the room. ''Yes?''

''It's us. Eustace and Minerva.''

''So I gathers,'' Lucy muttered. ''Come in.''

''We just wondered if you ever got Jeeves or Jem to answer the bell,'' said Eustace while his sister nodded vigorously.

''As a matter of fact, I didn't. But it's all right. I won't be needing them now anyway.''

''Oh. Well, then.'' Eustace, scanning the room, noticed the open window and rushed to close it. ''You mustn't sleep with this open, dear Mistress Moncrief!'' he declared. ''Our governesses always tell us the night air in London is poisonous.''

''Poisonous? Poppycock!'' said Lucy. ''I always sleeps wi— I mean, I sleep with my window open at home.''

''Where is your home, Mistress Moncrief?'' asked Minerva, rose-cheeked and innocent.

'' 'Ere, I'm beginnin' to think,'' Lucy murmured under her breath. ''Didn't you hear your father, you two? It is past your bedtime.''

''We just wanted to make sure you were settled in comfortably,'' Eustace assured her while his sister nodded again.

''Well, that I is—am,'' said Lucy. ''Now scoot, both of you. Go pop straight into your beds.''

Angels, they floated toward the doorway. ''See you in the morning, dear Mistress Moncrief,'' lisped Minerva.

"Sweet dreams," her brother put in.

"And the same to you."

When they'd gone Lucy dove for the window. Everyone else around here might be too busy to notice, but those two knew something was up, that was sure. She crawled onto the ledge, tried to wind the window shut from outside, and found she could not. She left it open and inched across the ledge to the drain. The street seemed a very long way below. "Wot the 'ell," said Lucy. "I can't stay 'ere, that's certain." She grabbed the pipe with both hands and shinnied down to the cobblestones.

The square was still deserted. Lucy darted toward the alley that gave on to the streets. Where she'd gone wrong, she reflected, was in leaving Shoreditch. She should have gone straight across to Joe Reilly's at the first hint of trouble, only she'd hated for him to know his forebodings about the rich strangers in her shop had been right. As she peeked from the alley to make sure the coast was clear, she thought it just went to prove what her pop always told her: *Rich folks 'n' poor is like fire 'n' water, pet. They just don't mix.*

There was no sign of Hawk-Nose anywhere as Lucy hurried through the unfamiliar neighborhood. It wasn't hard to retrace her steps to Shoreditch; she had the spire of Magdalen Church as a guide, and as she crossed Kingsland Road something else, too—a beacon of bright red flame shooting into the sky. Christ, Lucy thought, I hope nobody's been hurt. And then, Christ, she thought again, I hope it's not The Theatre that's on fire!

But when she came out of Green's Alley onto March Street she could see that the blaze was much closer to home than it had looked at first. She could hear men shouting for buckets and water, and women wailing, and a roar like thousands of horses running all at once. Sparks and bits of ash flew through the air, and all the ruckus seemed to be coming from her street, from Barkers Lane. Oh, Joe, she thought with a sudden hard pang of fear, I told you a million times not to toast your laundry too close to the hearth, now didn't I tell you? Heart pounding, she began to run.

"Lucy!" That was Nell Harper, emerging from a thicket

of smoke as Lucy gained her block. "Oh, Lucy, poor lass! Stay back, stay back!"

"Wot is it, Nell? Wot's on fire?"

"Oh, Lucy!" The old woman's face was stained with ashes and tears. "Lucy, sweet'eart, 'tis yer shop!"

"*My* shop?" Stunned, Lucy slipped out of the woman's sympathetic embrace and rushed to see. Nell's frantic voice pursued her through the swirling smoke: "Wait, Lucy, luv! That ain't the worst of it!"

"Oh, my God!" Lucy put her fist to her mouth as she saw what was left of the pawnshop: a ghostly skeleton ignited from within by a heart of red flame. "Oh, dear God!"

Another neighbor, Alf Smith, came and took her arm gently. "We did all we could, lass," he told her, leading her back across the street from the blaze, "but she went up so fast. Like gunpowder—boom! And then the whole place aflame—"

Dazed, Lucy clung to Alf's arm and tried to think what she might have done to cause the fire. Had she left the lamp lit downstairs? Candles up above? From the corner of her eye she glimpsed a crowd gathered around the gutter a few yards away. "Wot's that, Alf?" she whispered. "Wot's goin' on there?"

In the glow of the flames she saw his eyes were hollow, haggard. "Joe," he told her. "Joe Reilly. 'E got 'urt some'ow . . ."

"Joe!" Lucy called, pulling away from Alf, fighting through the jostling throng of neighbors. "Joe!" She reached the center and saw him lying curled on his side, his bald pate dripping sweat. "Oh, Joe. Oh, pet. Wot 'appened?"

He heard her voice and turned toward her, wincing, clutching his belly. His lips were blue despite the heat of the fire and the summer night. They moved faintly, briefly; she knelt down in the gutter beside him, bending her black head to his face to hear.

"Lucy." Why did his eyes look so wide and shiny? "Lucy. I tried to stop 'im—"

"Tried to stop who, Joe? Wot are ye talkin' about?"

"The 'awk man, Lucy." Her name was a strange sort

of gurgle. "The one with the nose. It was 'e set the fire. I saw 'im from me window, 'n' I come runnin' out—"

"Don't try 'n' talk, pet." Lucy cradled his head in her arm and looked up at the crowd. " 'As anyone fetched the doctor? Someone go for the doctor, dammit! Can't ye see this man is 'urt?" They backed away from her slowly. "Wot are ye, sheep, then?" Lucy cried angrily. "Never mind, I'll go myself!"

Joe's hand caught her wrist, tugging her back down beside him. "Lucy." His voice held such desperate urgency. "Lucy, luv, listen. 'E told me to tell ye—" He took a long, shuddering breath. " 'E told me to tell ye 'e'd be comin' back for ye, too."

"Would somebody fetch the man a bleedin' doctor?" Lucy cried to the crowd again, suddenly frightened by the way his body was quivering, how his cheek felt beneath her hand, so clammy and cold.

"Lucy, listen to me! 'E's comin' for ye, too!" Joe said insistently. " 'E said 'e would find ye! Ye've got to get far, far away from 'ere!"

A man in black pressed through the onlookers. "Oh, thank God!" Lucy called when she saw him. "Are ye the doctor?"

He shook his head. "Nay, lass. The priest."

"The priest . . ." Stunned, Lucy rocked back on her heels as he crouched down beside her, making the sign of the cross on Joe's pale forehead. "Do ye repent ye of all yer worldly sins, man, and are ye prepared in yer 'eart for the kingdom of 'eaven?"

Joe paid him no attention; his eyes were focused on Lucy's face. "Go, girl!" he whispered. "Go . . . far away . . . before 'e gets ye, too . . ."

The priest lifted Joe's hands up to fold them in prayer. Relieved of the pressure of his arms where he'd clutched himself, a great wide slit opened in Joe's belly, and a mass of glistening, heaving, steaming guts slithered out.

"Joe!" Lucy screamed. "Joe, Joe, Joe—"

" 'E's gone," said the priest, and closed Joe's wide, staring eyes.

Gentle hands were pulling at Lucy's shoulders, trying to raise her to her feet. As Alf Smith turned her toward him, Lucy vomited all over his chest. "Oh, Jesus, Alf," she gasped, "oh, Jesus, I'm sorry."

"There, lass, no 'arm done." He held her tightly. "It'll all come out in the wash. Come along 'ome with me, then, 'n' the missus'll make ye an 'ot cup of broth—"

"No!" Lucy wrenched free of his comforting arms. Joe was dead. The hawk man had killed him. And it was all Lucy's fault; the hawk man had seen her with Joe. What if he saw her with Alf now, or Nell, or any of her neighbors? They'd all be in danger; to know her, to touch her could be death. Joe had been right; she had to get away from here!

"Lucy, come back!" Alf cried as she darted away from him, running into the screen of swirling, billowing smoke. She had to get away; she needed to find someplace where she could think what to do—

"Let 'er go," Nell Harper told Alf, clutching his doublet. "Let 'er go on, then. Let 'er be by 'erself for a time."

Lucy ran from her shop and the fire and Shoreditch and Joe, ran until her chest was heaving, till her lungs were aching. When she got to the Kingsland Road she stopped and sat on a curbstone, pushing her tangled hair back with shaking hands. Think, Lucy, girl! she told herself sternly, beating back the horrible image of Joe in the gutter that kept filling her mind. Think clear and logical. Think like you do when you add your accounts at the end of the day. She said her six times tables, then her sevens, then her eights and nines and even her thirteens, and by then she could breathe again.

She had to get away, far, far away where nobody knew her. She had to go where the hawk man would never find her. But where? She thought of all the strange, exotic places in which the plays at The Theatre were set—Venice, Genoa, Araby, China. How could she get there? On a ship. But she would need money for a ship. She reached for her purse, then cursed as she realized she had left it on the counter in the shop when Hawk-Nose chased her away. No money, and that meant no ship.

But there was a coach. A coach that would leave on the morrow—what was it that fierce, scowling Lord Carlyle had said? To Derbyshire, that's where he was going. Wherever the hell that was, it sounded like a long way away.

Lucy began to tremble as she thought of the possible consequences of the deception taking form in her mind. She'd be found out in no time. But surely she could keep up the game at least until she got to Derbyshire. After all, there were only the children to hoodwink, and Jeeves . . .

She couldn't see any better option. She ran through the problems she might encounter. They would have to get an early start in the morning, to be gone by the time the real Claudia Moncrief arrived. And oh, Jesus, what about baggage? She'd said that her bags would arrive by the morn.

Half of Lucy wanted nothing more than to run back to Barkers Lane, to Alf and his wife, and cry her eyes out on their friendly shoulders. But the other half made her get up from the curbstone and head toward the house in the close, away from Shoreditch. You can do it, Lucy, she told herself firmly. You can pretend you're a governess. It will be just like being an actor up on Burbage's stage.

And then, as she passed the old dump that marked the end of the parish, she saw it—a trunk made of leather and wood, right at the edge of the heap. "There," she whispered, "now if that ain't a sign straight from 'eaven—" She dragged it away from the rubbish and into the street. It had all its straps and handles and everything, she noted in amazement. What kind of silly sod would throw a perfectly fine trunk away?

She started to haul it off with her, then paused. There was still one problem; it was far too light. Whoever packed it onto the coach would be sure to notice how empty it felt. Drat. She rummaged through the dump, pulling out wadded bits of cloth and rubbish and packing them into the trunk until it felt solidly full. There. She'd made the bloody thing five times heavier, but at least she'd have one less thing to worry about come the morn.

She pushed and pulled, dragged and carried the awkward load toward her destination. Though more than once she got lost in the labyrinth of unfamiliar streets, finally she stumbled on the alley that led to the close. It was black as pitch with the moon gone, but as she emerged in the courtyard faint streaks of light had begun to appear in the western sky. She hauled the trunk up to the stairs leading to the front door, thanked her lucky stars that she'd left the bedchamber window open, and inched back up the drainpipe to the iron ledge. All around her she heard sounds of people waking, stirring—footsteps, doors opening and closing, muffled sleepy voices. Just as she pulled her skirts in the window after her, she heard a knock at the door.

"Mistress Moncrief?" That butler fellow, sounding apologetic.

Lucy dusted off her gray skirts, ran her hands through her hair, and pulled the door open, smiling brightly. "Good morning, Jeeves," she said.

Chapter 2

"Dreadfully sorry to disturb you, Mistress Moncrief, but I was wondering about your baggage. You see, we—"

"Good morning, Jeeves!" a high voice piped as two golden heads appeared behind him in the doorway.

"Miss Minerva, Master Eustace. Good morning." The butler bowed to them. "I trust you slept well."

"So we did. My goodness, Mistress Moncrief," Eustace said, patting back a yawn, "you seem all out of breath."

"Do I? Well. I've been—been doing my exercises," Lucy said, and bent down to touch her toes. "Nothing like a good stretch to start the day off right. What were you saying, Jeeves?"

"Your trunk, Mistress Moncrief."

"You'll find it right by the front steps," Lucy told him briskly. "My men left it there not ten minutes ago."

"That's odd," said Eustace. "I didn't hear a cart come around, Minerva, did you?"

She shook her head. "No. And usually a cart makes an awful hubbub on those cobblestones."

"Don't say *hubbub;* it's a servant's word," her brother chided. His innocent blue gaze skewered Lucy. "You know, I'm quite sure I didn't hear any cart."

Lucy swallowed a distinct impression of uneasiness. She might be fooling Jeeves, but not those bright-eyed little angels. Still, all that mattered was to get on that coach and get out of here. "Well, I'm terribly sorry," she told the boy. "I'll just have them make more noise the next time. Now come along. It is time we were on our way."

Two sleek black carriages hitched to handsome bays were waiting in the courtyard. Lucy eyed the alley nervously, certain that at any instant the real Claudia Moncrief was going to appear. The drivers were loading the luggage onto the carriage roofs with impossible slowness. "'Tis a splendid day for traveling, Mistress Moncrief, don't you think so?" Minerva asked.

"Hmm? Oh, yes." Lucy sighed in exasperation as the drivers struggled to lift her trunk to the boot. "Eustace, why don't you give those poor fellows a hand?"

He turned to her with absolute incredulity. "What? I, Eustace Carlyle, do servant's work?"

Little prig in your fancy suit, thought Lucy. "Dear Eustace." She smiled. "I was making a jest, of course."

At last the coaches were loaded. Jeeves made a sweep through the house to make sure nothing had been forgotten—and took, Lucy thought, a damned lengthy time at it. But finally he emerged, took keys from his belt, and locked the door. "Everyone into the carriages," he ordered, clapping his hands at Jem and the sweating drivers. "Master Eustace, Miss Minerva, in here." He helped them up into the first of the carriages, then turned back for Lucy. "Mistress Moncrief?"

Lucy sneaked a last glance at the alley as Jeeves helped her onto the carriage step. So far, so good. She stooped low to fit inside. Eustace and Minerva sat, hands folded in their laps, one on either bench. "Do you prefer facing front, Mistress Moncrief?" asked Minerva, patting the place beside her.

"Or back?" Eustace indicated his bench.

Lucy had a sudden vivid mental image of Daniel entering the lion's den. "It doesn't really matter. Which does Jeeves prefer?"

"Oh, he won't be riding with us," Eustace assured her. "After all, a butler is hardly of our social class."

The carriage door slammed behind Lucy. "Front, then," she said weakly, taking a seat beside Minerva. Chin up, girl, she told herself, they're just a couple of kids. "How long a ride is it to Derbyshire?"

"Hours and hours and hours," said Eustace, settling back in his seat while his sister nodded agreement. "Just

think, we'll have all that time to get to know one another
ever so well.''

They lurched off over the cobblestones, squeezed
through the alley, and headed toward Kingsland Road at a
brisk clip. Lucy sat in the dim coach and though of Joe.
I'll be back, she promised him fiercely. *I'll come back
someday, somehow, and I'll get the bleeding bastard who
did you in* . . .

"Fruit, Mistress Moncrief?" asked Eustace, pulling a
bunch of grapes from a basket at his feet.

"No, thank you. I'm not hungry."

He scanned her drawn face. "You look rather peculiar,
you know. I do hope you don't get dizzy riding in
coaches.''

"I never have before," Lucy noted with grim humor.

"Perhaps you'd care to read," the boy offered, digging
deeper into the basket. "I've brought Plutarch's *Lives* and
Pliny's *Natural History*. And here's Aesop's *Fables;* Minerva likes to have them read aloud to her. Though, of
course, you have to translate it for her out of the Greek.''

"I'm sorry," said Lucy. "Reading in coaches does
make me dizzy.''

"Well, then," said Minerva, "whatever are we to do?''

Lucy blinked back a sudden swell of tears. Never in her
life had she felt so alone, not even when her father died.
But more than anything else, she felt drained of energy,
utterly exhausted. "I think," she told the children, resting
her head against the jolting coach and closing her eyes, "I
rather think that I shall have a nap.''

She woke some time later, cramped and stiff, with a
violent ache in her head from its bouncing against the seat
back. She opened her eyes warily. In the crack of light
from the barely open window Eustace was reading and
Minerva was dressing a china poppet in a red silk gown.
They looked so lovely and innocent, caught unawares at
play, that Lucy felt guilty for thinking such horrid thoughts
about them. She yawned and stretched to let them know
she was awake, and Eustace's first words immediately set
up her guard again. "What a long nap you've had," he
said with a hint of concern. "One would think you hadn't
been to sleep last night at all.''

"I never sleep well in strange surroundings," Lucy told him archly.

"I've never seen *anyone*," Minerva put in, "sleep like *that* in a coach."

"Don't overemphasize your words, Minerva; it's a sure sign of the lower classes," Eustace told her.

Stuffy little bugger, thought Lucy, and turned to the window. "Do you mind if I open this a bit more?"

"Not at all," Eustace said expansively, and then added, "There's a strange smell of smoke in here; we could use some air."

Lucy drew back the panel and drew in her breath.

The coach was just passing over a little stone bridge spanning a sparkling blue stream. Its banks were lined with nodding trees, their silvery branches hanging low to the water, and with flowers crowned with swarms of buzzing honeybees. Beyond the trees stretched great swaths of brilliant green meadow, and beyond the meadow rose shadowy gray-purple hills. Oh, Pop, Lucy thought, staring at the magical scene in wonder. You were right; there are such places! And even if nothing else good comes from this terrible tangle, at least now I know there are.

"Is something wrong, Mistress Moncrief?" asked Eustace.

"It's so beautiful!" Lucy breathed.

Minerva leaned across her to see. "It's Kettering," she said crossly, "and that means we've still got more than halfway to go." She tossed her doll onto the floor. "I am sick of riding! I want to *do* something."

"Don't overemphasize your—"

"Oh, shut up, Eustace!"

"I know," Lucy said brightly. "Why don't we play a game?"

Minerva eyed her sullenly. "What sort of game?"

"I don't know. What sort do you like?"

"I brought my chessboard." Eustace reached into the basket. "Do you play, Mistress Moncrief?"

"I hate chess," said his sister. "You always win. And anyway, only two can play."

Lucy was searching her memory for games she'd liked

to play as a child. Lord, that seemed such a long time ago. "How about Billingsgate Market?" she proposed.

"Don't know it," Minerva said, pouting.

"Then I'll teach you; it's very simple. All you do is pretend you are going to market—"

"Servants go to market," said Eustace.

"I said pretend," Lucy told him. "It's only a game."

"Go on," said Minerva, her pout fading slightly.

"You pretend you are going to market with a basket. And at the market you choose one of something and put it in. Then I choose two of something and put that in, too. Then you have to say what you first put in, and what I put in, and then put in three more of something."

"That," said Eustace, "is a stupid game."

"Do you mean," Minerva asked shyly, "I would put in an apple?"

"If you like," Lucy told her. "I'll put in two shoes."

"Then we have got an apple, and two shoes, and—" She paused, thinking. "Three cats."

"You can't buy cats at a market, stupid," said Eustace. "And even if you could, they wouldn't stay in the basket."

"Yes, they would, too," Minerva cried, "for it's a big basket with a lid. Go on, Mistress Moncrief." Eustace shook his head in disgust and opened his book again.

"Very well," said Lucy. "I went to Billingsgate Market with a basket. And in it I put an apple, two shoes, three cats, and four ripe plums."

"I went to Billingsgate Market," Minerva repeated dutifully, "with a big basket—with a lid. And in it I put an apple, two shoes, three cats, four ripe plums, and five—five peacocks!"

"There's going to be one hell of a row in that basket when the cats find them," Eustace observed.

"Mind your mouth, young man," Lucy said sternly. "I went to Billingsgate Market with a basket, and in it I put an apple, two shoes, three cats, four plums—"

"Ripe plums," said Eustace.

"If you want to play, play," his sister snapped. "If not, shut up!"

"*Do* you want to play, Eustace?" asked Lucy.

He closed his book. "I suppose I may as well. There's nothing else to do."

An hour later, after Eustace topped the basket with thirty-five Flemish fleeces, Minerva counted back as far as twenty-two yards of pink satin before collapsing in giggles. "I can't remember any more!" she told Lucy. "It makes my head ache."

Lucy rubbed her temples gingerly. "Mine aches, too."

"Our mother used to get headaches all the time," the little girl confided, "but she doesn't anymore."

"Really? How did she stop them?"

"She died," Eustace said flatly. "Didn't you know that?"

"I suppose I must have, but didn't remember. I'm very sorry, though."

Minerva was squirming in the seat. "Eustace, do tell Johnny I have got to stop."

Eustace hung his head out the window and shouted to the coachman, who reined in beside a dense thicket of trees. "Pull down the steps, Eustace, please!" his sister begged, crossing and uncrossing her legs with mounting urgency.

"Don't be ridiculous. You can wait another minute more."

Minerva did, though when the young coachman finally handed her down she darted into the shrubbery, already hiking her skirts up above her knees. Lucy followed her while Eustace headed for the other side of the coach. "Minerva, where are you?" Lucy called, entering the cool, quiet grove.

"I'm all right!" a small voice called back. "Don't come after me!"

"Don't you want some help?"

"I don't need any help!"

Shrugging, Lucy relieved herself behind a screen of branches. Minerva soon appeared, struggling with a dozen layers of stiff petticoats beneath her blue dress. "Here, then, sweetheart, let me get that," Lucy offered.

"I'm not your sweetheart." Minerva yanked her skirts straight and marched back to the coach.

Lucy followed her, chewing her lip, feeling sorry for

the girl. She knew how hard it was to grow up without a
mother; her own had died when Lucy wasn't much older
than these two. She supposed all the money in the world
didn't make that ordeal any easier to bear. She might as
well be a little nicer to them on this journey. After all, she
wasn't planning on staying around very long.

The sun was sinking low in the sky as they set out again.
Eustace handed out cheese and bread and grapes and a
flask that he pulled from the basket. Lucy nearly choked
as she tasted the strong liquor it held. "Does your father
know you've got that?" she asked incredulously.

"He wouldn't care," Eustace told her, and took a long
swig.

"He would if he knew that you'd swiped his—" Minerva began, then stopped as her brother kicked her shin.
She punched his arm; he pulled her hair, and in an instant
a full-fledged catfight had ensued.

"Eustace, stop that!" Lucy ordered as he lunged for his
sister. "Minerva, sit over here and keep still! I don't know
why in heaven's name your father doesn't ride with you on
a journey as long as this."

"Everyone knows gentlemen don't ride in coaches,"
Eustace declared, making faces at his sister. "It's sissy.
Gentlemen only ride horses. So shall I, just as soon as I
am old enough."

Lucy thought about that. It was true; she had only ever
seen women riding in coaches, though she'd never stopped
to wonder why. How silly the gentry were! Even this coach
had to be one hell of a lot more comfortable than a horse
on a long ride. But the information Eustace had imparted
fit in perfectly with what she knew about nobility. Everything they did was for show.

Minerva finished her meal and began fidgeting again.
"I am bored," she complained.

"Don't say *bored,* Minerva. Say *fatigued.* Or *ennuie.*"

"Eustace, why don't you just stick it right up your—"

"Why," Lucy proposed brightly, "don't we sing a
song?"

The children stared at her, their small faces blank. "Sing
a song?" asked Minerva.

"Aye, something good and rousing, like 'Hey-a-Down-

Derry' or 'Grannie Gammer.' Or 'When Barry Goes Bum-Di-Do.' "

"When Barry does what?" Eustace asked.

"We don't know those songs," Minerva confessed. "We don't know *any* songs."

"Nonsense," Lucy scoffed. "Everybody knows songs."

"Our father hates music," the little girl said.

"How can anyone hate music?" Lucy asked in astonishment.

She shrugged. "He does."

"We sing in church," Eustace offered, "but not any songs like those ones you said. Who is Barry, and why is he—what did you say he was doing?"

"Going bum-di-do. Look here, you two, are you gulling me? Do you really not know any songs?"

"No," Minerva said in her small voice, "but if they're like that game I should like to learn."

"The one about Barry," said Eustace.

But Lucy was having second thoughts about that one. It was just about the most lewd song she knew; she didn't know why it had popped into her head. "I'll teach you something else."

"We want to learn that one," Eustace insisted, and his sister began chanting "Barry, Barry, Barry, Barry" over and over until, faced with mutiny, Lucy gave in. What the hell; it wouldn't make any sense to them at their ages anyway.

"Very well. We'll start with the refrain."

"What is a refrain?" Minerva wanted to know.

"The part between the verses."

"What are the—"

"The part," said Lucy, "where we can all sing along. Ready?" She began to sing:

> *When Barry goes bum-di-do,*
> *When Barry goes bum-di-dee,*
> *The girls, they get giddy all over the city,*
> *When Barry goes bum-di-do.*

"That's the stupidest thing I ever heard," Eustace declared.

"Oh, hush, Eustace." His sister was smiling. "You have such a pretty voice, Mistress Moncrief. Sing it again."

Lucy sang it three times through, and eventually they joined in. Minerva's voice was wispy, but Eustace's turned out to be true and clear. When Lucy complimented him on it he accepted the accolade as his due. "Of course I've a fine voice," he said. "I'm a Carlyle. Sing the verse."

Little snot, thought Lucy, and without wasting any more guilt she did:

Now Barry the blacksmith's a fine piece of man;
His hammer strikes sparks 'twixt the anvil and pan.
And fathers can't stand him, but oh, daughters can,
When Barry goes bum-di-do.

"I still don't understand what this song is about," Eustace complained.

"It's *about* a blacksmith named Barry," Minerva told him. "Go on, Mistress Moncrief. Don't pay any attention to him."

Not without a touch of secret glee, Lucy dutifully sang all the verses of the old drinking song about Barry and his giant hammer. The risque innuendos went right over the children's heads; Eustace kept insisting he couldn't make any sense of it, and Minerva was content to shout out the chorus when its time came around. When that was finished she sang them "Lay Down, Nellie" and "King Cophetua and the Beggar Maid" and then "Love Me Little." By that time the sun had set and the moon was rising, and Minerva's head was nodding on her chest. But, "Don't stop," she begged when Lucy would have ended. "I'm awake. I'm listening." Lucy sang on softly, watching the moonlight glisten on the fields and trees:

Love me little, love me long,
Is the burden of my song.

Minerva crawled closer on the bench, resting her golden head against Lucy's shoulder. Eustace tucked his knees up under his chin. The carriage rumbled on through the quiet countryside, and long before it reached Derbyshire those inside were fast asleep.

"Are you waiting for me to carry you in as well?"

"Wot in—" Startled awake by the sensation of someone moving toward her in the darkness, Lucy kicked out blindly from a jumbled dream of the hawk man and Joe.

"I beg your pardon, Mistress Moncrief." The deep voice was cool, ironic; as Lucy opened her eyes she saw Lord Carlyle's hard, scowling face in the light of the lamp he held. All at once she remembered where she was—and who she was supposed to be. She sat bolt upright.

"The children—"

"None the worse for their journey. They're already inside. Won't you join us?" He extended his hand.

Her buttocks impossibly stiff from the long, cramped ride, Lucy followed him across a pebbly drive and through a set of carved oak doors. She was still half asleep, and her only impression of the building they were entering was that it was enormously large. She was yawning, eyes closed, as they went through the doors; when the yawn finally subsided and she glanced about, she nearly turned and ran out again.

"Gor, Lucy girl, look wot ye've stumbled into!" she murmured, staring at the vast marble-floored hall in which she stood. Its dark paneled walls were hung with lethal-looking spears and battleaxes and shields. She jumped as she saw, not two feet away, a fully armored knight, vi-sored and breast-plated, raising up an iron mace. "Eek!" she cried, backing away.

"There's no one inside it." That was Eustace, blandly disdainful as he stood on tiptoe to tilt up the visor. "It was our great-great-grandfather's. He wore it to fight King Richard at Bosworth Field. Which side did your family take in the War of the Roses?"

So far as Lucy knew, her ancestors had stayed home tending to the pawnshop in Shoreditch. But she replied, "Oh, the same as yours."

"How was your trip, Eustace, Minerva?" their father asked. Minerva started to answer, but her brother jabbed her in the ribs and spoke instead:

"Most edifying, Father. Mistress Moncrief gave us a very intriguing lesson in the economics of Billingsgate Market. And she told us a parable about a blacksmith."

"A parable?" his father repeated.

Eustace nodded. "In the form of a rhyme."

"Well. That does sound edifying," said Lord Carlyle. "Jem is waiting in the nursery to put you to bed. Go on. I'd like a word with your governess."

"Yes, Father," said the tousle-haired angels. "Good night, Father. Good night, Mistress Moncrief."

"Good night." Lucy watched them trail across the gorgeous polished floor, Minerva sucking her thumb, and disappear upstairs. The economics of Billingsgate Market indeed!

Lord Carlyle was scowling down at her. "Did the children cause you any problems along the way?"

"None at all," she assured him.

"Really. There were no difficulties?" He arched a thick brow.

"None I couldn't handle. Oh, Minerva fidgeted a bit, but that's to be expected. It's a very long ride. I daresay it would be easier on everyone if you were to have them stop for a good night's rest along the way."

"Stop along the way?" he echoed, the brow inching higher.

"Aye, in a tavern or inn or something. There must be one somewhere."

"Let the children spend the night in a tavern? What a novel idea." He laughed unpleasantly, and Lucy bit her tongue, realizing that, of course, the nobility didn't frequent taverns; he'd likely never been in one himself. "Suggest it to Eustace, why don't you?" he went on, and Lucy thought, Well, 'tis plain to see where those two inherited their snobbishness. Bloody fancy-dance lord . . .

"I've had your trunk taken up to your rooms," he said then. "As soon as Jem is finished with the children, she will help you unpack."

Lucy had to bite her tongue again, but this time to keep from laughing as she pictured what Jem's reaction might be on uncovering her chest full of rags. "Thank you, Lord

Carlyle, but I'd prefer to unpack it myself.'' He looked at her curiously, but what else could she say?

He shrugged his enormous shoulders. ''As you wish. I'll have Jeeves show you up, then. Jeeves!'' he called into the recesses of the house. The butler appeared, his black suit impeccable, not a single one of his scant hairs out of place. Aware of her own wrinkled skirts and mussed curls, Lucy could scarcely believe he had made the same coach journey as she. ''Show Mistress Moncrief to her chambers, Jeeves.''

''Very good, milord.'' The butler beckoned Lucy forward. She thought for a moment that Lord Carlyle was going to say something more, but then he shook his head.

''Good night, sir,'' said Lucy. He didn't seem to hear her; he paced off across the marble floor, the battleaxes and spears casting shadows across his broad back. Lucy followed Jeeves in the opposite direction, up the stairway the children had used.

''My Lord,'' she said as they reached the top and she peered down a corridor that seemed the length of Barkers Lane. ''This is an awfully large house!''

''Lockhaven Hall has one hundred and thirty-seven rooms in all,'' the butler said crisply, ''counting the old wing. Though, of course, that's no longer in use.'' He pushed open a door. ''Your rooms. I hope you will find them to your liking. Should you require anything, please ring.''

''Jeeves—'' Lucy was dying to ask him more questions about the house and its occupants, but the face he turned toward her was so prim and proper that she lost her nerve. ''Never mind. Good night.''

When he had bowed out she turned in a circle, contemplating her surroundings. They were every bit as sumptuous as the Carlyle house in London; if anything, they were even more grand. The bedchamber contained a huge canopied bed with a blue satin coverlet, a wardrobe and bureau of dark polished wood, assorted chairs and tables and footstools, and two large windows covered with blue drapes. She went to the windows and peered out, just in case. There wasn't any drainpipe or ledge; there was only a sheer drop of what looked to be a thousand feet, straight down a cliff into a ravine so deep that the bright moon couldn't pierce its depths.

"Jesus," she said, and quickly stepped back. She wouldn't be escaping from here that way, that was certain. Still, with a hundred and thirty-seven rooms in the place, she could probably hide out till doomsday in an emergency.

On the wall opposite the bed was a door; she opened it cautiously. Inside was another, smaller room, paneled in a reddish wood that gave off a lovely spicy smell. There were hooks hung all around its walls, and a great long mirror, and shelves up above. It had to be for getting dressed in, Lucy decided. Imagine having clothes enough to fill all those hooks! The thought reminded her that she really had to do something about those rags in her trunk before they started to smell.

She went to the huge fireplace that took up an entire wall of the bedchamber, found flint and steel on the mantel, and knelt down to light the fire laid in the hearth. As she struck a spark a vision of the pawnshop, all ablaze, rose up in her mind, and again she saw Joe lying in the gutter, slit open like a pig by old Hawk-Nose's sword . . .

She stared into the flames as they caught and leaped higher, her heart aching for her friend's senseless, brutal death. Suddenly she remembered the paper she'd taken from the lute, still tucked into her bodice. She pulled it out carefully, staring blankly at the squiggles and loops and lines. The letter, Hawk-Nose had called it. This was what he had wanted; it was for this piece of paper that Joe had died. Tears wetting her cheeks, Lucy started to feed the sheet to the fire.

Then she drew back her hand. If she burned this, Joe's death would be senseless. Hawk-Nose had wanted it badly enough to kill for it. Something that meant so much to him could only be useful when she plotted her revenge.

If only she could read! Hating her ignorance, Lucy stared through her tears at the mysterious scribbles. Then she got up and searched the room for a safe place to hide the letter. The long mirror in the dressing room caught her eye. Someone had pawned one like it in her shop once;

beneath the silvered glass it had a backing of wood that
slid out from the frame.

Carefully she lifted the heavy thing from its hook and
turned it around. Sure enough, when she pried at the back
it gave way. She tucked the sheet of paper against the glass
and slid it shut again. Then she hung the mirror back on
the wall and went to open the trunk.

A damp, sour stench poured out as she raised the lid.
Holding her nose, she plucked up a pile of rags and fed
them to the fire. They burned slowly, smokily. Looks like
no sleep for me for another night, she thought, resigned.

As she reached back into the trunk for more rags she
lifted her head, hearing a distant sound. Music—a sort of
music, anyway. Something like a lute, or more than one
lute playing at a time. There wasn't any melody as in a
song, only crashing harsh notes that jumbled all together
in a caterwaul.

She listened, wondering where the sounds might be
coming from. The jarring noise got on her nerves; she
hoped to hell it wouldn't go on all night. But even as she
listened it ended abruptly, and the house was silent again.

Lucy shivered, suddenly feeling alone and very vulner-
able. Then she shook herself. "Stop it," she said aloud.
It was only the tizzy—the *upheaval,* she corrected herself,
thinking of Eustace—of the last day that made her think
that way. At least she had managed, against all odds, to
fulfill Joe's dying command that she get out of London.
That was some small comfort to her in her predicament.

The distant music started up again with a crash. Lucy
began saying her nine times tables to block it out of her
mind and fed another rag to the fire. She'd gotten out of
London. She'd found a haven—what had Jeeves called the
house? Lockhaven Hall. She was safe—for now. The only
trick was to keep up her charade until she could figure out
what to do next.

Chapter 3

Lucy was awakened the following morning by a soft knocking at her bedchamber door. Pushing out from beneath the vast sea of covers, she struggled simultaneously to sit up and to remember where she was. The soft mattress and pillows reminded her; Lockhaven Hall. "Who's there?" she called.

"Me, mum. Jem. Brought up yer breakfast, I have."

Lucy realized with a start that she was starving. She glanced across the room to make sure no signs remained of her midnight bonfire the night before. Then, "Come in," she called, clambering out of bed in her pettiskirts.

Jem pushed the door open carefully, laden with a heavy tray. "What are ye gettin' up for?" she asked, looking at Lucy.

"Why—to eat my breakfast."

"Don't ye want it in bed, then?"

"Eat in bed?" Lucy blinked at the strange notion. "Of course not. Just set it down on the table, please."

"Yes, mum. Shall I draw ye a bath, mum?"

"Draw me a—" Lucy realized she sounded like Alf Smith's green parrot. The little brown-eyed maid was looking at her expectantly. "A bath. Yes, Jem, thank you. I'd like that very much indeed."

The maid bobbed a curtsy and disappeared into the hall. Lucy peeked beneath the covers on the tray and nearly swooned. Eggs and ham, toasted white bread with jam and butter, fresh blackberries and cream, muffins, sweet rolls, porridge—why, it was enough to feed everyone on Barkers Lane for a week!

She looked up to see Jem maneuvering a big copper tub through the doorway. "Wait, I'll help you with that."

"I've got it, mum," Jem plunked it down and started out again. "Water comin' right up."

"Jem, wait." The little maid spun around. Lucy gestured toward the breakfast tray. "There's much more here than I'll ever finish. Why don't you have breakfast with me?"

"What, me eat here with ye?" Jem snorted. "There's a laugh."

"Well, why not? I've come to work here the same as you do."

"I think we both know why ye're here," the maid said coolly. "I'll fetch up yer water now."

Lucy sighed and sat at the table. She'd hoped to make a friend out of Jem, perhaps ask her a few questions about this house and its occupants. She would hate to make another mistake like not knowing Lord Carlyle's wife was dead. But evidently Jem wasn't having any of that. In the meantime, Lucy's eggs were getting cold. She reached for a spoon, then paused. What a frightful lot of cutlery there was on the tray! Three different forks, two knives, four spoons—and all made of solid silver by the looks of them. What in heaven's name could they all be for? She heard Jem coming and quickly picked up a slice of bread; surely even the nobility ate their bread with their hands.

Jem brought up two pails of hot water and four of cold, with Lucy sneaking ravenous bites between each trip so as not to give away her ignorance of manners. When the maid poured the last bucket into the tub she curtsied. "Will there be anythin' else, mum?" Lucy shook her head, her mouth crammed with porridge. "Lord Carlyle asked that ye stop in his study before goin' on to the nursery, mum."

Lucy swallowed the porridge. "Where is Lord Carlyle's study?"

"Down the stairs, across the armory, through the portrait gallery 'n' the receivin' room to the monk's walk," the maid chanted easily, " 'n' then the third door on yer left."

"The monk's walk?" Lucy asked curiously.

"Aye, mum. That part of the house used to be a monstery, as they calls it."

"I see," Lucy said, hoping she meant a monastery. "Thank you, Jem."

Left alone, she devoured as much as she could of the breakfast; hungry though she was, that was less than half. Just in case of an emergency, she tucked a couple of muffins under her pillows. Then she stripped off her petticoats and stepped into the bath. "Gor, ain't this the life!" She sighed aloud as she rubbed sweet-scented soap over her face and arms. "A body could soon get used to this right enough."

She could have lingered there all morning, but the thought of grim, scowling Lord Carlyle waiting for her in his study made her cut the idyll short. She washed her hair as well, to get out the smoke smell Eustace had remarked on in the coach; she had hung her gown in the paneled dressing room overnight, and that seemed to have gotten the worst of the smell out of it. Then she plaited her damp black curls back into a single thick braid at the nape of her neck, put on her stockings and boots and clothes, and examined the end result in the long mirror. "I reckon ye looks like a governess," she told her reflection, cocking her head. "Let's go see wot Lord Carlyle says."

She tiptoed down the long staircase to the armory and wandered about until she found what had to be the portrait gallery—a long, dim hallway with rows and rows of Lords Carlyle, or so she supposed, gazing out at her with identical fierce scowls. "Jesus," she whispered, "they must go all the way back to the days of the Flood!" She emerged into what she hoped was the reception hall, blinking as she saw the walls and high ceiling painted with trees and birds and flowers and beautiful women, all lifelike as could be. "Gor," she muttered, staring at the extravagant display.

"Zuccaro," said a voice behind her. She whirled around and saw the butler, Jeeves, standing just behind her, impeccable in his black livery.

"I beg your pardon?"

"Federigo Zuccaro," the butler said, "though no doubt you recognized the style. 'The Abduction of Persephone,' he called it. My late mistress commissioned it; it is considered the finest example of his work in the country. Lady Carlyle herself modeled for Persephone. There.'' He pointed to the center panel in the ceiling. Lucy looked up and saw a painting of a gorgeous woman with great rippling tides of golden ringlets, clothed all in billowing green gauze, with garlands of flowers draped over her shoulders and circling her tiny waist. She was smiling and gay, but just behind her, in the shadow of the painted trees, loomed a faceless figure of a man in black. ''Remarkable, isn't it?'' the butler went on.

''Remarkable,'' Lucy agreed.

''What I find most intriguing is the way her eyes follow one all about the room,'' said Jeeves, staring up at the painting. Lucy walked a few steps to the left and then to the right and saw that it was true. She didn't much care for the creepy sensation it gave of always being watched.

''Could you please tell me, where is Lord Carlyle's study?'' she asked.

''Through the monk's walk.'' He nodded toward an arched entranceway across the room. ''Third door on the left.''

''Thank you, Jeeves.'' She left him gazing at the ceiling and walked down another dark corridor, then knocked timidly on the door he'd indicated.

''Yes?'' came Lord Carlyle's deep voice.

''Mistress Moncrief, sir.''

''Who?''

Gor, he was a strange bugger! ''Mistress Moncrief, sir. The governess.''

''Oh. Come in.''

She pushed at the latch. ''It's locked, sir.''

''Oh,'' he said again. She heard a key turn, and then the door swung open. She stood at the threshold, looking in curiously. This room wasn't fancy at all; it was a godawful mess. The walls were lined with shelves of books piled helter-skelter, and there were stacks of paper lying everywhere—on the floor, on an extra chair, all over the top of a handsome oak desk. ''Just a moment,'' Lord Carlyle told her, taking his seat again, bending over an open account book much like the one Lucy had used in her shop—though the numbers in it, she noted, standing on tiptoe to see, were much, much larger.

"You've forgotten to carry the four, sir," she told him.

He looked up at her, scowling. "What?"

"You didn't carry the four. There in the third column over."

"Really." He added up the long column of figures again. "Good at numbers, are you? See if you can drum some of that into their heads And the rest of the usual sort of thing. Reading, history, Latin. Any other languages you've got." He scratched out the erroneous figure he'd written with his quill. "You may go."

"Is that all?" Lucy blurted. It seemed odd to her that he should have hired a woman he'd never even met to teach his children—for if he had met her he'd know she wasn't Claudia Moncrief.

His blue eyes considered her dispassionately. "Should there be more?"

"I don't know, sir. They're your children."

"Then that is all."

"Yes, sir." Lucy turned to go.

"Mistress Moncrief." She turned back. "Are you—easily discouraged?"

After all she had been through in the past twenty-four hours, Lucy had to laugh. He stared at her as though she were some sort of heathen Moor. "No, sir," she gasped out. "I'm not."

"Really," he said coolly. "Close the door when you go out."

Back in the monk's walk, Lucy sagged against the stone wall, biting down on her fist as laughter threatened to erupt again. Crikey, she had little enough to worry about from him; she might have come there dressed in nothing but gauze, like the ladies painted on his ceiling, and he'd never have noticed anything amiss!

Of course, there was still Eustace and Minerva. Slightly sobered, she went to find the nursery and begin her new career as a governess.

The nursery was a big square sunny room on the second story, just down the corridor from Lucy's bedchamber.

The walls were plastered and painted yellow, and bright striped drapes hung at the windows lining two sides of the room. There was a big desk for Lucy and smaller ones for each of her charges. As Jem showed Lucy in, the children were sitting quietly, Eustace with a book, Minerva making chalk circles on a sheet of parchment.

Lucy sat down at her desk, hands clasped together to hide their shaking, and said, "Good morning, Eustace, Minerva."

"Good morning, Mistress Moncrief," they chanted, looking up from their labors with expectant smiles.

Now or never. Lucy gulped. "Your father has directed me to instruct you in reading, mathematics, and history."

"Don't forget Latin," said Eustace.

"Ah, yes, Latin." It was eerie how much his blue eyes were like his father's. "So, where shall we begin?"

"Latin," said Eustace.

"Ladies before gentlemen." Lucy turned to Minerva, praying this once she wouldn't be led by her brother. "What do you say?"

Minerva pursed her small cherub's mouth. "History."

"History! Well." It could have been worse; it could have been Latin. "Where did your last governess leave off?"

"The Peloponnesian War," Eustace declared with relish.

"You don't say." Lucy's heart sank. "What did you think of it?"

"It was *boring*," said Minerva. "It happened about a million years ago in a place a million miles away. Who cares about old Athens and Sparta? I wish they'd just killed each other off."

"It's your fault for picking history," her brother reminded her.

"It's better than Latin!" Minerva stuck out her tongue at him.

"History isn't boring," Lucy protested.

"Right," said Eustace, picking up his book.

"No, really!" Lucy didn't know beans about Athens and Sparta, whoever they were, but she hadn't listened to

London gossip for seventeen years for nothing. "Take our own Good Queen Bess. Or take Mary, queen of Scots."

"Who's she?" Minerva asked idly, scribbling with her chalk.

"Do you mean you've never heard the story of how Queen Mary had her husband murdered and then married his killer?"

"You're making that up," said Eustace.

"I am not!" Lucy told him indignantly. "It's history!"

"Tell us about it, then," said Minerva.

Lucy took a deep breath. "The story begins a long time ago—"

The little girl sighed. "They always do."

"But not so long as that," Lucy said hastily. "About forty years."

"Our father is thirty," said Eustace.

"Well, then, about ten years before he was born. Mary's father, King James of Scotland, was mortally wounded in a battle with our King Henry's soldiers. Henry the Eighth, that is. Queen Bess's father. And as he lay dying—"

"Who, Henry?" Minerva asked, puzzled.

"No, no, King James. As he lay dying he got the news that his queen had given birth to their only child—a girl. So she was crowned the queen of Scotland before she was even one year old."

"Fancy that!" said Minerva. "A baby queen!"

Lucy nodded. "Our King Henry wanted her to marry his son Edward, but the Scots didn't like that notion, so they sent her off to France, to be brought up there. And you know what the French court is like."

"What is it like?" asked Minerva.

Lucy lowered her voice. "Why, there's dreadful goings-on there! Debauchery, drinking, murders, and poisonings—"

"What's debo— debo—"

"Debauchery," Eustace told his struggling sister. "Immoral stuff. Men dancing with other men's wives."

"Right," Lucy confirmed. "Anyway, that's where Queen Mary was brought up, and that's where it all began.

When she was just fifteen Mary married the French prince, Francis—the Dolphin, they calls him.''

"Dauphin," Eustace said, snorting. "And it's *call* him, not *calls* him."

"Oh, shut up, Eustace, and let her go on!"

Watch your step, Lucy cautioned herself, meeting the boy's keen gaze. "Anyway, by this time King Henry had died, and his son Edward, and Bloody Mary, and our Bess had been crowned queen. But when Mary married the Dolph— the Dauphin, she proclaimed herself queen of England, on the grounds that Queen Bess was illegitimate.''

"What's illegitimate?" Minerva wanted to know.

"It means her mother and father weren't married, stupid," Eustace informed her.

"Were they?"

"That's a very long story; we'll save it for another lesson," Lucy told her. "Eustace, don't call your sister names. Where was I? Oh, yes. Mary declared herself queen of England, only nobody but the French paid much attention to it. A few years later, the French king died, and the Dauphin was made king of France, with Mary his queen. Then the Dauphin, who was now the king, died too—"

"Lord," Minerva marveled, "they just dropped off like flies!"

"Well, that's all history is, isn't it?" asked Lucy. "Men and women being born and having children and dying. Only some are reckoned important enough to remember, and others not. So. There's some say Mary poisoned her husband the Dauphin and some say she didn't. Anyway, the short of it is, she came back to Scotland, already a widow and hardly any older then me."

"How old are you?" asked Eustace.

"It's not polite to ask a lady her age," said Lucy. "I'm seventeen. Anyway, there's Mary back in Scotland as queen. But you know, Scotland's a harsh, wild country, and after living in France all that time, in the lap of luxury, Mary didn't like it. Besides, she was a Roman Catholic, and by that time Scotland was nearly all Protestant, just like us. So Mary already had troubles with her people and her nobles, but she only made them worse by acting scandalous. She brought a lover with her, a poet fellow, and he got caught up in her bedchamber one night. To hush it all up, Mary had the poet's head cut off.''

"She didn't," said Minerva, shocked and fascinated.

"Oh, yes, she did! Then she fell in love with another fellow, a young man named Henry Darnley. Oh, she's a regular she-devil, she is! She married Darnley, but she got tired of him quicker than you can drop a hat, especially after he got jealous of her Italian secretary and stabbed him to death.''

Eustace rubbed his palms together. "It's a good bloody story, isn't it?''

"Just wait; it gets better. Darnley, who wasn't any saint himself, got sick with the clap—''

"What's the clap?" Minerva asked, looking to her brother, who looked to Lucy.

"It's—well, it's a kind of a pox." Lucy rushed on to forestall further questioning on that subject. "When Darnley got sick, Mary put him in a little house by her castle, all by himself. And in the middle of one dark night—'' She paused dramatically.

"What?" they both cried. "What happened?''

"Boom!" Lucy said, so loudly that they jumped in their seats. "Gunpowder! And the little house was blown all to bits.''

"And Darnley," Eustace asked, wide-eyed, "was he blown to bits, too?''

"You'd think he would be, but he wasn't. They found his body outside the house, stark naked. He'd been strangled to death.''

"Who strangled him?" Minerva whispered.

"Ah, well! There was another fellow Mary had fallen in love with, Earl Bothwell. And the Scots lords brought him to trial for murdering Darnley so that he could marry the queen, but then they said there wasn't enough evidence to prove he was the one, though of course he was. And just three months later, with Darnley's body hardly yet cold in the ground, Mary married Earl Bothwell. But this time—'' She raised a finger. "This time she had gone too far.''

"Why? What happened?" Eustace demanded.

"Her own people rose up against her," Lucy said solemnly. "Bothwell turned chicken and ran away to France, and the Scots made Mary's son James, that she'd had by Darnley—only some say it was really by the Italian secretary—their king. They stuck Mary in prison on an island. But the she-devil got away and escaped to England, and she claimed protection from Good Queen Bess."

"After she'd once claimed Queen Bess's crown?" Minerva asked incredulously.

"Ooh, she's a brazen one is Queen Mary, and rotten right to the core! But you know, Good Queen Bess has got a mighty soft heart—too soft for her own good sometimes. Mary claimed protection on the grounds that she and Bess were family—cousins. Mary's grandmother was King Henry's sister Margaret, did I mention that? Well, all this was nearly twenty years ago. But ever since then Mary's been living off Queen Bess's charity here in England. Bess even gave her a castle of her own. It's called Chartley."

"Chartley!" Eustace got up from his seat and brought the map on the wall to Lucy's desk. "That's not more than forty miles from here, see?" He pointed to a spot on the map. Lucy tapped it with her finger.

"There's where she is, then. She's just a-sitting there in that castle, laying plots, making plans."

"Plans for what?" Minerva whispered.

"For stealing the crown of England from Good Queen Bess!"

The little girl's lips trembled. "I don't want her to be our queen! She's a bad, bad woman!"

"Oh, now, pet, don't cry." Lucy got up to hug her and felt her thin shoulders shaking beneath the fancy gown she wore. "Queen Mary will get her due one of these days, never fear. Her kind always do."

"You are such a baby, Minerva," Eustace said in disgust. The girl's shoulders stiffened, and Lucy pulled away.

Jem appeared in the doorway. "Dinner," she announced, bringing in a tray.

"Dinnertime already?" Eustace asked eagerly. "Goody! I'm starved!"

Lucy saw him nudge his sister as they took their places

at a table beneath the windows. She followed slowly, watching as Jem laid out three plates, a bewildering array of silver cutlery, and a sparkling crystal ewer filled with rosy liquid. "What's this?" she asked, peering into the pitcher.

"Wine, mum."

"These children are far too young to be drinking wine."

"But we always have wine with our dinner," Eustace protested.

"Take it away, Jem, please, and bring us some nice fresh milk."

"But we always—"

"Not anymore," said Lucy. "Jem, take it away."

The maid hurried off while Eustace muttered beneath his breath. "My, doesn't this look splendid," Lucy declared, sitting down and contemplating her plate. Roast beef nice and rare and sliced thin as paper, fresh green peas, mashed turnips with sauce—

"I hate roast beef," Minerva announced, pushing her plate away.

Lucy pushed it right back. "There are plenty of folks in this world who'd be more than grateful for a meal like this."

"Give it to them, then."

"That's enough, Minerva!" Jem arrived with the milk and poured it. Lucy felt someone's foot brush hers beneath the table; looking up she saw Eustace staring hard at his sister, a most unangelic expression on his small face.

Jem withdrew, taking the cart. Eustace shook out his napkin and tucked it under his chin. Minerva followed suit. So did Lucy. Eustace picked up his knife in his left hand. So did Minerva, and so did Lucy. Eustace took the smallest fork from the row of them beside his plate. He laid the knife on its side and, with the fork, shoveled peas onto its blade. Then he raised up the knife and, without spilling a single one, rolled the peas down the blade into his mouth.

Lucy looked at Minerva. She, too, was aligning peas on her knife-blade with the tiny-tined fork. Lord, thought Lucy, the nobility does have strange ways! She laid down her knife and proceeded to pile peas onto it.

With a different fork in his hand, Eustace pulled a slice of roast beef apart along the grain. Minerva, meanwhile, sculpted a neat mound of mashed parsnips onto the back of her spoon. Lucy ate slowly, cautiously, trying hard to master the tricky ways of eating that they used so naturally. "Father always says proper table manners are the mark of a person of class," Eustace observed, buttering bread with the bowl of a spoon. "Do you agree, Mistress Moncrief?"

"Oh, absolutely," she assured him, balancing peas on her knife.

Despite Minerva's complaint about beef, both children cleaned their plates by the time Jem arrived to clear the table. She blinked when she saw Minerva's empty trencher. "Ye've a hearty appetite today, little missy."

"Don't call her that," Eustace said sharply. "She's Miss Minerva to you."

The maid bobbed nervously. "Yes, Master Eustace."

"Now serve us our sweet and go."

"Yes, Master Eustace." The maid handed round fat slices of apple pie and yet another set of knives and forks, then hurriedly withdrew.

"You mustn't speak to Jem that way, Eustace," Lucy chided.

"Why not? She's only a servant." Blue eyes wide, the boy carved his pie neatly with his knife and fork and then ate the pieces with his fingers. So did Minerva and Lucy.

Jem came back one last time for the rest of the dishes. Eustace and Minerva washed their hands and went back to their desks. "What next?" asked Lucy.

"Another history lesson," Minerva proposed.

"It's my turn to choose." Eustace opened his book. "I say we read."

"What are you reading?" asked Lucy.

"This?" He glanced at the spine. "Can't you see from there?"

"Not quite."

"The Bible."

"Well, perhaps you would entertain your sister and me by reading it aloud."

"If you like." Eustace turned back the pages and began. " 'Tell me, muse, of the man of many resources who wandered far and wide after he sacked the holy citadel of Troy, and he saw the cities and learned the thoughts of many men, and on the sea he suffered in his heart many woes—' ' "

"Excuse me," Lucy broke in. "What book of the Bible is that?"

"Homer, of course."

"Oh," said Lucy, wondering whether the gentry even had a different Bible. "Go on."

"Dear me, I'm afraid I can't," said Eustace. "There's a word I don't know."

"Well—read around it," Lucy suggested.

"I can't do that, Mistress Moncrief. It might be important." He got up from his desk, bringing the book to her, pointing at a page. Minerva sidled up as well, peering over his shoulder. "There, that one." Lucy stared at the squiggly lines at the tip of his finger. "The one that begins with F."

"F . . ." said Lucy.

"Aye, F, R, A, U, D. Now what can that spell?"

"Ah—" Lucy felt a hot red blush crawling up her cheeks.

"Suppose I tell you, Mistress Moncrief. "It spells *fraud*," Eustace declared. "And that's what you are."

"That's right," Minerva accused. "You're not a lady!"

"What in the world would make you say such a thing?" Lucy tried bravely to brazen it out. "That's enough reading for today, children, don't you think? How about another history lesson?"

"You can't read, can you?" Eustace demanded.

"Of course I—"

"Go on, then," they challenged in unison. "Read it."

"Read a single word," Eustace dared her, "out of this book."

Lucy waved her arms to hush them. "Keep your voices down!"

"It isn't even the Bible," Eustace said in frank disdain. "It's Homer's *Odyssey*."

Lucy was cornered, and she knew it. "All right," she admitted, "you've found me out."

"I'm telling Father!" Eustace crowed, and darted for the door. Lucy grabbed his sleeve.

"But you can't tell him!"

"Why can't I? You just admitted you're a fraud, an imposter."

Lucy lowered her voice to a whisper. "I'll tell you why not if you'll just sit down." Reluctantly he came back to his desk. "My real name is Lucy Jones," she told the children. "I come from London. But a man there was trying to kill me, and I had to get away."

"You're making this up," said Eustace. "Just like that story about Queen Mary."

"It's God's truth!" Lucy told him. "You've got to believe me!"

"Why was he trying to kill you?" Minerva asked.

Lucy hesitated. She didn't want to tell the children about Hawk-Nose; it would be too dangerous. But she would have to give them something more or they would tell their father about her for sure. "He—he thought I had taken something," she said finally, cautiously.

"You mean you stole something," Eustace declared. "You ought to be in jail. We ought to have Father send you there."

"I didn't steal anything," Lucy insisted. After all, the letter hadn't belonged to Hawk-Nose, not really; it belonged to the other gentleman, the one who had brought her the lute. "And even if I had, that wouldn't make it right for him to murder Joe and burn down my shop!"

"Who is Joe?" asked Minerva.

"My friend. He lived across the street from me."

"And somebody murdered him?" the girl asked, wide-eyed.

Lucy nodded. "And he was trying to kill me, too. But I ran away, and I ended up in front of your house in London, and I saw that the door was open just a little bit, so I knocked on it. The next thing I knew, your father had opened it up and started calling me Claudia Moncrief. I didn't mean to take advantage of him, truly I didn't! But I had to get away from the man!"

"But who is he that was trying to kill you?" Eustace demanded.

"I don't know his name. I don't know anything about him except that he killed Joe and wants to kill me." Lucy looked into their suspicious blue eyes. "I know it all sounds crazy, but I swear on my mother's grave that it's true!"

"Nobody would lie on their mother's grave, Eustace," Minerva said nervously.

He pursed his lips. "You, Lucy Jones or whoever you are, go out in the hallway while I talk to my sister."

Lucy rose from her chair. "Are you going to give me away to your father?"

"I haven't decided yet. Go out in the hall."

Lucy left the room, closing the door, standing with her ear against it. She could hear the children talking in urgent whispers, back and forth, though she couldn't tell what was being said. At last footsteps approached the door, and Eustace flung it open. "Come on in," he invited with a cocky grin.

Lucy stood nervously before her diminutive judges. "Now, then," said Eustace, enjoying rendering their decision. "We've decided not to tell Father about you—at least, not right now."

"I'm indebted to you," Lucy said humbly.

"Of course you are. For the moment, we think it's best we go on calling you Claudia Moncrief."

"Even though," Minerva put in wistfully, "Lucy Jones is a much nicer name."

"Don't be stupid, Minerva," her brother said curtly. "It's lower-class." He turned to Lucy again. "Has it occurred to you that the real Claudia Moncrief is bound to be wondering why we left London without her?"

Lucy nodded. "I keep expecting her to show up any minute. And if she does, my goose is cooked for sure."

"I can fix that." Eustace went to his desk and pulled out a piece of parchment, a quill, and ink. "I'll write her a letter saying her services are no longer required, and sign it with Father's name. Then I'll have Johnny ride with it to London."

"But won't Johnny wonder why a letter is going to me in London," Lucy asked, "if I am here?"

Eustace shook his head impatiently. "Of course not.

Johnny can't read. I'll just tell him to take it to the Moncrief house.''

Lucy nibbled her lip. "That's a very clever idea, Eustace, but I don't want to get you in trouble—using your father's name and all.''

"It won't be the first time," Eustace said nonchalantly. "Now, what shall we say?"

"Put the date at the top," Minerva suggested. "I got a letter once and that's how it began."

"Very well." Eustace dipped the quill and made some squiggly lines, while Lucy watched enviously. She recognized the numbers he made—a 17, and then 1585—though they were ever so much handsomer than when she made them. He skipped some space and then squiggled something more.

"What does that say?" asked Lucy.

" 'Dear Mistress Moncrief.' " He skipped more space. " 'I regret to inform you that your services as gover—' How many S's in governess, Minerva?"

"How should I know?"

" 'That your services as governess to my children will no longer be needed, due to a change in plans. I sincerly—' " He squinted down at that and crossed it out. " 'I sincerely regret any incon— incon—'' He crossed that out, too. "—any problems this may have caused you. Very truly yours, Abraham Carlyle, Lord Carlyle.' "

"Do you think it will work?" Minerva asked anxiously.

"I don't see why not." Her brother folded up the parchment neatly, took a shiny red stick from his desk, and lit a match from his tinderbox. He held the stick to the flame and it melted, leaving a blob of red on the parchment edge. Then he squished a gold ring he wore into the blob, leaving a round impression in it. "There. Minerva, ring for Jem."

"Wait," Lucy said. "I don't think this is such a good idea."

Eustace arched a blond brow. "What about the man who is trying to kill you? Aren't you afraid of him?"

Jem bobbed in the doorway. "You rang, Master Eustace?"

He handed her the sealed letter. "Mistress Moncrief

would like Johnny to take this to her house in London immediately. Isn't that right, Mistress Moncrief?''

Oh, dear, thought Lucy, nibbling her lip. I have the strangest feeling that nothing good is going to come of this. But what choice did she have? ''Yes,'' she said faintly.

''Very good, Master Eustace.'' The maid took the letter, bobbed again, and went off with it.

''Now, then.'' Eustace grinned, flexing his small, white hands. ''I think that's enough lessons for one day, don't you, Mistress Moncrief? Perhaps you had better retire to your rooms. Minerva and I will manage to amuse ourselves somehow.''

Chapter 4

Jem brought Lucy's supper to her room that night. Lucy sighed when she saw the meal—chicken and asparagus, green salad, bread and butter, peaches, boiled custard. "A person wot lived very long in this 'ouse," she mumbled, "would soon be the size of it!" She couldn't eat much, but she diligently practiced the table manners she'd learned from watching the children at dinner. When Jem came back for the tray Lucy was just tucking the peaches under her pillows to save for an emergency.

"Beggin' yer pardon, mum," the little maid said, eyeing her curiously, "but I found some muffins under there this mornin' when I changed yer bed."

"Changed the bed?" Lucy blushed guiltily. "But I'd only slept in it one night."

"That was Lady Carlyle's way. She always insisted the linens be changed every day."

"I see," said Lucy, though she didn't. What a waste of labor! "Well. I am sorry about the muffins, Jem. It—ah—it's just that I've always heard if you leave some food under your pillow at night you'll dream about the man you're going to marry." Jesus, what a lie that was!

But the little maid looked intrigued. "Ye don't say. I ain't never heard that. But I reckon I'll try it. Even if it don't work, I can always tell Johnny it did."

"Johnny?"

"Aye, mum, the coach driver. I been tryin' to get that son of a— well, to get him to marry me for nigh on eight years."

"Well, why won't he?"

"Oh, it's just one excuse after another. We're too young,

64

he used to tell me. Now he says he's waitin' until he can better himself. Doesn't want to be coach driver 'n' courier all his life, 'n' he says I deserves better. As if I cared.''

"Don't you think it's nice that he wants a good life for you?''

Jem snorted. "Mum, 'tis thirty years old I'll be come next April. What I think would be nice would be havin' a husband—the rest can be damned.''

Lucy laughed, glad to have gotten the little maid talking at last. "If it's any consolation to you, I don't think you look a day over twenty.''

"That's on account of how short I is. Got its advantages, bein' short does, I suppose, though I can't help wishin' sometimes I was taller, like ye is. 'Twould make it a fair sight easier doin' the dustin' in this old house, that's sure.''

"How long have you been working here, Jem?''

"Been here all my life,'' the maid said proudly.

"Really? You must have known Lady Carlyle, then. I was looking at her portrait today.''

"Was ye now,'' said Jem.

"She was very beautiful, wasn't she? It must have been a terrible tragedy for Lord Carlyle and the children to have her die so young,'' Lucy hazarded. If only she could get Jem to answer even a few of the questions she had about this house and its occupants!

"Lord Carlyle don't like it spoke of,'' the maid said crisply, and from her suddenly wary expression it was clear that her master's word was the law, on that subject at least. "By the by, he wants to see ye in his study when yer supper's done.''

Lucy's heart sank. So those mean little creatures had tattled on her after all! Too bad Jem had taken those muffins; she might well be needing them before the night was through. "Well, 'twas grand while it lasted,'' she said grimly, getting up from the table.

"Beg pardon, mum?''

"Nothing,'' said Lucy, and marched down the stairs.

Bram Carlyle heard the knock on his study door and called "Come in'' without looking up from the volume of

verse he was reading. For some reason all that day he had
had Dante on his mind; there was a passage from the *In-
ferno* that he wanted to find but could not seem to locate.
How did it go? "There is no greater sorrow—" And then
something about the past . . .

"It's locked," said a tart voice. The new governess.
What was her name? Moncrief. Claudia Moncrief. The
name didn't suit her somehow, though he wasn't sure why.
How the devil did that passage from Dante go? He got up
to open the door, saw her green eyes, and remembered it
all in a rush:

> *Nessun maggior dolore*
> *Che ricordarsi del tempo felice*
> *Nella miseria.*

"There is no greater sorrow than to be mindful of the
happy time in misery." Why should he think of that now,
when he looked at her? She was no different from the
others, after all. He knew what had brought her here.

"I beg your pardon, Mistress Moncrief." He ushered
her in, noting that she seemed relieved. Probably because
he'd remembered her name this time. No surprise there,
really, not if she had talked to the others who'd come here
before her. There had been—what, ten? Twelve? And all
in the three years since Olive died. Was it any wonder he
could not keep them straight? They merged in his mind
into one long parade of rustling silk and sultry manners
and perfume and paint.

But this one wasn't painted; she needed no rouge to
highlight those fine cheekbones, no walnut juice to stain
her jet lashes black. What would she look like with her
midnight hair hanging loose over her shoulders? Shocked
at himself for wondering such a thing, he turned from her
quickly, clearing a chair of litter and gesturing her toward
it. "How did the first day's lessons go?" he asked gruffly,
taking his own seat again, watching from beneath lowered
lids as she went to the chair. She did not move like the
others. No coy gestures, no wasted motions, no fluffing
up of skirts or calling attention to her bodice with her
hands. Her breasts were small but full beneath the drab

gray gown she wore. Christ, why was he noticing her breasts? Angry at his thoughts, he repeated his question even more sharply, and saw her green eyes blink.

"I already told you, sir. Very well indeed."

"Did you? Well, speak up, dammit; I can't hear you when you mumble." But there was nothing wrong with her voice; he knew that. The fault was his. "What subjects did you cover?"

"History," said the girl sitting before him. "Reading. And some writing."

History . . . probably prying everything she could about him out of Eustace and Minerva. He scowled. "What do you think of the children?"

"Oh, they're very nice, sir." She paused. "Very clever. Plenty of gumption."

Now there was a word he'd never heard a governess use. But her language was just like her movements, simple and direct. And it certainly wasn't a word he would ever have applied to the two children upstairs. "You haven't found them—difficult?" he asked, scratching his chin.

"Well, they're high-spirited, sir. But I don't think that's such a bad thing for children to be."

There was that, too—the way she called him sir where the others had hastened to establish a first-name basis, winking and sly: You must call me Felicia, or Barbara, or Annabel, or whatever their bloody names had been. And all as if to say, this is only a game, this governess business. Shall we get on to more important things now, Bram? A simper, a primp of their hair, a seductive pout—

But perhaps *she* was being clever, this Claudia Moncrief. Perhaps she had spoken to the others and knew what hadn't worked; perhaps this was just a different tack. Aye, that must be it, Bram thought. "What a refreshing attitude you have, Mistress Moncrief," he said, his voice dripping irony. "Let us hope you last longer in your post than your predecessors."

"My—oh, yes, sir. Do let's hope that." She was blushing now, plainly flustered—which only went, Bram noted with satisfaction, to confirm his guess. He opened a desk drawer.

"We have not yet discussed your wages, Mistress Moncrief. Will fifty pounds a month be suitable?"

"Fifty pounds!" She gasped.

Bram's lip curled in a sneer. God, the greediness of these rich men's daughters never ceased to surprise him. "Seventy-five, then, if you find that low. First month in advance." He counted out gold sovereigns and pushed them at her across the desk. She made no move to take them, and his sneer intensified as he reached back into the drawer. "If you are going to insist on a hundred—"

"No!" she said quickly, and that did surprise him. "I mean—that is, seventy-five is quite adequate."

"If you want a hundred, Mistress Moncrief, I assure you another twenty-five pounds means nothing to me."

"I'm sure that's true, sir." Bram raised his eyelids slightly. Was that disdain in her voice? No, it couldn't be. But there was something unnerving about this one, something he could not quite put his finger on. She was different, and not only because she was more beautiful. He wanted her gone from this room, from his refuge. He wanted to be alone.

"That's that, then," he told her. "Close the door when you leave."

She didn't seem to have any purse, for she scooped the sovereigns into the front of her skirt and tied them there in a bundle. Where had she learned that? Bram wondered. He'd seen Jem carry apples from the orchard that way. "Thank you, sir. Good night." Graceful as a bird, she rose and went out. The door closed. The latch fell. Locked in his solitude, Bram looked down at the book on his desk. *There is no greater sorrow than to be mindful of the happy time in misery* . . .

Like a swan she moved. And those green eyes, so deep and still, like a cool, quiet forest. Black hair against her white throat, strewn across her white breasts . . .

He yanked open the dark drawer, groping for his brandy flask. Christ, he must have left the damned thing in London. He started to ring for Jeeves, then stopped. He'd go down to the wine cellar himself and bring up a bottle. She'd disturbed the sanctity of this refuge for the moment, and he needed a drink. Before he left he piled a stack of

books and papers back on the chair in which she had sat.
There. No traces left. And with enough brandy in him, he
knew, there would be no traces left in his memory of the
happy time.

With the enormous treasure tied in her skirts, Lucy hurried up the stairs to her room and let the gold coins spill
all over the coverlet, listening to the lustrous jangle they
made. Seventy-five pounds. Christ, it was a bloody fortune! She could go all the way to Turkestan or China with
this much money, go so far that old Hawk-Nose would
never be able to track her down!

Nor she him, she realized as she stared at the glistening
gold. She could run away, but where would that leave Joe?
Lying there in the gutter with his guts slithered out, and
no one in the world except she knowing why he had died.

Well, she and old Hawk-Nose. Her blood began to boil
as she thought of the names he had called her, what he'd
said about no one ever missing a cheap Shoreditch girl.
No doubt he thought nobody would miss Joe, either, just
because he'd been poor. "Well, ye was wrong, ye bleedin'
bastard," she said aloud fiercely. "I misses 'im. And
there'll be no runnin' away until ye gets wot's comin' to
ye, or my name ain't Lucy Jones!"

Strange. Her old Shoreditch voice was beginning to
sound unfamiliar. Just goes to show, she mused, what
comes of rubbing elbows with the gentlefolk! Another few
weeks here and no one back home would understand a
single word she said.

Another few weeks. She looked down at the gold on the
bed. It wasn't even hers yet, not really. An advance for
the month, Lord Carlyle had called it. Taking it now and
running away would be the same as stealing, and stealing
was wrong, even from somebody as rich as scowling Lord
Carlyle.

She'd save it, she decided, ripping a square from her
petticoat and wrapping up the coins. She'd hide it and save
it until she'd earned it, and then she'd decide what to do.
She could last a month here—assuming, that is, that Eustace and Minerva didn't give her away.

She put the gold with the letter, in the space behind the

mirror. As she closed the wood slat she thought of the strange, unmelodic music she'd heard the night before, floating up from somewhere in the house below. I must remember, she told herself, to ask the children what that is, and who it is that plays.

She yawned, stripping down to her pettiskirts and climbing into bed. Difficult, were they? Little wonder, with their poor mum dead and their father such a bleeding grim sort of man. She'd need to keep all her wits about her to last the month out. But at least, so far, she had Lord Carlyle fooled.

Black curls caught up in an austere bun, gray gown brushed and pressed, Lucy opened the nursery door the next morning, strode to her desk, and said, "Good day, Eustace, Minerva." The children made no reply, nor did they move from where they were sitting: Eustace on the windowsill with a book, his sister cross-legged on the floor with her china doll.

"If you'll take your desks, children, we can begin this morning's lessons." They stayed where they were. "Eustace. Minerva," Lucy said more sharply. "Kindly take your seats so that we can begin."

Eustace looked up, his blue eyes narrowed and cunning. "We don't feel like lessons today," he announced, and his sister nodded vigorously.

"Oh, you don't, do you?"

"No, we don't. And we particularly don't feel like taking lessons from you. After all, you're not really a governess, are you? You're an illiterate peasant. Frankly, we don't see what you could possibly have to teach us that would be of the slightest interest. So, dear Mistress Moncrief, what are you going to do about that?"

"That's right," Minerva said rather nervously. "What are you going to do about it?"

So this, Lucy thought wryly, is what comes of revealing your weakness to enemies! She contemplated the cheeky little brats. Then, "Nothing," she said.

"Nothing?" Minerva echoed, with a surprised sidelong glance at her brother.

"What can I do? Clearly you two have got me over a

barrel. You just go on with what you are doing, and I'll amuse myself somehow.''

She wandered over to the shelves across the room, putting her back to them, feeling their eyes on her. She looked at the map hung on the wall. She examined a bronze dog that served as a bookend. She picked up a carved wooden bird and laughed at its painted, unblinking expression. She straightened a jar full of paint brushes and set the lid back on Minerva's box of colored chalk. She found a pile of doll clothes and began to fold them.

''Don't touch them,'' Eustace said rudely. ''They're Minerva's.''

''I beg your pardon.'' Lucy smiled to herself at this evidence that she was still being watched, then looked in surprise at a familiar object: a square frame stretched with wires strung with shiny wooden beads. ''Whose is this?'' she asked, picking it up.

''Eustace's,'' said Minerva. ''Someone Father knows sent it for a birthday present. It's some kind of musical instrument. We think.''

''No, it's not. It's an abacus. My father used to use one in the shop.'' Lucy pushed the beads back and forth.

''Use it? For what?'' asked Eustace.

''For counting.''

''He must have been really stupid, then, for there are only fifty beads or so. Even Minerva can count that high.''

''He used it for doing sums,'' Lucy told the boy, holding her temper. ''Addition and subtraction and multiplication, too, though that's complicated.'' She smiled, picturing her pop, his work-worn fingers flying over the beads, racking up the most enormous sums just to amuse himself.

Minerva put down her doll. ''How would you use it to do sums?''

''Pick two numbers. Any two numbers.''

''Thirty-eight,'' said Minerva. ''Can they be that big?''

''Of course. They can be as big as you like.''

''Ninety-seven,'' said Eustace, getting up from the windowsill.

''Very well, thirty-eight and ninety-seven. Shall I add or subtract them?''

"Add them," Minerva proposed. "That will make a really big number."

"I can do that sum on paper," Eustace said disdainfully, heading for his desk, taking out his quill and ink.

"One hundred and thirty-five," said Lucy, having slid the beads around.

"That was fast!" Minerva marveled.

"Aye, but how do we know she's right?" Eustace figured the sum on paper, tongue between his lips. "Well, you were lucky that time," he admitted a few minutes later, very grudgingly.

"Now subtract them," Minerva challenged. "We'll have a race, Eustace versus Mistress Moncrief."

"Fifty-nine," said Lucy, before Eustace could even dip his quill. Glowering, he performed the subtraction, then looked up at Lucy.

"How does that thing work?"

"It's very simple, really. It just uses carrying over, the same as when you do a sum on paper."

"I hate carrying over," Minerva declared. "It always muddles me."

"You can't get muddled with an abacus," Lucy explained, "because every time you carry over, you just move the beads. Let's start with something simple, say, nine plus eight."

"I hate nines," said Minerva.

"Really? You shouldn't, you know. Nine is my very favorite number, because it's made up of three threes. Here, nine plus eight." Slowly, patiently, Lucy showed them how to move the counters on the frame to perform the sum.

"That is a pretty handy thing, isn't it, Eustace?" Minerva asked admiringly. "What do you call it?"

"An abacus."

"I don't suppose you know how to spell that," Eustace said cuttingly.

"Oh, shut up, Eustace. You're only jealous because she was faster than you." Minerva touched the shiny beads. "Let's do another sum."

In just a few hours, both children were doing simple addition on the instrument, with Minerva showing a genuine aptitude. "It's ever so much easier than doing sums on paper," the girl said happily. "Think, Eustace, how surprised Mistress Buxton would be if she could see me. That's our last governess," she explained in answer to Lucy's questioning look. "She smelled of camphor. You smell like Parma violets."

"Thank you," said Lucy. "How long was Mistress Buxton your governess?"

"Three weeks." Eustace giggled. "A new record."

"Why did she leave?" The children exchanged glances. Just then, Jem brought their dinner in.

But Lucy wasn't so easily distracted. "Why did Mistress Buxton leave?" she asked again when the table was laid out and Jem had gone.

"I hate sausages," said Minerva, grimacing at her plate.

"I like them because of how one is supposed to eat them." Eustace laid his big knife along the length of one and pushed down so the meat came squirting out of its skin.

"There is that," Minerva agreed, gleefully squashing down her own sausage.

"You haven't told me why Mistress Buxton left you," Lucy reminded them, copying their method of dining.

"She saw the ghost," Eustace said matter-of-factly, chewing sausage meat wrapped in bread.

"She *what*?"

"Saw the ghost. Haven't you seen her yet?"

"It's Mother," Minerva said helpfully.

"Oh, for heaven's sake!"

"Don't you believe in ghosts?" asked Eustace.

"I don't know if I do or not," Lucy admitted. Her neighbors in Shoreditch certainly had, but she'd never been convinced that they really existed. "I know I've never seen one."

"We believe in them," Minerva whispered. "Especially Mother's. She plays the virginals at night, down in the music room. Haven't you heard her?"

Lucy suppressed a tiny shiver. "I have heard something . . ."

"Well, that's Mother's ghost," said Eustace. "Pass the butter."

"Pass the butter, please," Lucy said automatically. "Why would your mother's ghost haunt Lockhaven Hall?"

"Because ghosts haunt," Minerva told her. "That's what ghosts do."

"She stays in the old wing, mostly," said Eustace. "Only sometimes she comes up the stairs from the music room. That's where she died, on those stairs."

"How did she die?" Lucy asked.

Again the children exchanged quick glances. Eustace answered, "She fell. Do you want to see where? We can take you down there after dinner, if you like."

Lucy had to admit she was curious. "All right," she said.

When the last of the sausages had been squished out, and the asparagus eaten with fingers, and the cup custard scooped up with knives, they slipped out of their seats. "Bring a candle, Eustace," said Minerva. "It's awfully dark down there."

With Eustace and the candle in the lead, they tiptoed past Lucy's rooms, then turned left at the end of the hallway. At the end of that corridor was a low door fastened with a pin stuck through the latch. Eustace unhooked it gingerly and pushed it open; Lucy saw a circular stone staircase winding downward, the steps worn in the centers by the tread of countless passing feet.

"There's a trick step halfway down to stop marauders," Eustace said, pointing. "Want to see it?" Lucy nodded, and one by one they ducked through the door and started down.

The trick stair was twice as high as the rest; Lucy could easily see how Lady Carlyle would have tripped and fallen in the cramped, narrow space. "Go all the way down, Eustace," Minerva whispered from behind Lucy. "Show her the virginals." Her small voice echoed eerily off the old stone walls.

"Come on, then." Around and around they went; the staircase seemed so long that Lucy thought they must be underground by the time they reached the bottom. Eustace ducked through a low arch, the candlelight dipping and wavering, and then the three stood huddled together in a small room, windowless and bare except for a square wooden box set up on legs.

"That's the virginals," Minerva whispered. Lucy tip-toed toward it. In the front of the box was an opening lined with small rectangles made of polished wood, white and black. She reached out to touch one, then jumped as a high, sweet note floated into the air.

"How does it do that?"

Eustace brought the candle closer and set it down on the box. He lifted up a panel in the back, and Lucy saw rows of strings, all different lengths, wound to pegs at each end and stretched across the box's insides. She ran a tentative finger along them, and the room was filled with a wonderful flurry of rich sound.

"Stop it!" Minerva hissed, snatching Lucy's hand away. "You'll wake up the ghost!"

But Lucy was captivated by the instrument. "Do you know how to play it?" she asked the children.

"Only Mother could," Eustace told her. "And now her ghost."

"It's a waste to leave it down here." Lucy plunked on the keys again. "We ought to ask your father to have it brought up to the nursery."

"Are you crazy?" Minerva whispered. "What if the ghost came, too?"

"I would ask it for lessons," Lucy said, and then laughed, picking out a note. " 'When Barry—' No, that's not right, is it? 'When Bar— When Barry goes bum-di-do—' " She sang along as she fumbled to find the right keys. " 'When Barry goes bum-di-dee—' Sing with me, why don't you?" she asked the children, turning around. Minerva was clutching her brother, her face very pale; he was staring toward the arched entrance to the stairway, his eyes very wide. Lucy stopped playing abruptly, hearing what they'd heard: slow, heavy footsteps descending the stairs.

"It's the ghost!" Eustace whispered, and Minerva began to cry. "Do something!"

"Ghosts don't make any noise when they walk," Lucy hissed back. "Do they?" The footsteps stopped—the trick stair—and then resumed. Closer and closer they came. Minerva, blubbering, hid behind Lucy's skirts. Lucy reached over to the virginals for the heavy brass candlestick. She had no idea whether one could stop a ghost by bashing its head, but she felt infinitely braver having some weapon in her hand. Above the faint sound of Minerva's sobs and those heavy footsteps she heard her own heart pounding, loud as a drum.

Again the footsteps stopped. Lucy gripped the candlestick, raising it over her head. An arm appeared in the doorway, and then a huge shoulder, and then—

"Why, it's your father," Lucy cried in relief, turning around to reassure the children.

But their faces had turned even paler; if anything, they seemed more terrified by Lord Carlyle than by a ghost. Even Eustace was cringing, and Minerva had buried her face in Lucy's skirts. Lucy, nonplussed, looked back at Lord Carlyle and had to fight down the urge to join the children in huddling on the floor. She had never, *ever* seen anyone look as angry as their father did.

"What is going on down here?" he demanded, his blue eyes blazing.

"It's her fault, Father," Eustace blurted from behind Lucy. "She made us come down here; it wasn't our idea."

Lucy, appalled by this blatant lie, whirled on the boy and was about to protest, but the genuine terror on his small face as his father advanced on him checked her tongue. Lord Carlyle yanked the children out from behind her, and Minerva screamed.

"Have I or have I not forbidden you to come into his room?" he thundered.

"Yes, Father," Eustace whispered, "but she made us do it! She made us come!"

Lord Carlyle, holding each of the children by an elbow, glowered at Lucy. "Mistress Moncrief, is that true?"

Eustace looked at her, his blue eyes pleading. "I—"

Lucy swallowed. "Yes, sir. It is."

He let the children go, and they scrambled toward the staircase. "This—room—is—off—limits," he said, his jaw clenched tight with fury. "Get out!"

"I'm sorry, sir. It won't happen again—"

"It had bloody damned well not! Now get out of here!"

he roared. Lucy darted through the arch, hearing Minerva and Eustace running up ahead of her as though the devil himself were in the room below. Though Lucy's steps were more measured, she did give a sigh of relief as she left the winding staircase behind her and came out into the light.

The children were waiting for her at the top. "Thanks," Eustace whispered. "We owe you for that."

Lucy glared at him. "You're damned right you do!"

Lord Carlyle's son and daughter were in no mood for lessons after that little adventure, and neither was Lucy. After a few attempts to interest them in doing sums, she put the abacus away and got up from her desk. "Where are you going?" Minerva asked.

"Out," Lucy said shortly. "I need some air."

She hadn't been outside Lockhaven Hall since her arrival. Stepping through the front doors of the dark armory and into bright sunshine was like stepping into paradise. The sky was deep blue and cloudless, the air mild and balmy, and gentle breezes the like of which never reached Shoreditch in summer ruffled her hair. Lucy crossed the drive to the iron gates in the tall wall surrounding the house and then paused, looking back. "Gor," she marveled aloud. If the place seemed big from the inside, it looked impossibly immense viewed this way; she had to tilt back her head to see the tips of the towers.

She went through the open gates and followed the line of the wall to her right. After curving around for what seemed like miles the wall finally ended, and the ground plummeted downward in the steep-sided cliff she could see from her bedchamber. In the daylight she saw there was another grand, huge house in the thicket of bristling trees far below. To her left was a forest, dense and dark and green; the tangle of branches and ferns and underbrush was intimidating to a city girl like Lucy. She retraced her steps along the wall and passed the gate, going to the left instead.

This way was more to her liking. A wide green meadow dotted with flowers sloped down to a sparkling blue pond on which long-necked geese paddled to and fro. Beyond the pond was an apple orchard, the gnarled black branches of the trees heavy with unripened fruit. How soft and green the meadow grass looked! Lucy thought of what her father had told her about the places where wildflowers popped right up between your toes. It seemed entirely possible here. She darted a quick glance back at the house to make sure no one was looking, then tugged off her shoes and stockings and walked through the luxuriant grass toward the pond.

The soft earth gave a little beneath her bare feet; the grass sent out a scent as she crushed it that was sweeter than any flower sold in the Billingsgate Market stalls. The birds on the water twisted their small heads around to face her as she came near them, their red eyes suspicious and malevolent. They paddled to the far side of the pond as she reached its edge: Lucy ignored their resentful stares and sat on the mossy bank, hiking up her skirts and dangling her feet in the cool water, watching the circles spread out from her toes.

The sun was deliciously warm on her face; she pushed up the sleeves of her gown and loosened her bodice strings, lying down on the bank and closing her eyes as the breeze rustled the leaves on the apple trees. She stretched her arms over her head, reveling in the exquisite luxury of idleness, of time to herself. Lord Carlyle and his sneaky children forgotten, she began to sing:

> O Western wind, when wilt thou blow,
> That the small rain down can rain?
> Christ, that my love were in my arms,
> And I in my bed again!

A shadow fell across her face, blocking out the warm sunlight. Now where in hell could that cloud have come from? Lucy thought crossly, breaking off her song. She opened one eye and then sat up abruptly, screaming in fright at the sight of the huge black figure standing over her. The geese flapped into the sky, honking madly; Lucy put her hand to her racing heart, recognizing the scowling man who loomed over her.

"You scared the devil out of me!" she cried angrily.

Lord Carlyle laughed. "Oh, I doubt that. Did you think I was coming to carry you away to hell, little Persephone?" He made a slow circle around her, his blue gaze raking her hiked-up skirts and white feet, the loose strings of her bodice. "I must say, you suit the role rather better than my late wife did. I think it's those green eyes of yours. Green as the leaves on the apple trees . . . ."

Lucy yanked down her skirts and tugged tight her bodice. "I think it horribly rude of you to come creeping up on me that way!" Having him stand over her made her feel nervous. He was so tall; beneath his billowing shirt she could see the rippling muscles of his chest and arms.

"Really?" he said coolly. "I suppose it is just coincidence that I find you here."

"Of course 'tis coincidence!" she told him. "What else would it be?"

"I thought someone might have mentioned that I go for a swim here every day, just about this time." His big hand moved with surprising quickness, catching her bodice strings. "I thought perhaps you'd come to join me."

Lucy sprang away from him, tensed like a cat. "Keep your bloody hands off me."

Something glinted in the depths of those stormy blue-gray eyes—something like surprise. "My bloody hands, Mistress Moncrief?" he asked softly, looking down at them.

Lucy blushed. Dammit, remember—you're supposed to be a lady, she reminded herself. And ladies don't use that word! "I'm sorry, sir," she stammered. "I meant nothing by it."

"Pity," he said. "If you had, I might have asked you to join me in my swim."

"I don't swim, sir."

"That's a pity, too," he told her, and stripped off his shirt.

Lucy stared for a moment in awe at his splendid, sun-darkened chest, the curly black hairs that covered it, the taut flesh of his belly and his brawny arms. God, she thought, what a man! Every inch of him seemed to exude power and strength. She raised her eyes to his face.

"Care to reciprocate, Mistress Moncrief?" he asked, and reached again for her bodice strings.

Lucy tore her gaze from him, pushed his hands away, and caught up her shoes and stockings, running back to the house. At the gates she paused to catch her breath and, against her better judgment, to look back. Her employer's clothes lay in a heap by the edge of the pond, but not a ripple disturbed its surface, and Lord Carlyle was nowhere to be seen.

Chapter 5

"Eustace," Lucy said the next morning in the nursery, "who is Persephone?"

"A Greek goddess," he told her. "The daughter of Demeter and Zeus."

"Oh," Lucy said, wondering why it was that in this house one question always led to ten more. "What's a goddess?"

"You know. A supernatural being."

"Like a ghost?" Minerva asked with a shudder.

"No, not like a ghost," he said. "The Greeks thought there were gods and goddesses who ruled over the earth. Sort of like giants in fairy tales. Demeter was the goddess of the earth, and Zeus was the chief god, the god of thunder."

"And what about Persephone?" Lucy asked.

The boy scratched his nose. "She was kidnapped by Pluto, the god of the underworld, to be his wife. He carried her into Hades—"

"What's Hades?" Minerva interrupted.

"Hell," Eustace said.

"Don't curse at your sister, young man," Lucy told him sternly.

"I'm not, that's what Hades is," he said impatiently. "The underworld, where the dead people live. Then Demeter got mad at Pluto and stopped everything on the earth from growing—"

"How did she do that?" asked Minerva.

"I don't know. That was her job as the earth goddess; she made things grow. Then Zeus got mad at Pluto, too, because all the mortals were dying because they didn't

81

have anything to eat, and he made Pluto let Persephone go.''

''This is more complicated than Queen Mary's husbands,'' his sister complained.

He gave her a withering look. ''What happened then?'' Lucy asked before an argument could erupt.

''Pluto had to let Persephone go,'' Eustace told her, ''but before she did he gave her six pomegranate seeds to eat. So after that she had to come back to the underworld for six months out of every year.''

''Why?'' Lucy and Minerva asked in chorus.

''Because,'' he told them impatiently, ''once you eat anything in the land of the dead you have to go back there. And that's how the Greeks explained why there was winter and summer. During the summer Persephone is on earth with her mother, but during the winter she's with Pluto in hell.''

''What a wonderful story!'' Lucy exclaimed. ''Do you know any more of them?''

''Tons,'' he said offhandedly. ''Only they're not called stories. They're called myths. Father used to tell them to us at bedtime.''

''I don't remember that,'' Minerva protested.

''You're too little to remember. It was a long time ago. He named his horse after somebody in a myth. Bellerophon, that slew the Chimaera.''

''What's a—'' Lucy couldn't pronounce it.

''A kind of she-devil.'' He sniffed. ''Some governess you are.''

''Mum?'' That was Jem, poking her head through the doorway. ''Sorry to interrupt yer lesson, mum. But Lord Carlyle's havin' guests for dinner tonight and he says ye should join 'em.''

''Me?'' Lucy echoed in astonishment.

''Aye, mum. Eight o'clock sharp.'' She ducked out again.

''Father must like you,'' Eustace said, with a quick glance at his sister. ''He never asks our governesses to dinner.''

''I'm sure I'm very flattered,'' Lucy said wryly. ''But I'm not going to go.''

"Why not?" asked Minerva.

"Just because I don't want to."

"You'd better go," the little girl warned. "He gets awfully mad when he's crossed. You saw him in the music
room yesterday."

"What can he do if I don't go?"

"He can dismiss you. Let you go," Eustace told her.

Lucy nibbled her lip. She'd only been here a few days;
she hadn't earned any of the gold he had given her yet.
"What would I wear?" she asked worriedly, looking down
at her plain gray gown. "This is the only dress I have."

"You'll be fine in that," Eustace assured her. "He's
just having the tenant farmers over. They talk about the
harvest. They're the only guests he ever has here anymore."

Still Lucy shook her head. "I haven't learned well
enough how to eat properly. I'd make a fool of myself."

"I know!" Eustace said promptly. "I'll go down and
find out from Cook what she's making, and Minerva and
I can go over how to eat it with you."

"You'd be willing to do that?"

"Of course! We owe you a favor for not telling on us
to Father yesterday."

"Well—all right, then," Lucy said tentatively. She really didn't want to risk Lord Carlyle's wrath again.

"Wonderful!" said Eustace. "I'll just pop down to the
kitchens, and then we'll get right to work."

He was back within minutes, armed not only with the
menu but also with fistfuls of cutlery. Lucy dutifully practiced with the silver most of the afternoon, while the children looked on. At last they declared her ready. Precisely
at eight she descended to the armory, her gray gown neatly
pressed, her hair tucked back into its bun.

Lord Carlyle was nowhere in sight, but Jeeves was
handing glasses from a tray to a dozen guests. Suddenly
shy, Lucy paused at the foot of the stairs. The women in
the room were all dressed much more finely than she,
farmers' wives or no; a few even wore jewels. The men
were hardy-looking fellows in doublets of leather; their
boots were well worn, but they'd been polished till they
shone. Clearly everyone knew everyone else, for they were

all chattering together. Intimidated, Lucy had just decided to duck back up the stairs when Jeeves saw her and announced in a loud voice, "Mistress Claudia Moncrief, governess to Lord Carlyle's children."

Every face in the room turned toward Lucy; the sounds of laughter and conversation died away. Twelve curious pair of eyes considered her from head to toe. There was a long moment of silence, while she stood frozen. Then the faces turned away, and the guests returned to their chats as though Lucy wasn't even there.

"Sherry, Mistress Moncrief?" Jeeves asked, coming toward her with his tray.

"Th-thank you." Lucy took a glass and gulped down the strong tawny wine, which steadied her a bit. She couldn't imagine why everyone was being so unfriendly to her. At last one of the women approached her. Lucy smiled brightly, glad for the chance to make friends.

"Claudia Moncrief. 'Tis yer father the baron what owns Tatworth Manor," said the woman. "I had a cousin farmed for him."

"How nice," Lucy said.

"He went short on the barley one year and yer bloody father sent him to prison," the woman went on. "He died there. Left a wife and five children. I reckon I'm lookin' forward to breakin' bread with ye about as much as ye is with me." She pursed up her mouth as though she was going to spit on Lucy right then and there. But instead she turned on her heel and walked back toward her companions, who'd been watching the encounter in silence.

"Guess ye told her all right, Mabel," one of the farmers muttered, and gave her a pat on the shoulder and Lucy a dirty glare.

But I'm not *really* Claudia Moncrief! Lucy wanted to cry to those stolid, stony faces. I'm much poorer than any of you seem to be; can't you see we are on the same side? She couldn't say any such thing, though, without giving her secret away. All she could do was stand ill at ease by the stairs, clutching her sherry glass and hoping that this nightmare would be over soon. At this point even the appearance of Lord Carlyle would be a relief. At least, thought Lucy, shaken by the farmwife's ire, he couldn't hate her because she was supposed to be rich!

Bram Carlyle was late to his own dinner party, but still he could not bring himself to hurry as he went though the elaborate sequence of putting on evening dress. These affairs for the tenant farmers and their wives were a duty, a tradition initiated God knew how many hundreds of years ago by some ancestor of his, and he perpetuated the tradition because it was expected of him as lord of the manor. He doubted, though, that there was any more pleasure for the tenants in these solemn twice-yearly assemblies than there was for him.

Still, the new governess would be there. He'd sent Jem to the nursery with the invitation on impulse that morning. When was the last time he had done anything on impulse? he wondered, pausing in the midst of buttoning his doublet to take a long swallow of brandy. It seemed like years. But the issuance of that invitation had been spur of the moment, prompted by a sudden mental image he'd had at breakfast of Claudia Moncrief's clear green eyes widening in alarm as he started to pull off his clothes by the goose pond. He'd never in his life seen innocence so well feigned.

A dinner with the tenants would put her to the test, though. From what he knew of her father, the baron of Tatworth, he was quite sure Claudia Moncrief had never dined in such company. She would show her true colors tonight. Suddenly Bram found he was anticipating proving once and for all that she was no different from the long line of others. He pulled down his cuffs, tugged his collar straight, took one last long swig of brandy, and strode out to the armory.

He saw her at once, standing by the stairwell, looking bewildered and out of place as she clutched an empty goblet. Christ, she hadn't even bothered to change that plain gown, he realized, his jaw tightening. Someone must have told her who the guests would be, that there would be no one here whom it was worth her while to impress. Still, he was here. And any of the others would have found this the perfect opportunity to show off one of those ridiculous court concoctions of satin and feathers and lace.

She looked up at him then, and in her green eyes he saw a strange, mute pleading. Begging me to rescue her from the rabble, no doubt, thought Bram, and proceeded to greet every one of the farmers before he made his way over to her.

"I see you have dressed appropriately for the occasion, Mistress Moncrief," he said coldly.

"Lord Carlyle," she said in an urgent whisper, "I appreciate your kindness in asking me to join you tonight, but I'm not feeling very well. Could you excuse me, please?"

Bram laughed. So she wanted out of the ordeal that desperately already! "Oh, no, Mistress Moncrief," he told her, tucking her arm atop his and holding it there so she could not escape. "We'll see this through to the bitter end, shall we? Ladies and gentlemen," he announced to the guests at large, "dinner is served. Shall we adjourn to the banqueting hall?"

Lucy could feel her escort's disapproval bearing down on her as they led the way to the table. How grimly he had scowled when he first saw her! And what had he meant by that remark about her dress? Well, there was no help for it now; she was trapped, and she'd have to go through with this wretched meal. Still, her knees were quaking, and when her employer held out her chair for her, she sank into it gratefully—only to find herself yanked abruptly upright again by Lord Carlyle, his hand at the back of her gown. Not until everyone else had taken his seat did he let her go. Lucy sat, a blush creeping over her cheeks. The children must have forgotten to mention that she was supposed to wait. From beneath the cover of her lashes she peeked up at Lord Carlyle and saw him glowering furiously down at her. She quickly averted her eyes, staring down at her plate.

She was relieved to see the silver cup of fruit salad laid before her. Eating that was easy; one simply speared the pieces with one's smallest knife and then drank the juice. Her hands folded in her lap, Lucy waited while Jeeves circled the table, filling the tall wine goblets. Lord Carlyle made a toast to the coming harvest, and then the meal began.

Lucy picked up her napkin and tucked it beneath her chin just as Eustace and Minerva had taught her. Everyone seemed awfully quiet. Staring steadfastly at her food, Lucy grasped her knife in her hand and speared a green grape, then popped it into her mouth and chewed.

Lord Carlyle made a noise like a growl. Nervously Lucy skewered a slice of melon. At the far end of the table a farmer cleared his throat and addressed his host: "So, milord, what think ye the market for corn will be like this year?" Lucy heard the reassuring clink of cutlery as those around her began to eat, too; Lord Carlyle answered, and general conversation at last ensued.

Having food in her stomach helped calm her, Lucy found, as did the delicious red wine Jeeves had poured. When she'd finished the fruit in her cup she lifted it to drink the juice, her little finger extended precisely as Eustace had shown her. Her mouth met the chilled silver. Silence descended on the room again. Lord Carlyle stopped speaking in the middle of a sentence, and didn't go until someone prodded him: "Ye was saying, milord?"

Bram tried to remember what he had been saying, but the thought had flown straight out of his head as he watched the girl beside him pick up her cup and slurp the juice from it. He'd never in his life seen so deliberate a display of bad manners as she was putting on. Her audacious rudeness was peculiarly riveting—rather, he supposed, like watching a hanging. He simply couldn't imagine what she would come up with next.

The farmers and their wives were doing their best to ignore the spectacle she was making; probably they hadn't expected any better of this haughty nobleman's daughter. And neither should he have, Bram thought angrily as Jem cleared away the fruit course. It was one thing for her to show her disdain for these people; it was another matter for her to do so when they were guests in his house! He tried to catch her eye, to let her know she had better not push him any further, but the arrogant creature kept staring down at her plate.

Jeeves made his way around the table with trenchers of

roast beef and peas. Lord Carlyle watched in utter disbelief as Claudia Moncrief picked up her butter knife and
salad fork and proceeded to pile the slippery green orbs
onto the blade, then lifted the knife toward her mouth with
infinite grace—

"That does it, by God," he growled, and grabbed her
arm, sending peas sailing through the air. "Would you
excuse us, please?" He pulled the governess right out of
her seat and through the door to the armory, nearly bowl-
ing over Eustace and Minerva, who for some reason were
crouching out there. "Get to bed, you two!" he roared at
them, dragging Claudia Moncrief along, and they darted
off up the stairs.

He didn't stop until he reached his study; he unlocked
the door and kicked it open, scattering papers from his
desk to the floor. Then he yanked her in after him and
glared at her. "Who in hell do you think you are?"

She blinked those wide green eyes at him, all innocent
confusion, but he wasn't about to be taken in by her again.
He ripped away the napkin she'd tucked in her gown. "You
think that because you are young and beautiful and your
father is a nobleman, that gives you the right to mock
those good people in there?" he asked furiously.

"M-mock them?" she stammered, and Bram fought
back an impulse to strike her, to shake her until she
dropped the naive facade.

"Aye, you heard me, mock them! Wearing that plain
gown, sitting down before they did, eating like a pig— My
guests may be farmers, but they're honest, hard-working
folk," he bellowed, "and I won't have any spoiled little
lord's daughter making London sport of them here in my
house!"

"But I wasn't—I didn't—"

"Shut up, damn you!" he roared, and saw with satisfaction that he'd gotten through to her at last; her lovely
face had turned pale. He reined in his temper, made his
voice ice-cold. "You may consider yourself on notice from
this moment, Mistress Moncrief. One more episode such
as this evening's and you are dismissed. Don't bother coming back to finish your meal. Now get out of my sight."

For a moment she didn't move; looking into her clear

green eyes Bram had the sense that she was coming to some realization—probably, he decided with satisfaction, that she had made a grave tactical error in her campaign to seduce him. "I'm sorry," she said then, softly, and if he hadn't known better he might have believed she was. Then she turned and left him—going off, no doubt, to plan a new strategy. Bram opened his desk drawer and had a celebratory swallow of brandy. She could try what she liked; he was immune to her now, green eyes and all, for he'd proven she was just like all the others at heart.

He went back to the banqueting hall in a fine humor, ready to apologize to his guests.

As she climbed the staircase, Lucy could hear muffled laughter from behind the closed door to the nursery. Lord, what must those people at the table think of her! She should have realized what was going on when she heard those awkward silences that filled the banquet hall as she began to eat. But she'd been so nervous, what with her encounter with the farmer's wife and then Lord Carlyle scowling right from the moment he saw her, that she hadn't dared look at anyone.

When it had dawned on her in Lord Carlyle's study what the children had done, she'd been ashamed at first, but now she was just plain angry. After all, she didn't know any better; she wasn't to blame. What had happened was the fault of those two little monsters who'd been crouched in the corridor outside the banquet room watching while she made a fool of herself. Seething with fury, she yanked open the nursery door.

"Why, Mistress Moncrief," Eustace said, and collapsed with laughter, clutching his sides.

"Don't ye 'Mistress Moncrief' me, ye snide little son of a bitch!" Lucy snapped, lapsing into her old Shoreditch tongue in her rage.

"You looked so s-s-stupid!" Minerva cried through a gust of giggles.

"Ye 'ad no right to pull such a cruel trick!"

"It's no more than you deserved," Eustace said coolly, "for pretending to be better than you are, you stupid shop-girl." He gasped as Lucy snatched him up by the collar of his crisp velvet suit. "Hey, what do you think you're doing?"

"Wot I should 'ave done to ye a long time ago!" She carried him to the chair at her desk, sat down, and pushed him over her knees.

"Hey, you can't—hey!" He twisted and squirmed, then screeched as she yanked down his trousers. "Ow!" Lucy smiled grimly as she gave him a good open-handed whack; she knew from experience that a spanking sounded far worse than it felt. "Minerva, for God's sake, go get Father!" But his sister stood rooted where she was, watching with wide blue eyes.

Lucy gave him three swats, then released him abruptly. He scrambled away, clutching his backside, tears rolling down his flushed cheeks. "All right, little missy, 'tis yer turn!" she said, and went for Minerva, who was still standing like a small shocked statue. The girl didn't let out a peep until Lucy turned her over her knees and smacked her behind. Then she wailed like a banshee, flailing her thin arms and legs.

"If you don't stop that," Eustace cried, "I am telling Father!"

"Go on 'n' tell 'im," Lucy dared. " 'N' when ye're finished, I'll be only too glad to tell 'im 'twas ye two tricked me into makin' a fool of myself in front of 'is guests."

"You do that," he threatened, "and I'll tell him you're an imposter!"

"Go right ahead! And I'll tell 'im 'ow ye've known all along 'n' said nothin' to 'im!"

Minerva had stopped wailing so she could listen. "She's got us, Eustace," she whispered. "If she tells Father that—"

Eustace looked nervously at Lucy. "Very well," he said, licking his lips. "I've got some money. How much will it take for you to hold your tongue?"

"Ye can't buy me off, bub," she told him, and then, as he backed toward a bookshelf, she added thoughtfully, "At least, not with money."

"With what, then?" the boy demanded, and his sister echoed him:

"What else have we got?"

"That." Lucy pointed toward the bookshelf.

Eustace turned and stared. "Books? Why, you can't even read!"

"I know. But you're going to teach me."

"Teach you to—oh, really." Eustace laughed. "That would take forever."

"Maybe not," said his sister. "She's awfully clever at sums. And at history, too."

"We're not teachers," Eustace scoffed.

"Neither is she," Minerva pointed out. "But she taught us how to use the abacus."

"I don't mean so I can read great huge books like you do," Lucy told Eustace. "Just a little. Enough so I can get by."

"Get by at what? Being a shopkeeper? Or a thief?"

"I am not a thief!"

"Eustace," Minerva said frantically, "if she tells Father—"

The boy frowned. Lucy waited, holding her breath. If he agreed, if they taught her to read, she would know what was in the letter she'd taken out of the lute. She would know why Joe Reilly died . . .

"Are you sure you wouldn't rather just have money?"

"Eustace, for glory's sake!" Minerva glanced fearfully toward the door; in the corridor outside Lucy heard heavy footsteps, and then Lord Carlyle calling:

"Eustace! Minerva! Jem says she heard someone screaming. What in hell's going on in there?"

"Oh, all right," Eustace hissed, and thrust his hand at Lucy. "It's a deal." They shook, parting just as the children's father opened the door.

"Dammit, I expect to be answered when I speak to you!" Lord Carlyle said, glowering. "Is something wrong?"

"Of course not, Father," Eustace said brightly, holding up his trousers, while Minerva shook her head so hard that her golden curls flew. "How could anything be wrong with our dear Mistress Moncrief here?"

* * *

"C," said Lucy as Eustace formed the letter on his slate with his sister's colored chalk. "C, A, T."

"Right," the boy told her. "Now what does it spell?" Lucy sneaked a quick glance at Minerva; she was pretending to pat something close to her shin.

"Dog?" Lucy ventured. Minerva surreptitiously shook her head, and Eustace sighed.

"How could it be dog? You just did B, A, T, bat, didn't you? This is C, A, T. It *has* to rhyme with bat."

"Oh! Cat!" Lucy smiled in triumph, while Minerva rolled her eyes.

"It's just like numbers, really," the little girl told her earnestly. "They mean something when they're alone, and something different depending on how you put them together."

"There are only ten numbers," Lucy pointed out, "but there are so many letters."

"Only twenty-six—and some of them hardly ever get used. Next." Eustace rubbed out the C with the back of his hand and made another letter. "Well?"

"D," said Lucy. "D, A, T." Minerva was shaking her head again. "What's wrong? D comes after C, doesn't it?"

"Aye, but D, A, T's not a word!" Eustace said in exasperation.

"Why not?"

"How should I know? Look at it, for God's sake!"

"Mind your mouth, young man. You weren't born knowing how to read, either." Lucy stared at the letter. One long vertical line and two smaller horizontal ones— "F! It's an F, isn't it? F, A, T spells . . ." She peeked again at Minerva, who had puffed out her cheeks as far as she could. "Fish!" Minerva collapsed in a paroxysm of giggles. Her brother glared at her.

"Minerva! Are you giving hints again?" He lunged for her, chasing her around the nursery, trying to tickle her ribs. Lucy watched them with downright fondness. It had been more than a week since the ill-fated dinner party, and so far her bargain with Lord Carlyle's children was going remarkably smoothly. Eustace clearly enjoyed his role of teacher—indeed, he seemed born to it. Already

Lucy had memorized the names of all the letters in the alphabet, though she still got a bit mixed up sometimes toward the end, and now she was learning to put the letters together to make different words. Minerva, who hadn't mastered all of this so long ago herself, was a great help, imparting tips that had helped her keep the trickier letters, such as M and W, straight.

Of course, thought Lucy as she went to rescue the girl from her brother's attack, the greatest help of all had been Lord Carlyle's departure. The children had seemed almost as relieved as she when Jeeves had come to the nursery the morning following the dinner party to announce that their father had gone off on business. Lucy did think it strange that he'd left without bidding his son and daughter goodbye, but when she mentioned this to Eustace he only shrugged. ''That's Father's way. He goes off like this all the time.''

''Well, when will he be back?''

''I don't know. When he feels like it, I guess.'' He lowered his voice to a whisper. ''The ghost won't play the virginals now.''

''Why—what do you mean?''

In the bright, sunlit nursery, Minerva had shivered, wrapping her small arms around her thin chest. ''It only plays when he is here.''

''There's no such thing as ghosts, pet,'' Lucy assured her. But she could not help noticing that the eerie nocturnal music did cease with the lord of the manor away.

Each evening, after she had supper with the children—unlearning all the made-up manners they'd taught her and learning proper manners at last—Lucy would go to her rooms and pull the lute letter from behind the mirror. She'd stare at the page, pointing out the characters Eustace and Minerva had taught her to recognize that day, trying to sound out the words they formed. She was still a long way from being able to read what was written there, but she was getting closer. Sooner or later—sooner, she hoped, for even Eustace had grudgingly admitted she was a quick study—she would know why Joe Reilly had died.

A fortnight after Lord Carlyle's unannounced disappearance he reappeared, also without warning. Lucy encountered him in the armory; he was coming in just as she set out for her afternoon walk, having failed so far to interest Eustace and Minerva in the benefits of fresh air. His chin covered with a thick growth of black beard, his clothes muddied and unkempt, he stalked out from behind the empty suit of armor so suddenly that Lucy could not suppress a little scream, thinking for one split second that he was an apparition. "Jesus!" she cried, and then relaxed as she recognized that grim, scowling face. "Must you go about creeping up on people all the time?"

He stood looking down at her, shifting the saddlebag he had slung over his shoulder. "It's my house. I come and go as I please."

Insolent bastard, Lucy thought. "While we're on the subject of coming and going," she snapped, "you might have the common decency to let people know when you are."

"I beg your pardon." He arched a black brow. "I wasn't aware my hiring you as governess made me accountable to you."

Lucy's temper flared; she found she'd been spoiling for this. "I didn't mean me, I meant your children. What sort of father just disappears for two weeks without even telling his children goodbye?"

His blue eyes were inscrutable in the dim room. "I was under the impression the children generally find my leave-taking an occasion for celebration."

"Well, can you blame them?" Lucy faced off against him, hands on her hips. "I've seen stray cats on the street that were better parents than you!"

His jaw tightened. "I give those children all they need. I feed and house and clothe them." He started to walk past her, but she grabbed his sleeve.

"That isn't all they need. They need time and love and caring and affection—"

"Then I'd suggest you add those things to the curriculum, Mistress Moncrief. Isn't that what I'm paying you for?" He stalked away, leaving her fuming, tempted to lower one of the battleaxes on the wall right down on his head.

That night she lay sprawled across her bed, studying the

lute letter, picking out the letters she knew. Lord, but
reading was hard; she didn't think she'd ever master it.
Some of the words in the note were as long as her arm.
She set her teeth together as, deep within the bowels of
the house, the virginals began to pound out their dissonant
refrain. Just what she needed to help her concentrate!

Suddenly she heard a frightened wail from the direction
of the nursery. When she rushed to answer it, she found
Minerva curled on her cot, a pillow clutched to her ears.
"What is it, pet? What's the matter?"

"He's back!" she sobbed, her thin shoulders shaking.
"He's back, and the ghost's back, too!"

"Oh, sweetheart." Lucy pulled the girl against her
chest. "It's not hurting anyone, is it? It's just making music—and not very good music at that."

"I don't care; I want it to go away!"

"Maybe it will go away if we sing. Shall we try that?"

"You sing," Minerva said in a small, muffled voice.

"All right, then." Lucy held her tight, rocking her back
and forth, and sang an old nursery rhyme her own mother
used to calm her fears at night:

> Pussycat, pussycat, where have you been?
> I've been to London to see the queen.
> Pussycat, pussycat, what did you there?
> I frightened a little mouse under her chair.

"That's a song for babies," Eustace said from the doorway of his bedroom.

"Shut up, Eustace." His sister snuggled closer to Lucy.
"Would you sing it again?"

Lucy sang it over and over, first loudly to drown out the
jangling sound of the virginals and then more softly as
Minerva nodded off to sleep. At long last the music
stopped. She tucked the girl in, then checked on Eustace.
He, too, was sleeping soundly. She tiptoed out of the darkened nursery, pulling the door shut behind her very quietly.

She turned back to her room, then froze as she saw a
thin, quavering light at the far end of the hallway, where
it turned off to lead to the music room in the old wing.

Her heart fluttered; she shrank back against the wall. The light grew brighter, and she put her hand to her mouth as an enormous black shadow fell across the floor—

Lord Carlyle rounded the corner, caught sight of her, and scowled ferociously. "What are you doing here?"

She walked toward him slowly in her white petticoats. "It is you down there playing at night, isn't it?" she demanded.

"What of it? This is my house."

"You have got those poor children frightened out of their wits!" she cried angrily. "They think it's a ghost!"

His blue eyes were dark in the flickering light of the candle he held. "There *is* a ghost in Lockhaven Hall," he told her, and laughed.

Lucy had to fight back an impulse to strike him. "I suppose it makes you feel very brave and manly to terrify two helpless children," she said cuttingly, and to her astonishment she saw his huge hand clench into a fist as though *he* would strike *her.* But he caught himself in time.

"I am sorry if my music disturbs you," was all he said.

"Music! That isn't music; it's caterwauling," she said hotly.

"We must all make our own sorts of songs, Mistress Moncrief."

She whirled around, starting back to the nursery, but he put his hand on her bare shoulder; Lucy trembled as she felt the force of his grip. "Where are you going?" he demanded.

"Where do you think?" she asked, turning, eyes flashing. "To tell those children that it's you playing, that there isn't any ghost."

"No," he said sharply. "I forbid you to."

"You forbid me—" Lucy shook her head in disbelief. "Why?"

"So long as they are afraid, they will stay away from that room."

"God have mercy on you," Lucy whispered. "You're a hard, cruel man."

"It's for their own good."

Lucy's eyes narrowed. "How would you know what is good for them? You know nothing about them," she told

him, and brushed past him to her bedchamber, slamming
the door.

Bram stood in the corridor holding the candle, staring
down at his hand, feeling his skin burn where he had
touched her shoulder. So that was how she looked with
her black hair hanging loose around her, tumbling down
her slim back in rippling waves. It was the sort of image
that might torment a man for years.

Bram knew about such images; he carried enough of
them already, branded in his memory so deeply that even
an ocean of brandy couldn't wash them away. One was of
Eustace on the day he was born, the first time he had ever
held him in his arms. Such a tiny, wrinkled thing he had
been, bright red and wailing. Bram had to lean against the
wall now as he remembered the wonder and awe and impossible joy that had filled his heart at that moment, when
he looked down at the bawling baby and whispered, "My
son . . ."

There was one for Minerva, too, just as vivid, just as
searing. Her first birthday—God, had there ever been a
more beautiful child? He'd been trying to teach her to
walk; she had on a blue dress, short enough to show her
small, chubby legs. Spring had come; they were out on
the lawn by the goose pond, and the whole world had been
drenched with sun.

"Come to Papa," he had coaxed her, holding out his
arms while she teetered uncertainly on her tiny feet.
"Come on to Papa, darling; I won't let you fall." And the
smile on her angel's face as she took that first step, the
trust shining in her blue eyes—he clenched his own shut
against a sudden rush of tears as he pictured that trium-
phant instant, that happy time so long ago.

And one more, of course. Olive standing here in this
corridor on the night she died, the night that ended all the
happy times forever. He waited for that image, that ghost
to visit him again, braced himself, eyes still clenched, for
the horror and guilt it evoked—

But all he saw was a black-haired girl in white petticoats
walking slowly toward him; all he heard was her voice as
she saw him: *It is you . . . It is you . . . It is you.* Aston-

ished, he raised his head. Jesus, what had that damned
girl done? Where was his old familiar ghost, the haunt he
was accustomed to?

"Olive?" he called in a panic. What was going on here,
what was happening to him? Black hair tumbling over bare
shoulders. Eyes green as apple leaves—

And his flesh on fire.

Impossible.

He said it aloud, angrily: "Impossible!" He said it
again, slammed his fist against the stone wall until he could
be certain the burning was only from pain. No more! Over
and finished. Closed. Ended.

Impossible. But, oh, God in heaven, what he would give
to believe there could be a happy time again!

Chapter 6

"I *hate* my name." Minerva, tongue between her teeth, was bent over a sheet of parchment, struggling to copy the elegant script Eustace had given her as a sample.

"I don't see why." Her brother guided Lucy's hand through the loops of an L; he'd decided she knew enough letters to learn how to write her name. "Minerva was the Roman goddess of wisdom."

"I don't care if she was the goddess of pickled beets; it's still a stupid name."

"What's wrong with it?" Lucy asked.

Minerva scrunched her small face. "It's not like other people's names. Nobody else has it. Do you know anyone named Minerva?" Lucy thought, then shook her head.

"You're a Carlyle," Eustace told his sister. "You can't have a name that's common, that's like everyone else's."

"Sometimes I wish my name wasn't Carlyle, too," she said wistfully. "Do you like your name, Eustace?"

"It's very old and distinguished. It's from the Greek, you know. It means 'fruitful.' It was the name of two saints and an Archbishop of Thessalonica."

"But do you like it?" Minerva pressed.

He shrugged. "It's all right, I guess."

"If I could have any name in the world," Minerva declared, her blue eyes dreamy, "it would be Lucy Jones. Now there's a good name. Plain and simple and easy to spell."

"Why, thank you, pet," said Lucy. "Did your father decide what to call you?" Considering what he called his horse—Bellero-something—she was sure it was he who'd saddled the children with their ridiculous names.

"I don't know. I guess so. All I know is I'd rather have any name except Minerva," the little girl said.

"I don't know anyone named Minerva," Lucy said thoughtfully, "but I had a neighbor in London whose name was Minnie."

"Did you like her?"

"Oh, very much indeed. She was a laundress."

"That figures," Eustace said.

Minerva stuck out her tongue at him. "I don't care what you say; I like it. I'm going to be Minnie from now on." She scratched out Minerva with her quill and began again. "How do you spell Minnie?"

"I'm not telling," Eustace said archly. "Not so you can go around calling yourself by some laundress's name."

"You're just jealous because you are still stuck with Eustace."

"I am not. If I wanted a nickname I'd pick one."

"Like what—Euey?" his sister asked scornfully.

"There's always Stacy," Lucy offered.

The boy glanced at her. "Did you know some slop-monger or horse drover in London named Stacy?"

"No. I don't know anyone named that. It just popped into my head."

"Stacy." He mulled it over. "Stacy Carlyle. It's not bad, is it?"

"It's a *million* times better than Eustace," his sister said feelingly. "Will you please show me how to spell Minnie now?"

He did, writing it out in his beautiful penmanship. Then he wrote Stacy beneath it, practicing different fancy flourishes on the final Y. "I like that one," Lucy told him, pointing to a particularly elaborate version. "Do it once more, slowly, so that I can—" She stopped; someone had knocked on the nursery door. Jem never knocked before entering, and neither did Jeeves on his infrequent forays to the children's rooms.

"Come in," said Lucy.

The door swung open, and Lord Carlyle entered, scowling and grim.

"Jeepers," Minerva whispered, and hurriedly crammed

the parchment she'd been practicing on into her desk. Lucy followed suit.

"Am I interrupting something?" Lord Carlyle demanded.

"Oh, no," Lucy said faintly. "We were just working on our penmanship."

"I see." He crossed the room, hands clasped behind his back. Eustace and Minerva perched on their chairs like two tiny scared sparrows, following his every move with wide eyes. "How are your lessons progressing, Eustace?"

"F-fine, sir."

"Minerva?" The girl let out a little squeak. Lord Carlyle's scowl intensified. "Have you been behaving yourselves for Mistress Moncrief?"

Desperate, pleading, their gazes flew to Lucy. "They've been as good as gold, sir," she said truthfully.

"I see." He paced around the room, looking at the toys and books and games on the shelves, the chalk drawings by Minerva that Lucy had tacked on the walls. Lucy felt his daughter's small, cold hand reach for hers and cling to it tightly.

"Was there something you wanted, sir?" she asked, taking the bull by the horns.

"Aye. To see what my seventy-five pounds is getting me," he barked. Then he stopped beneath one of Minerva's drawings, of a small gray cat curled up asleep on a sunny windowsill. "Did you do this?" he asked, taking a step toward her. Lucy felt Minerva flinch at her side.

"Say 'Yes, sir,' " Lucy prodded her in a whisper, but all she could manage was a brief bobbing nod.

Lord Carlyle looked at his tiny daughter for a long moment. Then he spun around and stalked out of the room, banging the door.

Eustace and Minerva exchanged wild glances. "Did you do something?" Eustace hissed frantically.

"No!" she hissed back, shaking her head.

"You must have done something bad; I know I didn't."

"Do something bad?" Lucy echoed. "What are you talking about?"

"What else would make him come here like that?" Eustace demanded. "He's never done that before."

"Silly geese, he came to see how your lessons were going."

"Why would he do that?" Minerva whispered in bewilderment.

"Why, because that's what fathers should do. Because he loves you."

"He doesn't love us," Eustace said with absolute certainty.

"Oh, pets, of course he does." Lucy looked into their small, frightened faces and sighed. "Don't you understand? It is just very difficult for some people to show their love. I imagine it is terribly hard on your father sometimes to have you near, reminding him of your mother and how much he misses her, how much he loved her, too."

"You're the one who doesn't understand," Eustace told her. "He didn't love her, either. He pushed her down the stairs."

"Eustace, for Jesus's sake!"

"It's true!" Minerva burst out, throwing her arms around Lucy, burying her face in her skirts. "It's true, it is! He killed her! That's why she's haunting the house, playing on the virginals. He killed her, and if we're not good he is going to kill us too!"

Lucy stared at her charges in horror. "You can't honestly believe that he—" But clearly they did. "Oh, Lord. Oh, my poor dears." She put an arm around each of them, hugging them tightly. "Now listen to me. There isn't any ghost in the music room." She knew Lord Carlyle had forbidden her to tell them this, but she could hardly let them go on thinking he was a murderer. "It's your father making the music. He's the one playing the virginals."

"How do you know?" Eustace demanded.

"Because I saw him the other night, when you woke up scared. Do you remember?" Minerva nodded. "Well, when I came out of your room I saw him coming up from the old wing, and I asked him, and he said it was him."

"He," Eustace corrected her, looking dubious. "Why would Father want to play the virginals in the middle of the night? He hates music."

Lucy hesitated. Even crueler than Lord Carlyle's playing to deliberately frighten his children would be to tell them that was what he was doing. She shrugged. "Well, you can't really call it music, can you, what he plays?" Eustace snickered. "Anyway, the point is, when you hear the virginals there's no reason to be afraid. It's your father playing. Mind you, don't you dare let on that I told you, or he'll be angry with me. And he does not want you down in that room. Do you understand? Minerva?"

"Minnie," the girl said firmly. "You're absolutely sure it is Father?"

"Absolutely."

"Well—all right then."

"Stacy?" He nodded, too. "That's better." She reached into her desk for the parchment she'd been writing on. "Let's get back to work. And no more nonsense about your father and mother, do you hear?"

Despite her assurances to the children, Lucy couldn't help wondering what had ever given them the idea that Lord Carlyle was responsible for his wife's death. That night when Jem came to take away her supper tray she broached the subject cautiously. "The children were talking about their mother today," she said. Jem didn't reply. "They don't talk about her very often," Lucy added.

"Lord Carlyle," Jem told her, tight-lipped, "don't like her talked about."

"So I gather. But the reason I ask is—well, they have got some wild notion that there's a ghost in the house. Her ghost."

"Little pitchers has got big ears," Jem muttered.

"What do you mean by that, Jem?"

"Oh—" Jem picked up the tray. "People will talk, won't they, when someone dies sudden, in the peak of health."

Lucy looked at her. "What do people say?"

"I shouldn't have spoke, mum," the maid said reluctantly.

"Jem. Please."

"Well—'tain't no secret, not really. There's talk about that the master done away with his wife."

"But why would he do such a thing?" Lucy asked.

"I'm sure he ain't told me, mum."

"You don't believe he killed her, do you?"

Jem shrugged. "They do say where there's smoke there's fire." Then she scurried to the door, clearly regretting having said that much. "Cook'll have my hide if I don't bring her down this tray."

Lucy sat at the table with her chin in her hand, thinking. Heaven knew she didn't much care for her employer, but still, it was hard to imagine he might be a murderer. He *was* a terrible father, but that wasn't a crime. If the truth be known, she felt sorry for the man. Here he was with all the money in the world, but he didn't enjoy it; all he did was sit in that little monk's room of his.

Still, he was a nobleman, just like old Hawk-Nose. Lucy sighed and fetched the lute letter from behind the mirror back. She was making progress there; she couldn't read any of the longer words, but she'd filled in some of the short ones: I, you, for, the, my. It was an enormously frustrating task; the more she knew, the more impatient she became. More than once she'd been tempted to just take the page to Stacy and ask him to read it to her. But the memory of Joe dying in the gutter always stopped her. Whatever the letter contained had to be terribly dangerous. She would just have to wait and be patient, until she could read it herself.

Lord Carlyle paid no more unannounced visits to the nursery. Early in August he disappeared, again without a word to Lucy or the children. She took advantage of his absence to spend the late afternoons out in the meadow, free of the fear of encountering him again on his way for a swim.

For a long time Minnie and Stacy wouldn't join her outdoors. Minnie was terrified of the geese on the pond, and Stacy preferred just staying inside, reading books or playing chess against himself. Lucy, unused to sitting still for as long as she did in the nursery each day, took to exercising by practicing the acrobats' moves she used to watch Burbage's actors do up on stage. One afternoon she came upright from a cartwheel to find both children standing by the gate, watching her.

"What are you doing?" Minnie called.

"Cartwheels," said Lucy, and turned another one.

"You look ridiculous," said Stacy.

"Really," said Lucy, and walked a few steps on her hands.

"I can see your drawers," Minnie squealed.

"That's all right," Lucy told her. "They're clean."

"Where did you learn to do that?" Stacy demanded.

"My father used to take me to a place called The Theatre in London to see the players. They were wonderful acrobats." Lucy did a somersault toward them.

"Father never takes us anywhere," Minnie said wistfully. "Is that fun, what you are doing?"

"I think so."

"Do you think you could teach me?"

"Of course I could. Take off your shoes and stockings and come on down here."

"What about the geese?"

"I won't let the geese hurt you, goose."

Minnie plopped herself down at the edge of the drive and pulled off her shoes and stockings. "What do you want to learn first?" Lucy asked as the girl tiptoed gingerly through the grass.

"The one where you roll over on your head."

"That's called a somersault. Here." Lucy demonstrated it for her, and after a dozen or so attempts Minnie turned one successfully.

"Stacy, Stacy, did you see me?" she cried. "Watch this!" And she did another.

"Big deal," said her brother. "I could do it, too, if I wanted to look as stupid as you."

"Bet you couldn't."

"Bet I could."

"Bet you couldn't," Minnie told him, and stuck out her tongue.

"Don't make faces at your brother, Minnie," Lucy scolded. "If he's afraid to try—"

"Who said I'm afraid?" Stacy demanded.

"Prove it," Minnie challenged him.

"I don't want to get my feet dirty."

"You're chicken," Minnie said.

"I am not!" He yanked off his shoes and squatted down while Minnie made small clucking noises. The somersault he turned wasn't pretty, but it was passable. ''There!'' he said triumphantly.

''Do you know what we ought to do?'' Lucy asked.

''What?'' said Minnie.

''Play leapfrog.''

''We don't know how.''

''It's easy. Just like somersaults,'' she told them. ''Minnie, you crouch down, and I hop over you, like this. Now, Stacy, you hop over both of us—'' Soon they were leaping and hopping all over the lawn, and even Stacy was giggling when Lucy sailed over his back with a whoosh of her skirts.

''This is fun!'' Minnie declared, her blue eyes shining. ''Do you know any more games?''

Lucy taught them all the ones she remembered from her own childhood, and after that they practiced tumbling or played hide-and-seek or hunt-the-slipper every day until the sun was going down. It felt strange to Lucy to play those old games on grass instead of cobblestones, with trees shading her instead of the dark overhangs of Barkers Lane. Tag, blindman's bluff, kick-the-bucket—they loved them all, but their favorite was pell-mell. They played it with brooms Lucy swiped from the maid's closet for mallets, and for balls they used apples from the orchard trees. Lucy fashioned a hoop out of an old barrel stave, and the children helped her stake out an alley in the meadow grass.

In the midst of a furious match one day Lucy stood barefoot, sleeves rolled up above her elbows, pondering a shot. ''Smack Stacy's apple,'' Minnie urged her, hopping up and down in excitement.

''No, hit Minnie's,'' her brother argued. ''Smack hers straight into the—'' He stopped, pointing toward the apple trees. Minnie looked up and abruptly stopped hopping. Lucy turned around curiously and saw Lord Carlyle, sweaty and travel-stained, sitting atop his black horse at the orchard's edge, staring at them.

He dug his muddy boots into his horse's sides and cantered out of the trees, his sharp gaze raking over the brooms, the apples, the wicket. He looked at Eustace and then at Minerva, and then back at Eustace again. ''What did you call your sister?''

"M-Minnie, sir."

Minnie crept a few steps closer to Lucy. "We've got new names," she said bravely. "Regular names. I'm Minnie, and he's Stacy."

"Are you?" Her father arched a brow. "Mistress Moncrief, where did you get those broomsticks?"

"The maid's closet, sir."

Without another word he galloped past them through the meadow and up to the house.

"We're going to catch it now," Stacy whispered. "I knew this was a rotten idea. I knew he'd be mad if he caught us going barefoot. Now he's going to—"

"Stacy, look!" His sister pointed up the hill. Lord Carlyle was running toward them, his own boots and stockings gone, waving a broomstick over his head.

"It's been a good twenty years since I played pell-mell," he declared as he reached the alley, "but I bet I remember how. What shall the sides be?" He looked at Lucy and the children; all three of them were standing open-mouthed. His blue eyes turned suddenly cloudy; almost shyly he asked, "Do you mind if I play?"

Lucy blinked, coming to her senses. "Of course not! The more the merrier, sir. Isn't that right, you two?" Minnie and Stacy didn't answer her; they were still struck speechless. "How about Stacy and me, sir, against Minnie and you?"

"Just what I had in mind. All right, then, Minerv—Minnie." He made a fierce, scowling face at their opponents, and she giggled nervously. "Let's show them how this game is played, shall we?" He plucked an apple to serve as his ball and strode to the top of the alley, carrying his broomstick over his shoulder like a soldier on parade.

"Stacy," Lucy hissed. He just kept staring at his father. "Come on," she urged him, "we can't let a challenge like that go by. We'll show *him* how it's played."

At first the children were timid and fumble-fingered in front of their father, but as he blundered about, missing shots completely or sending his apple careening off into the trees, they loosened up considerably. Before long Stacy was aiming his apple at Lord Carlyle's and, when he hit it, smacking it away without mercy. Minnie hopped up and down, cheering her teammate on and wailing in dismay when he flubbed his turn.

Lucy watched Lord Carlyle with her tongue in her cheek. It was plain that if he tried he could have sent his apple the whole length of the alley in a single shot; the muscles that bulged in his arms when he gripped his broomstick made that plain. When he came close to her to hit a drive she could smell the warm scent that clung to him, a scent of leather and horseflesh and musky sweat that reminded her of the Mermaid Tavern and the men her father used to drink with there. His long black hair kept tumbling down over his eyes, and he would toss it back impatiently in a gesture that made him look, in his billowing white linen shirt, more like a pirate or a highwayman than a lord of the realm.

Stacy and Lucy took the first round, causing Minnie to stomp her foot at her father's incompetence and demand new sides. "I warned you it had been twenty years," Lord Carlyle apologized, catching Lucy's bemused smile and returning one that made her catch her breath. Lord, but he was handsome when he wasn't looking grim. "Give me another chance?" he pleaded with his tiny daughter, his face so woebegone that she giggled and agreed.

The second bout was nip-and-tuck, with all players reaching the general vicinity of the wicket simultaneously. Stacy took his turn and knocked his ball just inches from the hoop, and it seemed certain he and Lucy would triumph again. Lord Carlyle took a long time lining up his shot, fussing over the lie of the grass, digging in his heels, while Minnie danced from one foot to another and urged him on. He hunched over his broomstick, face crinkled in concentration, and swung it between his long legs. His apple bounced over a molehill, was diverted by a twig, and finally rolled to a stop blocking Stacy's path to the goal.

"Your shot, Mistress Moncrief, I believe," he said, his blue eyes twinkling as Minnie cheered him.

Lucy looked to Stacy for advice. "What shall I do?"

"Hit Father! Knock him out of the way!"

"But what if I knock you away, too?"

"It doesn't matter. Minnie can never make it through

the wicket from so far out,'' he said with great superiority, while his sister stuck out her tongue. Lucy shrugged and took her shot. Her apple smashed into Lord Carlyle's and, sure enough, sent both it and Stacy's sailing away from the goal.

"My turn, my turn!" Minnie cried, running over to her apple.

"Better take your time," her father said gravely. "It's all up to you." Nibbling her lip, the girl bent over, eyeing the wicket, then pulled back her broom and let fly. Her apple careened across the green grass, heading straight for the wicket, and rolled through.

"Hurray, we win!" she squealed, running to her father, throwing her arms around him in a delirious hug. Lucy saw him start in surprise at the gesture, saw the way his body tensed at his daughter's touch. Minerva drew back from him quickly, as though astonished by her own boldness, and skipped toward Stacy. Lord Carlyle, having finally decided to return the hug, was left holding air.

"I did it, I did it, I did it!" Minnie sang, dancing around her brother.

"It was a good shot," he admitted grudgingly. "But let's have a rematch. Best out of three."

At the top of the hill someone cleared his throat. Lucy looked up and saw Jeeves standing there; if he was surprised to see his master playing pell-mell, his plain round face didn't show it. "Forgive me, milord," he said smoothly, "but your bath has been drawn for more than an hour. And you have an engagement at the countess of Sutherland's at eight."

"Oh, damn," said Lord Carlyle, scowling again, but this time in earnest. He looked at the children. "I am sorry. The rematch will have to wait."

"That's all right," Minnie told him shyly. "We'll get them next time."

"We'll see about that," Stacy cried, lunging for her and tickling her ribs. They rolled over and over in the long grass; their father watched them, hesitating. Then, "I'm sorry," he said again. "I really must go." And he ran toward the house, his long legs covering the distance in great strides.

In the fading sunlight Minnie turned to her brother, her eyes wide as saucers. "Wasn't that marvelous?" she asked, her voice tinged with awe.

"Marvelous," he agreed.

Chapter 7

The August air, so delightfully warm that afternoon, turned stifling and sultry by evening. Lucy lay on her bed stripped down to her petticoats, the door open wide so she could hear Minnie if she woke and cried; she was frightened by thunderstorms. She'd had a bath to try to cool off, but already her skin bore a faint sheen of sweat, and her black curls clung damply to the back of her neck.

She was trying to concentrate on unraveling the lute letter, but memories of the pell-mell match kept filling her thoughts, especially the shy, tentative way that Lord Carlyle had asked if he could play. And the way he'd drawn back when Minnie rushed to hug him—odd, it was as though he was as afraid of his children as they were of him.

In her mind's eye she saw him as he'd looked, barefoot beneath the dappled shade of the apple trees, in those long, tight leather riding breeches with his white shirt open at the throat. And when he'd smiled at her . . . She knew now what people meant when they said that their heart skipped a beat. His smiles had turned her knees to jelly, made her feel all quivery and hot. She could almost understand after that afternoon why Jeannie Paget from Shoreditch had fallen in love with her "young gentleman" despite everyone's warnings; there was something about the way Lord Carlyle moved, even clowning about at pell-mell. As though he owned the world . . .

She rolled onto her back, frowning, staring up at the ceiling. She could just hear what her father would say if he were here now: *Rich folk 'n' poor, pet, they're like fire 'n' water. They just don't mix* . . . And he was right, of course. Poor Jeannie was proof enough of that.

"Waiting for someone, Mistress Moncrief?"

Lucy sat bolt upright and saw Lord Carlyle leaning against the lintel, watching her from beneath half-lowered eyelids. "Sir!" She tugged down her petticoat skirts.

"You did leave the door wide open," he said lazily. Lucy looked up at him and then quickly away. How terribly handsome he was in his black evening clothes!

"Thunder frightens Minnie," she stammered. "I wanted to hear her if she cries."

"I see." He glanced at the table beside the bed, strewn with parchment and ink and the quill she used to practice her alphabet. "Were you writing to someone? A beau, perhaps?"

Lucy quickly turned the lute letter face down. "I haven't got a beau."

"A girl as lovely as you? With a father so rich? That's hard to believe." He took a step toward her. "You don't look anything like your father, you know. But I suppose you have heard that before. Such green, green eyes. Green as the leaves on the apple trees."

A gust of wind blew in through the open shutters, snuffing out Lucy's candle. She fumbled for the tinderbox to relight it, but before she could she saw a tongue of flame in the darkness, illuminating his cupped hands. He held the match to the candle, and light flickered through the room once more.

"Thank you," Lucy said. "And thank you for playing with the children this afternoon. It was very good of you. It meant a lot to them." She realized she was babbling, but it made her edgy to be alone here, only half dressed, with him so near.

"And what did it mean to you, Mistress Moncrief?"

"I don't know what you mean."

"It was a charming little scene that I stumbled on, wasn't it? Jeeves informs me you've been out there every day, frolicking barefoot among the apple trees. Next time I go away I'll let you know ahead of time when I am coming back. Perhaps you might arrange to be lolling naked in the goose pond when I return."

"Do you mean that you think I arranged that for—oh, really," said Lucy, and burst out laughing. "God, you are vain!" And for an instant she again glimpsed uncertainty in his heavy-lidded eyes. But then his customary scowl slipped back into place.

"Pell-mell's not your game, is it, Mistress Moncrief?" he asked softly, running his hand over the coverlet close by her knee. "You think you can get to me through the children—isn't that what you're up to?"

"All I am up to, Lord Carlyle, is to try to make your children happy," Lucy told him coolly. "Do you think just because you don't love them no one else can?"

"Noble little Mistress Moncrief," he murmured, his lip curled in a sneer. "Selflessly dedicated to making others happy." His fingers brushed her knee, and Lucy scrambled away from him.

"I've told you before, by God, keep your hands off me!"

"What's the matter, Mistress Moncrief? Don't you want to make me happy, too?" Lucy stared up at him as he loomed over her on the bed. The air between them seemed charged with fire, like the stormy skies; there was fire, too, in the depths of his indigo eyes. He reached down and caught a hank of her long, damp hair in his hand, his fingers closing around it so tightly that his knuckles went white. Then he jerked his arm back, pulling her toward him. Lucy let out a cry of pain, rising to her knees.

"Let me go, damn you!"

But he only hauled her closer, like a man who played a fish on a line. Lucy clapped her hands to the side of her head where he tugged at her hair. "Make me happy," he whispered, and the words were half challenge, half prayer.

"Leave me alone," Lucy cried in alarm as hot lightning flashed, as the night air crackled with life. Some force was surging within her as he raised her toward him, more wild and strong than the storm. He put his arm around her waist, letting go of her hair at last, but she was far from free, for his mouth touched hers, and a spark of fire fused them for an instant, so searing that it took Lucy's breath away.

Then a great rumbling crack of thunder shattered the

silence, so loud that it shook the very cliff on which the house stood. From the direction of the nursery came an ear-splitting scream. He raised his head, his grip on Lucy slackening so abruptly that she knew he had not believed her when she told him his daughter was frightened by storms. The realization made her furious; she shoved him away, her eyes flashing like the lightning. "If you'll excuse me," she spat at him, "I'll go to her now. She needs me."

"I—" he said hoarsely. But Lucy didn't stay to hear what he had to say. As she soothed trembling Minnie to sleep with the song about the pussycat that went to see the queen, she could hear above her own voice and the clamoring storm another sound in the distance: the discordant music of the virginals.

The thunder and lightning subsided by dawn, but the rain kept on for three straight days. The children, accustomed by now to their outdoor play, grew increasingly restless as the time dripped by, gray sodden hour by hour. When the fourth morning in a row dawned equally dreary, nothing Lucy tried in the nursery could interest them; rebels, they declared their own holiday. Stacy went down to the kitchens to torment grim old Cook. He must have swiped too many tastes from her mixing bowls, for by the evening he was groaning with a bellyache.

"Minnie," Lucy said, "run and tell your father that Stacy is sick. As for you, young man, pop straight into your bed."

Minnie reappeared in the nursery shortly afterward, with Lord Carlyle in tow. "What is wrong with him?" he asked, looking down at his son.

"He has a bellyache," Lucy said shortly; they were the first words she'd spoken to him since the incident in her bedchamber on the night of the storm.

"Is it serious?"

"Probably not."

Lord Carlyle stared at the wan, moaning boy. "Is there something you would like me to do about it?"

"I only thought," Lucy said between gritted teeth, "that you'd want to know."

"I have to go to Lord Babington's tonight," Lord Carlyle said.

"Well, go ahead! Why should a sick child stop you?" He flushed. "You don't understand. I must go."

"Oh, but I do understand," Lucy told him sweetly. "Do enjoy yourself. I'll look after Stacy. After all, isn't that what you pay me for?"

His jaw went so tight that she thought it might crack; he turned on his heel and strode from the room.

"Are you mad at Father?" Minnie asked hesitantly.

"No, pet," Lucy lied, and put her hand on Stacy's forehead. "Not getting a fever, are you?" His eyes were awfully bright.

"I'll be all right," he said bravely, wincing. "Maybe, Lucy, you could ask Cook to brew some chamomile broth?"

But when Lucy brought it to him not half an hour later he was sound asleep, and looking far less peaked. "Come on," Minnie said, tugging Lucy's arm. "I know what I want to do."

"What's that?"

The little girl pulled her into her bedroom next to the nursery. "Play Pussycat, Pussycat. I'll be the cat, and you can be the queen. Here." She reached under her cot and pulled out a box.

"What's this?"

"Queen's clothes. Go on, put them on." Lucy opened the box and looked down in wonder at the gorgeous apple-green silk gown.

"Minnie, where did you get this?"

"It belonged to Mistress Buxton. Our old governess. She left it behind when she went away."

"Left such a beautiful gown as this?" Lucy gingerly ran a hand over the soft, glowing fabric and caught a distinct aroma of roses on the air. "Why would she do such a thing?"

"I don't know," Minnie told her, and shrugged. "Look, she left this, too." She went to her wardrobe and brought out a handsome cape of deeper, forest-green.

"I wouldn't feel right playing dress-up with someone else's clothes," Lucy protested.

"But you have to dress up. You have to be the queen."
Minnie seemed on the verge of tears, and Lucy relented,
taking off her old gray gown and slipping into that cool
nest of smooth green silk.

"It feels wonderful," she said in awe. "I've never worn
silk before."

"It looks beautiful on you," the little girl said shyly.
"But you ought to unbraid your hair."

"Why is that?"

"In my books all the queens and princesses have long,
flowing hair."

"All right," said Lucy, laughing, and pulled loose her
curls. "How is that?"

"Perfect," Minnie declared.

Lucy turned to the looking glass and caught her breath
as she saw her reflection. Was that really her, Lucy Jones
from Shoreditch, that elegant creature looking back at her?
She whirled in a circle, and the long, full skirts spun out
in a glorious bell that shimmered and swirled on the air.
The waist was cut tight, and the bodice seemed shockingly
low. "Mistress Buxton must have been an odd sort of
governess," she observed, blushing to see how the tops
of her breasts swelled against the silk.

"She was," said Minnie. "Now, you go sit in that chair
over there, and close your eyes, and I'll sneak under it to
frighten the mouse."

Lucy did as she was told, settling onto the seat, giggling
at the way the silk crackled and rustled. "Close your
eyes," Minnie reminded her, and she did, just in time to
open them again at a horrible loud groan from Stacy's
room.

"Stacy!" She rushed in to find him curled in a tight
ball on his cot, clutching his stomach. "Stacy, what is
it?"

"I don't know." The boy groaned. "I am dying, I
think."

"Where does it hurt you?"

"Here," he moaned, "in my belly. Right here."

"I'll send for a doctor," Lucy said quickly.

"No!" He reached out and caught her wrist. "No! I
want Father. I want Father, please!"

''Very well, then, I'll send Johnny for your father, though I don't see why—''

''You've got to get him, Lucy. You go to Lord Babington's and get him,'' the boy pleaded, his face wretchedly pale. He was trembling all over. ''You go and get him, Lucy. He'll come home for you.''

''But Johnny can get there much—oh, Lord, Stacy!'' she cried, seeing his eyes rolling back in his head.

''Bring Father, please!'' he begged again, clutching her hand. ''Hurry!''

''I'll just change my clothes—''

''There's no time!'' Minnie cried, bundling her into the forest-green cape. ''I'll go and tell Johnny to hitch up the carriage, and then I'll get Cook here to watch him until you get back.''

''Stacy, are you sure—''

''Just bring Father,'' he croaked hoarsely, writhing on the cot. ''Bring Father and I'll be all right.''

Lucy ran downstairs and out to the drive, and in seconds, it seemed, Johnny drove round from the stables in the coach. ''To Lord Babington's,'' she told him, not bothering with the steps, just climbing in. ''Is it far?''

''No, mum. A five-minute ride.''

''Go, then, and hurry.'' Lucy slammed shut the coach door and leaned forward in her seat as though that would speed them along. Damn him! she thought of her gallivanting employer. How dare he go out when he knew Stacy was sick? This was all his fault.

The carriage ride *was* short; almost before Lucy knew it they'd come to a stop, and a liveried footman had opened the door. As Lucy stepped down she glanced back the way they had come and saw the huge sheer cliff behind her, with the turrets of Lockhaven Hall at its summit, just barely visible in the drizzle of dusk.

''I must see Lord Carlyle,'' she told the footman urgently. He handed her over to a doorman, who swept the cloak from Lucy's shoulders before she had a chance to tell him she wasn't staying. ''Take me to Lord Carlyle!'' she snapped. ''Immediately!'' The haughty doorman led her through a mirrored hall to a receiving room even bigger and grander than the one at Lockhaven Hall.

"May I announce you, madam?" he inquired at the entrance.

"Don't bother," Lucy told him, and hurried inside.

There must have been a hundred men and women in the huge room, all looking very elegant and gay. These weren't farmers, Lucy realized as she scanned the crowd for her employer; they were real lords and ladies, draped in velvet and satin and absolutely dripping with jewels. She couldn't help staring at one statuesque blonde in a close-fitting silver gown, cut so low in the front that Lucy thought she must use sorcery to keep it from slipping down and revealing her sizeable breasts.

Then she caught sight of Lord Carlyle, just behind the woman in silver; he was bent over a small gilt table, about to throw a pair of dice. Gambling, she thought, seething with fury. Stacy is home dying, and he is playing at dice. As she started toward him, she heard a long, low whistle at her side.

"Good evening, angel," said a smooth voice, high-pitched but male, with a courtier's affected lisp. "I do hope you are looking for me. Anthony Babington at your service."

Lucy glanced at the clean-shaven blond man who had caught her hand. His thin, bony face reminded her vaguely of someone she had seen someplace before, but she hadn't the time or the inclination to puzzle out where it might be. "I must see Lord Carlyle," she told him briefly, pulling her hand away. "Excuse me, please."

The young man laughed and followed her across the floor. "Abraham Carlyle," he called as they approached the dicing table, "you have been holding out on me. Who is this exquisite creature so intent on hunting you down?"

Lord Carlyle raised his dark head and saw Lucy, and the dice fell from his hand to the floor. My Lord, Lucy thought as his taut face turned pale with shock, he looks as though he has seen a ghost. He took a faltering step toward her, but just then the bosomy blond woman in the silver gown whirled around to confront him.

"So *you're* Abraham Carlyle!" she cried. "You naughty man, I have got a bone to pick with you!" She grabbed his arm. "I think it was absolutely despicable of you to dismiss me without even giving me a chance! Why, I just cried and cried for days when your letter came.''

Lord Carlyle tried to shake her off, as though she were a puppy pulling at his breeches leg, but she would not let go. "Who in hell are you?" he growled down at her.

"Who am I? Who am I?" The blonde slapped him playfully and laughed. "Why, Claudia Moncrief, you silly old thing.''

"Oh, my God," Lucy whispered, and knew she was the one turning pale now. She saw Lord Carlyle's face contort in a terrible spasm of rage as he stared at her across the room, and she whirled about in a swirl of apple-green silk and ran for the door.

"Johnny!" she screamed as she flew out onto the drive. "Johnny, where are you?"

" 'Ere, mum,'' he called from his driver's seat. "Are we waitin' for Lord Carlyle?"

"No. No, Johnny, just take me back to Lockhaven Hall." He'd be following her soon enough. She leaped into the coach, and Johnny's whip cracked, and she heard the wheels rumble over the cobblestones as they lurched off again.

Jesus in heaven, what a mess! Who in the world could ever have expected the real Claudia Moncrief to have been there tonight? From the expression on Lord Carlyle's face he'd been ready to murder her when that woman told him her name. But why in the world, she wondered, had he looked so shocked when he'd first seen her, before Claudia Moncrief even spoke up? Well, there wasn't time to find out now. She pushed back the carriage window and stared at the road behind the coach, but there was no sign of him or Bellero-whatever. Thank God! "Faster!" she shouted to Johnny. With any luck she would just have time to grab the lute letter and her money, say a quick farewell to Minnie and Stacy, and be on her way before Lord Carlyle ever got the whole story out of Claudia Moncrief.

It seemed that for once in her life she was going to be lucky. The carriage careened through the front gates and onto the drive at Lockhaven Hall, and still there wasn't any sign of a horseman behind them. "Stay right here," she told Johnny. "You'll be going to Hucknall for the doctor for Stacy—and taking me, too. I'll be back in five seconds.'' She raced through the door into the dark armory, tore toward the staircase—

And screamed in terror as something loomed up out of the darkness and grabbed her, wrestling her to the floor.

"Who are you?" It was Lord Carlyle's deep voice, unspeakably grim. How the devil had he got here before her? Lucy wondered, trying frantically to wriggle free of his grasp. She fought her way to her knees; he grabbed her arm, twisting it behind her back with such force that she screamed again.

"Who are you?" he thundered.

"Please," she cried, "you are breaking my arm!"

"By God, I'll break your neck!" He yanked her to her feet and shoved her against the wall with a horrible clanging of shields and axes and swords. His big hand circled her throat; she felt his fingers tighten mercilessly. "Who are you," he demanded again, "and why are you wearing my wife's wedding gown?"

His wife's wedding gown! Lucy went limp in his grasp. Jesus, no wonder he'd stared at her as though she were a ghost! It was another one of Minnie and Stacy's tricks. That was why Stacy had insisted he wanted his father, why he'd made her go to Lord Babington's instead of Johnny. She'd have seen through him right away if she hadn't been so worried about him, the little bounder. And she'd thought she and the children really were friends . . .

"Please, Father," a small, hesitant voice called from the top of the staircase. "Don't hurt her, please!"

Lucy looked up to see Minnie and Stacy in their nightclothes, carrying candles, hanging over the banister. "The dress is my fault," Stacy went on, "Minnie's and mine."

"What are you talking about?" Lord Carlyle demanded, staring up at their frightened faces, wreathed in candlelight.

"I gave her the dress to wear," Minnie said, her lower lip trembling. "She didn't know it belonged to Mother. I gave it to her."

"And I told her I was sick," Stacy confessed, "and sent her to Lord Babington's to get you."

"Why in God's name," their father roared, "would you do such a thing?"

"We wanted you to see how pretty she is," Minnie told him, and burst into tears. "We wanted—" She stopped, because Stacy had elbowed her.

"She hasn't got any clothes of her own," he put in, "except for one gown. She couldn't bring anything more because of the man that was trying to kill her."

Lord Carlyle whipped back to face Lucy. "Who the devil are you?"

"Her name is Lucy Jones," Stacy told him. "And she had a shop in London, in Shoreditch, only a man tried to kill her and killed her friend Joe, so she ran away and our door was open, and so she came in, and you started calling her Mistress Moncrief."

"What kind of lies have you been telling these children?" Lord Carlyle demanded, going for Lucy's throat again.

"It is true!" Minnie screamed, running down the stairs. "It is true, it is! Don't hurt her!"

"Shut up!" Lord Carlyle roared, and then bellowed for Jeeves. The butler appeared so quickly that he must have been listening from the banquet room. "Send for the sheriff, Jeeves," his master snapped.

"No!" the children cried in unison. Stacy, too, raced down the stairs, and both of them threw their arms around Lucy.

"We won't let you send her away," Stacy told his father.

"That's right, we won't!" Minnie said defiantly.

Lord Carlyle glowered. "Is this what she's been teaching you? Insolence? Disobedience?" By this time Cook and Johnny and Jem had all joined Jeeves and were staring at Lucy and the children and their irate master.

Minnie's blue eyes flashed. "She has taught us all sorts of wonderful things. Why, I can recite every king of England straight up from William the Conqueror."

"She is better at arithmetic than I am," Stacy put in, "or you, either, I bet. She showed us how to use the abacus; she learned by counting money in her shop."

"God in heaven," Jem whispered, "she's a bleedin' shopgirl!"

"She is really, *really* clever," Minnie insisted. "Why, Stacy didn't even start to teach her to read until a month ago, and already she's as good as me, almost."

"Jesus Christ Almighty," old Cook moaned. "She can't even read!"

"She can *too* read." Minnie was overemphasizing words right and left, but Stacy didn't stop her. "She *can* read, we'll prove it. Stacy, go and get the primer." He started up the stairs.

"Eustace!" his father roared, scowling furiously. "That's not the bloody point!"

Stacy scowled right back at him. "What is the bloody point then, I'd like to know?"

"Stacy!" Lucy cried, appalled. The situation had gotten completely out of hand. "How dare you speak to your father that way? Come back down those stairs." He hesitated for a long moment, his chin thrust out at Lord Carlyle, but finally he did. Lucy sat on the bottom stair with a child on either side of her and put her arms around them. "Both of you, listen to me. Your father is right to be angry with me. What I did was wrong; I deceived him."

"It wasn't your fault, it was his," Stacy said indignantly. "He opened up the door; he called you Claudia Moncrief. It was his mistake."

"Aye, but I let him go on thinking I was somebody I wasn't. And what's worse, I let him think I was a governess when I'm not. I can't teach you the things you need to know; I can't teach you Latin—"

"I don't want to learn Latin," Minnie sobbed. "I *hate* Latin."

Lucy kissed her forehead. "I know, pet, but you have to learn it anyway."

"Why?"

"Why, so you can take your proper place in the world, with the nobility. So you can make your father proud of you. You want that, don't you?" Minnie, glaring at her father mutinously, started to say something, and Lucy quickly went on: "Of course you do. Now, we have all had a wonderful time together these past several weeks, but it's time for me to go.''

"Don't leave us," Minnie wailed.

"I have to, sweetheart. Someday you'll understand."

"No, I will not!" Tears streaming down her cheeks, she clung to Lucy's neck. "And I will hate Father forever and ever for making you go away."

"Minnie!" Lucy pulled her back and looked at her sternly. "You'll do no such thing. Your father only wants what is best for you. Now, I want you to promise me that you'll work very, very hard for your next governess." The girl pouted and said nothing. Lucy tipped up her chin. "Please? For me?"

"All right," she whispered reluctantly.

"As for you, young man—" Lucy turned to Stacy; his eyes, too, were suspiciously moist. "I want you to apologize to your father for using bad language to him." He muttered something. "I can't hear you, Stacy."

He, too, was glaring at his father, but he did spit out, "I'm sorry. Sir."

"Thank you, Stacy," Lucy told him, and kissed his cheek.

"But where will you go?" he asked worriedly. "What will you do?"

"Don't worry about me," she assured him, and then looked up at their father. "I am sorry as well, sir, for having tricked you. I hope you'll believe that I never meant you or the children any harm. I'll return all the money you paid me, of course; I haven't spent any. And if you want to send for the sheriff, well, it's no more than I deserve."

"Shall I go, then, milord?" asked Jeeves.

"Wait," Lord Carlyle said.

The children stared at him, holding their breaths. "Minnie," he said slowly, "can you really name all the kings in order?"

"William the Conqueror," she plunged in. "William Rufus. Henry the First. Stephen. Henry the Second. Richard the Lion-Hearted. King John—he was a bad king. Henry the Third. Then three more Edwards. Then another Richard. And . . . and . . ."

"Three Henrys," Stacy prodded.

"Right! Three Henrys, two Edwards, another Richard, and then Henry the Seventh!" she finished triumphantly. "That brings us up to the House of Tudor. They're the greatest rulers England has ever had," she told her father gravely.

"Aye, so I've heard."

"Would you like me to tell you the names of Henry the Eighth's six wives? Or how Mary, queen of Scots, murdered Lord Darnley?" she offered.

"That won't be necessary. Stacy, say your nine times tables." The boy ran them off, lightning fast. "What is one hundred twenty-seven plus two hundred forty-eight?"

"I can do that," Minnie sniffed. "Three hundred and seventy-five."

"No it's not," said her father. "It's three hundred sixty-five."

"I think," Lucy said quietly, "you forgot to carry one. Sir."

Lord Carlyle looked at her. "Mistress—what in hell did you say your name is?"

"Jones, sir."

"Mistress Jones. I want to talk to you in my study. Privately."

She followed him across the armory, through the portrait gallery, and then across the reception room, with Lady Carlyle's eyes staring down at her from the ceiling as she passed below in her wedding gown. Then they went down the monk's walk and through the third door on the left.

She was sure he'd explode at her now that the children were out of earshot, but he just sat down at his cluttered desk, leaning back in his chair, his fingertips tapping together. "Are you really from London?" he asked, and she nodded.

"Shoreditch, sir."

"I'm not familiar with Shoreditch."

"I wouldn't expect you to be."

"Neither, I expect, were you overly familiar with the gentry. May I ask what made you think you could get away with pretending you were Claudia Moncrief?"

"I didn't see that I had much choice, sir. A man was trying to kill me. You opened your door."

''Why was he trying to kill you?''

''I don't know, sir.'' It was the truth, after all; she didn't yet know what the lute letter said.

He arched a black brow. ''He just came out of nowhere, I suppose, and murdered your friend and then tried to kill you?''

''Believe it or not, sir, that is just about what happened.''

He made a noise between a grunt and a snort and brought his front chair legs thumping down to the floor. ''The trouble is, Mistress Mon—Mistress Jones, I do believe you. You have got a very honest way about you. You must have done well in business.''

''Not so well as you, sir,'' Lucy said with a faint smile.

''I inherited my money,'' he said. Then he rocked back and forth on his chair legs, arms crossed over his chest, for a very long time. ''The children . . . seem fond of you,'' he said finally, stiffly.

''I am fond of them, sir.''

''They have changed since you came here. You've been good for them. If you want, you can stay.''

''Oh, sir!'' Lucy looked at him with wide green eyes. ''But all the things I can't teach them—''

''Just go on teaching them—what you can.'' He made the grunt-snort noise again. ''Now get out of that bloody damned gown and give it to Jem. She knows where it belongs.''

''Yes, sir! Right away!'' She whirled for the door before he could change his mind.

Stacy and Minnie were crouched right outside the door in the monk's walk. ''How many times have I told you two that it is rude to eavesdrop?'' Lucy demanded, pulling them up by their ears.

''We couldn't hear anything,'' Stacy hissed. ''What did he say?''

''Wot the 'ell d'ye think 'e said, child?'' grim old Cook barked from the end of the corridor where she was waiting with Jeeves and Johnny and Jem. ''That he's sendin' 'er straight to prison! That's where she belongs!''

''Actually,'' Lucy said, ''he told me that I could stay.''

"He did? Hurray!" Minnie cried, and Stacy hurled his nightcap high in the air.

"Now, as for you two," Lucy told the children, still tugging them along by their ears, "I've a few choice words for you about that stunt you pulled on me this evening. Upstairs! Now!"

"Are we going to get a spanking?" Stacy asked worriedly as she marched them right past the openmouthed servants.

"Oh, Stacy, who cares?" Minnie said joyously. "I'd take a million spankings to keep Lucy here!"

Part II

Chapter 8

"There now, wasn't that splendid?" Lucy stomped snow from her boots onto the armory floor, then knelt to unwind Minnie from a nest of mittens and scarves.

"It was cold," Stacy declared, blowing on his hands to warm them. "But great! Whoever would think those old serving trays would go so fast?"

"I thought it was kind of scary," Minnie put in as her small pink face emerged from its wrappings. "Especially when Stacy went near the goose pond."

"I told you, those old birds have all flown off south for the winter." Lucy wagged a finger at Stacy. "As for you, young man, stay away from that pond."

"It's frozen solid all the way down to hell," he grumbled.

"Bad word, bad word!" Minnie crowed, dancing up and down. "You owe tuppence to the Treasury!" Lucy had instituted a new rule, as much for her benefit as for theirs—anyone caught using a curse word had to pay tuppence to the Treasury fund. The children still hadn't decided what they would use the money for when there was enough of it. Minnie thought perhaps a trip to London to see the queen, but Stacy favored going on an adventure—to the New World, perhaps.

"I wasn't using it as a bad word," Stacy protested now, appealing to Lucy. "I was using it as a place."

"Then say Hades next time," she told him. "Minnie, how can you jump up and down like that when you've just been out sledding all afternoon? Scoot up to the nursery, you two, and sit by the fire while I put these wet things away. Ring for Jem to bring up some hot milk and biscuits if you like. I've got to have a word with your father.''

''What about?'' Minnie asked curiously.

''It's not wise to ask questions so close to Christmastime,'' Lucy said mysteriously. ''Now get up those stairs.''

She bundled their wet clothes together and took them back to the kitchens, hanging them up on hooks by the hearth to dry, hiding a smile as old Cook muttered and cast dirty looks her way. Cook resented Lucy's presence in the house more now than she had when she thought Lucy was rich. Jem, on the other hand, had warmed up considerably since learning Lucy was a commoner. As for Jeeves, well, he was still Jeeves, polite and unobtrusive regardless of what chaos might be going on around him.

It was from Jem that Lucy found out why Lord Carlyle had let her stay on even after he discovered who she really was. Apparently the other governesses he'd hired on for the children were a good deal less interested in Minnie and Stacy than they had been in him. ''Rich men's daughters they were. Very grand ladies, I'm sure,'' the maid confided, ''but that didn't keep 'em from actin' more like babies than the little ones. Always throwin' tantrums, demandin' this, orderin' that—'n' struttin' about the place in such outfits as ye can't imagine, tryin' to catch the Master's eye, sidlin' up to him—why, some of 'em tried to go out there to the goose pond in summer 'n' catch him naked while he was swimmin'! Poor man didn't have a moment's peace, the way they set their caps to marryin' him.''

Lucy laughed. ''He ought just to have married one of them, then.''

''Well, ye know what they says, Miss Lucy—once burned, twice shy.''

Shy. It was a strange way to describe Lord Carlyle, and yet it fit him. As gruff and grim and bellicose as he made himself out to be, Lucy sensed uncertainty beneath the bluster. She had glimpsed it that day in the meadow when he asked to join the children at pell-mell, and once or twice she had seen it since, when he came by the nursery to check on the progress of their studies. He never touched anyone, she had noticed, and no one touched him, unless you counted Jeeves handing him his cloak or his hat when he went away. He certainly hadn't touched Lucy since he found out she was from Shoreditch. But, then, she would have expected that.

He had been away for much of the autumn; there had been a meeting of Parliament in September and October in London. He had asked Minnie and Stacy if they wanted to go to the city with him, but they chose to remain at Lockhaven Hall. Lucy was glad. She would not have felt safe in the city, and besides she had been enthralled with watching the changing of the seasons, the way the trees in the ravine beneath her bedchamber window seemed to put on new clothes each day, always in more brilliant shades of crimson and ochre and gold.

Lucy had new clothes as well. With part of her wages she'd gone to market at the village of Hucknall and bought cloth—nothing fancy, just good, sturdy linsey-woolsey in dark blue and forest green. Her sole indulgence had been a length of handsome scarlet damask that she could not resist; it was the exact color of the oak trees beneath the cliff. She hadn't worn that gown yet, though; she was saving it for the holidays.

The trees had long since shed their brilliant attire; the countryside wore Puritan dress, shades of white and black and slate-gray. There was a somber beauty to the snow-covered hills, and on clear days the blue sky and bright sun made the icy branches of the apple trees in the orchard shimmer and glisten like jewels.

As she spread Minnie's cloak out to dry, Lucy ran her hand over its damp rabbit lining and frowned, thinking of another cloak faced with fur that clasped at the collar with a real jewel brighter than the ice-covered branches of the trees—the cloak worn by the young gentleman who had brought the lute letter to her shop. She'd been so busy with the children of late that she hadn't even looked at the letter in nearly a month, though she must have learned more of the words in it by now. Soon, she promised herself, with a twinge of guilt at her negligence. *Soon I will sit myself down and figure out just what that bloody letter says.*

With the wet clothes taken care of, Lucy headed for Lord Carlyle's study, pausing as she always did in the re-

ceiving room to glance up at the portrait of his late wife.
So gay and lovely she was, Lucy thought. Just like an
angel. Lucy could not imagine anyone wishing such a
beautiful creature any harm; even the dark figure of the
god of the underworld creeping up behind her would surely
have fled when he saw her exquisite face.

She knocked on the study door and heard her employer
call, "Come in!"

"It's locked," she called back without trying the knob.
If she could remember that it always was, why the devil
couldn't he?

"Oh." She heard a rustle of papers, and then the door
opened. "Yes?"

He looked tired, she noted; he hadn't shaved, and his
clothing was rumpled. But, then, he had been away on a
business trip for the past week and only got in the night
before; the thumping of the virginals had awakened her
near dawn. "If you'll pardon my saying so, sir, you could
use a bath and a nap," she told him.

"Thank you," he said, and scowled at her, opening the
bottom drawer of his desk and pulling out a glass. From
his doublet he produced a silver flask and poured the glass
full. "Do you want a drink?"

"What is it, sir?"

"Brandy."

"No, thank you. I'm not much of a one for strong spirits." He must have been, though, she thought, from the
way he gulped his down.

"Was there some reason why you interrupted my work
besides to comment on my looking like hell?" he demanded.

"I didn't say that, sir." Lucy gazed around the study.
"You know, it is none of my concern, sir, but I can't help
thinking you'd get a lot more done if you'd straighten up
in here."

"For your information, Mistress Jones, I know exactly
where everything is in this room, and I like it this way.
You are right about one thing, though—it's none of your
concern." He refilled his glass. "So, now that you've in-
sulted me and my working habits, what, pray tell, can I
do for you?"

"I am sorry, sir." Lucy shut the door behind her and took a step toward the desk. "But it's about Christmas. You know, it is only a fortnight away."

"Grnn," he said, and emptied the glass. "Want time off for it, do you?"

"Oh, no, sir, I've got no family to visit or anything. No, it's about the children. I've had them make out their lists." She pulled them from her sleeve and laid them before him. "I'm not saying they ought to get all they put down, for they shouldn't be spoiled. But they have been good. They've put what they want most at the top. I imagine some of these books Stacy asked for must be awfully expensive, but you see Minnie's just got a kitten at the top of hers, and that shouldn't cost anything at all."

Lord Carlyle rubbed his reddened eyes and stared blankly at the papers. "What are they?"

"Why—lists, sir. You know. Of gifts for Father Christmas to bring."

He held up one of the pages and read it aloud. "A gray girl kitten. Real balls for playing pell-mell with. A new tray for sledding because Stacy always gets the good one." He looked up at Lucy, who was biting her cheek.

"Well, it's true, sir. He usually does."

He pushed the pages back toward her. "Figure out what it comes to, then, and I'll write them drafts."

"What it comes to?" Lucy echoed.

"Aye, what it adds up to. The cost," he said impatiently. "That's the way I handle it every year. Give them money. Then they can buy what they like."

"I just thought, sir, you would want to pick out the gifts for them," she said hesitantly.

"Why should I? Here, look at this—a new tray for sledding. Christ, I haven't got the foggiest notion what she's talking about."

"But it would mean so much more to them, sir, if the gifts came from you."

"They do come from me if I pay for them," he said, exasperated.

"I mean, sir, if they knew you had taken the time to choose them yourself. Just giving them money—well, it seems a bit coldhearted, don't you think, after they've made out their lists and all?''

"Not particularly. It is what I've always done."

His thickheadedness was raising Lucy's hackles. "Maybe so, but it certainly doesn't show much thought or affection. Children need—"

"I'd like to know," he interrupted her rudely, "what makes you such a bloody expert on what children need. I will give them money, just as I always do. And as for you, Mistress Jones, why don't you just stop trying to change everything in this household to suit your liking? I don't need any lessons on raising children or anything else from you!"

Lucy's eyes flashed green fire. "Let me tell you something, Lord Carlyle. I may have grown up in a hovel instead of in a great fancy house like this. And maybe my father couldn't afford to give me much at Christmas, but by God he worked his fingers to the bone to make sure I got something! He picked it out himself, and he wrapped it up himself, too, in scrap paper and twine. And even if it wasn't anything more than a rag doll, I loved it. And I loved him for giving it to me." She took a deep breath. "I'll tell you something else, too. If you were any kind of a decent father, you'd know what Minnie meant by a tray for sledding. So there!" She spun on her heel and went out, slamming the door shut as hard as she could.

She half expected him to come after her and dismiss her right then and there, but he didn't. The only sounds from behind the closed door were the opening of a drawer and the glub of brandy filling a glass. Go on, she thought furiously, lose yourself in your bloody brandy and your bloody damned work! Those children deserve a proper Christmas, and I intend to see they get one even if I have to give it to them myself!

The very next market day she had Jem's Johnny drive her to Hucknall. He waited in the tavern while she made the rounds of the snow-roofed stalls. It was odd, she thought as she looked over the vendors' meager wares. When she lived in London she could never afford any of the goods she saw at market, and now when she had a purse full of money there didn't seem to be much to buy.

The bookseller only had some dog-eared copies of works Stacy already owned in much finer versions, and the toy-maker's goods were ordinary and crude.

She managed to find a game for Stacy that she knew he didn't have—backgammon, the toymaker called it, and as-sured her it was hard to play. And there was a quaint painted wooden top she thought Minnie would like; Lucy had had one just like it when she was a child. She spent the rest of the money at the confectioner's stall, on a sack-ful of comfits and nut-filled dates, peppermint lozenges and little animals molded from barley sugar, almonds and honey for making Christmas cakes.

"Ye've one hell of a sweet-tooth, mum," the grinning candyman told her.

Lucy laughed. "Oh, they're not for me. They're for Lord Carlyle's children."

"Ye don't say. So ye're the pretty new governess I've heard about. Livin' up there in the house, are ye?" Lucy nodded, and he shrugged, shoveling almonds into the sack. "Better ye than me."

"Why do you say that?"

"Why, there's strange goin's-on there, the way I hears it. Ghosts 'n' hauntings 'n' Lady Carlyle gettin' done in—"

"Lockhaven Hall isn't haunted," Lucy told him impa-tiently. "And Lady Carlyle fell down the stairs."

"Oh, aye, as ye says, mum," he told her quickly. "That'll be five shillin's, then, for the lot."

Lucy didn't see anyone at market selling kittens, but she'd already arranged for that wish of Minnie's to be grat-ified. Johnny had a cousin who owned a fine mouser. It had just given birth to a litter, and one of the kittens was a girl and gray. Johnny had promised to bring it to the house on Christmas eve.

Satisfied with her purchases, Lucy headed for the tavern to find Johnny. The smell of the dark, low-eaved common room—ale, damp wool, sawdust—brought back a rush of memories of the evenings she'd spent with her father at the Mermaid in Shoreditch. She stood on the threshold, eyes adjusting to the dimness, drinking in that smell.

Out of the shadows she heard Johnny's voice, a loud

whisper. "Aye, kept her on he did," he was saying, "even after he found out who she really was."

"Go on, get out," another voice objected. "Why would he?"

"Oh, she's a looker, she is. I'll grant ye that. Hair black as midnight, 'n' green eyes a man might drown in, 'n' a pair of bosoms I'd give a month's wages to get me hands on."

Cheeks burning, Lucy stepped forward to make her presence known just as Johnny's companion said ominously, "She'd better watch yer master don't get his hands on her. That wife he killed, she was a looker, too."

Lucy cleared her throat loudly, and Johnny's head popped up out of the darkness. "Oh! There ye is, missy. I didn't expect ye to finish with yer shoppin' so soon."

"Obviously," said Lucy, quickly dismissing her notion of having a cup of ale herself; everyone in the murky place had turned to stare at her. "I am ready to go."

"Right, missy." He drained his pint and followed her outdoors.

She turned to him in the snowy yard. "It isn't right for you to gossip the way you were in there."

It was his turn to flush. "Didn't mean no harm by it, missy," he mumbled, then peeked up sheepishly. "Ye is a fine-lookin' woman, though."

"I don't mean about me; I mean about Lord Carlyle!"

His embarrassment vanished. "Faith, missy, folks round here been talkin' 'bout him long before I came to work for the man. I can't help what they say."

"But you must know Lord Carlyle didn't murder his wife."

He returned her gaze with a touch of defiance. "Must I, now? I'll tell ye, missy, what I must know. The night she died the two of 'em was rantin' 'n' ravin' to beat the devil. Everybody there heard it; a soul couldn't miss that row lest he was deaf. The next thing ye know she's fallen down 'n' broke her neck." His voice dropped to a whisper. "They called me to help carry the body out of that there secret room. I saw the marks on her neck—the marks of two hands, big 'n' plain as day."

"Nonsense!" Lucy snapped.

"I saw what I saw."

"Johnny, that's absurd! There would have been an inquest—the coroner would have examined the body."

"Master's rich enough to buy this whole parish 'n' then some." He gave her a hand up into the carriage. "I reckon he could buy up the coroner, too."

That night after she'd tucked in the children, Lucy went down to the kitchens to seek out Jem; the maid had promised to help her make Christmas cakes for the holidays after grim old Cook refused to be bothered. "Jem," she said, punching out rounds of almond-flavored dough with a custard cup, "did you hear Lord and Lady Carlyle fighting on the night that she died?"

"Who's been telling ye tales, then?" the maid asked sharply.

"Your Johnny," Lucy confessed.

"Hmph. He's got a mouth bigger'n his brain, Johnny does sometimes."

"But did you hear them fighting?" Lucy pressed.

"There may have been some words 'twixt 'em," Jem said, tight-lipped.

"Well—could you hear what they were saying?"

"Certainly not—'n' I didn't care to." She frowned, jamming an almond into the top of a cake with her thumb. "I suppose Johnny told ye about them there hand marks he says he saw, too."

"Well, he did mention—"

"Miss Lucy," said Jem, "see here. Them two, they was married for more'n twelve years. They'd got their ups 'n' downs, I reckon, like anyone else. They was country 'n' city, d'ye know what I mean? She liked London 'n' he liked it here. They spent lots of time separate from each other, but that's the nobility's way. There's one thing I do know, 'n' that's that what he wanted more'n anything in the world was for her to come back here 'n' live for good. 'N' when she died, she *had* come back. Ever since Miss Minnie was born, she'd been livin' here quiet as ye please for nigh on three years. So why in the hell would he rock the boat when he'd got what he wanted, if ye get my drift?"

"They were wed for twelve years?" Lucy echoed incredulously. ''Why, they must have been just children when they got married.''

''He was, right enough. Just bare fifteen. Mistress Olive, she must have been a good ten years older. Daughter of an earl, she was. Very grand.'' She smiled, leaning her chin on her hand. ''Oh, my, he was head over heels with her when they was married. 'Twas a big huge wedding they had, right in Westminster Abbey. All the toffs was there.''

''And they were—happy together?''

''Well, like I says, they wasn't together all that much. After young Stacy was born, the master moved back here. He was happy, though. He just doted on that boy.''

''Really,'' Lucy said dubiously.

''Oh, aye. Apple of his eye, as they say. 'N' then there came Miss Minnie, 'n' Mistress Olive finally came home here to live just like he'd always wanted, all together at last.''

''You don't believe Johnny, then, about the marks he saw?''

''Oh, Johnny. I reckon he saw somethin' maybe. But he does tell tall tales.'' Jem made a face. ''Hasn't he been tellin' me he was goin' to marry me for the past eight years?''

''And you don't think Lord Carlyle killed her.''

''It's like I says, Miss Lucy—why would he when she'd finally settled down?'' She shrugged and pushed another almond in. ''Still, they do say quiet waters run deep, don't they? I guess ye never can tell.'' She glanced up at Lucy. ''Do ye think he did?''

''Of course not,'' said Lucy. ''I just couldn't help wondering about what Johnny said.''

''Well, I'd let what Johnny says go in one ear 'n' come out the other,'' Jem told her. ''That's what I do.''

Chapter 9

On Christmas eve morning Lucy ate breakfast hurriedly in her room, then wrapped the gifts she'd bought the children in tissue and string. Jem looked decidedly unfestive when she came to retrieve the tray. "Why such a long face?" Lucy teased her. "It's a holiday."

"Oh, Miss Lucy. It's—it's about the kitten."

"Did Johnny bring it by?" Lucy asked eagerly.

"No, he didn't—'n' he won't be." Jem nibbled her lip, on the verge of tears. "Somethin' terrible's happened, ye see. Johnny's cousin's dog got 'em."

"Got them? Do you mean—killed them?"

"Aye, all six of 'em," the maid said sorrowfully. "Johnny's just sick about it, truly he is. He spent all day yesterday lookin' for another, but he's had no luck. Winter's a bad time for kittens."

"Oh, dear. Do tell him not to worry, Jem; it surely wasn't his fault."

"I know, but he feels awful just the same." She brightened slightly. "His cousin says that mother cat's a right little tart, though. There'll be another brood along in no time; ye can tell Miss Minerva that."

"I will," Lucy assured her, even as she thought: Well, not a very auspicious beginning to the day.

Jem had no sooner gone than Minnie and Stacy burst in. When Lucy saw Minnie's tear-streaked face she thought for sure the girl had already heard about the kitten. "What is it, sweetheart?" she cried, rushing to hug her.

"It's Father," Stacy said flatly. "We went down this morning to his study to see if he would help us decorate the hall, and Jeeves said he was gone."

"Gone? Gone where?"

"B-b-business," Minnie sobbed. "Jeeves said he left last night."

"He didn't even say goodbye." Stacy's eyes were bright, too. "Christmas, and he couldn't even be bothered with that."

Damn you to hell, Lucy told her absent employer. *Damn* you, you thoughtless bastard.

"We didn't even do anything bad," Minnie wailed.

"Of course you didn't, pet." Lucy hugged her tightly, so angry with Lord Carlyle that she wanted to spit. How dare he disappoint them this way? Was it too much to ask that he spend some time with his own children one day out of the year?

"He forgot to give us our Christmas money, too," Eustace said in disgust. "We used to be able to count on him for that, at least."

Looking at their sad faces, Lucy wished she were a sorcerer, that somehow, by saying a few magic words and waving a wand, she could heal their hurt, bring their father back from wherever he'd gone. But she couldn't—and if he were here right now, she thought grimly, she'd claw out his eyes!

She pressed her handkerchief to Minnie's nose. "Blow, pet," she said gently. "No more crying. It's Christmas eve."

"So what?" said Stacy.

"So, we have decorations to hang, and treats to eat, and songs to sing, and presents to open—"

"Presents?" asked Minnie, rubbing her eyes.

"Of course! You don't think Father Christmas would forget about you just because your papa had to go away, do you?"

"What kind of treats?" Stacy wanted to know.

"All different kinds. Cakes and punch and biscuits and sugarplums—"

"I hate punch," said Minnie, then added wistfully, "I like sugarplums, though."

"Well, there you are." Lucy lifted her up and held out her hand to Stacy. "Come along. If this is to be a proper Christmas eve, we've got a lot of work to do."

* * *

Her arms piled high with greenery, Lucy kicked open the front door to Lockhaven Hall and held it with her shoulder while the children trooped past her, singing lustily:

> *The holly bears a blossom,*
> *As white as lily-flower,*
> *And Mary bore sweet Jesus Christ*
> *To be our own Saviour.*

Cook and Jeeves and Jem, hearing the commotion, came into the armory just in time to see them dump their loads of holly and ivy and pine branches onto the floor. "Now wot in blazes," Cook began indignantly.

"And a very Merry Christmas to you, too, Cook," Lucy said gaily, unbuttoning Minnie's cloak. "We're just going to pop upstairs and get into our fancy clothes and then we'll get to the decorating."

"Surely you ain't intendin' to 'ang that mess up in 'ere!" the old woman exclaimed.

"Why not? Don't you get tired of looking at all these battleaxes all the time?" Lucy glanced at her. "Come to think of it, I don't suppose you do." The children giggled, and she gave them her hands. "Would you build us a fire in here, Jeeves, please? A great big one that will burn for a good long time."

"Very good, Mistress Jones."

"Thank you, Jeeves. Minnie, Stacy, come along."

She had just finished buttoning the sleeves on her new red gown when Stacy and Minnie pounded on her bedchamber door. "We're ready!" they shouted.

"Come in and let's see. Oh, my!" She drew in her breath as they entered. "How handsome you are, Stacy Carlyle. And Minnie, you look so grown up in that pretty dress."

"Thank you." She dropped a curtsy. "You have a new dress on, too."

"Do you like it? I've been saving it just for tonight."

"It's beautiful," Minnie said, and sighed. "I only wish—"

"What, pet?"

"I only wish Father could be here."

"I feel sorry for him," Lucy told her, "because he is going to miss all the fun. Just give me one more moment to put up my hair."

"Do you suppose you could leave it down just for to-night?" Stacy asked shyly. "I like it when it's loose like that. It looks like waves on a midnight sea."

Lucy wagged a finger at him. "I pity the girls when you decide to come courting; you've a poet's tongue on you. Of course I'll leave it down. Now let's go see about brightening up that bloody—"

"Tuppence to the Treasury!" Minnie cried.

Lucy kissed her. "Quite right. That armory."

They sang while they draped garlands of green across the mantel above the fire Jeeves had built and festooned the weapons on the walls with holly and mistletoe. Stacy and Minnie even hung their great-great-grandfather's suit of armor with fir boughs and stuck springs of holly in his visor holes. Jem came to help, though Cook hovered in the doorway, exuding disapproval of the disrespectful transformation being wrought.

Lucy taught the children more of the carols she knew: "I Saw Three Ships," "Deck the Halls," "The Twelve Days of Christmas." Minnie liked this last one best, except for the line about geese. When the decorating was finished they sat on the rug in front of the roaring fire, and Jem brought them cups of steaming punch and the almond cakes she and Lucy had made. "Tell us a story," Minnie begged, curling up close to Lucy. "Tell us what Christmas was like in Shoreditch."

"Christmas eve in Shoreditch." Lucy smiled, remembering. "It was my favorite time of all the year. Just as the sun went down, all the neighborhood children would meet at Magdalen Church to go wassailing."

"What's wassailing?" asked Stacy.

"Well, we would have a big bowl with holly and ivy draped around it, and the boys would tie it up on big sticks. Then we would carry it around from house to house, singing carols and asking for alms."

"Asking for alms?" he echoed dubiously. "Do you mean you begged?"

Lucy laughed. "I suppose it was begging, though I never thought of it that way. I liked singing the carols, and the way the candles we held shone like stars in the dark."

Minnie put down the almond cake she'd been eating. "Were you so poor as that, that you had to go begging?"

"We were pretty poor," Lucy admitted cheerfully. "I remember one Christmas eve when all we had for our supper was cold gruel, because Pop hadn't got any money to buy wood for the fire. Don't you like the cake, Minnie?"

She pushed the sweet to and fro on her plate. "I don't like thinking about your having to beg at Christmastime. It makes me sad."

"It wasn't so bad as all that," Lucy protested. "I had a roof over my head, and a bed to sleep in, and a father who—well. Remember, the Baby Jesus had to sleep in a manger when he was born, his father was so poor. That's the story I ought to be telling, don't you think?" Minnie smiled and nodded. "Well. Once upon a time, a very very long time ago, a decree went out from Caesar Augustus, saying that all the world should be taxed. And to pay their taxes, everybody had to go to the city that their ancestors came from."

"Father would have had to go to Cumberland," Stacy noted. "That's where the Carlyles came from."

"Well, Joseph was of the house of David, so he went to Bethlehem. And he took his wife Mary, who was just about to have a baby. But the city was so crowded that there wasn't any room for them in any of the inns, so they went to a stable. And Mary brought forth her firstborn son, and laid him in a manger, and—"

"You forgot the swaddling clothes," Stacy pointed out. "What are you staring at?"

Lucy could have sworn she'd seen a face at the armory window, pale and round and covered with long white hair.

"Saints preserve us," Jem whispered, crossing herself as she followed Lucy's gaze. "It's the ghost!" Minnie saw it, too, and screamed, burying her head in Lucy's skirts. Lucy held her tightly while the front doors slowly swung open wide, letting in a gust of cold swirling wind and a flurry of snow and a great tall figure in a long black cape, with a big bushy white beard . . .

"No, it's not," she said in amazement, recognizing the blue eyes that showed through the forest of whiskers. "Minnie, Stacy—it's your father!"

"Father Christmas," the apparition corrected her in a hearty, booming voice. He slung down the bulging sack he carried over his shoulder and gazed about at the gaily bedizened armory. When he saw the ivy-draped suit of armor he crossed to it and made a flourishing bow. "How do you do, my good man?" he said gravely. "So kind of you to come."

Minnie peeked up nervously from Lucy's skirts. "Father, is that really you?"

"I told you, my name is Father Christmas," he boomed so loudly that she squealed and hid her face again. "Also known as St. Nicholas or Old St. Nick. I suppose you could call me Father, though, for short."

Stacy got up and sidled toward him. "What is in that sack?"

"Presents, of course! Presents for good girls and boys. Have these two been good?" he asked Lucy in his gruff, low voice.

"Very," she told him.

"Well, then." He peered at them through the white beard. "What's that you're drinking? Have you got a cup of it for poor old Father Christmas?"

"I'll bring some right away, sir." Jem hurried toward the kitchens, glancing back over her shoulder as though she still suspected he might be a spirit and would disappear.

Lord Carlyle dragged his sack across the floor and flopped down beside Minnie, pulling off his soaked boots. "Whew! That was a mighty long ride."

"Where did you come from?" Minnie asked shyly.

"Iceland." He took the cup of punch Jem had brought, tasted it, and smacked his lips. "Excellent, excellent—though it could use just a drop of brandy." He remedied that with a hefty pour from his pocket flask. "Where was I? Ah, yes. Iceland. I'd had a report there was a good boy there, but it turned out not to be true. Good children certainly are getting hard to find these days. Imagine there being two here. Could you please pass the cakes?''

"Certainly.'' Minnie did so. "Could we please see the presents?''

"Not so fast,'' he rumbled, with a white-bearded scowl. "What were you doing when I came in?''

"Lucy was telling a story,'' said Stacy, sitting down on the rug.

"Well, let's allow her to finish, then, shall we?'' He added more brandy to his cup.

"Where did I leave off?'' Lucy asked.

"Swaddling clothes,'' Stacy reminded her again.

"That's right. So Mary wrapped her baby in swaddling clothes, *then* laid him in the manger, and she called him Jesus, because an angel had told her to.''

She described the shepherds in the fields, and the angels in the sky, and the Three Wise Men, while the fire crackled and roared and threw dancing shadows over the children's rapt faces. Lord Carlyle warmed his red hands around his cup of punch, and even Cook and Jem came back out of the kitchens to hear, though Lucy suspected it was less because of her story than to see the astonishing spectacle of the master in a false beard. After the Wise Men had presented their offerings to the Christ Child, she ended the tale. "Presents now?'' Minnie asked, eyeing the bulging sack.

"Presents now,'' Lucy told her. "Why don't you sing a carol for your father while I run upstairs?''

"More presents,'' Stacy hissed, nudging his sister. Lucy smiled as she went up the stairs, hearing their sweet voices sing:

> *God rest ye merry, gentlemen,*
> *Let nothing you dismay . . .*

It just goes to show, she thought, giggling as she glanced back at Lord Carlyle's false beard, how wrong you can be.

They all looked up as she came down the staircase with her presents. "Where shall we begin?'' Lord Carlyle asked.

"With me,'' Minnie said promptly. "What is for me?''

"Here you are." Lucy handed her a bundle and watched as she pulled off the paper and string.

"A top!" she exclaimed in delight. "And such a pretty one." She set its tip on the floor and sent it spinning away.

"I had one like it when I was a little girl," Lucy told her.

"Did you? I like it even more, then." Minnie kissed her, then ran to retrieve the top before it smashed into her great-great-grandfather's steel greaves.

"Is that one for me?" Stacy asked of the package Lucy still held. She laughed and presented it to him. He removed the wrappings very neatly, unlatched the wooden box, and peered at the diamond-embossed board inside. "What is it?"

"A game," she told him. "It's called backgammon."

"How do you play?"

"I don't know," she confessed.

"I do." Lord Carlyle leaned over to see it. "Though it's been an awfully long time."

"I hope you are better at it than you are at pell-mell," Minnie said slyly, and darted away as he lunged for her ribs.

"Is it like chess?" Stacy wanted to know.

"A little. It's very ancient," his father told him. "The Romans played it. The object is to get all your men home."

"Then it's nicer than chess, I think," Minnie said.

"Will you teach me to play it?" Stacy asked his father.

"Certainly. We can start now if you like."

"Stacy." His sister glanced meaningfully at the still unopened sack.

"Oh. Perhaps a little later, Father?"

Lord Carlyle laughed and reached into the sack. "Who's first?"

"Me," said Minnie, dancing up and down.

"You went first last time," Lucy reminded her. "It's Stacy's turn."

"Here you are, then, Stacy." Lord Carlyle handed him a rectangular package. "I'm sorry for the wrapping," he apologized, wincing at the crinkled brown paper and untidy string. "I did it myself."

"There's nothing wrong with the wrapping, is there, Minnie?"

"It's beautiful wrapping," she said stoutly. "Now open it."

The brown paper fell away to reveal a book bound in handsome red leather. *"The Sonnets of Sir Philip Sidney,"* Stacy read from the spine.

"You're a bit young still for them, maybe," his father told him. "But then again, I suppose it is never too soon to learn wooing. I've marked one there with the ribbon that I especially like."

Stacy opened to it and read aloud:

Doubt you to whom my muse these songs intends,
Which now my breast, o'ercharged, to music lends?
To you, to you all song of praise is due;
Only in you my song begins and ends.

" 'Only in you my song begins and ends,' " Stacy repeated slowly. "I like that, too. Do you like it, Lucy?"

"Very much indeed." Her green gaze slanted toward the boy's father. "But I thought you didn't care for music, sir."

"I think I am beginning to," he said softly. "I am beginning to appreciate the beauty there can be in a song when Lucy sings it."

"When did you ever hear Lucy sing?" Minnie asked curiously.

"Once, by the goose pond, I heard her sing a love song. Something about the western wind."

"You've never sung us that one, Lucy," said Stacy. "How does it go?"

"I don't remember it," she said quickly, though it was a lie. *Christ, that my love were in my arms* . . . "Isn't it your turn now, Minnie?" She could feel her cheeks burning beneath Lord Carlyle's steady blue stare; was he, too, thinking of the night of the storm last summer, when he had held her?

He laughed, just as though he knew she was trying to distract the girl, and reached into the sack. The gift he drew out this time was nearly as big around as Minnie;

her eyes went enormously wide when she saw its size. She tore away the paper and string, and her cherub's mouth formed a delighted O at the huge pewter platter that lay within. "A new sled! Stacy, look, it has handles and everything!"

"It's a beauty," he said admiringly. "Will you let me use it sometimes?"

"It's my sled," said Minnie, and then added, seeing Lucy frown at her, "but I guess you can use it, too."

There were more presents in the sack: a gorgeous new doll for Minnie, a kite for Stacy, a book by Euclid that he'd been wanting for ever so long, and—Minnie sighed happily as she unwrapped the final bundle—"Real pell-mell balls, and mallets, too!"

"Cook was getting grumpy about never being able to find a broom," her father told her, grinning.

"They're wonderful," she declared. "Everything is wonderful."

"It sure is," Stacy echoed, surveying his bounty happily.

Lord Carlyle shifted to his knees on the rug. "Oh, my poor sore muscles. Iceland is awfully far away." He touched the front of his doublet. "Good Lord, I nearly forgot. There is one thing more. Minnie, come here." She came toward him tentatively, and he opened a button. Lucy heard a mewling squeak, and then out popped a small, downy gray head capped with two outsized ears.

"My kitten!" Minnie squealed in delight, throwing her arms around her father, showering kisses all over his silly false beard. "Thank you, thank you, thank you!"

"You must be very gentle with it," he cautioned, handing her the squirming ball of gray fluff.

"I will, I promise!" She took the tiny creature from him and smiled into its heart-shaped face; it let out an enormous yawn and then licked her nose. "Did you see that? She likes me already." She glanced at her father. "She is a she, isn't she?"

"That's what the fellow told me, though I don't know how he could tell."

"Here, love." Lucy reached for the kitten and turned it over, examining its rump. "Sure enough, she's a she."

"How can you tell?" Stacy demanded.

"Do you see these little marks here? A boy kitten has two dots, and a girl has a line like this and just one dot."

"Why?" Stacy asked.

Lord Carlyle was looking at Lucy with one black eyebrow arched. "You'll have to ask your father that," she told Stacy, and saw Lord Carlyle's bemused blue eyes turn alarmed.

"Some other time," he said hastily. "Suppose I teach you to play backgammon now?"

"Wait!" Minnie cried. "Lucy, you hold on to Reggie—"

"Reggie?" her father echoed.

"Aye, for Good Queen Bess—Elizabeth Regina. Someday I am going to take her to see the queen in London, just like in the song. But Stacy and I have presents to give, too. Stacy, come on!" She tugged her brother after her up the stairs.

Reggie curled up in the lap of Lucy's red gown and proceeded to wash her front paws. "She seems very much at home there, doesn't she?" Lord Carlyle asked. Lucy blushed again; she didn't know why everything either one of them said should seem so suggestive. He reached over to scratch the kitten's big ears, and Lucy shivered, a tingle running up her spine as his fingers rested against the inside of her knee. "I'm sorry," he said, and quickly drew back his hand.

Lucy set the kitten on the floor between them. "I'm the one should be sorry, sir. I was thinking the most awful things about you all day, and now it turns out you were planning such a lovely surprise. I am ashamed of myself." She hung her head, her long, loose hair falling over her face.

He brushed the silky black wave back across her shoulder. "Don't be. It is only because of you that I was brave enough to try."

Lucy looked up at him through the black fans of her lashes; his eyes were aglow in the firelight. "Try what, sir?" she whispered.

But just then the children came rushing back down the stairs. "Who first?" Stacy cried.

"Mistress Jones, of course. Ladies before gentlemen," his father told him.

"Why don't you call Lucy Lucy, Father?" Minnie asked.

"I haven't been invited to."

"Lucy wouldn't mind. Would you, Lucy?" Lucy hesitated, then shook her head. Why shouldn't he call her Lucy, after all? He called Johnny Johnny, and Jem Jem. And Mistress Jones did sound a bit silly. Jones wasn't a "Mistress" sort of name, not like Moncrief or Carlyle.

Minnie grinned and thrust a box toward her. "That's all settled, then. Now open this and see if you like it."

"Did you wrap this yourself?" Lucy asked, prying at the twine.

"Stacy did. He's much better at bows and things."

"Oh, Minnie. Oh, Stacy." Lucy lifted up a length of soft green wool from within the paper.

"Do you truly like it?" Stacy asked. "Minnie hemmed it, but I sent to London for the fabric."

"It's a scarf," said Minnie. "In case you couldn't tell."

"I knew right away it was a scarf." Lucy wound it around her head and tied it under her chin. "How does it look?"

"Beautiful," the girl told her, "because it's on you."

"Open yours now, Father," Stacy urged, handing a bundle to him.

"I only hope it's as nice as Mistr— as Lucy's present," Lord Carlyle declared, and unwrapped his gift. His gaze met Lucy's. The scarf inside was just as nice as hers. In fact, it was exactly the same.

"They match," Minnie pointed out unnecessarily.

"So they do," her father agreed, one black brow raised.

"We thought you could wear them together," she burbled on happily.

Lord Carlyle tried on his right over his bushy white beard. "We will have to do that. Only I fear I don't look nearly so nice in mine as Lucy does in hers."

"I think you look very handsome," his daughter assured him. "Lucy, don't you?"

Lucy blushed, suddenly ill at ease, and reached up to remove her scarf. Fortunately Reggie chose that moment to leap out of Minnie's lap and attack the mound of paper and string. By the time they'd stopped laughing at the kitten's antics the girl's question was forgotten. Jem brought out more punch, and the sweetmeats Lucy had bought in Hucknall, and Lord Carlyle gave Stacy a first quick lesson in backgammon and helped Minnie tie a bow around Reggie's tiny neck. Then Minnie wanted to sing more carols, so they did that, even though her father protested that he couldn't sing and then proved it quite conclusively. "You sound awful!" Stacy told him, doubled over in laughter.

"I told you. Lucy has a lovely voice, doesn't she, though? I could listen to her sing all night."

Lucy could feel color rising in her cheeks again. There was nothing wrong with what he had said; rather, it was the way he looked at her as he said it, with that same spark of fire that had shown in his eyes on the night of the storm. "No one is going to be singing all night," she announced, "because it is time for bed."

"I'm not tired," said Minnie, and let out an enormous yawn.

Lucy laughed. "Oh, yes you are. Come along and I'll tuck you in. You can bring Reggie if you want to."

"Perhaps Jem could tuck them in," Lord Carlyle proposed. "I thought you might have a cup of brandy with me, Lucy."

Stacy tugged his sister's arm. "We'll tuck ourselves in. Come on, Minnie."

"But—"

"Come *on*," he said again, with a pointed glance at his father and Lucy.

"Oh," said Minnie. "All right, then."

"Hug and a kiss?" Lucy held out her arms, and they came to her quickly. "And for your father?"

Minnie went first. "Thank you, Father, for everything. Especially for Reggie."

"Thank you for my beautiful scarf," he said, holding very still while she kissed his beard.

"It's been the best Christmas ever," Stacy told him shyly, and gave him an awkward embrace.

"Sleep tight," said Lord Carlyle, and watched as they trooped up the stairs with their gifts. "Merry Christmas!"

"Merry Christmas!" they chorused, smiling and turning around to wave.

Lord Carlyle looked at Lucy. "This fire's burned down. I can light the one in my study. And there's more brandy there."

"I'm really very tired myself, sir," Lucy told him, nervous now that the buffer of the children was gone.

"Surely you can keep your eyes open for one little cup of brandy." He offered her his hand to pull her up from the floor, but Lucy rose without his help, not wanting to risk his touching her again. "Please," he said quietly, drawing back his arm. "I want to know what you thought of the presents I picked out."

After he had gone to so much trouble for Minnie and Stacy, Lucy thought, she really shouldn't be so ungracious to him. What harm could there be in sharing one drink? "The presents were wonderful," she told him as they crossed the receiving room, followed by Lady Carlyle's watchful eyes, and went into the monk's walk. "Especially the kitten. I tried to get one for Minnie, but—" She explained about Johnny's cousin's dog. "Where did you find Reggie?"

"In London," he said, unlocking the door to his study.

"London!" Lucy stared at his broad back as he cleared a chair for her, then sat and opened his brandy drawer. "Do you mean you rode to London and back since just last night? In this freezing weather?" He nodded. "Oh, sir—"

"If I'm to call you Lucy," he said, filling a glass and handing it to her, "don't you think you might call me by my name? It's Bram. For Abraham."

"I couldn't do that, sir."

"Why not?"

"It just wouldn't be proper. After all, you're a lord and I'm a—" She stopped, then laughed. "I hardly know anymore what I am these days."

He pulled off his scarf and false whiskers. "Stacy and Minnie seem to think of us as equals," he noted, draping the green wool over the arm of his chair and gulping down his drink.

"They're just children, sir," Lucy said, embarrassed. "They don't know any better."

He poured himself another brandy, very tall. "They're not mine, you know."

Lucy was so startled that she spilled brandy all over her new gown. "I—I beg your pardon?"

"They—aren't—my—children," he said distinctly, and swallowed his second drink. "Their mother told me that . . . on the night she died."

Lucy stared at him, and despite her shock at his admission she felt as though a great door had opened in her mind, letting in a burst of light. Of course. So much made sense to her now where it hadn't before. The distance he'd imposed between himself and the children, his awkwardness toward them, their responding fear . . . Though she hadn't even wanted the brandy, she didn't object when he refilled her glass. She gulped it hastily; it burned like wildfire. Lord Carlyle smiled at the face she made.

"You aren't much of a drinker, are you? I drink too much."

"I'd say you have reason to," Lucy whispered, and set down her glass. "Are you sure? I mean, how do you know she wasn't lying?"

"Olive wasn't lying about anything that night," he said steadily. "She was even kind enough to tell me who her—who had fathered them."

"And before that you never suspected?"

He shook his head. "I had no reason to. I was . . . happy. I assumed Olive was, too. I am sometimes rather absentminded, I'm afraid."

Absentminded, thought Lucy, was a mild term for a man whose wife had borne someone else's child not once, but twice, without his noticing anything amiss! Still, she understood how it might have happened to Lord Carlyle when he was so cocksure, so confident of himself. "Minnie and Stacy—you've never said anything to them about it?" she asked tentatively.

"I've never told another soul in the world except for you." He smiled again, this time wryly. "Enough people already suspect that I killed my wife. They'd be sure of it if they knew I'd found out she was cuckolding me." He ran his thumb around and around the rim of his brandy glass. "It's an ugly word, that, isn't it—cuckold?"

"It's an ugly thing." Lucy paused. "*Did* you kill her?"

"No," he said quietly. "She fell down the stairs." He looked at her. "Do you believe that?" Lucy stared into his eyes, blue and gray as a stormy winter sky, and slowly nodded yes.

"But why tell me?" she asked uncertainly.

He tilted his chair back against the wall, his big hands propped on the edge of the desk; beneath his sleeves Lucy could see the muscles in his forearms slowly flexing and unflexing. "After Olive died, after what she told me that night, I hated those children. God help me, that's ugly, too, but it's true. Every time I looked at them, I saw her. I heard her laughing at me even from her grave."

"But you can't blame them for what she did!"

"Do you think I didn't know that?" he demanded, muscles coiled tight. "Do you think I didn't know I was being unfair? I am not a monster! Christ, by the time you came here I hated myself most of all, for what I had done to them, was doing to them still." He drew a long breath. "You changed everything, though, when you came here, Lucy Jones. I don't see her anymore when I look at them. That night when I wanted to send you away and they stood up for you—stood up to me—I felt I didn't even know them. They were so—so bold, so noble and fine. And it was because of you."

"I didn't do anything, sir," Lucy protested.

"God, you did! You loved them. You made me remember how sweet it was when I—when I loved them, too, when they meant the whole world to me. When we were . . . happy." He whispered the word, as though he were afraid to say it out loud, as though the mention of it might bring the house crashing down around their heads, as though happiness were a state he didn't dare contemplate deserving. "And you made me think that perhaps it wasn't too late. That maybe it could all be like that again . . . just as though she never told me at all."

"Oh, sir." Lucy wanted to cry for him, for his heartbreak, for the wretched secret he had kept to himself for so long. "Of course it isn't too late; you saw them tonight.

They've never stopped loving you, wanting you to love them. All you ever had to do was reach out to them. Love isn't something to be afraid of. You have to try!''

Something in her earnest words made him bring his chair legs thumping down to the floor—just as though, Lucy thought, he had finally reached some momentous decision. She hoped with all her soul it would be to forget the past and be a real father to Minnie and Stacy despite the circumstances of their births. He had made a good start at that tonight; it would only get easier now that he'd taken the first steps. She was about to tell him so when he reached into his doublet and pulled out one last small package. ''This is for you,'' he told her, pushing it across the desk. ''For Christmas.''

''For me?'' He nodded quickly, shyly, and watched from beneath half-lowered lids as she untied the twine, unfolded the crinkled brown paper. Inside was a roll of black velvet. She opened it curiously, and her startled gaze met his. ''Oh, sir!''

''I thought emeralds. Because of your eyes.''

Lucy looked back down at the golden eardrops set with fiery green stones that glittered in the firelight. ''They're magnificent,'' she breathed, holding one up gingerly, watching it shimmer and glow as it dangled from her fingertips. ''But I can't possibly accept them.''

''Why not?'' he demanded gruffly.

''They are far too dear!''

''Nothing could be,'' he began, and then stopped. ''I assure you, I can afford them.''

''It isn't just the cost, sir,'' Lucy said, embarrassed. ''It's the—the intimacy.''

''Oh, for Christ's sake. It's not as though I were giving you a corset!''

The way he said it, with such male disdain, made Lucy giggle even as she pushed the eardrops back at him. ''It's very kind of you, really, sir. But I can't.''

''Please,'' he said, and Lucy had the sense it was not a word that came easily to him, that he used often. ''Please take them. I want to give you something. For Christmas, for what you have done for the children.''

''But I—''

"Please," he said again, getting up from his chair. "They would look so lovely on you." Lucy couldn't deny she was flattered; at the same time her spine tingled, and her pulse grew quicker, as though there was danger near. He seemed to fill up the whole room when he stood; the air was charged with his scent, leather and horseflesh and sweat. With the false beard removed she could see the shadow of his own, coarse and black, across his cheeks and chin. With his doublet unbuttoned and his sleeves pushed up he didn't look like a lord—and yet Lucy knew she must think of him that way.

The eardrops lay between them on the cluttered desk. It was likely, Lucy thought, that he didn't even realize such a gift was inappropriate for him to give her—in which case it would be ungracious of her to refuse it. *For what you have done for the children*, he'd said . . .

"All right, then, sir," she said, picking them up. "Thank you very much. They are very beautiful. Good night." She hurried to the door, eager now to be gone, but he reached it before she could and opened it for her, held it as she left the warm glow of the firelight and went into the darkened monk's walk.

"Good night, Lucy. Merry Christmas," he said, and his voice sounded strange, as though something was caught in his throat. "Lucy—"

She turned back to him. "Yes?"

He caught her by the waist and pulled her into his arms.

His mouth crushed hers, fierce and hot and demanding, smothering her startled cry of protest. His tongue thrust into her, carrying with it a tangled rush of tastes, brandy and sweetmeats and salt, familiar in themselves but headily exotic when shared that way. With his arm still circling her waist he bent her backward beneath him; Lucy took a step away from him and felt the cold wall halt her retreat. He moved his hands to her shoulders, holding her there while he kissed her with furious abandon, his mouth pressing hungrily against her mouth, her ears, her throat, her hair.

Lucy was overwhelmed by a flood of sensation, by the wild intensity of his unexpected assault. He was kissing her, she thought, as though if he did not he would explode like gunpowder and shatter into pieces, as though there raged in him some fire only she could quench. At her skirts she felt the rock-hard bulge in his breeches as he thrust his groin against her. His hands slipped down from her shoulders to cover her breasts, and she shivered as he kneaded them through her damask gown, found her nipples and plucked at them with his fingertips, rubbed them over and over again while her flesh tightened beneath his touch.

Fire. He was on fire, and he was igniting a blaze within her, fanning her heart to flame with his hungry mouth and urgent hands. "Oh, Christ," she heard him moan as her nipples grew taut and round. "Oh, Lucy. Lucy." His loins ground against her, pinning her to the wall; she could feel his heart beating, frantic and wild. He yanked at the sleeves of her gown, pulling them down to uncover her breasts, and as he laid his hands on her bare flesh his whole body shuddered.

Lucy didn't know what to do, what to say. She realized she had to fight him off, but oh, God, what he was doing was driving all logic and reason straight out of her head! The fire, that was all she could seem to think of, the maddening, white-hot fire he had unleashed inside her, that was burning her blood and scorching her bone. She had never felt anything like that fire, had never imagined she could; it was as though all her life she had been waiting for him to strike the spark that would kindle the blaze. He kissed her mouth, his tongue thrusting inside her feverishly, and then lowered his head to her breast. As he seized the taut bud of her nipple between his lips she clenched her hands into tight fists—

And felt the emerald eardrops there.

The fire drained from her in a dizzying rush, doused by anger and shame. God, how could she be such a fool? She was going to wind up just like poor Jeannie Paget, falling for a gentleman who bought her a pretty bauble! What in the world was the matter with her?

Summoning all her strength, she shoved him away as hard as she could. He stumbled backward, caught off balance, and stood at arm's length, panting, his chest heaving wildly. She dropped the emeralds at his feet. "I may only be a girl from Shoreditch,'' she told him, her voice icy as the stones at her back, ''but I'm not so cheaply bought as that.''

''For God's sake, Lucy,'' he said hoarsely, ''don't do this to me. Not now!'' She pulled up her bodice and started away. ''The fire, Lucy!'' He caught her hand. ''Christ, tell me you feel the fire!''

She pulled free, turning her back to him, knowing that even in the darkness he would tell she lied if he saw her face. ''What fire?'' she asked coldly.

''Oh, God, Lucy—''

''I'll thank you,'' she shot at him over her shoulder, ''to call me Mistress Jones from now on.''

Chapter 10

New Year's eve.

Lucy knelt on the floor of the armory and buttoned Minnie's winter cloak beneath the girl's small chin. "And don't unbutton it, either," she warned, "or you may catch cold."

"If you came with us," Stacy pointed out, "you could make sure she wouldn't unbutton it."

"You, too, young man." She clapped his hat on his head. "Keep this on."

"Why won't you come with us, Lucy?" Minnie asked earnestly. "You'd like Margery, honestly you would."

"I'm sure she's very nice, pet. But I hardly think she would want a Shoreditch shopgirl visiting for the holiday."

"You're not a shopgirl anymore," said Stacy. "You're our governess."

"You're a governess, and she's a countess," said Minnie. "Both ess-es. Aren't they the same?"

Lucy laughed. "Hardly. A countess is the wife of an earl."

"Widow," Stacy corrected her. "Her husband's dead, and Father says she is lonely, so that's why we're going to see her. She likes company. I know she'd like you."

Lord Carlyle spoke from the doorway where he'd been watching Lucy bundle up her charges. "Mistress Jones seems to have her mind made up; I wouldn't bother trying to change it." There was an edge to his tone.

"Why don't you call Lucy Lucy anymore, Father?" Minnie wanted to know.

Lucy answered for him. "Because it's more fitting this

way. I call your father Lord Carlyle, and he calls me Mistress Jones.''

''You could call him Bram,'' the little girl suggested. ''That's what Margery calls him. Why don't you?''

''Because,'' said Lucy, giving the girl's bootlaces a final tug, ''it wouldn't be my place. Just as it's not my place to go with you to the countess's. As for you, your place is in that carriage.'' She steered her toward the door. ''Now go.''

''Margery has a dog that she lets us play with,'' Minnie noted—one last hopeful bribe.

''You go play with the dog, then, and I'll look after Reggie for you.''

''If we go to Margery's to keep her from being lonely and leave you here, then won't you be lonely?'' Stacy asked anxiously.

''Mistress Jones,'' Lord Carlyle observed with a sneer, ''has her pride to keep her company.''

Lucy flashed him an angry glance. ''I'm sure you'll find plenty of company, milord. So many places to look for new friends—the laundry, the scullery. Did you bring any pretty trinkets in your pockets?'' She saw his jaw muscles tighten and was glad.

He threw open the door. ''Minnie, Stacy. Let's go.''

''I'll miss you, Lucy,'' Minnie cried, giving her a hug.

''I'll miss you, too, but it's only for a few days. Be good, now. Best behavior. No naughty words,'' she cautioned, standing in the doorway and waving as their father helped them into the coach.

''We won't! Don't worry!'' they called, waving back. Lord Carlyle pushed up the steps and shut the carriage door.

''Happy New Year, Mistress Jones,'' he said, his eyes as frosty as the snow-covered drive. Then he leaped up onto Bellerophon, signaled to Johnny, and galloped off, with the carriage rumbling behind.

Lucy felt oddly bereft as she closed the door against a blast of icy wind. She would miss the children—though not, God knew, their father. Since the incident in the monk's walk on Christmas eve she'd been barely civil to him; he was equally distant in return. It was a shame he had spoiled that wonderful evening with his clumsy attempt to bribe her into his bed.

He was trying, though, with the children. How excited they'd been when he proposed this visit to the countess. "Lucy, too?" Minnie had cried, jumping up and down. "Will Lucy come, too?" Lucy told her she had other plans, and she did. The coming of the New Year had reminded her again that nearly six months had passed and she still had not figured out all the words in the lute letter; she still did not know why Joe Reilly had died. That, she'd determined, was how she would spend her time while the rest of the household was away.

Darkness came early to Derbyshire in winter. That night she lay with Reggie on her bed, bundled up in blankets, and stared at the piece of paper in front of her. *Dear,* it began. The next word had to be a name, though she hadn't worked out what it was yet. Then, *If you hadn't*—she could read that much. W, R, I, T, T, E, N—itten, like the end of kitten. W, R. Wuh-rr, she sounded it out. Written! *If you hadn't written, I never would have* B, E, L, I, E, V, E, D. That was much too long; she skipped it and went back to the name.

A, N, T, H, O, N, Y. Ant like the insect. H, O, N, Y, that was almost like honey. Ant-honey. Anthony! she realized. Just like the name of the man with the house in the valley, the one whose house she'd gone to when Stacy was sick. Anthony Babington.

Heartened by this success, she went back to the long word that began with B. Be-lie-ved. She said it aloud, but it wasn't any word she knew. Sometimes though, Stacy had taught her, when two vowels were together you sounded the second one instead of the first. That would make it be-lee-ved. And then she knew it, of course.

Dear Anthony, If you hadn't written I never would have believed you C, O, N, S, I, D, E, R, E, D. Con-sid-er-ed. *Considered reviewing my*—she flattened the paper with her hand, and Reggie, always ready to play, growled and pounced on her hand. "Not right now, if you please," she told the kitten, and moved her down to the foot of the bed. She ran right back up, and kept on attacking Lucy until finally, sighing, Lucy set the kitten on the floor.

S, U, G, G, E, S, T, I, O, N, S—Jesus, such huge words! She broke it up into pieces, then frowned at Reggie, who was mewing frantically and scratching at the crack beneath the door to the hall. "Reggie, please, I am trying to concentrate!" But the kitten only cried more loudly, and at last she sat up and got out of bed. "What is it, then, a mouse?" Shivering in her nightdress, she opened the door.

The kitten skittered through her legs and down the corridor toward the old wing. "Reggie, no!" Lucy called, chasing after the fleet ball of fluff. "Reggie, get back here!" Naturally the cat paid her no attention. Cursing, Lucy went back to her room for a candle and started after her.

"Bad kitty," she said sternly when she found her, scratching and pawing at the foot of the door to the music room. "No, you can't go in there, I'm afraid; no one's allowed except our lord and master." Making a face, she bent down to scoop up the kitten in her hand. To her astonishment, the tiny thing hissed at her and dug its claws into her palm.

"Ouch!" She set the candle on the floor, holding Reggie in the other hand, sucking blood from where she'd scratched her. A sudden draft blew the flame out. "Now see what you've done," she scolded crossly, and then fell silent; on the chilly air she smelled the distinct aroma of roses, heavy and sweet.

She reached back for the candle, then let out a little scream: in the darkness her hand brushed something else, something like cloth, whispery as silk. "Who's there?" she called sharply, but the only answer was a rustle as though whatever it was was moving away. She grabbed for it blindly, and her hand met the door. Nothing, then. Only the wind . . .

But the wind didn't explain the scent of roses in January. More unnerved than she cared to admit, she ran back to her room.

In bright light again, with a fire blazing, she was heartily ashamed of having let her imagination get the best of her. "This is all your fault, Reggie," she sternly told the kitten, who yawned and curled up, promptly falling asleep.

I won't do the same, Lucy vowed in expiation for her momentary lapse of reason, until I have got this whole bloody letter read through!

T, A, P, E, S, T, R, Y. Tap-es-try. P, R, O, C, E, S, S, I, O, N. Pro-cess-ion. B, L, A, C, K, S, M, I, T, H. Black-smith. That was certainly strange! The name of the song she'd taught Minnie and Stacy was in the letter— "When Barry Goes Bum-Di-Do."

Finally only one word remained that she could not read: it was in the signature, where the spidery hand-writing was most elaborate, right after the name Mary. R, she thought it began with. R, E, G, I, N, A. Reg-i-na, *Regina*, like Minnie's kitten! Regina, Latin for queen. Mary queen.

With mounting excitement, Lucy realized there was only one Mary queen that she knew of: Queen Elizabeth's arch-enemy, Mary, queen of Scots. She went back to the top of the page and read the whole letter through:

Dear Anthony,

If you hadn't written, I never would have believed you considered reviewing my suggestions for the tapestry plan! My maid and I think perhaps it is best to begin and be sure it's workable. The absolute final finishing date still should be soon, but may not be until next Lammas or Soul's Day, or because of stiff fingers maybe next year. Please forgive the wait. My situation here is splendid. My cousin's most generous annual allowance arrived. Procession of my appeals to Westminster are slow but surely will be successful. My months here pro-vide quiet and the chance to perfect my embroidery— such opportunity! France sends no money, and I say devil take the French and the Pope! I will stand always ready to support the queen with heart and arms, soul and spirit. Her men came to comfort and assure me of the dear love she harbors me. Crowns you sent most welcome! Transfer and confirm the tapestry pattern de-tails with sketches in your next, your anxiously awaited reply.

Fondly, Mary Regina.

And then there was something more at the end: "I heard a most amusing London tune recently, all about a blacksmith, called 'When Barry Goes Bum-Di-Do.' "

Lucy's elation at having figured out all the words deflated like a bladder stuck with a pin. What in the hell was this? Some silly nonsense about tapestry patterns, compliments to Elizabeth—good God, there was nothing in here worth killing Joe Reilly for!

She read the letter through again, more slowly, thinking perhaps she had missed something important, some clue as to why Hawk-Nose had wanted it badly enough to commit murder, but it was perfectly innocent. From the looks of this letter, Elizabeth's archenemy was an empty-headed chatterer who liked needlework and risque songs.

And for this Joe had died. Oh, Jesus, Lucy thought hopelessly, why the devil didn't I just give the letter to that bloody bastard Hawk-Nose when he asked for it? He must have burned down her shop just for spite, just to show he wasn't going to let a shopgirl from Shoreditch get the best of him. And Joe? He'd killed Joe because he knew he could get away with it, because he was rich.

If only she'd listened to Joe's warnings about those men; if only she hadn't been so greedy for a bit of extra gold. What had Hawk-Nose paid her in all—five, six shillings? So cheap a price for sweet, silly, muddleheaded Joe. She stuffed the letter back behind the mirror. She would keep it as a rebuke, a reminder of her greed and willfulness.

The clock in the armory tolled twelve long strokes. Happy New Year, Lucy thought, tears burning her eyes. What a fine way to bring in the year 1586—by finding out she'd gone and got her best friend killed for no reason at all.

Minnie and Stacy came home from their holiday at the countess's two days later, rambunctious and restless, like two overwrought colts kept penned up too long. "Hello, pets," Lucy greeted them as they tumbled out of the carriage. "Did you have a nice time?"

"The food was good," Stacy offered. "Margery has a much better cook than Cook."

"There was a ball with dancing," Minnie put in. "Father didn't dance, even though a lot of ladies asked him to.''

"Really. Where is your father?''

"He stayed to talk business or something with Margery. He'll be home later, he said. Come on, Minnie, let's change clothes.'' Stacy grabbed his sister's hand and raced into the armory.

"Where are you going?'' Lucy called, laughing at their eager energy. Minnie paused on the staircase.

"Well,'' she said, "Margery is awfully nice, but she's awfully old, and so Father told us not to make much noise, and her cook, even though she is good, wouldn't let us borrow any trays, and besides, Margery's house is in the middle of this big flat place without any hills anywhere around—''

"We've been dying to go sledding,'' Stacy summed up for his sister. "Can we?''

"I think you had better,'' Lucy said, laughing again, "or you'll be up all night.''

The day was icy cold, the snow fresh white and glistening. "I love being the first one to touch new snow, don't you?'' Stacy cried, running to the hill and throwing down his tray. "I want to go really, really fast.''

"Back over here, Stacy,'' Lucy cautioned. "You're too close to the goose pond.''

"It must be frozen solid about a million feet down by now,'' he protested.

"Stacy—''

Sighing, he dragged his tray back. "I'm going to aim right for that great big snowdrift,'' he announced, getting a running start and then flopping onto the tray belly-down. "Whee!'' He careened down the slope, rocking back and forth and screaming at the top of his lungs. Minnie was tugging at Lucy's sleeve.

"Do you see any geese?'' she whispered.

"Only you, goose. They've all gone south for the winter,'' Lucy assured her. "Get on and I'll give you a push.''

Minnie perched cross-legged in the center of her sled, holding tight to the handles. "Not too fast,'' she reminded Lucy.

''Don't worry.'' Lucy gave her a gentle shove, and the tray skidded over the snow.

''Where's Stacy?'' Minnie called back over her shoulder.

Lucy looked, but didn't see him near the snowdrift he'd been aiming for. ''Stacy, where are you?'' she called. Minnie's sled gathered speed as it slid down the slope. All of a sudden, out of the snowbank just ahead of her, a dark shape rose up, honking and flapping its arms.

''Stacy, don't tease your sister!'' Lucy cried. But the damage was already done; at the first honk Minnie had tumbled from her sled and gone running off, gloves over her ears, screaming, through the snow.

''Minnie, stop!'' Lucy tore down the hill after her. ''Stacy, catch her, she's headed straight for the pond!''

''Minnie, it's only me,'' the boy shouted, chasing his sister. ''It was only a joke!'' But Minnie, ears filled with her own screams, kept running straight toward the gray mush that marked the edge of the pond.

''Minnie, stay back!'' Lucy screamed, and ''Minnie, don't!'' Stacy screeched, but Minnie's high, hysterical cries were the loudest of all. She blundered onto the ice; for a moment the surface held her. Then she tripped on her skirts, skidding toward the center, and the ice gave way with a horrible, loud cracking sound.

''She can't swim!'' Whiter than snow, Stacy watched as his sister plunged into the water. ''She can't swim, she'll drown, she'll die and it will be my fault!''

''Stacy!'' Lucy reached the water's edge and grabbed his shoulders, giving him a shake. ''Run to the house. Get Jeeves. Have him bring a rope.''

''She's going to die!''

''Stacy, do as I say!''

He started up the hill. Lucy stripped off her cloak and boots. She couldn't swim, either, but there wasn't time to think about that. She lay on her stomach and shimmied across what was left of the ice toward the gaping black hole in the center. There was no sign of Minnie's curly golden head.

Jesus, what if she was trapped beneath the icy surface? Frantic with fear, Lucy smashed it with her fists. As it shattered and moved apart she caught a faint glimpse of something pale in the water beneath her. Taking a deep breath, she held her nose and plunged in.

The water was so cold it numbed her instantly; she could barely move her arms or legs, and her lungs seemed to swell and fill up all her chest, crowding out her heart. She groped down in the direction where she thought she'd seen Minnie, clawing at the darkness, and felt her limbs turning stiff and useless as sticks.

Give up, her fading heartbeat urged. Give up, it is hopeless. The black water swirled around her, pounded in her ears. But then through the deafening pounding she remembered Stacy's anguished cry—*She'll die and it will be my fault!* Lucy knew all too well what that burden felt like. She made one last desperate effort to reach down—

Her fingers brushed something—cloth? Hair? A hand? She forced them to close on whatever it was and pulled up, kicking her legs, dragging it in her wake. Her head bumped the ice on the surface; she reared back and hit it again, as hard as she could.

It gave way; she saw sunlight on its shards as it shattered, bright white like diamonds. She yanked at the weight beneath her, wrenching it up, and saw Minnie's small head, blond curls soaked, cherub's mouth open and gasping for air.

She was still alive! Lucy wrapped an arm around her and heard her name called from the shore. Stacy and Jeeves—the butler flung a length of rope over the ice, and Lucy caught it with frozen fingers and slipped the loop at its end over Minnie's shoulders, then held on as tight as she could. "Pull!" she tried to shout, and heard her voice come out all wispy and weak.

"Too—heavy." Jeeves grunted as he and Stacy tried to haul in the line.

"Hang on, Lucy!" Stacy cried. "Don't let go!"

"Can't—do it!" the butler shouted.

"We can do it, we've got to!" Stacy told him frantically.

Lucy tried to see them on the shore, but she couldn't; all the world seemed to be going black in front of her eyes. She and Minnie weren't moving. Jeeves was right.

"Lucy, don't!" Stacy screamed. But she let the rope slide through her hands, and Minnie sprang toward the shore. With the boy's voice echoing in her ears, she slipped below the surface again . . .

And then she heard a terrible crashing sound, as though all the ice in the universe must be breaking, and felt herself flying into the air, and someone else was calling her name, saying, "Lucy. Lucy. I've got you. It's all right. I've got you." But after that she heard nothing more.

Chapter 11

Barkers Lane was dark as pitch except for the plume of red fire in the distance. Lucy ran toward it, panting, her skirts caught up in her hands. She could feel the awful heat of the blaze as she got closer, felt it burn her face and throat and arms until she was sure she was on fire as well as her shop.

A figure loomed up out of the thick smoke in front of her: Joe Reilly, smiling, bald head shining, purse clenched to his chest. "Give us an 'and 'ere, luv; ye knows I can't make 'ead nor tail of me money . . ." He held out the purse, and his guts slithered down to the cobblestones. Lucy screamed and tried to turn, to run, but someone was holding her shoulders in a grip like death. "No!" she cried, thrashing to break free of the hands that restrained her. "No, Joe, oh, dear God, no!"

The smoke cleared; the haze lifted. She was on the hillside above the goose pond at Lockhaven Hall. Barefoot, in her crimson gown, she ran toward the water through long green grass, wildflowers springing up, tickling her toes. She threw out her arms to embrace the dazzling summer sunlight that shone off the water. Its surface rippled and broke, and a small blond head rose up, hair choked with scum and weeds. She saw Minnie's face, white as snow, cornflower-blue eyes blank and staring, thick black water streaming from her open mouth.

Lucy screamed and tried to dive in to get her, but again someone's hands were holding her back. "Let me go!" she cried. "Let me go, I've got to save her." But something cold as ice lay across her forehead, weighing her down. Ice. She had to break through. Flailing, fighting, she felt the weight fall away, but before she could catch her breath it was there again, reforming into a solid sheet that was crushing her head. Time after time she broke through the surface, and each time it reformed, until she could struggle no more and fell back into the water again.

When she woke the horrid weight was still there, smothering her, suffocating her. She clawed at it with her hands, tearing it away so that she could breathe. There was a strange sound ringing in her ears, something that reminded her of her father. The weight lifted, and she was in her bedchamber at Lockhaven Hall, Jem standing over her, a folded towel in her hands.

"Oh, Miss Lucy." The little maid let out a sigh of relief. "Saints be praised, I never thought ye'd make it. Here, now, ye've got to keep this on ye." She laid the towel back across Lucy's forehead, then held a cup to her mouth. "Take a bit of water, can ye? There's a good girl."

Lucy drank thirstily; the water tasted cool and sweet. Jem grinned, watching her. "Parched, ain't ye? Well, that's the fever. More?" Lucy nodded weakly, then licked her lips.

"Minnie—" she whispered hoarsely.

"Miss Minnie's right as rain. Didn't have nary a sniffle, she didn't. Don't ye worry 'bout her; she's just fine."

"What's—" Lucy raised a weak hand, pointing to her ear. "Noise—"

Jem laughed quietly and pointed to the other side of the bed. Lucy turned her head and saw Lord Carlyle sprawled in a chair at her bedside, fast asleep and snoring in long, loud rumbles, like thunder on a distant mountaintop.

She looked back at Jem. "What's he . . . doing here?"

"Been here night 'n' day both, ever since he pulled ye out of that water. Don't ye remember?" she asked, seeing Lucy's uncomprehending stare. "Why, he came thunderin' down over the hill on that big black horse of his 'n' yanked ye up just like a rag doll. Then he sent to Hucknall for the doctor, 'n' when that one said there weren't no hope, he sent Johnny all the way to London to fetch up another! That one said the same, but the master, he wouldn't give up. He just kept tryin' everythin' he could

think of to bring ye back. 'N' ye know, they do say nothin'
is impossible to a willin' heart.''

"How long . . . have I been here?" Lucy managed to
ask.

"Been more'n a fortnight." Jem put her finger to her
lips. "Hush now, 'n' get back to sleep. Ye needs yer rest."
She winked and nodded toward Lord Carlyle. "He needs
his, too." Then she tiptoed away. Lucy sank back on the
soft white pillows and drifted into sleep again.

The next time she opened her eyes she felt much more
clear-headed. Minnie and Stacy were hovering over her,
their small faces wrinkled with worry; she smiled at them
and they let out a cheer, and both began talking at once.

"Oh, Lucy, we were so scared for you."

"The doctor from Hucknall said—"

"And the other one, too."

"I promise I'll never, *ever* tease Minnie about the geese
again."

"All right, ye two." That was grim old Cook, pulling
them back from the bed. "One at a time, 'n' if ye don't
keep yer voices down I'll 'ave both yer hides."

"Minnie." Lucy touched the girl's shining curls.
"You saved my life," she said happily.

"Stacy helped." Lucy smiled at him. "You were strong.
Brave."

"Not as brave as you. If Father hadn't come just then,
you would have drowned."

Lucy squeezed his hand. "Everything is all right now."
She turned her head toward the chair where she'd last seen
Lord Carlyle sleeping. No one was there.

"He's in his study," Minnie told her. "But he was here
all the time until you woke up."

"He cried when he pulled you out of the water," said
Stacy, awe in his voice. "I never saw Father cry before."

"That's enough for today, ye two," Cook announced,
and herded them toward the door. "Get on now. Miss
Lucy, see if ye can take a wee bit of this broth."

Lucy sipped the warm liquid from the spoon the old
woman held out for her, then looked into her shrewd eyes.
"Did he really cry?" she whispered in disbelief.

Cook dipped the spoon into the broth again. "Master?

Well, 'e was all covered with water 'n' snow 'n' such; 'twould be 'ard to say. Still, I reckon 'e might 'ave.''

"It must have been over Minnie," Lucy mumbled.

"Wot's that?" old Cook asked, cocking an ear.

"I said, the broth tastes good."

"Well, of course it does. I made it, didn't I?" And she stuck the spoon into Lucy's mouth again.

Lucy was confined to her bed for another ten days. The children came each morning and evening to read to her and play games; Minnie even gave up Reggie so Lucy could have the kitten for company. Cook stuffed her with broth and warm milk; Jem tended to her linens and chamber pot; even Jeeves came by to apologize for not being strong enough to haul both her and Minnie out of the pond. Only Lord Carlyle stayed away, conspicuous by his absence. As the time went by, Lucy began to believe she had only dreamed seeing him asleep in the chair by her bed.

Still, Stacy had said his father cried. Why? Had he cried for her? Lucy held that thought in her heart, a small question mark, all the time she was recovering; she asked it of herself over and over again on the chilly afternoons when she watched from the nursery window while he frolicked with the children in the yards below. Minnie and Stacy would look up at her all the time to wave, but he never did.

The more Lord Carlyle avoided her, the more Lucy wondered. She tried to tell herself it ought not to matter whom he had been crying for—if he had been crying—but somehow it did. She felt at a disadvantage; she was beholden to him, and he had not even given her the chance to thank him. She wanted to know why he had kept that silent vigil beside her bed.

When she'd been up and about for a week and still hadn't spoken to him, she decided she should simply go and see him. Wasn't that the logical thing to do? She had a question; he had the answer. She wanted to thank him; what could be more natural than for her to go to his study and do so? Why was she so timid suddenly?

The reason came to her when she was halfway across the receiving room, and nearly sent her scurrying back up the stairs: because she preferred imagining that he might have been crying for her to finding out once and for all that he hadn't. That realization frightened her so much that she had to force herself to knock on his study door.

"Come in," her employer called.

"It's locked, sir."

There wasn't any sound for a good two minutes; Lucy was just about to flee when the door opened at last. "What is it?" he asked brusquely, scowling down at her.

"May I come in, sir, please?"

He turned his back to her, going and sitting down at his cluttered desk. Lucy followed, closing the door behind her. "Make it quick," he told her, fussing with a stack of papers. "I have work to do."

"You saved my life," Lucy said softly.

"What did you expect? That I would watch you drown?"

"But the rest of it—the doctor from London. And they say that you stayed with me. Stacy said—" Lucy's voice trailed away; now that she was here, she found her question absurd. This curt, scowling lord had surely never cried for anyone, much less for her.

"So?" he asked abruptly.

"So it seems a lot of trouble and expense to go to for a—"

"What? For a shopgirl from Shoreditch?" he asked, watching her from beneath half-closed eyelids.

"Actually, I was going to say, for a piece of tail."

"What makes you so certain I am after your tail, Mistress Jones, as you so delicately put it?"

Lucy was flustered in the face of his evident composure. "I thought—what you did on Christmas eve, trying to bribe me with those jewels—I've seen what happens when a girl like me takes presents from a man like you."

"A man like me." He leaned far back in his chair. "Tell me, are all the poor men in Shoreditch honest and righteous and stalwart and loyal and true?"

"Of course not."

"Then what makes you so certain all noblemen are monsters?"

"With all due respect, sir, I didn't hear you asking to

marry me there in the monk's walk," Lucy said with a hint of temper.

"What if I had?" he asked, arching a brow.

"What?" Lucy blurted.

"What," he said slowly, "if I had asked you to marry me?"

"Why, I would have said no."

"Why?"

This was hardly fair, Lucy thought crossly. She had come to ask him a question, and he was firing them at her instead. "It's like my pop used to tell me," she said impatiently. "Rich folk and poor are like fire and water. They just don't mix." At her mention of fire his grim expression changed; for a moment he looked wounded, sad.

"Do you really think I am so different from you?" he asked quietly.

"Of course you are."

"How am I different?"

"Oh, really," Lucy said.

"Really," he insisted. "I want to know."

Lucy cast her memory back to Shoreditch. "How could you know?" she asked passionately. "Have you ever had people in fur cloaks walk by you, looking through you as though you weren't even there, while you are shivering with cold in the winter? Have you ever had someone spit on you because you got in their way, or heard them talk about you as if you don't even exist, as if you couldn't feel or see or hear? That's what the gentry did when they came to Barkers Lane—if they came there at all."

"I am not like that."

"But you are. That night in London, if I'd come to your door and told you I was a shopgirl named Lucy Jones and a man was trying to kill me, would you have let me in?"

"If I were a stablehand, would you have gone to bed with me on Christmas eve?" He saw her eyes go wide and laughed. "Don't worry. The question is hypothetical, like yours."

"I don't know what that means," she told him, her chin jutting out.

"It means," he said, his voice suddenly distant, "that we'll never know."

Lucy looked down at him as he sprawled in his rich leather chair. "What is it you want from me?" she demanded.

"What I want from you." His blue eyes closed completely; beneath black velvet his broad chest rose and fell. "What I want from you is . . . impossible." Then he opened his eyes again. "Why do you ask?"

"I owe you a debt," she told him stubbornly. "I like to pay my debts."

"Very well, then. I would like you to call me Bram."

"Call you—that's all?"

He laughed at her suspicious expression. "Well, you might let me call you Lucy, too. Unless, of course, you think that's too great a demand for me to make in return for having saved your life."

Lucy couldn't help it; she laughed as well. "You really are a very strange man, sir."

" 'You are very strange, Bram,' " he corrected her, grinning.

Lucy hesitated. "If I call you Bram, are you going to try again to take advantage of me?"

The grin abruptly disappeared. He shook his head. "No. We will just be—friends."

"Well, all right then. Bram," Lucy added, blushing a bit. His name sounded strange on her tongue. "And thank you very much for saving my life."

"You're welcome," he said.

Well, thought Lucy as she left him alone, that settled that. They were to be friends. He was to call her Lucy; she would call him Bram. Everything certainly had worked out splendidly. How lucky she was!

And then, for no reason that she could fathom, she burst into tears.

"Whee! Lucy, look at us go!" Minnie cried as she skidded down the snowy hill above the orchard straddling Bram, who was lying belly-down on her Christmas sled. Look at you, indeed, Lucy thought, watching as the little girl clung to Bram's broad back with all her might, one arm thrown around his neck. They plowed into a drift and went tumbling head over heels together in a flash of black hair and golden curls and laughter.

"Come on, Lucy, let's get them!" Stacy tugged at her cloak, and they ran downhill after the sled, scooping up handfuls of snow and pelting their victims mercilessly.

"I've got you," Bram growled, hauling Stacy into the drift in a flurry of powder.

"And I've got you," Minnie declared, pulling at Lucy, who obligingly let herself by yanked to her knees and have a fistful of wet snow rubbed into her face.

"Father, do the Great Snow Monster from the North," Stacy pleaded as he came up for air, rubbing his runny nose with a mitten. Bram got to his feet and lurched across the snow toward Minnie, grunting and making horrible faces. Minnie squealed and clapped her hands over her eyes, and he grabbed her and slung her over his shoulder, stomping back up the hill.

"Save me, save me!" Minnie begged between gusts of laughter.

"I shall slay the dreaded Great Snow Monster," Stacy cried, running after Bram and lunging at his legs. Bram grabbed him, too, tucking him under his arm and continuing to stomp toward the house. "Oh, no!"

"You're the only one who can save us, Lucy," Minnie shrieked. "Help! Help!"

Bram turned and leered at Lucy, his tongue hanging out while he made slurping noises. "Tender young kid flesh in the pot for my supper tonight!"

"That's what you think, Snow Monster." Lucy darted after him and shoved him, and he went sprawling down in the snow, while Minnie and Stacy jumped onto his back. "Oof!" he grunted. "Lucy, you're strong."

"She's as tough as nails," Stacy said approvingly.

"That she is, son. That she is."

Lucy smiled to hear how easily the word *son* came to him now—more easily, really, than his name came to her. Old habits died hard, and despite their agreement she still slipped up from time to time and called him Lord Carlyle. More often she just tried to avoid the issue by not addressing him directly. The use of his first name, for her, implied an intimacy between them that did not exist.

He was trying hard to make up for the time he had lost with the children. In the fortnight since Lucy had gone to his study, he'd been out sledding every day, playing backgammon with Stacy in the evenings, even trying to help Minnie teach Reggie how to jump through a hoop. But though he called Lucy by her given name and spent hours with her—and the children—the gulf between the two of them seemed wider than ever before.

Lucy knew it was her own fault. She could not stop thinking of that question he had asked her—about whether, if he were a stablehand, she would have slept with him. She had never been attracted to another man the way she was to him; when she touched him, even something as brief as the shove she gave him into the snow, she could feel sparks at her fingertips, the embers of that blazing white fire still left from Christmas eve, when he had held her in his arms. When he looked at her with those stormy blue-gray eyes she felt all muddled and hot, even if she was covered with freezing snow.

She would lie in her bed at night and remember the way he had kissed her, the exquisite sensation of his mouth against hers, his hands at her breasts, and she would tremble more violently than she had when the fever raged through her blood. It frightened her that she felt that way. The neighbor women in Shoreditch had never spoken of anything like that fire; on the contrary, they only complained of being always at their husbands' beck and call. Or else, like sad-eyed Jeannie Paget, they said nothing at all.

But he was right: the question was hypothetical. She'd looked the word up in Stacy's dictionary after asking the boy how to spell it. She would never know if she would have gone to bed with him, because he hadn't touched her again since that night, not in that way. They were friends, united in their affection for the children, sharing afternoons of play and suppers in the nursery. Clearly he was content with that—and so, Lucy told herself time and again, was she. After all, he was a great lord, and she was only a shopgirl from Shoreditch. It would have been mad to hope for anything more than friendship with him.

Cook rang the supper bell from the kitchens just then; the children let their groaning father up from the ground. "I'm starved!" Stacy said happily.

"Can we play Snow Monster again tomorrow?" Minnie wanted to know. Bram hoisted her onto his shoulders, carrying her toward the house.

"I'm afraid not. I have to go away on business."

Lucy looked at him in surprise. For some reason, since he had told her his secret about the children, she had assumed his business trips had only been an excuse to get away from Lockhaven Hall, from his memories. He hadn't gone anywhere since Christmas, and that was nearly two months past.

"Can we go with you?" asked Stacy.

Bram laughed. "You wouldn't like it. Very dull, my business."

"Why? What is it you do when you go away?"

"What do you think? I gallop about on Bellerophon and rescue damsels in distress."

"What's a damsel?" asked Minnie.

"A lady, stupid," her brother told her.

"Oh."

It had never occurred to Lucy that he might be visiting a woman when he went away, but now it made perfect sense. He could hardly bring her here, after all, not with the children. Of course. He had a lover. Why had she never thought of that before?

"When are you leaving?" asked Minnie.

"Tonight."

"Can we have supper with you in the banquet hall before you go?"

"If you like. A damsel rescuer has to eat to keep up his strength." They had reached the front doors.

"How many places for supper tonight, milord?" Jeeves asked as he let them in.

"We'll be eating in the banquet hall, Jeeves. And we'll be four."

"Three," Lucy said, and then, as Bram and the chil-

dren turned to her, she added, "I have a headache. I think
I'll just eat my supper up in my room."

She stayed there even after she'd finished her meal; she
did not come downstairs to see him off, though she heard
Minnie and Stacy calling goodbye to him from the front
drive.

That night she woke trembling from a dream of him.
She sat up in bed and then noticed the room was pitch-
black; there wasn't even a faint glow of coals from the
hearth. "Fool," she told herself aloud as she climbed from
beneath the blankets. She'd forgotten to build up the fire,
that was all.

As her feet touched the icy floor she stiffened, catching
a whiff of some sweet, heavy scent on the air. Roses . . .

Silk rustled in the darkness at the foot of the bed. Was
there some shape there, a deeper black against the blackness, or did she only imagine it? Stealthily she moved her
hand toward the cord that would summon someone to the
room. Out of the cold, eerie stillness came a voice, a low,
throaty whisper. "Go," it said.

"Who's there?" Lucy cried, and yanked the bell cord
as hard as she could. "Who is that? What do you want
from me?"

"Go!" the voice commanded again. Lucy grabbed a
candlestick from the table and hurled it into the darkness.
It crashed against the far wall; above the whispering swish
of silk she heard a strange, high-pitched laugh. And then
all was silence again.

She stood by the bed, hearing the pounding of her heart
in her head. Then a glow of light appeared in the corridor.
"Miss Lucy!" It was Jem, carrying a lamp. "Miss Lucy,
is ye taken sick again?" she cried, hurrying into the room.

"Jem," Lucy said slowly, "what do you smell?"

"What do I—" The maid stared at her. "Ye got me out
of my bed in the dead of night to ask what do I smell?"

"Please, Jem, just tell me. Do you smell anything?"

Her nose probed the air. "Peat," she offered. "Burned
peat."

"That's all?"

"Well, what else would there be?"

"I thought I smelled . . . roses," Lucy whispered uncertainly.

"Saints preserve us!" Jem crossed herself, quaking. "That's Mistress Olive's ghost, then. That's what she always wore—attar of roses. Did ye see her?"

"I didn't see anything, not really. But I thought I heard—"

"What, Miss Lucy?" the bug-eyed maid demanded. "What?"

Lucy frowned. Now, in the bright lamplight, it all seemed so unreal. "Nothing," she said. "It must have been a bad dream." She crossed the room and picked up the candlestick she had thrown. The maid eyed her dubiously.

"Usin' that to ward off a dream, was ye?"

"Hush, Jem," Lucy told her, going to rebuild the fire. "It was nothing. I'm sorry I woke you. Please, just go on back to bed." All the same, she decided as she rekindled the coals in the hearth, she was going to keep the door to her room locked at night from now on.

Chapter 12

One week later Lucy again awoke in the night, but this time not to the scent of roses. Instead she heard the distant thumping song of the virginals in the music room below. Bram, she thought, sitting up in bed, pushing her hair over her shoulders. Home from his visit to his lover. What was she like, Lucy wondered, this woman whom he visited so regularly, at such length?

She would be a noblewoman, Lucy was certain of that. An earl's daughter, perhaps, like Olive, or a countess or baroness. She would be beautiful, of course, and very cultured; she would speak Greek and Latin and French and Spanish and Portuguese even, probably. She would never have to ask him what words like *hypothetical* meant. They would sit all day on velvet pillows, sipping brandy and talking about Athens and Sparta and the Peloponnesian Wars; at night they would lie naked together and he would make that sweet, hot fire flame in her blood. Her name . . . her name would be something exquisite and fine. The Lady Penelope, perhaps, or Anastasia or Isolde or Phyllis, like the names of the women the poets in Stacy's books wrote their verses to.

And when he came home he played this strange, discordant tribute to her, the Lady Penelope or Anastasia or Isolde or Phyllis, down there in the room where his wife had died; he made music for her the only way he knew how. It might not be pretty, but it was passionate. And it was more than he would ever play for Mistress Lucy Jones.

The music broke off abruptly. Lucy pictured him sitting at the virginals in that strange room at the foot of the stairs, his black head bowed, already dreaming of the next time he would see her, his darling, his beloved, and hold her in his arms again.

Lucy slipped out of bed, barefoot, in her white night-dress, and unlocked the door to her bedchamber. She wanted to see him when he came up the stairs, see what those blue eyes might look like while they still burned with love for the Lady Penelope, while the notes of his artless serenade still hung on the air. Candlelight fell across the end of the corridor to the old wing, and then his shadow, and then he turned the corner and saw her waiting there.

"Lucy." Surprised, that was how he looked, she thought, and annoyed, and perhaps faintly guilty. "What are you doing awake at this hour?"

"I heard you playing. Your song."

He laughed, but not really as though he found anything amusing; his sleepy-lidded eyes were nearly closed as he looked at her standing in the doorway in her white night-dress, her black hair tumbling down her back. "Cater-wauling, you called it once, I remember. It's a wonder Reggie doesn't howl along, I suppose. I'm sorry it woke you. How are Minnie and Stacy?"

"They're fine. How was your—business trip?"

"Exhausting," he said with a wide yawn. "Well. Good night." He moved past her down the hall.

"What is she like?" Lucy asked softly.

He whipped around to face her. "Who?" Every trace of sleepiness was gone from his eyes.

"The lady you go off to see."

"What makes you think I go to see a lady?"

"You said so, didn't you, to Minnie? You and Bellero-phon riding off to a lady in distress—"

"That was a jest, nothing more," he said quietly. "Meant to amuse a child."

"A jest with a kernel of truth. Really, it was very stupid of me, I think, not to realize it sooner," Lucy said gaily, brightly. "I mean, it is hardly likely that a man like you would live like a monk. I do hope she isn't married, this lady of yours; it would be rather unkind, don't you agree, to cuckold someone else after you'd been cuckolded?"

"Be quiet, Lucy."

"Ooh, so she is married. Well, that certainly explains

why you don't bring her here. Very nasty, wouldn't it be, with the children. After all, they're so curious, so bright—''

"I said be quiet!" he snapped.

Lucy dropped a curtsy, holding her skirts. "I'm very sorry, milord. Pray forgive me, milord. For a moment I forgot my place."

She saw him clench his huge hand in a fist; all his muscles were rigid, and his jaw was tight as he fought to hold on to his temper. The effort cost him so much that a vein pounded on his forehead, and sweat beaded on his lip. "Go to bed, Lucy," he said between gritted teeth.

"Yes, milord. Right away, milord." Lucy's eyes burned with tears, and she blinked them back angrily. "You play that you're a monk, I'll play that I'm a teacher, and we'll just pretend the rest of our lives away!" She ran back into her room and slammed the door, turning the key with shaking hands.

She hoped wildly, illogically, that he would pound on the door and demand to see her. She would have let him in that night, into her room and even, God help her, into her bed. But there was no sound from the corridor for a long time; then she heard his footsteps, heavy and slow, as he went away.

Furious at herself, furious at him, Lucy flung herself down on the bed and gave vent to her tears. There was no sense in pretending any more. She had gone and done the one thing her pop and everyone else in Shoreditch knew only led to disaster, the one thing she'd sworn she would never, ever do no matter what. She'd gone and lost her heart to a nobleman.

Bram Carlyle did not sleep for the rest of that night. He sat at his desk in his study, a bottle of brandy at his elbow, and considered the choices open to him.

He could send her away.

Just the thought made his hand tremble as he picked up his glass. Never to see her again, never hear her bright laughter or watch as her smile lit up her green eyes— impossible. He knew what it was like to be parted from her even for a week: as though the whole earth was draped in darkness, as though spring would never come again.

He could do nothing. That would be the coward's way. He could go on acting as though his body didn't ache for her when she was near him, deny the awful need he felt in his soul, but that was impossible, too. She was young, she was—oh, God, beautiful as a dream. She was so full of life—how could he think to keep her here in this house of the dead? She was growing restless already, and who could blame her? There was no man worthy of her at Lockhaven Hall. There was no man worthy of her in all the world.

He could try, though, to find someone who might make her happy. Like a fond, doting uncle, he could launch her in society, then look on as the young men gathered around her—for he was sure they would. He would be the chaperone when they came courting, sit discreetly in a chair in the receiving room while other men held her hand and whispered endearments, and when finally she chose one to marry he would give her away, stand by the altar as she promised to love and cherish someone else for all time. Christ, how would he bear it? "Impossible," he said aloud, slamming down his brandy glass.

Well then, if he could not withstand the agony of that, suppose he sent her to Margery's? Margery could be the chaperone, serve the port wine and cakes to Lucy's beaux. He could take the children to visit, catch glimpses of her that way. Perhaps Margery's own grandson, Gordon, would marry her; she would live at Harten House, close but not too close. That would be ideal. She would have children; he would watch them grow. She would be happy. And he—he would know that she was. He had no right to hope for anything more than that.

There was one more choice, of course, but that he did not even contemplate, for it truly was impossible.

Margery's, then. Through the long, cold hours before dawn he drank and mulled it over in his mind, and by the time the morning came he had convinced himself it was the only answer. When Jem brought him his breakfast he sent her to fetch Lucy. He might as well get it over with now.

He heard her knock and poured a sizeable shot of brandy into his glass. "Come in."

"It's locked."

"No, it's not." He had not wanted to risk getting up to let her in, being that close to her. He watched as she tried the latch and entered, dressed in the old gray gown she had worn the first time he had ever seen her, when she came to his door in London. At the sight of her his heart leaped into his throat just as it had then. Christ, he had not reckoned how hard this would be.

"Sit down, Lucy, please," he told her as steadily as he could.

"Sir." Her green eyes were dark, abashed. "About last night. I am sorry I made such a scene."

"It doesn't matter." He couldn't look at her; he toyed with his quill, straightened papers absently. "I haven't been very fair to you, Lucy, have I?"

"Not fair?" she echoed, sounding surprised.

"Aye. I haven't considered how—how lonely it must be for you here. Oh, I know you have the children, but still . . ." Keep going, he told himself, keep talking. "You must miss having company your own age. Parties, dancing. Balls. That sort of thing."

"We didn't have many balls in Shoreditch," she told him.

"Oh. I don't suppose you did." He pawed hurriedly through the piles of papers on his desk, found a creamy vellum envelope containing a card, and consulted it. "The countess of Sutherland is having one, though. Tonight. Would you like to come?"

"Me?" He glanced up at her, saw her wide green eyes, and quickly looked back at the invitation. "I can't even dance!"

"Neither can I."

"What would I wear?"

"I thought you looked rather nice in the red gown you wore on Christmas eve." That, Bram thought wryly, was as great an understatement as he'd ever made.

"But—would she want me there?" she asked tentatively. "I mean—does she know about Shoreditch?"

Bram nodded. "The children told her at New Year's. She wants very much to meet you. In fact, I am hoping—" Hoping she will take you in, he meant to say, hoping you will fall in love with her grandson Gordon and marry him. Hoping you will leave here, leave me in peace with my misery. But he could not form the words; his throat had gone dry. "Hoping you will enjoy it," he finished lamely. He would wait and tell her that night, at the ball. It would be easier there, once he saw her with other men, once he saw how happy she would be. He would be certain then that he had made the right choice.

"I'd be honored to go," she said softly.

"Well! That's fine, then!" he said in a loud, hearty voice. "I'll ride Bellerophon, of course, but I'll tell Johnny to have the carriage ready for you at seven, shall I? It isn't far. About an hour's ride—" He went on about the details, still in that false, cheery tone, fiddling with his pen and papers, not looking at her, until at last she broke in:

"Excuse me, Bram—"

"Yes?" He looked up at last, saw her smile blaze at him, and flinched.

"The children are waiting for their lessons. And if I'm to be ready at seven, I've a great deal to do."

"Of course." That was how she looked when she was happy. That was how she would look all the time without him. "I will see you there, then."

"Aye," she said, already halfway to the door. "I will see you there."

Never in her life had Lucy prepared for an occasion so carefully. She soaked in a warm tub full of violet-scented suds until her toes were wrinkled; she washed her hair and brushed it until it shone. She plucked all the cat hairs that Reggie had left from her red damask gown; she pressed her petticoats beneath a damp cloth, sprinkled them with starch, and pressed them again, until whenever she touched them they gave off a splendid crisp, crinkling sound.

For there had never in her life been so momentous an occasion. Abraham Carlyle had actually asked her to go with him to a ball! She could scarcely believe it; while she worked she kept pinching herself to make sure it wasn't a dream. She had gone to his study that morning expecting him to give her her notice, and instead he had invited her to the countess's!

He'd felt strange about asking her; she could tell that from the way he had started and then stopped his sentences, avoiding her gaze and rummaging through the mess on his desk. No doubt he wasn't sure she would behave properly, but Lucy intended to show him she could be every bit as much a lady as the lover he went off to visit. This was her chance, and all she had ever wanted was a chance. She could make him forget about that other woman, she knew she could. And just the fact that he'd asked her to go with him proved he was thinking now that they might be more than friends.

Minnie and Stacy watched her labors intently; they were as delighted as she at the news that she was going with their father to the ball. When the armory clock struck six, she chased them out of her room while she got dressed and then stared in the mirror, trying ten different ways of putting up her hair. Finally she settled on a loose chignon at the nape of her neck that left her throat and shoulders bare. Almost perfect, she thought, frowning at her reflection. Almost—but not quite.

"Lucy?" Minnie rapped at the door.

"Come in, pet."

"Here." The girl held out her hand and pressed something into Lucy's palm. Lucy looked down at the emerald eardrops.

"I've already told your father I can't take them from him, sweetheart."

"You aren't taking them from him," Minnie said patiently. "You're taking them from me. He gave them to me just now, and I am lending them to you to wear to Margery's."

"Well—I'll just see how they look." Lucy fastened the jewels and considered her reflection again.

"Oh, Lucy," Minnie said in awe. "You have to wear them. See what they do to your eyes." Lucy laughed at the girl's hushed tone, but she had to admit the eardrops were just what her outfit was lacking; they made her green eyes sparkle magically.

"I'll borrow them just for tonight, then. Thank you." Lucy leaned down to kiss her cheek.

Stacy burst in just then. "Johnny's ready with the carriage,'' he announced, and then stopped in his tracks, staring at Lucy. ''Damn,'' he said admiringly.

''Tuppence to the Treasury,'' Minnie told him.

''I don't care; I'll pay. You look—you look—'' For once in his life words failed him; he just shook his head.

Lucy laughed. ''Well, thank you very much, I think. I had better go.'' She caught up her cape.

''Don't forget this.'' Minnie handed her the Christmas scarf. ''Father wore his.''

''And don't be afraid,'' Stacy told her as she tied on the scarf. ''You'll be the belle of the ball. The most beautiful lady there.''

Snow was falling slowly outside Lockhaven Hall—big, soft, lacy flakes that swirled and glowed in the light of the carriage lamps. ''Enjoy your evening, Mistress Jones,'' Jeeves said as he helped her up the coach steps.

''Thank you, Jeeves.'' Minnie and Stacy were standing in the entranceway, waving; Lucy blew them a kiss. Then Jeeves shut the coach door, Johnny whistled to the horses, and she was on her way.

Lucy pulled over her knees one of the fur robes Jeeves had so thoughtfully provided and leaned back in her seat, wondering what her pop would do if he could see her now. As if she didn't know, really—give her a good scold, that was what. Rich folk and poor . . . but Bram didn't look down on her, or he would not have asked her to the countess's tonight. And if she showed him that she wasn't intimidated or afraid, then he would forget all about Lady Penelope or Phyllis or whoever and fall in love with her; she was certain he would.

He would marry her. They would be a family, he and she and Minnie and Stacy; they would live in Lockhaven Hall. She would never do wrong to him the way Olive had; she would never in her life look at another man . . .

Her head filled with dreams, Lucy was surprised by how quickly the hour's ride passed; in no time at all the carriage rolled to a stop. A footman in a fancy blue livery opened the door to her, and Lucy blinked; there was a carpet laid across the snowy drive leading to the house, and a canopy stretched overhead to protect her from the drifting flakes.

The footman helped her down the carriage steps and led her through a lavish entranceway into the house. Candles gleamed in sconces along the tapestried walls, and the floor was covered with more plush carpeting. The footman relinquished her to a doorman, who helped her off with her cloak and scarf and even knelt down to dry her shoes with a fluffy towel, though she tried to protest that they weren't damp.

The doorman rang a little brass bell that summoned a butler dressed all in blue velvet, who bowed low to Lucy and asked her name. "Mistress Jones," he exclaimed when she gave it. "The countess has been expecting you. Won't you please come this way?"

She trailed along behind him to an absolutely cavernous room in which hundreds of bright torches flickered, lighting up the pink marble floors and halls. There were perhaps fifty men and women inside, all dressed very elegantly, sipping wine from long-stemmed goblets; in a gallery stretching midway between the pink floor and gilded ceiling a quartet of musicians played.

Lucy searched for Bram among the guests and finally spotted him kneeling beside a tiny chair on which was seated the most patrician creature imaginable. She was very old, white-haired and frail, but her pale skin was seamless, almost translucent in the warm torchlight. She was dressed in sky-blue watered silk, with ostrich plumes of the same color tucked into her elaborate coiffure; circling her throat was a string of huge, lustrous pearls. She looked like a porcelain doll, so delicate and perfect that she might shatter if one touched her. "The countess of Sutherland," said the butler, leading Lucy toward her. "Madame, Mistress Jones."

Though Lucy had sworn not to be intimidated, she dropped her gaze to the floor as she curtsied. "Milady," she whispered.

The woman seated before her laughed, a surprisingly robust sound coming from so fragile a soul. "There, Bram, didn't I tell you to forget that silly business about gentlemen and coaches and ride with her? Now she has had all that time alone in a cold carriage to fret. Call me Margery, my dear; everyone does. And for heaven's sake, get up from the floor. Whoever invented marble floors, anyway? They are utterly impossible to keep warm. Bram, where are your manners? Fetch Lucy a chair. She and I have just got time for a nice chat before the dancing begins.''

This rather lengthy speech was delivered without a single pause for breath. Lucy looked into the countess's merry blue eyes, and her shyness vanished; no one could have felt timid in the face of such warmth. Bram fetched another of the dainty chairs and set it by the countess's, and Lucy sat down. ''What am I to do, pray tell, while you two are becoming acquainted?'' he asked.

''Why don't you go and have a drink?'' the countess suggested. ''You are so good at that.''

He laughed. ''Shall I get you one, Lucy?'' She nodded, blushing, and he strode off across the marble floor.

The countess looked at Lucy and sighed. ''Lord, it's been years—no, let's be honest, decades—since I blushed like that, Lucy. Do you mind if I call you Lucy? From everything that Minnie and Stacy told me about you I feel as though we are old friends. I am so glad someone finally gave those two decent names. I always thought Bram mad to let Olive call them Eustace and Minerva. I have a theory, you know, that a person's name is the key to his personality. Take your name, for instance. Did you know— uh-oh. The wolves are gathering.''

''I beg your pardon?'' Lucy asked. The countess nudged her and pointed. An elderly man with a long white beard and drooping, dark-ringed eyes was approaching them.

''Margery.'' He kissed the countess's cheek. ''I have never seen you look more radiant.''

She sniffed. ''As though you came over here to see me.''

The man grinned and squinted at Lucy. ''Oh, is there someone else with you? My eyesight is grown so poor—''

''Not so poor that you can't still spot the prettiest girl in the room. Get on with you, William Cecil.'' The countess gave him a poke of her ostrich-plume fan.

''William Cecil?'' Lucy echoed in awe. ''The queen's William Cecil?''

''None other,'' the countess said briskly. ''William, allow me to present Mistress Lucy Jones.''

''Mistress Jones.'' Queen Elizabeth's lord high treasurer bent to kiss Lucy's hand. "Delighted to meet you. May I have the honor of fetching you something to drink?"

"Bram has beat you to it, William, you old lecher," the countess told him as he arrived with two glasses of wine.

"Bram!" The two men shook hands. "Is this ravishing creature with you?"

"Mistress Jones is governess to my children, Sir William."

"Lucky little devils," Cecil said enviously. "I never had a governess looked like that."

"Excuse me, William." Another man, short and sharp-eyed, with a bushy black beard, caught Cecil by the shoulders and moved him a few steps to the side. "Do you mind? You are blocking my view. And what a view it is." He smiled at Lucy. "Won't someone introduce me?"

"Mistress Lucy Jones," the countess said with a sigh, "Sir Francis Walsingham. I can see I shall be at this all night."

"Mistress Jones," Cecil put in, "is governess to Bram's children."

"Mistress Jones," said the queen's secretary of state, kissing Lucy's hand, "is the only thing that could ever lure me back to a schoolroom. How do you do? Do you know, you have got my very favorite sort of eyes; I adore green eyes. Only don't tell my wife, please, because hers are brown."

Lucy laughed just as a blond-haired young man bounded over to the countess. "The musicians said to tell you they are ready, Grandmama. Oh, I say." He'd just caught sight of Lucy. "Hello. I'm Gordon. Margery's my grandmama. Will you marry me?"

"Gordon, behave yourself!" the countess scolded him. "This is Mistress Lucy Jones."

"Enchanted," the young man exclaimed. "If not marriage, Mistress Jones, then perhaps this dance?"

"I'm afraid I don't dance," Lucy admitted apologetically.

"You cannot possibly be a bad dancer, Mistress Jones. You are far too lovely. And anyway, I have two left feet, isn't that right, Grandmama? I shall make you shine by comparison.'' He reached for her hand.

''I really don't dance,'' Lucy tried to protest even as she giggled at his eagerness; he reminded her of a young puppy let loose from its leash. ''I mean, I just don't know how.''

''I shall devote my life to teaching you,'' Gordon said solemnly. ''Starting now.'' With a helpless glance back at the countess, Lucy set down her wineglass and let him pull her toward the center of the floor. ''If you please, something slow,'' he shouted up to the gallery.

The musicians began to play; Lucy and Gordon took their places at the end of a line of lords and ladies. ''This one's very simple,'' he assured her, patting her hand as he laid it on his arm. ''Just left foot, right foot, left—or is it right, left, right? Well, we'll just watch everyone else and follow them, shall we?'' Still giggling, Lucy agreed.

It wasn't hard to mimic the movements of the other dancers, she found. ''Unfair!'' Gordon protested as she caught on to the pattern. ''You lied; you do too know how!''

''It is just that you are a good teacher,'' Lucy told him, although that wasn't true.

''Really? Do you think so?'' He beamed at her. ''Whenever I dance I always feel as though I have on someone else's shoes, if you know what I mean.'' Lucy laughed aloud; imagine a countess's grandson needing reassurance from her!

When the dance was finished he suggested another, but Sir William Cecil appeared to claim Lucy's hand. ''Age has its perquisites, Gordon,'' the lord high treasurer growled, and sent him on his way. ''Come along, Mistress Jones, and make an old man's day.''

''I don't know the steps, milord,'' Lucy objected.

''Nonsense—I was watching you on that last dance, along with every other man in the room. You're the soul of grace.''

Lucy watched the rest of the dancers for a moment; the hop-skip-and-step they were performing wasn't much different from the hornpipe she'd seen danced at the Mermaid Tavern, though it was slower and more stately and the men weren't swinging mugs of ale. She and Cecil joined in on the second go-round. He wasn't much better than Gordon, but Lucy scarcely noticed. She was overwhelmed to think that the man beside her had actually walked and talked and ate and maybe even danced with the queen herself!

She was dying to ask him about Good Queen Bess, but while they were dancing she had to pay too close attention to that, and when they had finished another man was waiting to ask for an introduction. His name was Lord Rupert Something-or-other; Lucy didn't quite catch it. "You must be related to the Northampton Joneses, milady," he told her as they took their places. "I knew your great-uncle—I presume your great-uncle—Sir Edward quite well." Lucy didn't see any point in disabusing him, especially while she was concentrating on the steps. Besides, he didn't leave her much room in which to say anything; he spouted on and on about his own family and how important they were. He, too, wanted another dance, but the countess of Sutherland came to Lucy's rescue, calling them to her side.

"Forgive me, Sir Rupert," the countess said smoothly, "but I must have a word with Lucy. Will you excuse us?" And then, as he bowed and walked away, she nudged Lucy with her fan and whispered, "God, isn't he a bore?"

Lucy laughed. "Well, he did seem a bit full of himself," she whispered back.

"Now, where was I before all these men started panting over you? Ah, yes, names. Did you know that Lucy means—oh, dear."

"What is it?" Lucy asked, following the woman's gaze toward the entranceway. A buxom blond woman in a low-cut silver gown was standing there, her pale eyes scanning the room.

"Over there." The countess sighed. "The baron of Tatworth's daughter. His manor's quite close to here. I heard she'd been sent away from the court for a few months for some infraction—probably wearing those indecent gowns. And one doesn't like to be unneighborly. But the plain truth is, I can't abide the girl. You think Sir Rupert is bad, you ought to hear her go on about the stellar lineage of her family. Eight dukes, twenty earls, fifty barons—and her father is even worse. Artemis, his name is, if that's not enough to tell you right there. Artemis Moncrief."

The moment she heard the last name, Lucy recognized the haughty blonde she'd seen at Anthony Babington's. Claudia Moncrief . . . "But that's the woman that I—"

"Yes, dear, I know."

"But what should I do?"

"If I were you," said the countess, leaning down to pick up Lucy's glass, "I should finish this wine."

Gordon Sutherland came over just then with a plate of sweetmeats for his grandmother and Lucy, who nibbled nervously on a tart while keeping watch on Claudia Moncrief from the corner of her eye. She nearly choked as she saw Bram, looking impossibly elegant in his black evening clothes, stroll over to the woman, bow, and kiss her hand. Claudia Moncrief's pale eyes lit up; she curtsied coquettishly, affording him an even more obvious chance to admire her décolletage. They began to talk, Bram leaning against the wall, Claudia laughing gaily, plying her feathered fan.

"I say," said Gordon, who'd been making cow's eyes at Lucy, "if you find it dull to be told how beautiful you are, I could stop."

"What?" Lucy asked, her gaze on the couple by the doorway.

"Never mind," he told her, crestfallen. "I don't suppose you'd care to dance again?"

Lucy saw Claudia drop her fan and Bram gallantly retrieve it. "As a matter of fact, Gordon, thank you. I would."

While he led her through another course on the floor, Lucy kept sneaking glances at Bram. Whatever he was saying to the blonde, she certainly seemed to find it amusing; she kept laughing, her hand at her breast, lashes fluttering seductively. Though the music was lovely, Lucy couldn't keep her mind on the steps now at all; finally she apologized to Gordon and asked him to take her back to her chair. Before long there was a cluster of men surrounding her, asking the countess to introduce Lucy, plying her with compliments. But all Lucy could see was Bram flirting with Claudia Moncrief while he leaned lazily against the wall.

Finally the countess rose from her chair with a sigh.

"Gentlemen," she told the bevy of Lucy's admirers, "would you excuse us, please? There's something I would like very much to show Lucy in the next room. Lucy dear, come along."

Lucy followed her reluctantly, glancing back at Bram. He paid no attention to her as she crossed the marble floor, but Claudia Moncrief's pale eyes narrowed slightly, watching her go.

The countess of Sutherland paused halfway down the long corridor outside the ballroom. "We were speaking of names earlier, my dear," she said softly. "Do you know what the name Lucy means?" Lucy shook her head, looking back over her shoulder, wishing she could see what Bram was up to with the blonde. "It means light-bringer," the countess went on, tugging Lucy's chin around so that Lucy looked into her eyes. "You have done a remarkable job of bringing light back into the lives of Minnie and Stacy. But there are some people in whom the darkness lies very deep."

"He has scarcely looked at me since I got here!" Lucy cried.

"No, he hasn't," the countess agreed, her blue eyes shrewd. "I should think that would tell you a great deal." Then her gaze widened slightly as she looked beyond Lucy's shoulder. "Oh, dear."

Lucy turned and saw Claudia Moncrief bearing down on her; the blonde was no longer laughing, and her pale eyes were narrowed to slits. "You little bitch," she snarled, and slapped Lucy's face with her fan. "Oh, Bram's been telling me all about how you weaseled your way into his house by posing as me. I suppose you think you are very clever, don't you? Of all the colossal nerve—how dare you impersonate me? Why, you're nothing, nobody—a conniving little peasant who can't even read her own name!"

Lucy shrank from her, the blood draining from her face. So that was what Bram had been saying to her, what they'd been laughing about. God, what a despicable man! To think she'd imagined he had asked her here because he cared about her when instead he'd been mocking her behind her back, jesting with this haughty noblewoman at her expense!

Claudia Moncrief turned her wrath on the countess. "And

as for you, all I have to say is you should be ashamed! Have you no sense of your class, of your station? Do you think I or anyone else would have come here tonight had we known you would even let such filth through your door?"

"You listen to me, young lady," the countess began, but Lucy stopped her, putting a hand on her arm.

"Thank you very much for your kind hospitality," she said as steadily as she could, "but I am going home now."

"Go back to the gutter, why don't you?" the irate blonde cried. "That is where you belong!"

"Lucy—wait, please!" the countess pleaded. But Lucy caught up her skirts and ran down the corridor to the front doors.

"Are you leaving so early, Mistress Jones?" the surprised butler asked.

"I'm afraid so. Could I get my cloak, please? And would you have my coach brought round?"

Not until she was back inside the cold, dark confines of the coach did she give vent to her despair, huddling on the seat, the cloak wrapped around her shoulders. She pulled open the window and let the freezing wind batter her tear-streaked face, let the snow swirl in, wishing it would fill up the carriage and bury her completely, leave her dead and frozen like her heart, which lay in her chest like a lump of ice.

God, why hadn't she listened to her pop, to reason, to her own good sense? She wished she'd never come to that door in London and seen Abraham Carlyle; she wished she had let Hawk-Nose kill her and leave her lying in the gutter with Joe. Bram had been laughing at her. Christ, she could have borne anything but that.

Through the rage of the storm she heard the thunder of hooves and his voice, bellowing, roaring: "Stop the coach, Johnny! Stop that bloody damned coach!"

She put her head through the window. "Keep going, Johnny!"

"Stop that damned coach now!" Bram roared as he galloped up beside her on Bellerophon.

"Don't stop, Johnny!" Lucy cried, ducking back into the carriage, trying to pull the window shut. Bram's hand caught the wooden panel, holding it open even as he rode along. The carriage bounced to a halt; Lucy clawed at

Bram's fingers, but he would not let go; he leaped down from Bellerophon, thrust his whole arm in through the window, and pried up the latch, throwing open the door.

"I thought gentlemen didn't ride in coaches," Lucy cried, kicking at him as he bent his great shoulders and squeezed through the doorway. A burst of wind followed him in, scattering the snow that lay over the floor and seats. He yanked the door shut with a bang that rocked the whole carriage.

"What is the matter with you?" he demanded, blocking her flying feet, pinning her to the seat by her shoulders. "Why did you run away, for God's sake?"

"Why did I— Why do you think, you bastard?" Lucy raged, trying to reach his eyes with her nails. "Because you told her about me—that woman, that creature. Because you were laughing at me."

"And what if I was? There were ten—twenty men there tonight who would fall in love with you if you gave them the chance."

"Not if they knew I was only a—a conniving little peasant," she cried. "A nothing, a nobody. A shopgirl from Shoreditch—"

"That wouldn't make any difference at all to any decent man."

"It matters to you, though, doesn't it? I am good enough to—to kiss in the dark, is that it? Good enough to corner in hallways, and to try to—to try to—" She caught her breath in a sob. "But there, in front of all those people, you didn't even look at me, did you? You were looking at her, laughing with her—her eight dukes and twenty earls and fifty barons! What a fine jest it makes, doesn't it? 'Can you imagine, Claudia darling, I actually believed the little nobody was you?'"

"Yes," he said. "Yes, that's what I told her—"

"God, I hate you!" she spat at him.

"Good! Hate me!" he roared, shaking her shoulders.

"Damn you, damn your black soul!"

"Aye, damn me to hell, Lucy! Hate me and damn me!" And even above the wild, angry wrath of the storm she heard the desperation in his voice, remembered the countess's words that night: *There are some people in whom the darkness lies very deep* . . . She stopped fighting him, but still he held her, clutching her shoulders, his grip like iron. "Hate me, Lucy," he said again, only this time the words sounded like a prayer. "Hate me. Please . . ." His hands slid up over her throat, cupping her face, catching in her hair. "Oh, Christ, Lucy," he whispered brokenly, "I want you so much that I think it will tear me apart."

And then he kissed her, put his mouth to hers and crushed her beneath him, drank in the taste of her like a man who'd been dying of thirst for a thousand years.

"Milord—" Johnny said, peering in through the window. Bram raised his head long enough to say, "Drive. Home." Then he slammed the window shut and turned to Lucy again.

The coach sprang forward, and he pulled her down from the seat to the floor in a tangle of fur robes and wet wool and white snow and red damask. She lay sprawled atop him, and he tugged her hair, kissed her eyes, her mouth, her throat. "I have waited—so long for this," he murmured, his mouth at her ear. "If you could feel what you do to me, Lucy—the hunger, the fire—" But she did feel it; she knew what he meant. Sparks were flaring in her everywhere he touched her. "Hold me. Kiss me, Lucy," he said hoarsely, and she put her mouth to his timidly. His tongue thrust between her parted lips, slipping inside her, savoring the taste of her. Through the tangle of fur and wool he reached for her bodice strings, tore them open, and groaned as his hands found her breasts.

His fingertips closed on her nipples, kneading, caressing the rosy buds, and the sparks inside Lucy burst into flame as they grew taut and hard at his touch. His loins moved beneath her as the carriage rattled and jarred over the rough country road; against her skirts Lucy felt his manhood throbbing like a third urgent heart. He reached up and pulled the pins from her hair so that it tumbled around them both; he drew her up until his mouth closed on her breast, teased the hard nipple with his tongue.

Lucy's head was spinning with the wild swirl of sensations around her: cold snow, hard wood, wet cloth, silky fur, his eager hands, his warm mouth, the dark air, the shimmering fire. He could not stop kissing her, touching her; he could not kiss her enough. He tore at her skirts, yanking them upward, thrusting them aside until he could reach beneath the red damask and starched white linen to caress the bare flesh above her stockings. As his fingers stroked the softness of her thighs he let out his breath in a rush of longing, of passion that shook Lucy to her soul.

But he drew back then and sat up against the seat, drawing her into his lap, pushing her black curls from her face. "What is it?" Lucy whispered, terrified that she had done something wrong.

"I can't," he said raggedly. "Not like this, not this way. Not for your first time."

Lucy sighed with relief. "What makes you so sure it is my first time?" she teased.

His arms went rigid around her. "Is it?" he asked, with something like fear in his voice.

She found his mouth, traced it with her finger. "Yes."

He caught her hand and kissed the palm. "Then I must make love to you in the way you deserve." He pounded on the side of the carriage. "Dammit, Johnny, can't you go any faster?"

"We're there, milord!" Johnny shouted back indignantly. The carriage stopped; Bram kicked open the door and gathered Lucy into his arms, robes and cloak and wet skirts and all, and carried her into Lockhaven Hall.

The house was dark and silent except for his echoing footsteps as he crossed the armory, went through the portrait gallery and receiving room; Lucy still shivered, though, as they passed beneath Lady Carlyle's unsleeping gaze. He bore her as though she was weightless, more precious than diamonds, all the way down the monk's walk to the room at its very end.

Inside all was pitch blackness. Lucy felt herself sink down into a sea of soft blankets and feathers; his mouth brushed hers, and then he pulled away. "I want to look at you," he whispered, and then a flame flared in the darkness as he lit the fire at the hearth to warm the cold air. He took a box of candles from atop the mantel and lit them as well, one by one, setting them up all around the room until it glowed with soft, golden light.

Lucy had never seen his bedchamber before; it was neat and plain, like a religious cell, in striking contrast to his chaotic study. Even the bed on which she lay was stark and simple as a child's cot; the one in her own room was far more grand. He turned from lighting the candles, saw her staring at the sparse furnishings, and smiled. "I don't have many visitors here." Lucy smiled too, knowing he was trying to put her at ease, but still she was trembling. He came and sat beside her, prying her fingers from the edge of her cloak, kissing her as he pulled it open. His eyes were glowing like the candles, hot indigo flames.

He pushed the sides of her bodice apart and laid his hands on her breasts while his mouth still covered hers, his kiss gentle as a whisper; still she felt hot force simmering beneath his patient caresses. "We must have these clothes off," he murmured, and she looked at him with wide green eyes. He moved to the foot of the bed and unbuckled her boots, slipped them over her heels. Then he reached beneath her skirts and petticoats and rolled down her stockings, his fingers barely grazing her skin.

Slowly he unfastened the band at her waist, lifting her so he could reach the buttons on either side, undressing her as though she were a helpless child. Then he took the hems of her gown and petticoats in both hands and raised them up inch by inch, uncovering her ankles, her knees, her thighs, and sealing each new bit of flesh he revealed with a tender kiss.

When he had lifted the skirts to her waist he drew her up again and pulled them over her head, easing her arms from the sleeves, kissing the soft whiteness of her wrists and arms. He let the bundle of damask and linen slip to the floor; he even unfastened the emerald eardrops while his tongue traced the shell-like delicacy of each ear.

He stretched out beside her and untied the string of her drawers, then slid them slowly down over her hips and knees and ankles. She lay before him naked and trembling; shyly she put her hand down to cover the nest of curling black hair below her belly, and crossed her arm over her breasts. He put his hand over hers and eased her arm away gently. "Don't. You're so beautiful, Lucy, like a goddess, an angel—"

She felt herself blushing, embarrassed by the awe, the wonder in his eyes as he drank in her nakedness. "Don't stare at me so," she mumbled, rolling onto her side, hiding her face in the bedclothes. He ran his hand over her shoulders, down her spine to the soft, rounded mounds of her buttocks; then his hand went away, and she heard the sounds of him undressing, unbuckling his belt, pulling off his doublet and breeches and hose.

"Lucy." He kissed the nape of her neck, his fingers twining through her hair. "Have you ever seen a man naked?" She shook her head, still hiding from him. "Will you look at me, Lucy?" She shook her head again, more emphatically. "Please?" he whispered, his hand at her shoulder, pulling her toward him. She clenched her eyes shut. "Look at me, love." She opened them ever so briefly, intending only to peek, to please him. But what she saw made them stay open wide. His body was so different from hers, long and lean and hard where hers was soft, in the tight coiled muscles of his shoulders and chest, his taut belly and—she swallowed, knowing she was staring now but unable to help herself as she saw the stiff, swollen manroot that thrust up between his legs.

He was watching her closely, his blue eyes narrowed and dark. She raised her gaze to his, and her surprise seemed to reassure him; he took her hand in his. "Now, will you touch me?"

"No!" Lucy burst out, intimidated by that thick, hard rod, by the strange bulging sacs of taut flesh that lay beneath it. But he had already touched her fingers to its tip, closed her small hand over its length.

"Oh, God. Oh, Jesus," he groaned, his whole body shuddering as he held her there. She felt his life's blood pounding in her hand, felt his flesh quicken and throb at her hesitant touch; then with a ragged moan he pulled her away. "No more of that . . ."

He drew her into his arms and kissed her, her breasts crushed against his chest, his tongue teasing hers, making circles around it while his hand traced the same circles at the small of her back. Then he ducked his head to her breasts again and teased them, too, his tongue licking, darting, circling the rosy tips. He reached down to her belly, stroking it gently with his long fingers, his touch soft as feathers against her skin. Then he reached lower, down to her thighs, to the mound of flesh between them, all the while plucking at her nipples with his tongue.

Lucy shivered as he touched her there, as his hand rubbed in smooth, slow circles. "Don't be afraid," he told her. "I won't hurt you. I love you—" He slipped his hand between her knees, brought it upward to part them, caressing her tender white flesh. "Don't be afraid," he whispered again, and one long finger inched upward and touched her most secret place.

"No," Lucy cried, not believing him, not knowing what he was doing. "No . . ."

"Yes, love. Yes." His finger reached forward, slipping into her warm, tight sheath and sliding out again.

Lucy felt muscles she had never known she possessed convulse in a quivering pulse of fire. He reached inside her again, more deeply, pushing down with his hand, and in her belly the fire began to spread, to flow in a burning river through her blood and bone.

Then he withdrew his finger and knelt over her, bending down to suck at her breasts, one after the other, while his hard shaft rubbed against her belly. Lucy lay utterly still, afraid to move, afraid to even breathe lest he stop, lest that magical river of fire stop flowing. He reared back, raising his head to look at her, and Lucy closed her eyes. "Lucy," he said, "Lucy—" He shifted downward, and the swollen head of his manhood slipped between her thighs; his tongue traced circles on the bright aureoles of her breasts, flicked across the stiff buds of her nipples again and again.

Lucy clenched her hands into fists at her sides, rigid with wonder, certain there could be no sensation in all the world so thrilling and sweet. Then he moved back on his haunches, and his fiery rod thrust into her, straight and sure as an arrow let loose from a bow.

In the midst of the tide of pleasure Lucy felt a sharp stab of pain that wrenched a cry from her throat. Bram pulled back from her hurriedly, touched her cheek with his hand. "I'm sorry," he whispered. "Christ, I am sorry." She opened her eyes and looked up at him, saw his taut, strained face, and she wanted to tell him not to be, that it didn't matter, that all she wanted in the world was for him to start the fire burning again.

But before she could speak he drove into her once more, his hands cupping her buttocks, raising her up against him, plunging her down beneath him with wild, frenzied force. Lucy thought each hard, burning thrust would drive her to madness, that the fire raging between them would melt them to nothingness. The pleasure was so fierce, so intense that she wanted to cry out once more, but she could not bear the thought that he might stop again if she did. She was so unsure of what he wanted from her now, what the proper response should be to the rushing flood of sensations that enveloped her; Christ, she thought, Christ, am I pleasing him? What should I do?

And all she could think to do was to lie there beneath him in silence, surrender to him and let him do as he would. The bed rocked against the floor with each wild thrust he made; Lucy had to fight with all her will not to cry out to him now. The fire had turned so brilliant and hot that if he stopped now she was certain she would die.

And then suddenly the light folded in on itself, became flame no longer but light, pure and incandescent and holy, white as a lily flower, more blinding than the sun. Bram called out her name, his shaft sunk to its hilt in her flesh, his face buried against her black hair. Lucy opened her mouth at last, but her long scream of ecstasy was soundless; she could think of no words to express her emotion at that moment of knowing, of truth. Her nails cut into her fists; deep in her belly she felt a final burst of flame. Bram fell against her, shuddering, but Lucy slipped away into unconsciousness, her senses strained to breaking by the force of that terrible, wonderful fire.

Chapter 13

When she opened her eyes, Lucy was alone in the bed; the candles around her had burned down more than an inch. Puzzled, she pushed up on the pillows and saw Bram was already dressing, pulling on his boots in a chair by the hearth.

"Bram," she whispered.

He turned to her, his blue eyes furtive, guilty. "I—I have to go away."

"My God," she said in disbelief. "You are going to her. To that other woman."

"There is no other woman, Lucy. There never could be. I—I wrote you a note. It is there on the bed."

"Bram, what are you—"

"Just read it, Lucy. I'm sorry. I have to go."

"Bram, please!" Lucy cried. She had so much to tell him, to share with him; she had to know if he, too, had felt that magical white light, that river of fire. But he jammed his hat down onto his head and started for the door. Just before he went out he paused for the length of a heartbeat, looking down at the floor.

"I mean every word I wrote there," he said hoarsely. And then he was gone.

Bewildered, Lucy looked among the tangle of clothing and bedding and found a piece of parchment, stared down at it. The candlelight was too dim for her to see; she scrambled out of bed and took it closer, terrified of what it might say.

"My beloved Lucy," she read. "I love you with all my heart and soul. Will you marry me? I'll be back for your answer in a week. Love, Bram." And then there was one more sentence tacked onto the end: "If you don't want to, I will understand."

What in God's name— Clutching a blanket around her shoulders she ran from the bedchamber, calling for him.

The monk's walk was empty; so were the receiving room and the portrait gallery. In the armory, Jeeves, a lantern in his hand, was closing the front door. "Jeeves," she cried, "where is Bra— Where is Lord Carlyle?"

"I'm afraid you've just missed him, Mistress Jones," said the butler, not batting an eye at the blanket or her bare feet that showed beneath its hem.

"Gone—" Lucy flung open the door and saw only a muddle of footprints and hoofprints and then only hoofprints in the clean, fresh snow. "Gone where?"

"I'm afraid I don't know. Is something amiss?" he inquired politely.

"Is something—" Lucy pushed the door shut and leaned her head against it. "Oh, Jeeves, I don't know."

"Well," said the butler, heading toward his rooms, "if there's anything at all I can do, you have only to ring."

"Thank you, Jeeves," she told him, and then retraced her steps to the bedchamber.

She read the letter through three more times, but it still made no sense to her. If she'd done something wrong, if she hadn't pleased him the way he had pleased her, then surely he wouldn't be asking her to marry him! But if he loved her, as the letter said, then why had he rushed away? Why had he looked so guilty? It just wasn't logical.

Slowly she gathered up her scattered clothing from the bedchamber floor. A week, he'd written. He'd be back for her answer then . . .

There were so many differences between them, she thought, pulling on her petticoats. Still, in the night, in the glow of the candles, none of that had mattered; they hadn't been servant and master, lord and peasant, rich and poor. They had been man and woman, filled only with hunger and longing and need.

And with love. God, how she loved him! And he loved her; she looked down at the tangled bedclothes, shivering with pleasure as she remembered the way he had plunged that fiery rod into her, crying her name. Would she marry him? She didn't need a week to decide; if only he had stayed, she'd have told him right then and there. "Yes, Bram," she whispered, and then laughed aloud at the sound and tried it again. "Yes, Bram. Oh, my love, yes!"

Cook said spring had never come to Derbyshire so early before, and allowed as how she ought to know, seeing as she'd lived there nigh seventy years. "Geese back by St. Matthias' Day" she went about muttering. "Snowdrops 'n' jonquils, 'n' Lent barely begun. Wot's this world comin' to?" She seemed, Lucy thought bemusedly, to take the countryside's unseasonal exuberance as a personal affront. "Nothin' good'll come of it," the old woman kept saying darkly. "Ye mark my words." But Lucy thought the early thaw was only too fitting: the bright sun and budding flowers matched the warm unfurling of love in her heart as she counted the days until Bram would return.

The morning after Bram's departure the children were waiting for her in the nursery. "Well?" Minnie demanded.

"Well what?"

"Well, did you have a good time?"

"I had a splendid time."

"And Father?"

"I think," Lucy said, hiding a smile, "that your father enjoyed himself, too. By the by, he had to go away on business unexpectedly. He'll be back in a week. He would have said goodbye to you, but you were both asleep."

Stacy eyed her suspiciously. "Is something going on that you're not telling us about?"

"Of course not. Could we please get to work, now? I am in the mood for some good hard sums, aren't you?"

She said nothing to them of Bram's proposal; she would tell him her answer first; that was only fitting. Then they would tell the children together, as a family—for that was what they would be from now on. Together forever and ever . . . Lucy could barely wait to share such grand news with them. The temptation was so great that she began to take long walks alone in the afternoons, in the forest beyond the wall, just so she could tell her secret to the unheeding trees.

It was on one such walk, just at dusk on the day before Bram was due to return, that she finally made her peace with her father. "Pop," she told him, looking up at the brilliant blue sky through the branches of a strong oak tree, "you were a very wise man, probably the wisest man I'll ever know. And you were right about most everything that you ever told me. But you were wrong about rich folk and poor. People are people, Pop; there are good ones and bad ones. And Bram's a good man, I know he is. You'd like him even if he is rich. And I'm going to marry him. And I hope, Pop, wherever you are, you'll understand."

Then she turned to go, and right there beside the toe of her boot, though she could have sworn it hadn't been there a moment before, she saw a tiny wild crocus, bright as a blessing. "Oh, Pop," she whispered, her tears spilling over. "I knew you would!"

She could scarcely sleep that night for her tremulous excitement. She kept imagining herself in Bram's arms again, his lean, hard, naked body pressed tight to hers while his mouth and hands worked their magic, awakening the fire in her belly and blood. She remembered the way he had whispered her name, his eyes like indigo flames, and the gentleness with which he'd stroked her to readiness: *I won't hurt you. I love you . . .* At long last she drifted to sleep, praying that the morning would come quickly, that the day would pass soon, that her love would hurry home to her.

She woke in darkness, unsure at first what had roused her. Then she smelled the faint odor of roses that surrounded her bed. She lay perfectly still, listening to her heartbeat, and out of the darkness there came the silvery rustle of silk. She held her breath, waited, felt the cold air stir around her as the scent of roses grew stronger. Then, "Go," a voice whispered, so close to her ear that Lucy screamed in fright.

"Who are you? Who's there?" she cried, backing up against the headboard.

"You know who I am," the eerie voice answered. Lucy lunged with both hands in the direction of the sound, but there was nothing there.

"What do you want?" she demanded, trembling. It was someone playing a trick on her; it had to be. Oh, God, let it be!

"Go," came the ghostly voice. "Go now! Before it is too late!"

"Too late for what?"

Something moved across her throat, soft and silky as wind. "Before," came the whisper, just as soft and silky, "he kills you, too."

The feathery touch on her throat grew tighter. Lucy gasped, clawed at it with wild fingers, the rustle of silk and strange high-pitched laughter ringing in her ears. But whatever it was vanished into nothingness; she was left holding air. "Go!" the voice commanded once more.

Lucy grabbed for the tinderbox and knocked it onto the floor, found it, dropped it. By the time she'd struck a spark and lit the candle, the room was empty. She ran to the door, tried to yank it open, and realized with a shock that it was locked, with the key still hanging in the latch. She turned it with trembling hands, looking in both directions down the corridor. There was no one anywhere to be seen.

She leaned against the doorframe, blood pounding in her head. She wasn't dreaming; she was awake. Someone or something had been in her room and vanished into thin air. She put her hand to her throat where she'd felt that silky touch and shuddered uncontrollably. *You know who I am . . .*

Lady Carlyle's ghost, Lucy thought, and then hated herself even for thinking of it. Bram hadn't killed his wife; she knew he hadn't! If she didn't believe him about that then everything else he had told her would be nothing but lies.

It was someone playing a trick on her, that was all. Someone who hated her, who wanted her gone from this house . . . but who could it be? Not the children, surely none of the servants—and who else was there? Who was her enemy?

She went back into her room, locked the door, and stoked the fire to a fearsome blaze. She lit a dozen candles and lined them up on the table beside her bed. Bram will be home tomorrow, she told herself sternly. Bram, who loves you with all his heart and soul. He'll find out who it is playing tricks on you.

She climbed under the covers, staring at the locked door. Tomorrow, her heart beat out above the fire's crackling, comforting roar. He'll be home tomorrow . . .

But even so she did not sleep for the rest of that night.

Bram didn't come in the morning, or by dinnertime. Lucy ate the noon meal in the nursery with the children; as Jem served them she found herself watching the little maid suspiciously. "Did you sleep well last night, Jem?" she asked, searching her face for any sign of guilt.

"Who, me, Miss Lucy? Right enough. Just like a babe," Jem told her, not missing a beat as she handed the dishes and cutlery round. Lucy, looking at her cheery smile, couldn't believe she'd been the one playing ghost.

"Is anything wrong, Lucy?" Stacy asked when the maid had left them.

"Wrong? Of course not. Why do you ask?"

"I don't know. You seem sort of edgy."

"You're imagining things," Lucy said more sharply than she'd intended. He raised wounded blue eyes to her, but Lucy was too preoccupied to apologize, and the children were uncharacteristically quiet for the rest of the meal.

Cook, then, Lucy decided, going down to the kitchens in the afternoon. The old woman hadn't ever like her; hell, she didn't like anyone. Lucy found her rolling out crust for pies. "Master'll be 'ome tonight," she said when she saw Lucy. "Loves my cherry pies, that 'e does."

"Anyone would," Lucy said. "You make wonderful pies."

"I reckon I ought to, after seventy years," said the old woman, thumping the dough.

"Cook, can I ask you something?"

She cackled. "Sure enough, long as it ain't for my crust recipe. That's a deep, dark secret, that is."

"Do you believe in ghosts?"

Cook looked up, her eyes shrewd among their surrounding webs of wrinkles. "Why? 'As ye seen one?"

"I don't know," Lucy said.

Cook raised her rolling pin. "Listen to me, girlie. Ghosts 'n' spooks 'n' such, they come from the devil 'imself. They don't do nothin' but try to frighten honest folk with whispers 'n' lies. Ye've done a damned sight of good for everyone in this household, so don't ye be lettin' no evil spirits scare ye away. 'Ere." She dusted flour from her hands, then hobbled over to an earthenware jar and pulled out a garlic head. "Keep this about ye," she whispered, pressing it into Lucy's palm. "This'll keep the ghosties away."

Lucy took the garlic with thanks, feeling vaguely foolish. It surely hadn't been Cook in her room the night before; old as she was, she could never have disappeared from the hallway before Lucy got there. She must have been dreaming. Had she been dreaming? Nonetheless, she went to find Jeeves. He was in the receiving room, running a cloth over the murals painted on the walls.

"Jeeves—"

"Yes, Mistress Jones?" he asked, straightening from his work.

"Can you tell me, please, who has the key to my rooms?"

"I do hope nothing is missing, Mistress Jones."

"No, no, there's nothing missing. I just wondered, that's all."

"Naturally, I have keys for all the rooms in the house in my keeping," the butler said briskly. "So does Lord Carlyle. And there are spare sets in the kitchens as well as in the stables."

"In the stables?" Lucy asked in surprise.

"Yes, Mistress Jones. In case of a fire."

"I see." Lord, Lucy realized, that meant anyone could have got into her bedchamber. She would just tell Bram what had happened when he came home; after all, he would be there that night . . . "Thank you, Jeeves."

"You're welcome, Mistress Jones," said the butler, and went back to his dusting.

Lucy fetched her cloak from her room and headed outside, seized by a sudden longing to see again the crocus that had sprung up beneath the oak tree; she wanted the reassurance of knowing the sign of her father's blessing was still there. It was, the bright golden petals shining as bright as the sun. She sat with her back against the strong tree; through the branches she saw a sky as cloudless and blue as Bram's eyes. She realized she was still holding the head of garlic that Cook had given her; laughing, she tossed it off into the trees. Ghosts! Honestly, as if anything could ruin her happiness now. With the spring sun pouring down on her, she closed her eyes and drifted off to sleep.

She awoke at dusk; the air had turned so cold she could see her breath, and the forest was draped with shadows. She glanced at the crocus and saw it had folded in on itself with the coming of night. Then she raised her head, hearing the clashing, discordant song of the virginals.

Bram was home! She scrambled up from the ground, brushing dust from her skirts. God, how could she have slept so long? She was still in the old gray gown she had worn from London; she'd meant to put on the red one he preferred. Even though she was in a hurry, she could not help pausing to listen to the thumping sound of the virginals. He'd said it relaxed him to play. He must be nervous about what her answer to his proposal would be; she had never heard the music sound so loud.

It grew even louder as she made her way out of the woods, following the line of the wall overlooking the ravine. A half moon was rising in the sky, casting its silvery pallor over the face of the cliff. Lucy stopped suddenly, arrested by the sight of a figure climbing right up the sheer rock. She blinked in confusion, then saw that there were stairs cut into the stone; the faint moonlight showed their outlines in clear relief. So that explained how Bram had gotten back to Lockhaven Hall before she did on the night she'd gone to Anthony Babington's!

Who could that be now, climbing toward the house under cover of night? A man, tall, rather thin; she could see moonlight shine between his breeches legs as the wind swirled back his cloak. Probably some neighbor coming to complain about Bram's playing, she decided, biting her lip. It really was astonishing how clear and loud the virginals sounded from this vantage point.

The man's cloak was black, clasped at the throat with a gold-set jewel, but it was lined with something lighter that showed white as snow in the moonlight. A faint sensation of uneasiness swept through Lucy. She didn't like the cloak; it reminded her of something unpleasant, something she could not quite put her finger on. Near the top of the cliff the man paused, nearly losing his footing in a sudden gust of wind that blew back his hood. Beneath the white lining his face was bony and thin, his hair wispy and pale.

And then he disappeared. Lucy was staring at him one moment, and the next instant he had vanished. Jesus, she thought, rubbing her eyes, am I going mad? First I see ghosts in my room, and now men are disappearing right in front of me! Curious, she found a toehold in the wall and climbed up atop it. From that angle she could just glimpse a patch of darkness against the moon-pale cliff face—a cave, or a tunnel. So that was where the climber had gone! She looked up at the huge house towering above her, counting windows. Wherever the black hole led had to be underground, in the old wing. The music room? That would explain why the virginals sounded so loud.

That black cape lined with white was still bothering Lucy; she wracked her memory for where she had seen one like it before. Then, from the mouth of the tunnel, she heard a man's voice, high-pitched, with a faint trace of a lisp. Anthony Babington's voice, that had sounded so familiar when she met him at his house in the valley below. *Good evening, angel. I do hope you are looking for me.* A young man, thin-faced and tall, with a lisp and a black cape lined in white fur . . .

Dear God! Lucy was so startled that she nearly fell off the wall. Of course! Anthony Babington was the gambler, the young gentleman who had first brought the lute to her shop! Only he had a beard then and had since shaved it off. No wonder his voice had sounded so familiar to her.

She shivered, crouched on the wall in the cold moonlight. What was Anthony Babington doing climbing up the cliff under cover of night? What business could he have with Bram? Her uneasiness growing, she crept along the wall toward the side of the house. She knew she shouldn't eavesdrop; hadn't she told Minnie and Stacy that a thousand times? But there was something so strange about the way Babington had appeared in the darkness—almost as though Bram were summoning him with the song of the virginals.

From the corner where the wall met the house she could understand what the voices from the tunnel were saying. She heard Babington first: "Was there any trouble?"

Bram answered him, lazily reassuring: "There never is."

"And you have the letter?"

"Right here."

Lucy's heart began to beat unsteadily. The letter? What letter? *Dear Anthony*—that was how the lute letter began. Had it been written to Anthony Babington? Oh, God, she prayed, let this letter be from anyone else in the world except the Queen of Scots. Let Bram have a secret lover, let him have ten thousand of them, but please, dear God, don't let him be mixed up with those letters, with the men who had caused Joe Reilly's death!

"How lucky it was, Bram," Anthony Babington said in his lisping courtier's voice, "that I saw you murder your wife. Wouldn't you agree?"

Saw him murder his wife! Lucy waited for Bram to deny it, to toss Babington right out of the tunnel and over the cliff, but he only laughed. And Lucy, hearing that rich, cold laughter like the jangling of coins, felt as though he had wrenched her heart out from her chest. "Surely you know by now, Anthony," he said smoothly, "my sympathies have always been with Queen Mary's cause."

Lucy began to tremble uncontrollably. She thought she would be sick, she thought she would die, she wanted to throw herself headlong into the ravine and be battered to pieces. He *was* mixed up with Joe Reilly's murderer; Christ, he was a murderer himself! Oh, she cried silently, oh, you rich, treacherous noblemen, damn you all to hell, damn you and your lies!

She could bear no more; she inched backward along the wall. The ghost had tried to tell her, but she wouldn't believe it. In her mind she heard that eerie whispering voice: *Go now . . . before he kills you, too . . .* By God, she believed now.

She climbed down from the wall and then leaned against

it, trying to concentrate, to think through the awful tearing pain in her soul. She couldn't stay here now. She couldn't even bear to set foot back inside that house. She knew if she saw Bram, if she looked at him, she would never be able to pretend even for a moment that she hadn't heard what he'd just said.

Think, Lucy, girl, she told herself sternly, her arms crossed over her chest to quiet her trembling. Think clear and logical. Think what you're going to do. Seven times one is seven. Seven twos, fourteen. Seven threes—God, what were seven threes?

She would run away. She would go home to Shoreditch, back to her own kind, to Alf Smith and Nell Harper and all her old friends. But what if Hawk-Nose was still looking for her there? Even worse, what if Bram came searching for her? No, that wouldn't do. Oh, Jesus, Lucy, she told herself frantically, think!

And then the answer came to her, so clear and complete that its simple logic took her breath away. Of course! She couldn't think of anything wrong with the idea, though she twisted it back and forth in her mind.

"All right, Lucy girl," she whispered aloud. "That's it, then." She caught up her skirts, darted into the woods, and ran.

Part III

Chapter 14

The grand doge of Venice drifted down the canal in a gilded gondola poled by his trusty servant Rodrigo. Past the marble-fronted *palazzi* they sailed, Rodrigo's strong brown arms moving in steady rhythm to the grand doge's heartfelt sighs.

"I shall never look on her again," the white-bearded doge said mournfully, reclining on his nest of silken pillows.

"You must not give in to despair, milord," the faithful servant told his master. "Bianca lives; I know it. I feel it deep in my soul."

The old man raised his head. "So," he said softly. "You loved her, Rodrigo."

"Who would not love the beauteous Bianca, fair as an angel, bright as the summer sun?"

The grand doge brought his fist crashing down on the side of the boat. "A thousand curses fall upon the head of that villainous traitor Orlando, who stole my Bianca, my pride, my only child from me! Would to God I had named him my successor as he bade me do. But I never dreamed he would go so far as to spirit Bianca away. Ah, woe is me! She is gone forever, Rodrigo, and with her is gone all my joy."

From a window far up in one of the huge marble palaces a voice drifted over the water, high and clear and achingly sweet, singing an old song of love wounded and defiled:

> *The promises he made me*
> *Were warm as summer rain;*
> *But oh, he has betrayed me,*
> *And left me tears and pain . . .*

The doge started up from his pillows, his ancient lined face astonished, disbelieving. "Rodrigo," he whispered, staring toward the window, his hand on his heart. "Rodrigo, do you hear? It is a miracle—it is my Bianca! She lives! God in heaven, she lives!"

His servant had stopped rowing; he, too, was gazing toward the window, and there was hope, fierce and wild, shining in his eyes. "Bianca," he breathed. "Oh, my dear love—"

He flung a line from the gondola to the palace dock and leaped out. "Rodrigo, where are you going?" cried the grand doge.

"To rescue the flower of Venice!"

"But Orlando and his men—they will kill you!"

"Let all the devils of hell try to stop me," Rodrigo cried. With the line from the gondola clamped between his teeth, he began the long climb up the wall of the palace toward the sound of his beloved's voice.

The doge watched anxiously from the gondola below, casting fearful glances at the doors to the palace. Inch by slow inch Rodrigo ascended. When he reached the balcony beneath the window he secured the line to its railing. "Bianca!" he called, and the singing broke off; a face appeared in the casement, a woman's face, pale and lovely, framed by long curling golden hair.

"Rodrigo! Oh, Rodrigo, I knew you would find me!" Bianca threw open the window and leaned out to embrace him, sobbing with joy.

"Soft!" he warned, peering past her into the palace. "Who is here with you?"

"Only my faithful handmaiden Esmeralda." Another woman came to the balcony, this one taller, with black hair.

"Master Rodrigo!" The maid gasped when she saw their rescuer. "You must take the lady Bianca away from this terrible place. Orlando, he is a beast, a monster!"

"Do not fear, good Esmeralda. No harm can come to you now. Come, we must away before Orlando tries to stop us."

"Rodrigo, beware!" the doge cried from the gondola. The palace doors had burst open, and a dozen of Orlando's guards poured out. Rodrigo thrust the women to safety behind him, then beat back the guards one after another as they swarmed toward him up the palace walls. With bloodcurdling screams they fell to their deaths on the docks, their blood spattering the pale marble. When the last man had been dispatched, Rodrigo turned back for Bianca. "Now, my love, let us fly—"

"Not so fast, Rodrigo," came a deep, chilling voice from within the palace window. Out stepped Orlando, tall and slim and mustachioed, dressed all in black, with a long, lethal sword in his hand.

"Swine," Rodrigo spat at him, lowering his own bloodied sword. "Come and have at it, and I'll send you to hell with the rest of your pigs."

Orlando advanced on him along the narrow balcony. "You were a servant fighting servants," he said derisively, surveying the dead soldiers below him with no hint of regret. "But now you face the master. I shall finish you off, and then that mewling old man, and then I shall be the grand doge of Venice—and fair Bianca mine to do with what I will."

"You will never be doge," Rodrigo told him bravely, "and you never shall have Bianca! On guard!"

He sprang at his opponent, his sword flashing in a great arc. A wild, deadly fight ensued in the narrow confines of the balcony. Rodrigo's mobility was hampered by the two women huddled behind him for protection; Bianca watched the lethal contest with wide eyes, but Esmeralda covered her face with her hands and screamed.

The air rang with the clangor of steel upon steel. In the gondola the grand doge watched impotently as Rodrigo fought with valiant desperation to save the republic and fair Bianca's honor. But the strength of the evil Orlando was too great; he landed a blow to Rodrigo's shoulder that sent a great fountain of blood spurting, and Rodrigo's sword went flying over the edge of the balcony.

"I've got you now," Orlando snarled, coming in for the kill. "Prepare to die, lackey scum!" Esmeralda screamed, and Bianca sobbed. But just as Orlando moved toward him, Rodrigo whipped a dagger from his boot, ducked low beneath the flashing sword, and thrust the dagger deep into Orlando's heart.

Orlando clutched his chest, letting his sword fall, and collapsed across the balcony railing, panting and gasping for breath as blood seeped through his hands. "Thus dies . . . my dream for Venice," he cried, writhing in the throes of death.

Rodrigo stared at him coolly. "Thus die every usurper's dream." Orlando clung for a long moment to the railing, and then plunged head over heels to the dock below, landing with a gut-wrenching thud.

"Rodrigo!" Bianca cried, her face wreathed in smiles. "Oh, my brave Rodrigo!"

"I must take you to your father now." He grabbed her up in one arm, grabbed the rope with the other, and stepped off the edge of the balcony, swinging toward the boat where the doge was waiting. With a mighty cry of victory he let go of the rope and leaped into the gondola, which promptly broke apart into pieces with a resounding crash.

Doge and daughter and the brave Rodrigo went tumbling onto the hard, blue-painted water of the canal. Bianca's golden wig flew off her head and landed in Orlando's lap. The dead men on the docks burst out laughing, and Esmeralda nearly fell off the balcony because she was giggling so hard. The doge picked himself up slowly, rubbing a sore shin, and glared at fair Bianca's rescuer. "Goddammit, Dick," he snapped, "now look what you've done!"

"Sorry, Father," the red-faced Rodrigo mumbled. "Here, Willie, are you all right?" He offered his hand to Bianca, pulling the boy to his feet in a flurry of tangled skirts. Orlando had risen from the dead and was doubled over on the docks, helpless with hilarity, holding Willie's wig. Willie stopped laughing long enough to feel a sudden cool breeze on his backside; he groped at the waistband of his gown.

"Jesus Christ, I've torn my bleeding dress!"

"That's all I need!" James Burbage roared, yanking off his grand doge's turban and stomping on it. "That and a bloody gondola that's in eight million pieces. How in God's name any son of mine can be so bloody clumsy—''

''I said I was sorry,'' Dick tried to apologize again.

''Aye, well, sorry doesn't fix the gondola, does it, or my shin, or Willie's bleeding gown!''

''James, James.'' Toby Mifflin, costumed as the evil Orlando, tried to smooth things over even as he kept laughing. ''I can fix the gondola by tomorrow. Don't worry; we'll open on time.''

''Or,'' Willie Reilly suggested, twisting to peer at the rip in his skirts, ''we could always set the play someplace else. Someplace without canals.'' The men on the docks lost any semblance of lifelessness at this suggestion, rolling onto their backs and flailing their legs in the air.

James Burbage surveyed them coolly. ''Since everyone is having such a bloody good time, why don't we just run through the whole fifth act once more?'' he proposed, and the laughter turned to loud groans.

''But, Father, how can we,'' Dick asked, ''with the gondola smashed?''

''We'll pretend,'' The Theatre's owner snapped. ''We're players, aren't we? That's our job, to pretend.'' He clapped his hands. ''Set the stage for Act Five, scene one. Willie, for God's sake, show my knuckleheaded son how to swing down on that rope.'' Willie grabbed his wig from Toby and tugged it on, then clambered nimbly back up the rope to the balcony, hand over hand.

''It's simple, Dick, truly it is,'' he said, and pushed off from the balcony railing to sail down to the dock in a perfect arc.

''Simple for you, maybe,'' Dick muttered as his father stomped off the stage with a ferocious roar:

''More blood! More blood and more gore, that's what I want to see this time! That's what the people pay their pennies for!''

Willie and Dick ducked behind the facade of the grand *palazzi* of Venice, and this time Willie took a ladder up to the platform behind the windows that showed from the front of the stage. Tom Shoemaker, playing the loyal Esmeralda, joined him there, grabbing his arm. ''Here, feel this.'' He clapped Willie's hand to his chin.

"Feel what?" Willie asked, puzzled.

"Can't you tell? My beard's coming in at last! No more of this bloody makeup and skirts and wood heels for me," the boy said proudly. "I'm going to play the heroes instead of stupid old Dick."

"Don't call Dick names," Willie muttered absently.

Tom cocked his head. "You're weird, Willie, do you know that?"

But just then James Burbage bellowed up at them: "Willie, Tom! Get your asses out through those windows now!"

The second run-through of the act went smoothly enough, considering that there wasn't any gondola, and Burbage pronounced himself satisfied with the performance at last. Tired and thirsty, the players trooped down to the dressing room below the stage. "Willie!" Burbage shouted from the door to his office. "Get in here and let me see that dress!" Willie dutifully followed him into the small, cluttered room, overflowing with bits of costumes and vials of cosmetics and scraps of paper on which The Theatre's owner was always jotting down ideas for improving the plays. He shut the door behind Willie and turned him around, examining the rip in his skirts. "Well, better the back than the front, I suppose, eh? By the by, Willie Reilly, you've got a new nickname from your multitude of admirers."

"Have I? What?"

"Toby heard it last night. They are calling you the Rose of Shoreditch." Willie's back stiffened, and Burbage looked down at him curiously. "What's the matter? Don't you like it?"

"I'm not all that fond of roses, sir."

Burbage caught Willie's chin in his hand and looked into his green eyes. "Is anything the matter?" he asked, his loud actor's voice softening.

"I'm just tired, sir."

Burbage grunted. "Aren't we all? 'Tis a hell of a life, the stage. I tried to tell you."

"Oh, it's not that, sir. I love the work, honestly I do."

"Well, you're still new at it. Just wait—the excitement wears off after thirty years." Then he frowned. "I'd better go see about that damned gondola. Can you fix that gown yourself?''

Willie grinned and nodded. "That's just another of the advantages I neglected to mention when I came to you for this job.''

Burbage laughed and yanked Willie's fake blond curls. "The bloody Rose of Shoreditch," he muttered, shaking his head. "Who would ever have imagined it three months ago, eh? See you later at the Mermaid?'' Willie nodded, and Burbage went out, leaving him alone.

The Rose of Shoreditch sat down in front of the looking glass, tugged off the blond wig, and ran her fingers through her close-cropped black curls. Then she took a rag from the pile beside the mirror and rubbed the white paint and rouge from her cheeks. As her own face emerged from beneath the layers of makeup Toby had taught her to apply, she studied the image thoughtfully. It was astonishing what a difference the short hair made; sometimes when she caught a glimpse of her reflection in a window nowadays she herself thought she was a boy.

Her plan had gone far more smoothly than she ever expected when she fled Lockhaven Hall on that chilly March evening. She'd snatched a shirt and a pair of breeches from some unlucky farm wife's laundry line near Hucknall; she tore her gray dress into strips and wound them around herself to flatten her breasts. Her hair she hacked off as close to the roots as she could with a sharp stone; it wasn't pretty, but it did the job. No one in Hucknall recognized her as she trudged into town, barefoot and dusty; the kindly candyseller she'd done business with so often cursed her for a beggar and chased her away from his stall. Reassured by that success, she started off southward, begging a ride from a farmer with a cart. He took her as far as Derby; from there she begged another ride, and another, walking when begging failed. Five days later, sunburned and dirt-encrusted, she reached the gates of London Town.

She made her way to Shoreditch; in her rolled-up breeches and filthy shirt she strolled all along Barkers Lane and March Street and the square, passing not three feet away from old Nell Harper. She even begged a bit of day-old bread from Alf Smith at the baker's shop. When none of her friends so much as blinked to see her, she screwed up her courage and went to the Mermaid Tavern, cornering James Burbage there.

"I want to be a player, sir," she announced as he sat with his companions, drinking and playing cards.

"Sure you do, lad," said The Theatre's owner. "Doesn't everybody? Who knows what's trump?"

"I can read and write and tumble and dance and sing," Lucy told him stubbornly.

"Is it diamonds, then?" Burbage asked, not looking up from his hand.

One of the other men at the table, a tall, slim fellow with lazy dark eyes, was looking at Lucy. He nudged James Burbage. "Take a peek, James. Under all that dirt there's a handsome boy." He wet his kerchief in his mug of ale and wiped dust from Lucy's cheek. "No beard yet. How old are you, son?"

How old should she be? Lucy wondered. "Thirteen."

"There, you see?" the man with the dark eyes appealed to Burbage. "He's got two more good years in him. Turn around, son." Lucy did. "Good long legs, a strong back, and a pretty face—what more could you want?"

"Watch out, boy," another of the men at the table warned, and laughed. "Toby's taken with you."

Burbage glanced up from his cards. "Look at him; he's fifteen if he's a day. What year were you born, boy?"

"Seventy-three, sir," Lucy told him, calculating rapidly. "I'm just tall for my age."

"Where are you from?"

"Born in Shoreditch, sir. But I've been living out in the country. At my uncle's."

Burbage grunted. "Run away, have you? Where are your parents?"

"They're both dead. Sir, if you'd just hear me sing—"

"Let's hear him, James," the man named Toby urged. "What harm could it do?"

"It could interrupt my bloody card game when I am winning," Burbage rumbled in his rich actor's voice, glaring at Lucy.

"Tom's not getting any younger, you know," Toby told

him, nodding toward a freckle-faced youth who was watching the game.

"Oh, for God's sake, all right," Burbage snapped. "But be quick about it. Jesus, if you knew how sick I am of listening to every Tom, Dick, and Harry who comes around here—"

Toby reached for a lute by his chair. "What's your name, son?"

"Willie," said Lucy. That was for her father. "Willie Reilly." That last was for Joe.

"Well, Willie Reilly." Toby toyed with the tuning pegs. "How about 'O Western Wind,' do you know that one?" Lucy nodded, and he strummed a chord. She took a deep breath and began to sing.

She was shaky at first, and the boy with the freckles snickered, but by the time she reached the refrain she had found her full voice:

> O Western wind, when wilt thou blow,
> That the small rain down can rain?
> Christ, that my love were in my arms,
> And I in my bed again!

The clamor in the noisy tavern slowly died away. Burbage forgot his cards and leaned back in his chair, watching Lucy closely. She sang all the verses she knew, and as she sang she found herself thinking of the time that Bram had made love to her in his bed at Lockhaven Hall, surrounded by candles. When she finished the song there were tears in her eyes.

No one said anything for what seemed a very long time. Then Toby set down the lute. "Ever been in love, Willie Reilly?" he asked.

Lucy forced a laugh. "What, me, sir? At my age?"

Burbage cleared his throat. "Come round to The Theatre tomorrow morning, lad, and we'll see what else you can do."

"Yes, sir!" Lucy told him happily.

The next day he had her read from a script, the part of Bianca, and do somersaults and pretend to die a tragic death and leap from the balcony down to the stage. Afterward he took her into his office and offered her a job with the troupe, at two shillings the week. Not until then did Lucy confess to the trick she had played, knowing that in the close confines of The Theatre her deception would be far easier to carry off with Burbage's help.

He exploded. She had to use all her powers of persuasion just to keep him from tossing her out on her ear. "Think of it, sir," she pleaded. "My voice won't ever change; I'm not going to grow a beard. And I already know how to act like a woman—"

"Exactly!" he roared. "It's a boy you don't know how to be!"

"Begging your pardon, sir, but I fooled you last night, and all the others, too."

He let out a short, unamused laugh. "So you did. But how long do you think you could go on fooling them?"

"It wouldn't be forever, sir. Just until I have time to save some money, make other plans."

"It's against the law."

"Nobody but you would know, sir. And if somehow the authorities did find out, I'd swear up and down that you didn't."

"Sooner or later someone would be bound to recognize you."

"You didn't, and you just watched me for two hours straight. Besides," Lucy argued earnestly, "I'll be all the way up on the stage, in a costume and wig—"

But Burbage shook his head. "I'm sorry, girl, but it's just too risky. The answer is no."

"Oh, but sir, you've got to let me try. You don't even have to pay me anything for the first month; I'll work for free. I'll make money for you, I know I can."

That caught his attention. "God knows we need money," he admitted reluctantly. "And you do sing like an angel. Which reminds me." He tipped her chin toward him, searching her eyes. "You lied last night, didn't you? Not just about being a boy, but about never having been in love." Lucy nodded. "Hurt you badly, did he?" She nodded again. "Hmph," he said. "And would it be a pregnant boy actor I was hiring?"

"No, sir." To her enormous relief, Lucy had begun her

menses just that morning. She couldn't bear to think what she would have done if she'd been carrying Bram's child.

Burbage leaned back in his chair and sighed. "I remember your father, Lucy Jones, from the old days. Lord, he was a winsome soul; he could have talked a Scotsman into giving him his last penny. Full of big dreams he always was. Big dreams, big plans."

"He was a great talker, was Pop." Lucy smiled remembering him too.

"After your shop burned down, the gossips said you threw yourself in the Thames and drowned. Did you know that?" She shook her head. "I never believed it myself; there was too much of your father in you for giving up. Still, I never imagined you'd turn up on my doorstep and talk me into a harebrained, cockamamie scheme like—"

"Talk you into? Do you mean you'll let me? That I can stay?"

"We'll try it. For one month. With no pay."

"Oh, thank you, sir!"

"What the hell." He grinned. "I'd put a naked Chinaman on stage if I thought it would bring in the audiences. Why not try a girl?" He raised a cautionary finger. "Mind you, if anyone finds out, both of our gooses are cooked for sure."

"They won't, sir. I swear it."

"See that they don't. Have you got a place to live? No? There's a spare pallet in my attic; you can put up there."

Lucy reached for his hand. "You won't be sorry, sir."

"Hmph," said James Burbage. "You've got exactly one month to prove that to me."

Lucy had proved it. Right from her first performance she was the talk of Shoreditch; the pit was filled every night thereafter with Willie Reilly's admirers. She worked hard, she didn't complain, and she earned her keep. Her secret stayed a secret. And here she was, three months later, the Rose of Shoreditch.

Being a boy, Lucy thought, making a face at her reflection in Burbage's mirror, wasn't nearly as hard as being a lady. And best of all, she was back with her own kind of people, back where she belonged.

She took off her gown and put on a shirt and breeches,

then walked through the familiar streets of the city to the Mermaid for a good, honest tankard of ale.

She found Tom Shoemaker sitting in his usual corner, where he had the best vantage point from which to see buxom Emmie, the barmaid, each time she leaned down to work the taps. "What do you think it's like?" he asked, sighing happily as Emmie's hefty bosom strained against the low-cut white linen of her bodice.

"What do I think what's like?" Lucy asked, signaling the barmaid for a half pint.

"You know," Tom hissed. "Getting your hands on them."

"Jesus, don't you ever think of anything else but that?" Lucy asked, and laughed.

"What else is there?" Tom leered at Emmie as she brought Lucy's mug and reached out to pinch her.

"Grow up," the barmaid told him, with a withering glance.

"I am grown up," the boy boasted. "My beard's coming in; want to feel it?"

"By God, I think you're right," Emmie told him, bending down for a closer look. "Now, how would you like to feel something?" As Tom, wide-eyed, reached for her breasts she grabbed his crotch; the rest of the players roared with laughter as he yelped in pain. "Maybe that'll teach ye to pull in yer eyeballs," Emmie said sweetly, and sashayed away.

"I don't know what you're laughing at," Tom told Toby Mifflin, lashing out at the closest target in his hot embarrassment. "At least I like women; at least I'm not queer!"

"Tom!" Lucy said in shock.

But Toby only grinned and said, "Who says I don't like women? I adore Emmie."

"And I'd sooner have Toby pinch me," Emmie told Tom, "than a snot-nosed boy." She gave Toby a lusty kiss, and Tom, wounded and defeated, hobbled off in misery to the other side of the room.

Lucy knew well enough what Tom had meant. Not long after she'd joined the troupe, Toby asked her out to dinner. She'd had a marvelous time listening to the stories he had to tell about life at The Theatre; the food had been splendid, and so had the ale; they had talked for hours. Then, while they were walking home, Toby stopped in a shadowy doorway and tried to kiss her. Lucy's first thought was that Burbage must have told him her secret, but as she pulled away from his embrace he smiled ruefully and said, "I'm sorry. I shouldn't have done that, Willie. Have I shocked you?"

"N-no," Lucy said, as it dawned on her that he did think she was a boy.

"I only thought—there is something about you, Willie Reilly. Something special. You're not like Tom, always panting over anything in a skirt."

"I haven't got time for such nonsense," she told him. "I've got too much to learn about The Theatre."

"Hard-working Willie." Toby held out his hand. "My mistake. No offense intended. I hope we can still be friends."

"No offense taken," said Lucy, smiling. "I hope so, too." And they shook on it.

They had become friends. Burbage was in charge of words and action on The Theatre's stage, but Toby was its master of illusion. It was he who could paint a length of wood to look like a palace in Venice, or create out of cheap wool and paste gems a dazzling gown. It was through his skill with cosmetics and paint that freckle-faced Tom became an Italian maidservant, or young Dick Burbage a wrinkled old man. He even wrote the music for Burbage's productions, and the ferocious villains he played had earned him the fierce devotion of the crowds in the groundling pit.

He came and sat beside Lucy now in the seat Tom had vacated. "Thanks for springing to my defense," he said wryly, "but Tom didn't mean anything by it; he's just a foolish boy. Can I buy you more ale?"

"No, thanks." Lucy frowned at her mug. "Funny. The ale here doesn't taste as good as I—"

"As good as you what?" he asked curiously.

As good as I remember, Lucy had almost said. She laughed instead. "As good as I always expect it to after such a hard day. It went well, don't you think? Except for the gondola, of course."

"Well enough." Lucy knew by now that he never liked to jinx a new play by praising it before the opening. "James ought to be pleased. There's enough blood on that stage at the end to fill a Venetian canal."

"Well, that's what the audiences want, isn't it, just as he says? Plenty of blood and gore?"

Toby shrugged. "Maybe. Or maybe we just give them that because it's easier."

"Easier than what?"

"I don't know. You take Orlando. He's evil incarnate. Rotten to the core, just like every other villain I've ever played on that stage."

"And what's wrong with that?"

"Real people aren't like that—one-sided, with no redeeming qualities at all." He waved his hand impatiently. "Even the worst cutthroat degenerate ought to have some virtue. He might keep terriers, or look after his poor aged mother. Anything to earn him some sympathy."

"The audience isn't supposed to sympathize with the villain," Lucy protested.

"Why not? Aristotle said every tragic hero should have one fatal flaw. I think every villain should have one fatal niceness."

"You've got strange notions," Lucy told him, but she was smiling. That was why she liked talking to Toby; he made her mind stretch.

"It's not strange at all. Think now, just for a moment, of the person you hate the most in all the world." Lucy thought of Bram. Toby chuckled. "My, you do hate whoever it is, don't you? What a face! Isn't there something, one tiny little thing about that person that you like or admire?"

"No!" Lucy said emphatically. But in her mind she was picturing Bram sitting patiently on the floor of the armory next to Minnie, his big hands struggling to tie a red bow around Reggie's neck. And the way he would make Stacy happy by letting himself be beaten at backgammon again and again . . . or, oh God, the way he'd made love to her, the touch of his hands, his mouth on her skin while he whispered her name . . . But she must not think of that; she would not think of that. Only at night, alone in her cot in James Burbage's attic, did she let herself surrender to those sweet, seductive memories.

"Liar," Toby said softly. "There is, too. I see it in your green eyes, Willie Reilly. And that's what I mean. In real life people aren't purely evil like Orlando or purely good like Rodrigo. That's what makes real life so interesting."

"Interesting." Lucy laughed shortly, bitterly. "People don't come to The Theatre for real life, Toby. People have had it to here with real life. They come for a spectacle, for a show."

"That's what we give them," Toby mused. "But sometimes I can't help wondering—who's to say they wouldn't like it better if Rodrigo fell there at the end and smashed the gondola to pieces? If he wasn't perfect?"

"Or if Orlando kept dogs."

"Aye, if Orlando kept dogs. Then instead of just cheering madly when Rodrigo kills me, they'd feel sorrow, too."

"Why would you want them to feel sorry for the villain?"

"Death ought to be sad no matter who's doing the dying," Toby said softly.

"I don't know about that. I can think of one person I'd be glad to see dead." That was what Bram deserved, wasn't it, for what he and his cronies had done to Joe Reilly? But just the thought of his dying made Lucy's stomach churn. She changed the subject quickly back to safer things. "Why don't you write a play like that if you're so sure it would work?"

"I'm no wordsmith or I would."

"What does James think about all this, pray tell?"

"He says I'm mad. 'All we need is blood!' he keeps saying. 'Blood and more blood!' " Lucy laughed at Toby's imitation of Burbage's thunderous voice. "Dick agrees with me, though," he went on, to Lucy's surprise.

"Does he really?"

Toby nodded. "That young man's star will eclipse his father's one of these days."

"Dick?" Lucy said in disbelief, looking across the tavern at James Burbage's gangly son.

"Aye. You'll see. Someday a playwright will come along who is brave enough to hold a mirror right up to the world, create villains and heroes that every one of us can see ourselves in. Dick has got the vision and the range to portray them. Mark my words, Willie, his name will go down in history.''

"Willie! Willie Reilly!" James Burbage roared from his table. "Give us a song to distract these cardsharps; they are beating the breeches off me!"

A chorus of other voices echoed him: "Aye, let's have a song!"

"A song from the Rose of Shoreditch!"

Toby grinned at Lucy. "Pity you won't be around to play the heroine to Dick's heroes; your beard is sure to come in before then."

That's what you think, Lucy said to herself, and got up to sing.

Chapter 15

"I *won't*," said Minnie, and stomped her foot. "I won't, and there's nothing you can do that will make me."

Bram Carlyle set his brandy glass down on the floor and knelt before her. "Please, Minnie," he pleaded. "Be a good girl. Put Reggie down and get in the tub."

"No!" she said even more vehemently, and the cat spat and clawed Bram's hand.

"Dammit, Minnie, I am tired of fighting with you over every little thing I ask you to do. You need a bath!"

"I hate baths," she told him coldly. "And I hate you."

"Stacy." Bram turned to the boy reading in the window seat of the nursery. "Talk to your sister."

"Go to hell," said Stacy, not looking up from his book.

"I've had about all I intend to take of your insolence, young man," Bram snapped, scowling fiercely.

"Leave him alone, why don't you?" Minnie cried. "It's your fault, not his, that Lucy ran away!"

"Minerva Carlyle, get in that bloody tub!"

"Make me," said Minnie, and stuck out her tongue.

Bram drew a long, deep breath. "Jem, for God's sake, can't you handle this?"

"Don't look at me, sir," the maid told him. "I can't do a thing with 'em, never could. Only Miss Lucy—"

"I am sick to death of hearing about Lucy!" Bram said explosively. "Lucy this, Lucy that—listen to the lot of you! Lockhaven Hall existed before Lucy Jones ever came here. We had a life before she came here."

"Not much of a one," Stacy said icily from the window seat. Bram snatched up his brandy glass and stormed from the room before he said or did something he would regret.

233

In the corridor he leaned against the wall, drinking thirstily, refilling the glass from the flask he always carried with him now. Enough brandy in him and he could almost forget his pain, the memory of the hell of that chilly spring evening when he'd come up from the music room to find that Lucy was gone.

The children were right, of course. It was his fault she'd left them. Christ, why had he pressed his luck? Why couldn't he have been content to watch her and love her from afar? But he knew the answer: because his need for her had burned in him like wildfire, torturing him, consuming him; he couldn't concentrate, couldn't think, couldn't breathe. Because she was a miracle worker; because she had brought the children out of the darkness and into the light. Because he had hoped and prayed she could save him, too. What was it she had said at Christmastide? *Love isn't something to be afraid of.* And those words had given him the courage to take those first few hesitant steps out of the hell he had lived in since the night Olive died.

At least she hadn't told Minnie and Stacy why she was leaving; at least she had spared him that humiliation. She had simply disappeared from their lives the same way she had entered them, as abruptly as that year's strange, sudden spring.

He walked down the corridor toward the old wing, clutching the brandy glass and the flask, and the ghost rose up before him: Olive as she'd looked that last night in her splendid silk gown, the lovely face he had fallen in love with turned haughty and cold. The angry, bitter words she'd flung at him still rang in his ears. Desperately he downed more brandy, but even its numbing power couldn't drown out what she'd said. *Yes, he's my lover. Yes, I'm going to him now. And do you want to know why, Bram, do you? Shall I tell you why?* God, why wouldn't that ghost let him rest? Damn his memory, damn her for what she had done—

Because he is a man, Bram, and you are nothing but a boy. Relentlessly his mind played out the scene. *I found that out on the night we were wed. You've never satisfied me, never made me feel like a woman—*

He stared at the ghost in horror, remembering his

wretched confusion: *You lie,* he had whispered. *I know that you lie.*

And she laughed. *Why? Because when you climb onto me I whimper and moan? That was lies, Bram. That was when I lied.*

Olive, for pity's sake! You don't mean that.

For pity's sake, that was why I did it! Out of pity for you, you sad little boy!

Hush, Olive! Hush. The children.

The children.

Oh, God, ghost, don't say it!

The children? Do you think those children are yours? You couldn't give me children, you're not a man! They are his children, Bram, not yours.

No. No, you're lying, it is all lies!

Useless, the ghost snarled.

No!

No better in bed than a eunuch—

No!

Pitiful puny mewling humping little boy!

That was when he had gone for her.

When she was dead, when her laughter stopped, he might as well have killed himself, for he was sure in his heart that her words had been true. She would know; she was so much older, more experienced than he. That was what attracted him, virgin, scarcely fifteen years old, to her, that sly seductive power that she oozed. Eve, evil, friend of the snake, she knew; it was true. When she lay dead, the fire in his loins had died, too.

Then the governesses began, greedy daughters sent by their greedy fathers, after his gold; they had flirted and flaunted themselves before him, preening like peacocks, trying to beguile him into marriage. But he felt nothing, no glimmer of heat, no spark of fire; he saw Olive's ghost in their eyes, heard the words she had flung at him. And one by one, thwarted, they packed their silk gowns and jewels and went home again.

But then there had been one girl . . .

One girl that he opened the door to in London on a steamy summer night—a girl with tangled black hair and flushed cheeks and eyes green as apple leaves. One girl, long-legged and lithe as a bird, lying by the goose pond, her white feet dangling in the cool blue water, singing to the sky. And his long-dead heart had heaved up in his chest at the sight. And—oh, worker of miracles, Lucy, light-bringer—the fire had flared in his loins again.

She hadn't wanted his money. She hadn't wanted anything from him except that he love those children the way she thought he should. *I don't know, sir. They're your children.* And by God, she had done what he thought was impossible: exorcised Olive's ghost, stilled that harping voice of accusation, so that he was free to love them again as if they were his own. And by the time he did, he was head over heels in love with her, too.

Hating himself, knowing what it would cost him, he went into her room, stared at the bed she had slept in, the things she had touched, the clothes she had worn, that once had been next to her skin. That skin, whiter than almond-milk. Her hair black as midnight, falling in soft, shining waves. Her proud, high breasts crowned with rosered nipples. The curve of her thigh in his hand— Christ, Christ, he remembered it all; the fire had burned her image into his heart forever. And her eyes, those emerald eyes, clear and far-seeing and brave. Those eyes—*Love isn't something to be afraid of*—that had given him courage, the courage to touch her, to try, to make love again after all those years of loneliness and shame.

But even she had been able to tell, virgin though she was. She lay beneath him silent and still as death; God, she hadn't even had the art to feign her pleasure as Olive had. That one brief cry of pain, that was all he had caused her; no fire, no flame. And when he had finished, when he had made love to her as best as he knew how, when his seed burst into her and he fell against her, shuddering, still she said nothing, and he knew once and for all that the angry words Olive screamed at him were the truth.

Coward, failure, still he could not bear to relinquish his love for her, and had scribbled that hasty note: *If you don't want to, I will understand.* And then she sat up in his bed, still so unspeakably beautiful, this angel that he had ruined, and he could not look at her, could not stand to see the ghost of Olive in those wide, proud eyes.

And when he came back she was gone. It was no more than he had expected; it was why he delayed his return as long as he could that day, even first summoned Babington to the music room. He would have done anything to prolong his hope, put off the inevitable moment when he walked through this great, empty, echoing house and knew, finally, that the answer to his question was no.

He looked at himself in her mirror. Two ghosts now stared back at him: Olive's, hers. There would be no more; he would not try again. The monk's walk, that would be home to him for the rest of his days.

"Here's to you, ladies," he whispered, draining the brandy he held and then hurling the cup—empty cup, empty loins, empty life—at the looking glass. His reflection shattered into thousands of bright shining shards, pieces of a man, not a man.

As the silvered glass flew through the room, a sheet of parchment fell at his feet. Messages to the dead from the living. He bent over, staggering, to pick it up, and scanned it with brandy-clouded eyes.

His head cleared instantly.

"Father? We heard a noise—"

He whirled toward the bedchamber door. Minnie and Stacy, wide-eyed, fearful. "Father, what is it?" Minnie whispered. "What have you got there?"

He folded the letter from the queen of the Scots into a small, neat square and tucked it into his doublet. "I have to go away," he said steadily. "On business."

"When will you be back?" Stacy asked.

"As soon as I—" He stopped. "As soon as I can."

"Thus die every usurper's dream!" the dashing Rodrigo declared. Orlando contorted in great, lurching spasms of death, then slowly fell over the railing of the balcony to the dock below.

"Rodrigo! Oh, my brave Rodrigo!" Bianca cried.

"I must take you to your father now."

Lucy held her breath as Dick tucked her under his arm and swung down from the balcony toward the reconstructed gondola; she imagined everyone else in the company was doing the same. But this time Dick landed cleanly; the ship held together; Dick headed back up the rope for Tom while Bianca tearfully embraced her father the doge.

"Would that I might give you my Bianca's hand in marriage, Rodrigo," the doge said sadly when they were all assembled in the gondola, and a shout went up from the crowd in the pit: "Give 'er to 'im!"

"But alas," the doge went on, a bit more loudly, "though loyal and true, you are but a low-born servant—"

"Oh, no, 'e ain't!" a woman in the pit shrilled.

"And as such, unfit to marry her," the doge concluded above a growing swell of cries of "Tell 'im, Rodrigo!" "Tell 'im who ye is!"

"Milord." Rodrigo made a jaunty bow. "I must confess that I have deceived you. When first I came to Venice long years ago and joined your service, I withheld my true identity from you. My name is not Rodrigo."

"What's this?" the doge screamed, and fair Bianca gasped.

"My father sent me abroad to learn more of life than mere bookish lore," Rodrigo continued, "so that when my time came to succeed him I might rule wisely and well."

"Succeed him?" echoed the doge.

"Aye, milord. My father is Frederico, the king of Naples. And I am Alfonso, his only son and heir."

"Alfonso, Prince of Naples—" The doge stared at him. "Can it be? The son of the noble Frederico, my ally and friend?" Laughing, he embraced the man he'd thought a servant, kissing both his cheeks, and a satisfied sigh rose from the audience. "Gladly then do I give you my Bianca's hand," he cried, leading the happy couple forward. "Let the nuptial celebrations begin!"

The crowd applauded wildly at this grand conclusion, and tossed flowers at the stage as Lucy and Dick came forward hand in hand to take their bows. "Willie!" they shouted. "Hooray for Willie Reilly! Hooray for the Rose of Shoreditch!"

Toby got up in his blood-spattered doublet to take his bows, to a chorus of good-natured boos and hisses for his villainy. And he wants to give them real life, Lucy thought wryly, looking out at the delirious throng. In real life Rodrigo would never have turned out to be a prince. And if he had any damned sense, he'd have steered far clear of the nobility of Venice and all their intrigues.

The audience slowly gave up applauding and drifted toward home, well satisfied with their pennies' worth of blood and gore. The players adjourned to the dressing rooms, where the usual mayhem that attended a successful opening prevailed. Lucy, engaged in a furious shoe-hurling battle with Tom, heard her name called above the uproar and saw James Burbage gesturing to her from his office door. Leaping out of the path of a flying sandal, she climbed over the benches toward him, wigless but still clad in her woman's gown.

"What's up, then?" she asked, ducking another well-aimed shoe. Burbage caught it and winged it back at Tom, landing a blow that made the freckled boy yelp.

"Keep the noise down," Burbage roared, "we've got a visitor!" Then he pulled Lucy into the office and shut the door.

Toby was already inside, with another man, bald and hugely fat, whom Lucy had never seen before. One look at his gleaming black boots, his embroidered doublet and golden rings, and she knew he was a nobleman. On guard, she stood as Burbage made introductions: "Sir Christopher Dalton, may I present my co-shareholder in The Theatre, Tobias Mifflin. And of course, Willie Reilly, the Rose of Shoreditch."

"An honor," Dalton told Toby, and then to Lucy, "A very great honor." His fleshy palm swallowed hers. "I came to The Theatre today solely because of what I heard about you, young man. I must say, you didn't disappoint me. Splendid singing. A remarkable actor, too."

"Thank you, sir," said Lucy, wondering what all this was about.

"Now then, Sir Christopher, I believe you wanted to propose some sort of investment to Toby and me?" Burbage asked, and Lucy understood then that this was about money, of which The Theatre and its owners were perennially short. Attendance had been up lately, a fact Burbage attributed in part to Willie Reilly, but expenses were rising, too. There were plays to be commissioned, players to be paid, scenery and props and costumes to be secured, advertising bills to be printed—not to mention money for the copious amounts of ale downed each night in the Mermaid, and sums lost at cards. To top it all, Lucy knew, the landlord who owned the spot of ground on which The Theatre was built had just raised the rent again.

"Hm. Yes," Dalton drawled, settling back down in Burbage's favorite chair. It let out a creak of protest, and Lucy hoped it wouldn't break beneath his great weight. "Most of the acting troupes in the city, as I'm sure you're aware, enjoy the patronage of some great lord at court. There are the earl of Warwick's men, the lord chamberlain's, the lord admiral's—"

"As you say," Toby noted dryly, "we are aware of that fact. Could you get on with it, please? We've all had a long day."

"Just take your time, Sir Christopher," Burbage said quickly, and glared at Toby, mouthing, "Shut up!"

"Yes. Well. Then you also must know that having such a patron increases the prestige of a theatrical company immeasurably."

"Prestige be damned," said Toby. "What we need is cash."

Dalton shot him a withering look and addressed himself solely to Burbage. "Such patrons also serve the purpose of calling a particular troupe to her majesty's attention. And I need not tell you—"

"But you will." Toby sighed.

"—the advantages of that. Command performances for the queen provide immeasurable honor—not to mention publicity that money can't buy—to any troupe fortunate enough to secure them."

"Don't we know it," Burbage said longingly.

Sir Christopher Dalton toyed with his heavy golden chains. "You, Master Burbage, have no patron."

"No," Burbage confessed, with a hint of apology. "We haven't. Not yet. We're still a fledgling company compared with some of the others."

"Nonetheless, you have managed to build a reputation of sorts. A reputation enhanced considerably by the addition of this young man to your company." Dalton smiled at Lucy, a big, greasy smile.

"You are very kind, Sir Christopher," Burbage said humbly. Lucy bit her cheek at the deference the proud actor was showing this pompous man. The things folks will do for money, she thought bemusedly.

"Yes. Well, suppose, Master Burbage, I was to tell you that there is a group of noblemen at court, very notable ones, who are interested in becoming your patrons."

"Who?" Toby demanded.

"I am not at the moment at liberty to say. But I can assure you they are all close to the queen's ear—very close indeed."

"Leicester," Toby guessed. "Is it Leicester? Or maybe Northampton?"

"I am not, at the moment—"

"I know, I know. At liberty to say." Toby's sloe eyes held a speculative gleam as he looked at Burbage, who was stroking his chin.

"The problem with patronage, I've heard," he said slowly, "is interference."

"Interference, Master Burbage?"

"Aye. These noblemen lend you their name, and then they're always expecting you to put on some bloody masque for their daughter's wedding or the birth of their child."

Dalton's laughter was rich and thick and heavy. "I can assure you, you wouldn't have to worry about that with these lords. No, all they would ask in return for their invaluable patronage is, of course, the boys."

"The boys?" Toby's voice was suddenly sharp.

Dalton smiled at Lucy. "That one in particular. I know my masters' tastes, and he is just the type. Of course, they might want the other one, too, now and then, for a change. Or both, perhaps."

Toby got to his feet. "You fat bloody pimp," he said in disbelief, while Burbage and Lucy stared at the knight, astonished by his bald temerity. "You big, slimy, pandering barrel of lard. Get out of here before I throw you out."

"I beg your pardon!" Dalton huffed.

"You heard me," Toby told him. "Out. Out!" He

yanked the knight's golden chains, pulling him straight out of Burbage's chair, and shoved him toward the door, his face an awful vision of rage; not for nothing had he been playing villains for twenty years.

"How dare you handle me this way!" Sir Christopher Dalton bleated. "Why, you're nothing but theater scum, the lot of you!"

"And tell your bleeding lords to stick their patronage right here!" Toby bellowed, landing a kick squarely in the center of the knight's wide rump, which sent him tripping through the door that Burbage had thoughtfully opened. He careened into one of the benches, staggered to his feet, and was hit in the head by a shoe untimely thrown by Tom.

"Sorry, your honor, sir!" The frightened boy gulped.

"Don't be!" Toby roared. "Hit the bastard with everything you've got!"

"Really?" asked another of the players.

"Really!" Toby hurled a rouge pot himself; the others joined in gleefully, and Dalton, bright red and shaking, fled up the stairs.

"You'll regret this!" he shouted in parting. "I'll see to it that you never play before the queen, by God!"

Toby growled ferociously and started after him with a prop sword. Besmirched with lampblack and walnut juice and paint, Sir Christopher Dalton turned tail and disappeared.

"The bloody nerve," Burbage muttered, shaking his head. Lucy giggled. "What's so funny?"

"I was just picturing what those patrons' faces might have looked like," she whispered, "when they got Willie Reilly undressed!"

Burbage chuckled, but he quickly sobered as Toby came back to join them. "You shouldn't have gone after him that way," he chided. "We could use friends at court."

"Not friends like that," Toby said darkly. "Unless— Willie, did you like him? I'm sorry; I ought to have asked."

Lucy laughed. "Are you daft? If I ever do decide I want to sleep with men, Toby, it will be someone like you."

"Aha! Hope, I have hope!" Toby cried dramatically, falling to his knees at Lucy's feet.

"I'm glad," Burbage said morosely. "But I still haven't got the rent."

"Come along to the Mermaid." Toby jumped up and threw one arm around him and the other round Lucy. "Maybe you'll be lucky at cards for a change."

So they went to the Mermaid and drank ale and celebrated the opening of *The True and Tragicomic History of Alfonso, Prince of Naples.* Tom Shoemaker made mooncalf eyes at Emmie; Toby and James Burbage got gloriously drunk and strode about shouting lines from their favorite plays. Someone brought out a fiddle; someone else played the pipes, and the players danced.

Lucy sat in a corner with her breeches legs rolled up, hands wrapped around a mug of ale. Her mind was far away, in a coach rattling along a snowy road in Derbyshire. *Oh, Christ, Lucy, I want you so much I think it will tear me apart . . .* And then he had kissed her, there in the darkness; she could taste his mouth against hers even now.

Don't be such a bloody damned fool! she told herself fiercely. To hell with him, to hell with Hawk-Nose and Anthony Babington and Sir Christopher Dalton and all the nobility, all those rich, treacherous men. This was where she belonged, here in Shoreditch with her own kind, who threw flowers if they liked you and rotted plums if they didn't. At least with them a girl—a boy—knew where he stood.

She got up to dance with her friends, the actors, the artificers, the masters of illusion, and in their rough jigs and antics found an illusion of happiness.

The *True and Tragicomic History* enjoyed an extended run at The Theatre—all of ten days. But long before the last performance had been given, Burbage's players were already hard at rehearsals on a different work. The London public's appetite for novelty was voracious; to Lucy, who had been to see plays only infrequently as a child, it came as a surprise to learn that the troupe's repertoire numbered in the hundreds. And even with all of those to draw on, Burbage was constantly in search of new writers, new plays.

When he couldn't find anything new, he would rehash an old chestnut, rejuvenating it with different names for the characters, a change of scene, new songs. The forthcoming production, a gory bit of business set in Ethiopia, wherever that was, would be one of these. Toby, struggling to write new music for the lyrics Burbage assigned him, confided to Lucy that he wished it would die of old age.

Lucy sat by his side at the virginals in the mornings, watching him work, learning how to read and write something new—music. It was worth the ribbing she took from Tom Shoemaker about being Toby's lapdog to have such an opportunity. Toby would plunk out a line on the keys and then jot it down with his quill, while Lucy tried to hum it from the written notes. She found learning to read music much easier than learning to read words had been. "It is all mathematical, isn't it?" she asked Toby. "Just like numbers. It has all got to do with the spaces in between."

He nodded as he scribbled, pleased by the analogy she'd made. "That's why I like music. It is as much a matter of what you skip as what you write." He set her to work copying out parts for the musicians; before long she didn't even need to use the keys of the virginals to see how many spaces she should leave on the staff, for she could hear the notes and spaces in her head.

Despite his talent, Toby was finding these new songs hard to compose. Once, as Lucy worked beside him on the empty stage, he brought both his hands crashing down on the keys in a jangled, angry chord, then stared as she clapped her hands over her ears. "What is it? What's wrong?" he asked.

"Don't *do* that!" Lucy cried. "It reminds me—"

"Of what?"

"Of a song," she told him grimly. "A song that I hate."

On the night before the final performance of *The True and Tragicomic History of Alfonso,* Lucy was at the Mermaid with the rest of the players, looking on as James Burbage lost rather badly to Toby at a round of post and pair, when the door to the street suddenly burst open with a force that made the lamp wicks flicker. The door crashed against the wall, and every head in the place turned that way.

A very tall figure, bundled in black cloak, gloves, and hood, despite the summer night's heat, appeared on the threshold; the hood was pulled down to cover his face, and the cloth of his outfit was the very finest. In one gloved hand he carried an elaborate basket-handled sword nearly as tall as he. "James Burbage?" the black-clad figure said, and Lucy felt the hairs on the back of her neck prickle; the man's voice was so deep and cold that it might have come yawning up through the ground all the way from hell.

Burbage folded his cards carefully and laid them on the table, then stood. "I am James Burbage," he said evenly.

"James. Don't." Toby tugged at his doublet. "It could be one of that wretch Dalton's friends."

But Burbage shook him off, taking a step toward the ominous black figure. "Identify yourself," he said. "What business do you have with me?"

"Identify myself?" The man in black chuckled darkly. "I am called by many names among men. Some know me as Baal; some as Sammael, some as Rahab, some as the Leviathan. My name is unimportant; you know who I am." He thrust back his hood with a sudden gesture, and Lucy screamed as she saw the blank, bleached eye sockets of the skull beneath. "And my business," the ghastly creature went on, with another chilling laugh, "is to call you to account for your sins!" Before anyone could move, he rushed toward Burbage and ran him straight through with his sword.

Burbage's eyes bulged out horribly as the cold steel sliced him; he clutched his stomach, bending over, writhing as he fell to the floor. He twitched, he kicked, he foamed at the mouth, while his killer watched through those sightless, staring sockets. Burbage stumbled up to his knees, reaching out an imploring hand to the avenging angel of death, trembling violently. The angel tilted back its bony head and laughed. "May God have mercy . . . on my soul," Burbage gasped out, and dropped to the floor again, to lie stone-still.

The figure in the death's-head began to applaud. "By

Christ, you always did know how to die, James," he said in a quite different voice, not ominous at all.

"And you always knew how to make an entrance." Burbage grunted, pushing himself up from the floor. "Give me your bloody hand."

As Lucy watched in astonishment, the man hauled Burbage to his feet, took off the staring white skull and tucked it under his arm, then shrugged off his cloak. Beneath its built-up shoulders his real head and body emerged; he was elderly and rather stooped, with sparse white hair and merry blue eyes nearly lost in leathery, wrinkled skin. "Been a long time, James, hasn't it?" he asked.

"Too long," Burbage agreed, and the two men embraced. "Here, Dick!" he called then, searching for his son among the crowd in the tavern. "Remember Richard Tarlton, Dick, from the old days in the provinces? You were named for him."

"Uncle Richard!" Dick Burbage came forward, chuckling. "You scared the bejesus out of me in that outfit!"

"Well, look at you!" the old man exclaimed, clasping Dick's hand and looking him over at arm's length. "When last I saw you you were the size of a sparrow. Lord, the years do fly."

"Sit down, sit down," Burbage urged his visitor, leading him to their table. "Emmie, a dozen cups of the Mermaid's finest over here! You do still drink, don't you, Richard?"

"Do fish still swim? Do women lie?" Richard Tarlton winked. "And at a certain inn in Warwickshire, does the landlord still curse and spit on the ground at the mention of James Burbage's name?"

Burbage laughed, clapping his back. "Lord, the times we had when we were young, didn't we, Richard?"

"What's this about an inn in Warwickshire?" his son Dick wanted to know.

"Something about the landlord's wife or daughter, I seem to recall," Tarlton began, and Burbage elbowed him sharply.

"It was, of course, Dick, a long time before I married your mother."

Tarlton snorted into his mug. "I beg your pardon. Very strong ale," he apologized, eyes twinkling.

Burbage sighed. "It has been a lot of years since then. Still, the time has treated you well, eh, Richard? Leader of the Queen's Men, her majesty's favorite clown—" There was only a hint of envy in his voice.

"Just the luck of the draw," Tarlton said modestly. "She took a fancy to me."

"A pretty lucrative fancy, I'll wager," Toby put in. "We've not met, Master Tarlton, though of course I've long been your admirer. Tobias Mifflin, at your service."

"Call me Richard, please," Tarlton invited, shaking Toby's hand. "James's partner, aren't you? Well, I'd say you two have done all right for yourselves. Got the busiest playhouse in London, I hear."

"Aye, and all the headaches that go with it," Burbage told him. "What do you think has made my hair go gray? But tell me, what brings you from the luxury of Whitehall to the squalor of Shoreditch?"

"Would you believe I just longed to see that handsome face of yours again, James?" Burbage shook his head, grinning. "Ah. Rightly so. Actually, I'm here about a flower. The Rose of Shoreditch." Those merry eyes scanned the players at the table, settling on Lucy. "Willie Reilly, I presume?"

She nodded, surprised that he knew her. Of course, she'd heard of him. He was the most famous player in all England, celebrated for his verse-making and mimickry; it was said Queen Elizabeth never let him far from her side.

"I've heard that you sing like a nightingale, Willie Reilly," Tarlton went on.

"He does," Burbage said with pride, and then added hastily, "though if you're thinking of trying to steal him away, it's no use. He won't go with you. He knows his friends, and he's loyal to them."

Tarlton winced. "I suppose I deserve that. I haven't done much for you, have I, James, since we parted ways?"

Burbage was embarrassed. "I didn't mean— I know, Richard, if I'd ever come to you for help you'd have given it freely. Just as I'd do for you."

"Still." The little man began to cough, and quickly held a kerchief to his mouth. Lucy saw the cloth was spotted with blood when he pulled it away; she knew Burbage had noticed it, too. "You never did come to me, did you? And now I'm getting old. The queen's doctors don't think I'm long for this world. Something in my lungs—" He broke off, coughing again.

"Pah, what do doctors know?" Burbage said stoutly. "I say laughter's the best medicine, and if it is you'll outlive all of us here."

"That could be," Tarlton acknowledged. "Especially if this is the finest ale the Mermaid's got!" Emmie, bringing another round, glared at him, and he pinched her and leered expertly. "But it does make you think, when those black-coated fellows start gathering around you like vultures. As you say, I've done well, James. I've got it all now—money, fine apartments, the queen's favor. I'm respected—"

"Well," Burbage broke in slyly, "let's not get carried away!"

His friend laughed. "You know, James, it's the queerest thing. Everything I've got, and yet when I look back, do you know what I find myself thinking of? Those times in the provinces, when we hadn't a decent pair of shoes among the company, and we played for pickles and bread and a mug of ale. It's true what they say. The best days are the old days."

Burbage laid a hand on his. "We did have fine times."

Tarlton shrugged off his mood the same way he'd shrugged off his black cloak. "Anyway, as I say, I've been thinking. And I said to myself, I said, why not do something nice for James Burbage now he's in his dotage—"

"I'll show you my dotage!" Burbage declared, giving him a mock cuff.

"—and even though the Lord knows he doesn't deserve it, not after that time in Penzance when he stole that old blighter's roast pig and then stuck the gnawed bones in your bedroll to sic the law on you—"

"Richard, please!" Burbage clapped his hands over his son's ears. "Not in front of the boy!"

"—or that time he got caught in the sack with that

butcher's wife in Hereford and yelled as he escaped out the window that his name was Dick Tarlton, and even spelled it out for the fellow—''

''Youthful pranks,'' Burbage told his laughing companions. ''Nothing more than youthful pranks!''

''In spite of all that,'' Tarlton continued, grinning, ''I thought I ought to do something for you, since 'tis plain that without my help you'll never amount to a goddamned thing. So I mentioned to her majesty that this latest play of yours, the piece about the prince of Naples, was said to be quite good, and that you had got this boy, Willie Reilly, who was the toast of all Shoreditch, and wouldn't she perhaps like to see your play?''

''What did she say?'' Burbage asked eagerly.

Tarlton scratched his chin. ''Well, 'tis a bit odd, James, what she said then. It seemed someone else has been talking to her about you before me. She'd heard you were all a bunch of crazed, violent sodomizers.''

''Sir Christopher Dalton.'' Burbage and Tony groaned in unison, and Toby added, ''Goddamn his fat, febrile soul.''

''You've a nice touch with a curse,'' Tarlton told him appreciatively. ''What's Sir Christopher got to do with this?''

Burbage explained briefly about the knight's visit to The Theatre. Tarlton nodded knowingly when he was done. ''Well, that certainly explains it. There have even been rumors going around that The Theatre may be closed down.''

''Closed down!'' Burbage turned milk-pale.

''Aye. That's why I thought I had better step in. I've managed to convince the queen that she should at least hear the singing of the Rose of Shoreditch. So I've arranged for a recital for Willie, the day after tomorrow, at Whitehall!''

''Well, I'll be damned and hallelujah,'' James Burbage said.

Lucy blinked. Sing for the queen! Why, it was an honor she had never even dared to dream of! Oh, Pop! she thought. How proud you would have been to see your little girl go to sing at Whitehall, for Good Queen Bess and her court—

And her court. "My God," Lucy whispered. "I can't go."

"Can't go?" Burbage echoed incredulously. "Can't go—what do you mean you can't go? You've got to! This could be a whole new beginning for us—a chance to gain the queen's favor, maybe even find a patron at the same time."

"I know that, sir. But you don't understand."

"You're bloody right I don't!"

Lucy looked at him imploringly. "If I could talk to you for a moment in private, please, sir?"

Burbage rose, holding Tarlton in his chair. "You stay right here, Richard. Don't move. Don't leave. I'll get this straightened out in no time. As for you, come on." He grabbed Lucy's arm and pulled her out the doors of the tavern to the street. "Now what's all this about?" he demanded as the doors slammed behind them.

"I can't sing at court," Lucy hissed frantically. "There could be someone there who might recognize me!"

"Oho," Burbage said after a pause. "So he was a nobleman, was he, this fellow who broke your heart?" He wagged a finger at her. "Clever as you are, Lucy Jones, I'd have thought you'd got sense enough to keep to your own kind."

"Well, I've learned my lesson now. Why do you think I won't go to Whitehall?"

"But think of what it could do for the rest of us," Burbage argued.

"Listen to you. You just told me to keep to my own kind; you ought to take your own advice!"

"This is business, girl," he snapped, "not some silly affair of the heart." He saw the pain in her eyes and sighed. "Jesus, don't tell me you're in love with this bastard still."

"Of course I'm not. I don't want to have anything to do with him or anybody else like him ever again!"

Burbage frowned. "Look here, this man's not likely to be at Whitehall on the one day you sing there, is he?"

"No," she acknowledged. "But there are other people—important people that he introduced me to."

"Introduced you to his friends and all, did he? My, my, it sounds as though he led you a merry dance. Still, you've been playing in front of your old friends and neighbors for months now," the actor pointed out. "No one has recognized you."

"Aye, but that was from the pit, with me way up on the stage."

"Christ, girl, you know Toby; he can paint you so your own mother wouldn't recognize you. And he and I will both go with you. There's no reason for you to be afraid." He took her hands in his. "And think of it, Lucy—singing for the queen herself! How many people have a chance like that in their lifetimes? Why, think of what your pop would say."

"Oh, sir." Lucy nibbled her lip. "I wish you hadn't put it that way."

He sensed she was weakening and pressed her. "I took a chance for you, Lucy, when I took you on. I've worked all my life for an opportunity like this. Won't you take a chance for me now?"

Lucy sighed. "Well—"

"That's my girl—my boy, I mean," Burbage cried, grinning and slapping her back. "Come on, now, let's go tell Richard. You and Toby will have to figure out what you're to sing and to wear—"

Still talking excitedly, he led Lucy back into the tavern and thrust a celebratory mug of ale into her hands. What the hell, Lucy thought with resignation as she saw how excited Toby and the rest of the players were at the news. The chances that Bram would be in London two days from now had to be more than a million to one.

Chapter 16

Barkers Lane, Shoreditch, London.

Bram Carlyle, a thick growth of black beard shading his face, stared down from Bellerophon's saddle at the heap of burned rubble before him. So this was where Lucy Jones had lived.

This was where the story began—and, so far as he had been able to learn, where it ended. Despite a fortnight of meticulous searching, he'd found no one who had seen Lucy after she disappeared from Lockhaven Hall last March. Though she seemed to have dropped off the face of the earth, he could not risk the chance that she might turn up unexpectedly, not now that he knew she had read one of Queen Mary's letters. And so he had come here, back to the beginning, in the hope that something in this mute pile of charred brick and timber might give him some clue as to where she had gone.

He glanced down the dark, cramped street in both directions. Women in petticoats sat on their stoops, eyeing with mild resentment this stranger who had appeared in their midst. Skinny, long-limbed children chased one another under the eaves of the rickety houses, their skin pale as mushrooms that never saw the sun. Worn men stood by the gutters and watched him through half-closed eyelids, suspicious and wary, their conversations left dangling in mid-sentence until he moved on.

He tried to picture Lucy here among them, to imagine her sitting on a curb in her underclothes with the stink of dung and garbage and unwashed bodies thick as Thames fog, but he found it impossible. He wished he had come there sooner, though; seeing Barkers Lane brought home to him in a way nothing else could the courage and strength of the slim, green-eyed woman he had set himself to finding whatever the cost.

A wizened old woman sidled toward him, her eyes lively with curiosity. "Somethin' I can do for ye, guv'nor?"

Bram looked down at her. "This place. This shop—"

"Aye, milord?"

"The woman who owned it—where is she now?"

The old woman crossed herself. "Wot, our Lucy? At the bottom of the Thames, they say, God rest 'er soul.

Bram's pulse quickened. "She's dead? When did she die?"

"Oh, la, a year or so back. Drowned 'erself, that's wot they say, the same night Joe got killed 'n' the shop burned." She considered the fire's debris. " 'Tweren't nothin' left but my old black kettle when the flames died down."

"No one's seen her since?"

"Well, 'ow could they, then, when I just told ye she was dead?" The crone toed the curbstone; her feet were bare and gnarled like apple bark. " 'Twas my fault, I reckon. Alf Smith, 'e wanted to take 'er 'ome to 'is missus, but I said let 'er go, let 'er be; she needs time to 'erself. La, she was such a pretty thing." Shielding the late sun from her face, she peered up at Bram. "Thinkin' of buyin' the place, are ye?"

"Could be. Whom would I see?"

"I don't rightly know. Alderman, I reckon. She'd got no kin. The city likely owns it now."

The beginning and the end. "Thank you kindly," he told the woman.

She shrugged. "Ye're welcome, I'm sure."

Bram wheeled Bellerophon about, then stared at the bizarre apparition coming toward him through the dusk: a knot of gay, elegant courtiers and ladies, as aberrant in the grim poverty of their surroundings as preening peacocks in a flock of crows. They carried wine bottles and hampers as they picked their way over the cobblestones in their high wooden heels; their bright laughter hung heavy on the shimmering air.

"Bram? Bram Carlyle?" One brilliant bird detached

herself from the covey. "Well, I never—it is you!" It was
Claudia Moncrief, her blond coif studded with jewels, her
silver skirts raised above the filthy street.

"So it is," said another voice, and Bram saw Anthony
Babington's bony face, saw, too, the way Babington's eyes
darted beyond his shoulder to the burned-out shop that had
once been Lucy's. Amateur, Bram thought scornfully. The
fool might as well have worn a sign reading "I know a
secret about this place." It was a wonder the queen of
Scots' cause hadn't foundered completely on such idiocy.
"What are you doing here?"

Bram looked to see if any of the other courtiers had
noticed Babington's edginess; one could never be certain
in this game who was on whose side. They seemed obliv-
ious. Bram laughed coolly, easily. "Thank God!" he said.
"I was headed for Bethnal Green and took a wrong turn
somewhere; I've been wandering lost for an hour. Tried
to get directions from these bloody idiots, but I can't understand a single word they say."

Babington, he saw with relief, looked calmer. "Hello,
Claudia," Bram went on.

"I'm not speaking to you," the blonde announced with
a sniff. "Not after that countess friend of yours had me
put out of her house. I've never been so outraged in all
my life!"

"Suppose I try to make up for her rudeness," Bram
suggested, "by giving you a ride. No one as beautiful as
you should have to walk through a hellhole like this. What
the devil are you doing here?"

"We're on our way to The Theatre," she told him coyly
as Babington boosted her into the saddle in front of Bram.
"To hear Willie Reilly."

"Who is Willie Reilly?"

"Some snot-nosed little Shoreditch wonder," said a
courtier in a red doublet, and laughed. "He's coming to
Whitehall tomorrow to sing for the queen."

"You're jesting!"

"No, he's not," Babington confirmed. "The queen's
clown, Tarlton—he arranged it."

"Then it is a jest—a clown's joke?" Bram asked.

"Tarlton says not," Claudia told him, leaning back

against his chest. "Though we have our doubts. And so we've come to see for ourselves. If I'd any notion of what Shoreditch is like, though, I'd have taken a carriage." She glared at the silent, staring men and women around them and took a deep breath from a scented kerchief. "Honestly, can you imagine pigs living in such a stench?" Her pale gaze slanted slyly toward Bram. "Oh, forgive me—that little governess of yours that Margery Sutherland was so hot in defending was from Shoreditch, too. You must be quite used to this stink."

"Charming Claudia." Bram grinned. "She is long since gone."

"Does that mean," the blonde purred, her hand brushing his thigh, "that you're in need of a new teacher? For your children?"

"I might be. Would you care to apply for the post?"

"If you come to The Theatre with us, I'll consider it," she told him coyly. Bram laughed, shaking his head.

"I'm not fit company tonight, I'm afraid. I've been drinking."

The man in the red doublet belched. "Christ's sake, man, so have we! Do you think we would come here sober?" He hurled an empty wine bottle at a boy who was edging toward the band of courtiers, a thin arm outstretched. "Get the hell away from me, you disgusting urchin!" The bottled shattered at the child's feet, and he skittered away.

"Well, in that case—" Bram pulled his flask from his doublet and took a long swallow. "Why not?"

"Lead on!" Babington cried. "To The Theatre!" The cluster of glittering aristocrats flitted on down Barkers Lane. At the end of the street Bram turned in the saddle and glanced back. The ranks of the residents had closed in behind them, just as though the unwelcome intruders had never been there.

At the gate to The Theatre the ticketseller gaped when he saw the lords and ladies swooping down on him. "How many tickets?" Anthony Babington demanded, counting jeweled heads. "Twelve, sirrah. How much are twelve of the best seats in the place?"

"The play is almost over," the startled man stuttered. "Ye'll not get yer money's worth."

"As if," Claudia sniffed, "there were ever any question of that!"

"Will Willie Reilly sing yet?" Babington asked.

"Oh, aye, sir. In the last scene."

"Then we'll go in." He flung a purse at the ticketseller's feet. "There. And you can watch this gentleman's horse as well." He headed in, and the man grabbed his sleeve.

"Not there, sir—that there's the pit. Go on up to the gallery, then, if ye must go in." He pointed to the stairs.

Babington loosed the man's fingers from his doublet and brushed off the cloth with disdain. "To the gallery, then. Ladies, gentlemen, prithee, follow me."

Halfway up the rickety staircase Bram paused to drink from his flask and cursed, finding it was empty. "Oh, dear," Claudia said with a pout. "None left for me?"

"Don't worry," he told her, grinning and heading back down the stairs. "I've got more in my saddlebag."

"I'll keep a seat warm for you, Bram darling."

"You do that, Claudia, my sweet."

"Psst! Willie!" Toby Mifflin crooked a finger at Lucy, beckoning her toward the balcony window. "Word that you're to sing at Whitehall has traveled fast. Look and see what's come to take the fine Shoreditch air."

"Where?" she asked, trying simultaneously to pull on her shoe and look out through the window without being seen.

"In the gallery. There, to the left."

"My God." Lucy stared at the knot of exotic courtiers stumbling out of the stairwell with their wine bottles and hampers. "What are they doing here?"

"Come to see you, I reckon, so when you sing for the queen tomorrow they can all act *veddy* superior and say, 'Oh, Willie Reilly? Of *cawse;* we discovahed him *ages* ago, while he still sang in *Shaw*ditch.'" His lofty accent made Lucy snort and drop her shoe. "Here, look at that blonde in the silver gown," he urged her, and then caught her arm as she swayed on the platform. "What's wrong?"

"Nothing. These bloody shoes." But what had made Lucy lose her balance was recognizing Claudia Moncrief. She stole another peek at the buxom blonde. "Do you like her dress?"

"Like it? It reminds me of a dream I had once after I ate a plum pudding that had gone bad."

Lucy giggled. "I love you, Toby, do you know that?"

" 'I love you, Toby.' " Tom Shoemaker, climbing the ladder to the platform, puckered his mouth and made lewd smacking noises. "Christ, what a couple of pansies. You both make me sick."

"Why don't you mind your own business, Tom?" Lucy asked sweetly.

"Toby!" another of the actors hissed from below. "Come and give us a hand, would you? This bloody door's jammed again."

Toby hurried down the ladder. "Swisher," Tom hissed after him.

"Dammit, Tom," Lucy whispered as, at the front of the stage, the grand doge of Venice lamented the kidnapping of the fair Bianca. "Why are you so beastly to him?"

" 'Beastly,' " he mimicked. "Christ, you're starting to sound just like him. I'll bet you love that scene where he kisses you."

"He's my friend!"

"Oh, that's right, you're great chums together, aren't you? Going up to Whitehall tomorrow to see the queen—"

"Is that what this is all about?" Lucy demanded. "Singing for the queen? Are you jealous, is that it?"

"Of course not. Why should I care if you two want to get dressed up like a couple of bloody pansies and prance around Whitehall?"

"Toby doesn't prance."

"Willie! Tom!" Toby was glaring at them from down below. "Stop your damned bickering and listen for your cues!"

"Faggot," Tom whispered in Lucy's ear.

"Idiot," she hissed back.

Up in the gallery the visitors from court were attracting attention. "God, can you believe the stench in this place?"

Claudia Moncrief exclaimed, holding a perfumed kerchief to her nose.

" 'Ey!" A burly man in the benches ahead of her turned and shook his fist. "Shut the 'ell up, why don't ye? I'm tryin' to watch the bleedin' play!"

"Well, you surely can't watch it if you're staring at me," Claudia shot back. "Cheeky peasants. Where is Bram with that brandy?"

"Shut up!" someone shouted from the groundlings' pit, and hurled a rotten peach into the gallery.

"A thousand curses fall upon the head of that villainous traitor Orlando," James Burbage said from the gondola on stage, sneaking a look up into the two-penny seats to find out what had got the audience riled, wincing as he saw the courtiers.

"*There* you are," Claudia cried in relief as Bram stumbled up beside her. She snatched the flask from his hand.

"Claudia, darling," the man in the red doublet hissed, "keep your voice down!"

"Don't tell me you are intimidated by this riffraff, darling," she said airily.

"Keep it down up there!" an apprentice bellowed from the pit below.

Burbage was rushing through his speech to Rodrigo; he knew only one thing would quiet the unruly audience, and that was Willie Reilly's singing. "She is gone forever, Rodrigo!" he shouted desperately above the growing rumble in the pit. "And with her is gone all my joy!" Come on, Lucy! he urged silently, and then relaxed as her ethereal voice floated from the balcony window, impossibly sweet and clear, so hauntingly beautiful that even the obnoxious blonde in the balcony closed her mouth:

> *The promises he made me*
> *Were warm as summer rain,*
> *But oh, he has betrayed me—*

Lucy looked up at Claudia Moncrief again, saw the tall, black-haired man who now stood beside her, and broke off in mid-note.

" 'And left me tears and pain,' " Tom Shoemaker hissed, thinking Willie had forgotten the words. But Willie didn't hear him; he just stood looking out from the window, his face gone ghost-white.

In the gondola below, James Burbage and his son exchanged uncertain glances. Behind the painted *palazzi,* Toby got the doors unstuck, noticed that the musicians had stopped playing, and turned on them. "What's the matter with you?"

"It's not us—it's Willie, man!"

At first the crowd in the groundling pit thought the abrupt halt in the song was intentional, but as the silence stretched they began to turn ugly. "Wot's goin' on?" someone shouted, and a host of his companions took up the cry.

"So that's the great Willie Reilly," Claudia said with a disparaging wave at the stage.

"Where?" Bram asked, taking his brandy flask from her.

"There in the window. The blonde who is staring up at—Bram!" She saw him start to fall and grabbed for him, but it was too late; he stumbled forward drunkenly, pulling down half a dozen benches and making a terrible commotion.

"My God," Anthony Babington muttered, blanching as the groundlings turned their attention that way once more. "We had better get out of here!" He and the rest of the gentlemen managed to haul Bram back to his feet and hustle him down the stairs.

Burbage heaved a sigh of relief as the courtiers disappeared. "All right, Willie!" he called up to the balcony in a loud stage whisper. "Go on! Keep singing!" But the blond head had vanished from the window; behind the painted scenery Toby searched the stage for Willie, but he couldn't be found. Toby held a rushed conference with Tom, and after a moment the loyal Esmeralda appeared on the balcony, tearing at her hair. "Woe is me!" she cried, sounding genuinely shaken. "The lovely and virtuous Bianca has thrown herself into the canal and drowned!"

* * *

The promises he made me
Were warm as summer rain—

Bellowing at the top of his lungs, Bram staggered into the yards of Whitehall Palace, one arm around Claudia Moncrief's bare shoulders, the other circling Bellerophon's withers. A stableboy came running to take the reins from him; as the boy pulled the big black horse away, Bram stumbled and banged his knees on the cobblestones. Claudia tumbled down atop him in a flurry of silver skirts, giggling madly. Anthony Babington yanked them both up again, frowning as he brushed dust from Bram's black doublet.

"I say, old man," he hissed in Bram's ear, "pull yourself together. Can't have you making a spectacle of yourself here; we don't want to call attention."

"I shall be the soul of discretion," Bram promised, and pulled out his flask. Babington snatched it away.

"And I think you've had enough to drink."

"Oh, Anthony, leave him alone," Claudia said crossly, taking back the brandy. "This is a celebration! I'm to be Bram's new governess."

"And perform certain other services," he reminded her, leering as he groped at her bodice.

"Mmm. Certain ones," she agreed, twisting her head for a kiss. "I am *so* glad we happened to run into you, Bram."

"So am I." He grabbed the flask and drained it, then tossed it onto the cobblestones.

"Well, I'm not," Babington muttered. "Straighten up, Carlyle, and stop pawing her, or we won't even get in the door."

The doormen did look askance at the throng of revelers returning from The Theatre, but Bram drew up his shoulders and stalked right past them. "Abraham Carlyle, Lord Carlyle," he said as he breezed by. "Is her majesty receiving?"

"Aye, milord. In the Presence Chamber."

Bram squinted down the long corridor beyond the entranceway. "Where's that?"

"I'll take you," Claudia told him, slipping her arm through his. "This way."

With Babington and the rest of the group trailing after them, they headed down the hall.

The queen's Presence Chamber was illuminated by hundreds of torches; the huge high-ceilinged room was thronged with courtiers and ladies-in-waiting. A quartet of musicians was playing in the gallery; servants circulated gingerly through the crowd carrying trays of sweetmeats and wine. The queen herself was seated at the far end of the chamber, in a gilded chair canopied with cloth of gold. She wore a resplendent gown of crimson velvet, the bodice and sleeves studded with thousands of tiny pearls. More jewels hung from her ears and circled her throat, and atop her elaborate red coiffure rose a golden crown. She was speaking to the earl of Leicester, laughing gaily at some jest he was making, her black eyes sparkling brighter than her jewels or crown.

"Look, there is Daddy," Claudia cried, tugging Bram toward a distinguished-looking white-haired gentleman in blue, golden chains of office hanging heavy against his fine doublet. "Let's go and tell him the good news. Daddy!" She waved, and the white-haired man pushed his way through the crowd to her side. "Hello, Daddy." She pecked his cheek. "Do you know Bram? Lord Carlyle, my father, the baron of Tit— of Tatworth. Father, Lord Carlyle."

Lord Moncrief eyed his daughter. "Claudia. Have you been drinking?"

"Just a teensy-weensy bit of brandy. We went to The Theatre in Shoreditch to hear Willie Reilly sing and met Bram on the way."

"Shoreditch!" Lord Moncrief looked appalled. "Isn't that part of London supposed to be filled with rabble and ruffians?"

Claudia shuddered. "So it is. Never fear, none of us will ever be caught dead there again. Oh, but Daddy, do listen, I have got the most thrilling news. I am going to Derbyshire to be Bram's governess!"

"I should hardly think a man his age needs a governess," Lord Moncrief said coolly.

"Oh, Daddy!" His daughter giggled and slapped his

arm. "For his children, I mean. Two of them. Erasmus and Millicent or something."

"The last time you engaged my daughter's services," Lord Moncrief told Bram, frowning, "you proceeded to cancel them—rather rudely and abruptly, I might add."

"Not I, sir. My children." Bram grabbed a goblet of wine from a passing tray. "The entire story is rather difficult to explain."

"Some little tart of a commoner showed up on his doorstep," Claudia put in, "and told him she was me."

Lord Moncrief looked worse than appalled; he looked horrified. "What sort of man could mistake a commoner for my daughter?"

"I'm afraid, sir, that I can be rather absentminded at times."

"Absentminded! Why, you would have to be blind!" Lord Moncrief sputtered. "I hope to God you had this audacious imposter horsewhipped and sent to jail."

"Oh, Daddy, there's no sense getting all worked up over it now," Claudia told him. "It is all in the past, and Bram is going to make amends."

"I shall take the matter of your going to Derbyshire under advisement, Claudia," her father said briskly.

"Daddy." She stood on tiptoe to whisper in his ear. "His title goes all the way back to William the Conqueror. And he has an income of seventy thousand pounds a year."

"I said I would take it under advisement."

"Daddy, he is the biggest catch in all of England! And you said before that I could go!"

"Aye—before I heard about this business of his mistaking a commoner for you!"

"Daddy!" she wailed, and stomped her foot. "I want to go!"

"We'll see," was all he said. "And by the by, young lady, I saw you come in with Lord Babington. Stay away from him; he is a pernicious influence." He bowed to Bram, his pale eyes cold. "Lord Carlyle."

Bram returned the bow with drunken dignity. "Lord Moncrief."

"Dammit, Bram," Claudia snapped as her father stalked

off, "now look what's happened! And all because of that little slut of a—"

"You are very beautiful when you are angry," he interrupted, gulping down his wine. "Come on. I want to dance with you."

The queen and Leicester had gotten up to lead a pavane. Bram and Claudia joined the lines that were forming, men on one side and ladies on the other. Claudia frowned, her hand on Bram's as they started off, his movements clumsy and slow. "You are too drunk to dance," she accused him, hearing several of the courtiers laughing behind their backs.

"Don't be ridiculous," he said thickly, and knocked away the countess of Surrey's fan as he made a turn.

"I think we had best sit down," Claudia said between gritted teeth as Bram galloped her through the next progress, his boots thudding on the marble floor. The queen had glanced once or twice in their direction, and she did not look pleased.

"We'll just finish out this round," he told her, panting with exertion, tossing back his black hair in a careless gesture that made him lose his balance and grab her for support. The rest of the dancers were regarding him in alarm.

"Bram, I think we should—oh!" Claudia froze. Bram's leaden foot had caught the train of the queen's red gown as they paraded past her; it ripped with a horrible wrench. The musicians in the gallery stopped playing; the dancers stared. Queen Elizabeth turned around slowly, her black eyes ablaze.

"Who are you, sirrah, that dares to tread upon our skirts?" she demanded.

He bowed cockily, staggering again. "Abraham Carlyle, your majesty," he said loudly. "Lord Carlyle."

"Lord Carlyle." She tapped her foot, considering him imperiously. "Ah, yes. Aren't you the man who murdered his wife?"

Bram jerked up his head. "Aren't you the daughter of the man who murdered two?"

There was dead silence in the enormous room. Elizabeth stood very still; only her thin lips moved, and those barely, as she asked, "What did you say, sirrah?"

He laughed, still holding tight to Claudia's hand. "You heard me. The allegations against me have never been proven, but the whole world knows your father had your mother beheaded when he found out that she was a—"

"Jesus Christ, Bram!" Claudia cried, and wrenched away from him.

"Whore," he finished succinctly. "And another one, too." He clucked his tongue. "Poor man, he had dreadful luck with wives."

The queen raised her arm, pointing one long finger at him. "Remove this knave from our presence."

Bram grinned. "What's the matter, your majesty? You can dish it out but you can't take it served back to you?"

"We warn you, sirrah!" The queen was visibly shaking with rage. "One word more and you go to the Tower!"

He swayed on his feet. "One word, eh? I shall have to make it a good one. How about 'doxy's daughter'? Oh, dear, that's two."

Elizabeth struck him with such force that he sprawled backward to the floor. "To the Tower with him," she cried. "By God, we shall have your head, swine!"

Half a dozen guards armed with pikestaffs swarmed forward and wrestled Bram up from the floor, dragging him from the room. The queen's jeweled head swiveled as she searched the crowd of courtiers and ladies who looked on, aghast. Then she found the man she was seeking. "Lord Moncrief."

The white-haired lord stepped forward nervously. "Yes, your majesty?"

"Is this your daughter?" Elizabeth demanded, lowering her finger at the trembling Claudia.

Lord Moncrief's pale eyes were colder than ice as he glared at his errant offspring. "Aye, your majesty."

"You would do well, milord," the queen said softly, "to advise her to choose her companions more carefully."

"Rest assured, I will, your majesty." The white-haired lord yanked Claudia toward him and hustled her away. A growing buzz of comment followed them; Anthony Babington ducked out of the Presence Chamber through the closest door.

"We will retire now," the queen announced, and the courtiers quickly cleared a path for her. "Leicester, prithee take us to our rooms."

Looking as though he might be auditioning for a role as the god of thunder, James Burbage stomped into the stable of the Mermaid Tavern, slammed the doors, and swung aloft the lantern he held. "Lucy! Lucy Jones, where are you?" he shouted.

"Hush!" came a small, frightened voice from the hayloft. "For God's sake, don't say my name!"

"I can think of a few names I'd rather call you at the moment, believe me." He barged toward the ladder. "First you ruin one of Toby's best songs, then you ruin the entire play—next I suppose you'll tell me you can't sing for the queen tomorrow."

"That's right," she said timidly. "I can't."

"You can't." Burbage kicked a feed bucket, sending it crashing against a wall. "Well, I'll tell you one thing more you can't do, and that's act on my stage ever again!"

"That's all right, sir," said Lucy, her breath catching in a sob. "I couldn't anyway."

Burbage stared up at her small face, ghost-white in the lantern light. "What is it, child? What's got you spooked?" he asked more gently.

Lucy began to cry. Burbage sighed. "All right, lass. Come down here and tell Uncle James all about it."

"I can't!" she sobbed, her face buried in his hands.

"Then I'll come up there."

He climbed the ladder slowly, pausing at the top to catch his breath and hook the lantern on a nail. "Hmph. I'm not the athlete I used to be," he muttered. "Now what in God's name is all this about? Don't tell me you found out you're pregnant."

"It's much worse than that."

"Hard to imagine anything worse than one of my boy actors getting pregnant," Burbage said, so gravely that Lucy hiccupped a little laugh. He patted her shoulder. "There, you see? There's nothing so horrible that you can't tell me about it. I've proven I can keep a secret, haven't I?''

''I can't tell you,'' Lucy said again.

Burbage squatted in the straw beside her. ''Lucy, listen to me. Your singing for the queen is the biggest break of luck I've had in the eleven years I've owned that bloody theater. If I'm to lose that chance, don't you think I deserve to know why?''

Lucy chewed her lip. He had been a good friend to her; she owed him some explanation. ''The man that I—the one who—''

''The nobleman you were in love with?'' he asked, and she nodded. ''What about him?''

''He was at The Theatre today. Up in the gallery. He came in with those Whitehall toffs.''

''But surely he didn't recognize you,'' Burbage said dubiously. ''In your wig and makeup and costume, from all that distance—''

''I don't know if he did or not. But he looked straight at me. Sir, I just don't know!''

''Look here, is this fellow still in love with you?'' Burbage demanded.

''He never was in love with me,'' she said miserably. ''He was just toying with me. And then I found out something horrible about him.''

''Found out what?'' Burbage asked curiously.

''He—he murdered his wife,'' she whispered. ''And he is mixed up in something—I don't know exactly what— that has got to do with the man who burned down my shop and murdered Joe Reilly.''

''What sort of something?''

''Something to do with the queen of the Scots.''

''My God. Lucy, if you know something like that, you must go to the authorities!''

''There's no point in it, sir,'' Lucy told him impatiently. ''It would be my word against his, and who is going to believe me when he is a rich lord and I'm a nobody? He bought his way free when he killed his wife; he'd just buy his way free of this, too. And then—'' She shuddered. ''Then he'd come looking for me.''

The bells of Magdalen Church chimed the hour of nine.

Burbage cursed and ran his hand through his thinning gray hair. "Christ, you really have got yourself into a mess, haven't you? I was supposed to meet Tarlton in the tavern half an hour ago. And Toby's brought the costumes by—they turned out beautifully. Look here, Lucy, you can't be sure this fellow will be at Whitehall tomorrow."

"He was with those courtiers tonight," she said stubbornly. "And if he was there, sir, I wouldn't do you any good with the queen. The same thing would happen that happened up there on that stage. I wouldn't be able to sing a single note."

He sat back on his heels. "What will you do now?"

"Run away from him again. Only I'll go farther this time. This time I really will go to Venice or Persia or Araby. Sir, I've got five pounds I saved sewn up in my cot in your attic. If you could give me five now, then you could take those and I could leave tonight."

Burbage sighed and reached for his purse. "Here, take seven; that's all I have. I—" He stopped; Lucy had heard hoofbeats coming toward the stable and shrank back into the shadowy loft. The stable doors opened. "Who's there?" Burbage called nervously.

"James? Is that you?" Rich laughter, clown's laughter. Lucy let out her breath, recognizing Richard Tarlton's voice. "What the devil are you doing up there? Actually, I can't say I'm surprised what with everything else that has gone on tonight. It must be a full moon. What a scene there was at Whitehall! That's why I'm late. You know how it is when you've spent your lifetime in the theater; you just can't stand leaving until you have seen the last act."

"Listen, Richard," James tried to break in, "I have bad—"

But Tarlton kept on talking as he climbed down from his saddle. "This great big scowling fellow came blundering into the Presence Chamber stone drunk, with Lord Moncrief's daughter, who, by the by, is a story all in herself, and—"

"Richard, I have to—" Burbage tried to interrupt again, but Lucy had grabbed his arm and was listening.

"While they were dancing, this big fellow tore the

queen's gown. Then the queen accused him of murdering
his wife, and he called the queen's mother a whore! Would
you believe it, James? He said it right to her face!''

"God in heaven," Lucy whispered. "The scowling fellow—what was his name?"

"Well, hello, Willie Reilly," Tarlton said gaily, seeing
her hanging over the railing. "All ready for your big day
tomorrow?"

"His *name*," Lucy repeated urgently, "do you know
his name?"

Tarlton scratched his head. "Began with a C, I think.
Carruthers? Carstairs?"

"Carlyle," Lucy said in disbelief.

"Aye, aye, that's it. Abraham Carlyle." The queen's
clown peered up at her curiously. "Hope you're not fond
of him, lad."

"Why is that?"

"Why, the queen's sent him to the Tower. She says she
will have his head for what he said to her."

"I'll be damned," James Burbage muttered, seeing the
shocked expression on Lucy's pale face. "That's him, isn't
it? The nobleman you're afraid of?" She nodded faintly,
and he clapped her back. "Well, it's perfect then, isn't it,
what's happened? He'll be in the Tower of London tomorrow. And if he does lose his head, it will be the answer
to your prayers. Won't it, now?"

It ought to have been, Lucy knew, but somehow it
wasn't. Bram in the Tower. Bram beheaded. Her careless
words to Toby came back to haunt her: *I can think of one
person I'd like to see dead . . .* What was it her father
used to tell her when she was a child? *Beware of what you
wish, for it may come true.*

"Say," Tarlton called to them, "what are you two doing
up in that loft, anyway?"

"Willie was having some second thoughts about singing
for the queen tomorrow," Burbage told him. "But he's all
right now. Aren't you, Willie?"

*Oh, Christ, Lucy, I want you so much I think it will tear
me apart . . .* And then he had kissed her—

"Willie?" Burbage said again.

"Yes," Lucy told him in a small, dead voice. "I'm all right now."

"Good!" Tarlton rubbed his hands together. "I can't wait to see what Toby's come up with for you and him to wear, Willie," he said as Lucy followed Burbage down the ladder. "What did you decide on?"

"Venus and Adonis," she told him absently.

"Uh-uh," said Burbage. "Toby changed his mind. He's come up with something better."

"What?" Lucy asked in surprise.

"Pluto and Persephone."

"Pluto and— Dear God," Lucy said, and stumbled a bit as they left the dark stable and went into the brightly lit Mermaid. Out of the darkness and into the light . . .

"What's wrong with that?" Burbage demanded, catching her arm as she began to cry.

"Nothing," Lucy whispered, tears streaming down her face. "Nothing at all. Everything is just perfect now, sir. Just as you said."

Chapter 17

"Come away with me to the underworld, my sweet," Toby Mifflin said in his oiliest villain's voice, leering at Lucy through the eyeslits of his black hood. "I will give to you all the pleasures of hell. Everlasting fire!" And he pawed at the skirts of her forest-green gown.

"Stop it, Toby. Please." Through the window of the carriage James Burbage had hired that they might arrive at Whitehall in style, Lucy could see the four spiky minarets of the Tower of London in the distance; the sight brought a harsh tightness to her throat.

"Don't tell me you're nervous, Willie." Burbage patted her knee. "What could possibly go wrong now? Toby's costumes are spectacular, don't you think?"

"They really are, Toby," Lucy admitted. In addition to his black hood, Toby wore a long black cape, black hose, and a scarlet doublet. Lucy's green gown was embroidered with tiny flowers and leaves; a wreath of roses and myrtle crowned her golden wig. But what was most startling was the way Toby had painted her face: half young and beautiful, to represent her half life on earth, and the other half tortured and in pain, symbolizing her time in the underworld. Lucy hadn't even recognized herself in the mirror when he had finished; it was a masterpiece of cosmetic art.

"We both know the songs forward and backward," Toby went on. "And Willie Reilly's voice would charm the Prince of Darkness himself. Don't worry, Willie. Everything is going to be fine."

"I quite agree," Burbage declared, "even though I

ought never to trust you again, Toby Mifflin, after that debacle you engineered on the stage last night.''

''Debacle?'' Toby echoed, highly offended. ''I thought it was brilliant!''

''Bianca committing suicide? Orlando killing Rodrigo and becoming Doge? Evil triumphing over good? What the hell kind of play is that?''

''Real life, James,'' Toby said with great satisfaction.

''You are one crazy bastard,'' Burbage told him, shaking his head.

''Maybe I am. But you have to admit, the audience cheered when I ran that goody-goody Rodrigo through. And Tom Shoemaker gave the performance of his young life when Orlando tried to kiss him there at the end.''

''Christ, don't remind me of Tom,'' Burbage said morosely. ''What am I to do with him? He's getting too old to play women, he won't learn his lines—all he wants to do any more is pick fights and arguments.''

''Ah, puberty.'' Toby sighed. ''Sooner or later it comes to us all. Except, perhaps, for Willie Reilly.'' Through the slits of the mask his dark eyes held a speculative gleam.

''What's that supposed to mean?'' Burbage demanded.

''Oh, just a wild notion that came to me when Willie stopped singing so suddenly last night.''

''Well, keep your wild notions to yourself,'' Burbage told him. ''At least until this performance for the queen is through. Are you going to be all right, Willie?''

''Yes, sir,'' Lucy said quietly. She would be, though her whole body felt numb. Burbage and Toby had a lifetime of work riding on her singing today. She would not let them down, even if she could not share in their jocular mood.

''What do you think, Willie, about having evil triumph over good?'' Toby asked her.

The spires of the Tower disappeared from the window. ''I think,'' said Lucy, ''real life is stranger than any play ever could be.''

The coach clattered on through the city and came to a stop at last before a set of huge iron gates. Burbage opened the door and stared at the vast white bulk of Whitehall

Palace. "Here we are," he said gaily. "Where fortunes are lost and made! Let's go."

Richard Tarlton was waiting for them just inside the palace. He looked awfully edgy, Lucy noted with some surprise. Well, he had recommended them to the queen; she supposed he had a high stake in their success, too. "I've got to have a word with Toby," he said in greeting. "It's about—about the music. This way, Toby." They went off together, vanishing down a long corridor. That left Lucy and Burbage standing before a host of curious footmen and pages. "Are you Willie Reilly that's come to sing for the queen?" one of the youths asked Lucy. She nodded. "Well, if you're a boy, why are you wearing a gown?"

"We're players," Burbage told him. "From The Theatre."

"Oh," said the page, and eyed Lucy's green skirts. "What do you wear underneath?"

"Same as you," she said, and lifted her gown to show him her boy's boots and hose.

He backed away, shaking his head. "Gor, players is strange!"

Tarlton hurried back toward them down the corridor. "Where's Toby?" Burbage asked.

"He's already at the virginals. Willie, here's the plan. I'll take you in and present you to the queen. You bow, and if she asks you any questions, answer them. Don't forget to call her your majesty. James, why don't you wait here until we see how everything goes?"

For the first time Burbage showed a hint of alarm. "What do you mean? What could go wrong?"

"Oh, nothing, nothing," his old friend said hastily. "Still, it couldn't hurt to make sure. Ready, Willie?" Lucy nodded. "Then come along."

He led her through the corridor he'd traveled with Toby, turned to the left, then turned left again. Despite her confusion over Bram's fate, Lucy felt her numbness start to wear away. She wanted to take in all the grandeur around her and hold it forever in her memory. After all, this would be a moment to treasure, to tell her children and grandchildren about. If, that is, she ever married . . . if she ever found anyone besides Bram who could make her feel that magical white fire.

But she would not think of that now; she would concentrate instead on her surroundings. Marble floors strewn with meadowsweet. Gilded walls lined with tapestries. Servants bustling by in the queen's white-and-green liveries—she had never seen those liveries so close up before. Great lords in dark, solemn robes and heavy gold chains of state . . . for some reason she found herself mumbling the silly nursery rhyme she sang Minnie to sleep with:

> *Pussycat, pussycat, where have you been?*
> *I've been to London to see the queen—*

God, what would become of Minnie and Stacy when Bram was beheaded?

"Willie?" Tarlton was tugging at her arm; she'd stopped dead in the hallway. "Come on!"

The room to which Tarlton led her was the biggest she had ever seen, dwarfing by far anything at Lockhaven Hall or even at the countess of Sutherland's house. There must have been a thousand people inside, she realized with amazement, and wished for a moment that she'd stayed with Burbage. She'd never dreamed there could be so much gold and jewels in the whole world as there was in that room; the courtiers and ladies seemed to glitter bright as the sun.

She looked for Toby in the crowd and finally saw him, sitting at the virginals on a little dais at the far end of the chamber; he waved to her cheerily, and his confidence fired her courage. Bravely she followed Tarlton as he made his way through the knots of lords and ladies who leaned languidly against the great carved pillars, murmuring to one another in their silky, cultured voices, occasionally sparing a glance at Lucy as she went past.

And then, suddenly, Lucy saw her: Queen Elizabeth herself, grander even than Lucy had imagined her, dazzling as a star. She was dressed in bright jeweled satin and seated on a golden chair beneath a purple canopy, with a golden crown atop her high-piled red hair. In her hands she held a huge feathered fan; diamonds weighted her throat and her fingers and hung from her ears. She was breathtaking, overwhelming, so perfect, so—so *regal* that Lucy had to fight back an urge to burst into tears.

"Your majesty." Tarlton reached the throne at last and bobbed a low bow. Elizabeth turned her jeweled head toward him on a white neck as long as a swan's. "Pray permit me to present Master Willie Reilly, your majesty. The fine singer I told you of. The one they call the Rose of Shoreditch."

Elizabeth Tudor's imperial black gaze swept over Lucy from head to toe. "Who?" she asked, without a great deal of interest.

"Willie Reilly, your majesty. The boy who sings at The Theatre in Shoreditch."

"A boy, is it?"

"Aye, your majesty."

Elizabeth frowned down her nose. "And what is it he does? Does he juggle?"

"He sings, your majesty," Tarlton said rather desperately.

"Does he? So do canaries," said the queen, and turned away.

"Forgive me, your majesty, but you said you would hear him sing," Tarlton burst out.

"We do not recall saying any such thing."

"But you did, your majesty."

The queen looked back at him, and her black eyes flashed. "We do not care to be contradicted, Tarlton. And neither do we care to hear any beggar boys from Shoreditch sing."

Lucy stared at the queen in disbelief. Was this the Good Queen Bess she had been brought up to love and revere? Why, she was every bit as haughty and cold and disdainful as the worst of her courtiers! And Lucy had been so sure she would be different, would be as fond of her poorest subject as she was of her glittering courtiers. Wasn't that what her pop and Joe and everyone in Shoreditch said, that she had the love of her people because she loved them?

Lucy's disillusionment was so sharp that she felt it as a physical pain. "Please, let's just go," she whispered to Tarlton.

"You! Boy!" The queen was pointing a long finger straight at Lucy's nose. "Who gave you permission to speak?" The lords and ladies snickered; Lucy trembled. She wanted nothing in the world but to be gone from the place.

"N-no one," she stammered.

"No one, your majesty," Tarlton hissed.

The queen glanced at him, then back at Lucy. "You say the creature sings?"

"Yes, your majesty."

"Very well, Tarlton. Let us hear it sing. This may prove amusing." She settled back on her throne, smiling a thin, cold smile.

"Yes, your majesty," Tarlton murmured again, grabbing Lucy's arm and pulling her toward the virginals where Toby sat waiting. The faces of the lords and ladies they passed were taunting and hostile; Lucy recognized among them some she had seen at the countess of Sutherland's, including William Cecil and Francis Walsingham. So this is how they would have behaved toward me had they known I was from Shoreditch, she thought bitterly.

As calmly as she could, she took her place on the dais across from Toby, the virginals between them. The first song they'd decided on was an air by the late Sir Thomas Wyatt. " 'Forget Not Yet'?" she whispered, and Toby nodded behind his black mask. It wasn't likely he and Lucy could salvage this disastrous performance now, but she was determined to try. She clasped her hands before her and looked down at her toes, breathing in as deeply as she could, waiting for Toby to strike the first chord.

No sound came. Lucy held the breath as long as she could and then let it out. The courtiers tittered. " 'Forget Not Yet,' " she hissed to Toby again.

"I'd say he has forgot it," a sneering voice called out of the crowd.

What in the world was the matter with Toby? "It starts on a B," Lucy said pleadingly. "For God's sake, just give me a B!"

"A bee!" One of the grinning young lords began swatting the air around him. "Where is there a bee?" His circle of companions made loud buzzing noises while he jumped about and cried, "I am stung, I am stung!" Lucy looked at the queen; she, too, was laughing, her jeweled head thrown back.

"Play something, Toby," Lucy begged him. "Just give me a note!"

A courtier reached for his purse. "I'll give you five pounds," he offered, "if you'll head back to Shoreditch and stop wasting our time."

"Aye, back to Shoreditch!" "Get on back to Shoreditch!" a chorus of rude voices echoed. Even if Toby played now, Lucy could not have heard him above all the shouts and jeers.

Someone hurled a fistful of coins at her, and she leaped out of the way. "Look there! He can dance even if he can't sing!" a loud voice roared. "Dance, Willie Reilly!" Another shower of gold coins came winging her way. Others took up the cry, letting loose a torrent of shillings and crowns that clanked and spun about on the marble floor. "Dance, Willie, dance!" they chanted. Lucy saw fat Sir Christopher Dalton doubled over with laughter, fumbling for his purse, and it was more than she could bear. Flushed with humiliation, she caught up her skirts and ran blindly down from the dais, pushing through the taunting, sneering lords and ladies toward the nearest wall.

She reached a door, ran down a corridor, heard footsteps pounding behind her. Christ, they were going to run her right off the palace grounds! But it was only Toby, she realized; he caught up to her, black cloak flying, and pulled her out of the hallway into a small stone-walled room furnished with nothing more than a table and five chairs. Lucy collapsed against the wall, yanking off her wig, rubbing smudged paint from her face with her sleeve. "Damn you, Toby," she cried, "why did you make us look like such fools? Why the blazes didn't you play?"

"I had to think of some way to explain why Willie Reilly never sang in public again after his Whitehall performance for the queen."

Lucy stared at the tall figure in the black hood, every drop of blood draining from her face. That wasn't Toby's voice. She knew whose voice that was.

"It's been a long time, Lucy," Bram Carlyle said, pulling off the hood.

Lucy ran for the door, screaming as loud and as hard as she could. He caught her from behind, his hand clamping over her mouth. She tried to twist away, kicking at his legs, but his grip was too strong. "Promise me you won't scream again," he ordered. "Promise?" She nodded, and he took his hand away, and she let out another bloodcurdling yell.

"Dammit, Lucy!" He clapped his hand back over her mouth, then cursed again as she bit him. "Stop that!" For answer she ground her heel down onto his foot with all the strength she had. "Very well," he said grimly, "if that's how you want it—" Quickly, efficiently he gagged her with his hood and bound her hands behind the back of the chair with the belt from her gown. "Now, are you ready to listen to me?" She tossed her head, her green eyes flashing fire, straining at her bonds.

Someone knocked at the door. Lucy tried to scream through the gag but could not; instead she banged her chair against the wall, backed up into the table, and sent it crashing over onto its side. Bram lunged for her, but he was too late; the door had already opened wide.

"Dear me," said the tall, elegant redhead in jeweled satin who stood there plying her ostrich-plume fan. "I did warn you, Bram, that she was going to be angry. That was a perfectly horrid trick you made me play!"

Chapter 18

"Thank God!" Bram sighed as he looked up and saw the queen. "She won't listen to anything I say; she just keeps screaming."

"I rather think we heard her," Elizabeth Tudor said wryly.

"And I can't say I blame her," Francis Walsingham declared, following his sovereign into the room.

After him came William Cecil. "Lucy, my dear. So good to see you again." He crossed the floor to kiss her hand, noticed her bonds, and blinked. "Good heavens, Bram, don't you think you might—"

"All right, but cover your ears," Bram said grimly, and removed Lucy's gag and the belt from her hands.

"You know," the queen chided her sternly, "you really ought not to yell like that; you will ruin your voice."

Lucy backed slowly away from the four of them, right up to the wall. "Where's Toby?" she whispered. "What have you done to Toby?"

Walsingham answered her: "He is on his way back to Shoreditch with James Burbage. He knew nothing about any of this until he got here, Lucy, so you mustn't be cross with him."

Lucy looked at Bram, her green eyes narrowed. "Why aren't you in the Tower where you belong?"

"I never was in the Tower, Lucy. After you saw me last night at The Theatre I knew you'd never come to court today if you thought there was any chance I'd be here."

"So," Elizabeth put in, "he came here and created a scene. He just went on insulting me and I kept threatening punishments until finally I got to the one that he wanted."

She glared at Bram, wagging her ostrich fan. "Did you have to pick my poor mother to insult?"

"You started it," he told her easily, "with what you said about my wife."

She sniffed, then turned to Lucy, still huddled against the wall. "My dear child, there is nothing to be afraid of. I am sorry about that scene out there with the courtiers; it was simply disgraceful. But those stupid sheep all take their lead from me, at least when they are in my presence, and Bram told me I had to be rude to you for your own good."

"He doesn't give a cat's damn about my good," Lucy burst out, "nor yours either! He is a spy!"

"Well, of course he is, child. He works for Sir Francis here," the queen agreed.

"Oh, no, he doesn't! He is working for the queen of Scots!"

"My God." Bram stared at her. "How the devil did you find out about that?"

"I was out by the cliff the night you came back to Lockhaven Hall. I saw Anthony Babington come up to meet you. And I heard everything you said—about the letter you brought him, and how you'd always been true to Mary's cause, and about how he saw you kill Olive."

"Oh, dear," the queen said worriedly. "Francis, Bram, do set that table upright again. William, would you be a pet and ring for wine? And then, Bram, I think you had better do some explaining."

Walsingham frowned as he and Bram raised the table Lucy had knocked over. "I don't think an explanation is necessary, Bess. After all, the fewer people who know what Bram's up to—"

"Dear God, Francis," the queen said impatiently, "we can't have Lucy thinking Bram is a murderer."

"How do we know Lucy is trustworthy?" the secretary of state demanded.

"Oh, honestly, Francis, must you be so suspicious of everyone all of the time?" the queen asked crossly, settling herself at the table with a swish of her skirts.

"It's my job to be suspicious—and to keep you alive."

"All right, you two," Cecil said bemusedly, carrying

in the tray a servant had brought in answer to his summons. "Stop bickering; you are as bad as children. Lucy, do sit down." He held out a chair for her, and she perched on its edge, feeling completely bewildered.

"Wine, my dear?" the queen asked, filling a cup and pushing it toward her. "Heaven knows I need some, and I can't abide drinking alone." She poured for the men as well. Walsingham and Cecil sat down; only Bram remained standing.

"Go on, Bram," Cecil said. "Just begin at the beginning."

"I'd like my objections to this breach of security noted," Walsingham announced.

"Consider them noted, then, Francis," the queen told him. "Bram, go on."

"Begin at the beginning." He shook his head, pacing back and forth across the small room. "I suppose that would be when I married Olive. I don't know, Lucy, how much you've heard about her. She was much older than I—very beautiful, very glamorous. I was very young and very foolish. I had just turned fifteen; my father had died the year before, and I'd come into my inheritance and come to court for the first time. When Olive took an interest in me, I could scarcely believe it. She was everything a boy that age dreams of—experienced, sophisticated, worldly-wise. I fell for her—I fell hard. I asked her to marry me, and when she said yes I thought I was the luckiest—" He swallowed. "The luckiest man in the world."

"If Bram hadn't been so new to court," Cecil said quietly, "he would have known that Lady Olive Montague came with a reputation in addition to her more obvious charms."

Lucy looked up at Bram; he was smiling sadly. "As I recall, William, you tried to hint as much to me and I challenged you to a duel. God, it is hard to believe I was ever that young."

"It was the event of the season, that wedding," Elizabeth noted. "No one could quite believe Lady Olive had snagged herself a husband at last. But Bram—well, do you know what they say, Lucy, about people having stars in their eyes? That day in Westminster Abbey, when we watched Bram waiting for Olive at the altar, was the first time I really saw anyone with stars in his eyes.''

"For a long time," Bram said, his voice wistful, "those stars blinded me. She didn't care for Derbyshire; I bought her the house in London, so she could be close to court. Anything she wanted, I gave her—clothes, jewels, money. A lot of money. I never asked what she did with it. I was happy. I assumed she was happy, too. The short of it is, after five years I'd damned near bankrupted my estates. I told her we would have to move back to Derbyshire so I could put my affairs in order. She refused. I would have insisted, but then she told me the most wonderful news. After all those years, she was finally with child." For a moment his blue eyes met Lucy's, and she realized that she knew something even the queen and her ministers did not—that Olive had told Bram the child was not his.

"So I let her stay in London," he went on, "to be near the best doctors, have the finest care. I went home to Derbyshire, worked hard, lived like a monk, managed to hold on to my lands."

"While his wife was carrying on all over London," Walsingham put in. "By that time Lady Olive Carlyle had come to my attention. She'd taken up with a man named Anthony Babington, a romantic young Catholic devoted to Queen Mary's cause."

"I don't think I would have cared if she'd taken up with the devil." A spasm of pain crossed Bram's face. "Because by that time she had given me a son. And it all began again. Nothing was too good for her. I came back to London and gave her everything she asked for. Before long, there wasn't more to give. I begged her to come home with me, but she told me she was with child again. And I let her stay here. She gave me a daughter. And then, miracle of miracles, she came to live at Lockhaven Hall. I thought having the children had domesticated her at last. The truth, though I didn't know it at the time, was that a man named Anthony Babington had just bought the manor down in the ravine. And Olive began to spend a great deal of time down in the music room.''

He drew a deep breath. "For three years they carried

on right under my nose, and I never even guessed it. I was busy with the children. I loved them—so much. I might never have caught on if it weren't for the money. She ought to have needed less since she was living at home, but she wanted more. One day I had a great deal of gold in my study—nearly five thousand pounds, the wages for the tenant farmers for the autumn crops. It disappeared. And somehow—I guess I was growing up—I knew Olive had taken it. I went looking for her, and I found her in the corridor by the old wing. By the stairs to the music room.''

''Bram, don't you want this wine?'' the queen asked. He shook his head, turning his back to the table.

''She had the money with her. I asked her where she was taking it, why she needed it, but she wouldn't say. That was when I remembered the secret passageway from the cliff to the music room. Christ, I had shown it to her myself; I used to play down there when I was a child. And all the whispers, all the rumors I had heard about her came back to me. I accused her of having a lover, and she didn't deny it. She admitted it proudly, said it was all my fault, that I wasn't—that I couldn't—'' He swallowed. ''She told me his name. She laughed at me.''

''The row that Jem and Johnny heard,'' Lucy whispered.

''Aye,'' Bram said hoarsely. ''She said I wasn't man enough to stop her from going down to Babington. I went for her, started after her, and she ran down the stairs. And then she missed the step and fell. By the time I got to the music room, she was dead.''

''Then you didn't kill her?'' Lucy cried in confusion.

''No. I did something worse.'' He drew a long breath. ''God forgive me, I was so filled with hate and rage! I hated her for not letting me kill her. I wished I had killed her. And I—I grabbed her, put my hands around her neck and just—I just— Jesus, it was inhuman, what I did.''

''It was all too human,'' Cecil told him softly. Bram leaned his head against the far wall, his shoulders shaking, unable to go on, and so the lord high treasurer picked up the tale. ''Just at that moment, Babington came in through the passageway from the cliff. When he saw Bram kneeling over Olive with his hands at her throat, naturally he assumed he'd just missed witnessing a murder. And he didn't exactly waste time in mourning for his dead mistress.''

"What did he do?" Lucy asked, wide-eyed.

"He blackmailed Bram. It turned out that the money Olive had been taking was going through Babington to a group of men who were working to depose Elizabeth and crown Mary queen of England in her place. If Bram agreed to keep paying him, Babington said, he wouldn't tell the authorities what he had seen. Bram kept his head remarkably under the circumstances,'' Cecil said with admiration. "He professed to be an admirer of Mary's and asked if there wasn't something more he could do. Babington took him up on the offer and gave him the job of smuggling letters in and out to Mary at Chartley Castle. They shook hands, Babington left, and Bram came straight to London and told the entire story to Francis and me.''

Lucy stared at Bram's broad back. "That's where you go when you go off on business? To Chartley Castle? To Mary?''

He turned to face her, nodding. "When Babington has a letter to go to Mary, he leaves it in the music room. There's a tavernkeeper in Sheffield whom he pays to make special ale barrels for him, barrels with false bottoms. I hide the letter in a barrel, deliver it to Chartley, and wait for Mary to write an answer. That goes back in the ale barrel, and I bring Mary's letter to Babington. My playing the virginals is the signal to him that the letter is ready for him.''

"Naturally," Cecil put in briskly, "before he hands over any of the letters to either Mary or Babington, he makes copies for Francis and me.''

"So Babington thinks Bram is on Mary's side," Lucy said slowly, "but really he is working for Elizabeth.''

"Precisely," Cecil told her, beaming.

Walsingham was still frowning. "I really do wish we didn't have to go into all this.''

"Well, I really wish," said the queen, "someone else would have some of this wine.''

"What we need to know from you, Lucy," Cecil said,

"is where you got the letter from Mary that Bram found in your mirror at Lockhaven Hall."

"It has something to do with the man that was trying to kill you, doesn't it?" Bram asked her.

She nodded hesitantly. "I had a pawnshop in Shoreditch, you see." And as briefly as she could she explained about Babington and Hawk-Nose and the lute letter and the fire and Joe. Walsingham listened closely, making notes in a small book he took from his doublet.

"And this Hawk-Nose—he never told you his name?" Lucy shook her head. "Well, what the devil did he look like?"

"Like a gentleman," she said rather helplessly. "White hair, pale gray eyes, and a nose like a hawk."

"That describes half the noblemen in England," the queen said, "or maybe more."

"Lucy, why the devil didn't you show that letter to me?" Bram demanded. "Why didn't you tell me the whole story?"

"I was afraid!" she said passionately. "I didn't trust you! And then by the time I started to, I had figured out what the letter said, and there wasn't anything important in it. So I just thought Hawk-Nose must have killed Joe and tried to kill me out of spite."

"She has a point, Francis," said the queen. "There isn't anything in any of those letters from Mary except silly prattle about needlepoint and songs and compliments to me."

Walsingham rolled his eyes. "And you believe her when she writes that she wishes you nothing but long life and happiness."

"Why not? That's what I wish her."

"Bess, you can't judge other people's motives by your own," Cecil told her.

"Oh, honestly, William, you are starting to sound like Francis, always seeing conspiracies lurking behind every bush. Mary is a weak, foolish woman who couldn't conspire to see past the nose on her face."

"Bess," Walsingham said wearily, "you are the brightest woman I know, but when it comes to your cousin Mary you're the one who can't see; you are blind as a bat. She wants your crown. She wants you dead."

"Don't be ridiculous! She is grateful to me; it says so in every one of those letters she writes."

"At least let me arrest Babington," the secretary of state argued. "A few days with that bastard on the rack—"

"No," the queen said quietly but firmly. "You know what I think of such methods of persuasion; they don't lead to truth, only to more lies. My mother died because of the falsehoods a weak, silly boy had pulled out of him by the rack."

"Dammit, Bess, I am sick to death of fighting you on this," Walsingham snapped. "That woman's string of dead husbands and lovers is proof enough for me of what lies in her heart, no matter what she might say in those letters. Had it been up to me she would have been executed the moment she stepped over the border from Scotland."

"But it's not up to you, is it, Francis?" The queen's voice held a glimmer of anger. "Perhaps you can forget that she is my cousin, my own flesh and blood, but I cannot. And I don't like beheadings—especially beheadings of rulers who have been dethroned by their subjects. It sets a dangerous precedent." Her long fingers pulled at the diamonds circling her throat.

"You've never even met the woman, for God's sake," Walsingham said belligerently. "How can you have any family feeling toward her?"

Elizabeth's black eyes burned. "She has Tudor blood in her veins. And her son is the last of us, God help him. If King James of Scotland is to become King James of England *and* Scotland, I won't risk his punishing my people and my country after I am dead because he believes I had his mother executed unjustly!"

Cecil intervened. "Then what would you have us do, Bess?"

"Bring me proof. Bring me hard, solid proof."

"When her scheming succeeds and you are dead and buried in your grave," Walsingham said angrily, "will that be proof enough?"

"Francis, how the devil can she kill me? Nothing leaves Chartley that isn't checked by your men except the letters

Bram carries, and we have copies of them! For God's sake, let the poor woman live out her life in peace with her embroidery and her songs and her dogs. She means no harm to me.''

''Your majesty,'' Bram said quietly, ''I have met Mary. And I would not make the mistake of underestimating her. She has a dangerous ability to seduce men into doing her will.''

''I will hear no more talk of her,'' said the queen.

''But, your majesty—''

''I said no more, Bram Carlyle!'' Elizabeth cried, and hurled her wine cup across the room. In the silence that followed her outburst Lucy looked at her and saw she was shaking. Lord in heaven, she is jealous of Mary, she realized suddenly. They were opposites, these last two Tudor women: the Virgin Queen and the Harlot Queen. And it was Mary's scandalous power of seduction that Elizabeth envied, even feared, because it was the one weapon the queen of England did not include in her own arsenal, the one that, given her mother's tragic history, she had never dared use.

Cecil, who had served the queen from the first day of her realm, recognized that these were dangerous waters. ''Bess.'' He reached for her hand. ''We worry about you because we love you.''

''Do you? Are you sure? Perhaps you would rather have Mary as your queen, if she is as seductive as Bram says. Perhaps you would prefer a woman who is not so pig-headed and blind,'' Elizabeth said accusingly, ''who is still young, who isn't dried up and ugly and old!''

''Ugly? Old? You?'' Bram laughed. ''Good God, you're a hundred—nay, a thousand—times more beautiful than Mary!''

''You are only telling me that because you have made me angry,'' the queen of England said with a pout as childish as Minnie's.

''And she looks a good ten years older than you.''

''Oh, go on, Bram Carlyle.'' But the pout faded, just a bit. ''I have seen portraits of her, you know. She's a fine-looking woman.''

"She chooses imaginative portraitists. I've seen her in the flesh—of which she has, incidentally, a great deal."

"Putting on weight, is she?" Elizabeth primped at her own tiny waistline. "Pity. But then one really couldn't expect anyone as self-indulgent as she to maintain her figure, I suppose. How is her complexion these days?"

"Dreadfully pasty," Bram told her. "The last time I saw her she was breaking out in some sort of red blotches."

"You don't say. Dear, dear. The cousinly thing to do would be to send her some of that special cream I use," Elizabeth mused. Then she laughed. "I don't think, though, that I shall." She smiled at Lucy, her good humor restored. "My dear child, is there anything else you need to know?"

"As a matter of fact, I would like to know what Bram meant when he said he had to make sure Willie Reilly never sang in public again."

He met her gaze, hesitated, and then spoke quietly, quickly: "I know you won't come home to Lockhaven Hall, Lucy; I know you won't marry me. But you can't stay in London."

"Why not?" she asked.

"Because it is far too dangerous. I recognized you up on that stage. What if you had played for the queen and Babington realized who you were—or, even worse, the man with the hawk's nose saw you?"

"No, no," she said impatiently. "I mean, why wouldn't I marry you?"

He dropped his gaze abruptly. "We both know why."

"Bram Carlyle, are you blushing?" the queen asked in disbelief.

"I'm sure I don't know why," Lucy said, completely bewildered. "The only reason I ran away was because of what I heard you saying to Babington, and you've explained all that."

Slowly he raised his head, his blue eyes wary, shy like a skittish wild thing, but with a flicker of hope in their indigo depths. "The only reason? Then it wasn't because of—" He stopped.

"You're right, Bess. He is blushing," Walsingham declared, and chuckled.

"Francis. Bess." Cecil was making little nodding motions toward the door, getting up from his chair.

"Where are you going?" asked the queen.

"Don't you think we ought to leave them alone together?" he asked rather pointedly.

"Must we?" She saw his expression and sighed. "Oh, I suppose we must. Francis, come along."

When they'd gone Lucy looked at Bram. "Why did you think I left you?"

"Olive didn't just tell me—she didn't just say Babington was her lover and that he fathered the children, Lucy. She said that I didn't—that I couldn't satisfy her. That it was my fault that she took lovers, because I wasn't a man."

"Oh, Bram!" Lucy didn't know whether to laugh or to cry. "And you believed her?"

"Well, isn't it true?"

"I don't know whether she was telling the truth about Babington and the children, Bram, but I *know* she lied about that. I have dreamed about your making love to me every night for the past four months."

"You have? Really?"

"Oh, my love, yes!"

"But—you didn't say anything, Lucy. You didn't cry out or call my name—"

"I was afraid, Bram—afraid that you would stop. And afraid that it wouldn't be—you know. Ladylike," she confessed, abashed.

"Oh, Lucy. You damned little fool!" He laughed then, shaking her by the shoulders. "You put me through four months of hell because you thought there was an etiquette for making love?"

"Well, it certainly seemed as though there ought to be," she said indignantly. "It was one hell of a lot more exciting than eating peas!"

"Oh, goose." He cupped her face in his hands, looking down into her clear green eyes. "What am I to do with you?"

"Would you consider—giving me another chance?"

"I would. Oh, God, Lucy, I would!" He took her into his arms, pulling her right out of her chair and showering her with kisses, kissing her eyes, her mouth, her throat, her hair. She returned the kisses joyously, tears streaming down her face; it was heaven to be in his arms again. "Don't ever leave me, Lucy," he begged her, and she knew that he was crying, too.

"I won't Bram. I promise I won't, no matter what that old ghost might say!"

He pulled away from her, holding her at arm's length. "What ghost?"

"Oh—" She blushed, lowering her gaze. "I kept dreaming there was a ghost in my bedchamber, telling me that you had killed your wife."

"And you thought it was real?" he asked incredulously.

"Well, not until after I heard what you said to Babington, that night out on the cliff."

He tipped up her chin, forcing her to look into his eyes. "A logical creature like you, believing in ghosts?"

"You told me yourself that there was a ghost in Lockhaven Hall," she reminded him.

"I never meant the sort of ghost that creeps up behind you in dark hallways or rattles the pots in the cupboard, love. I only meant the ghost of Olive's memory. But all of that is in the past now. I'm not afraid of her anymore. And I don't want you to be."

"I thought perhaps it was someone playing a trick on me," Lucy said hesitantly. "Someone who wanted me gone, someone who hated me."

"No one at Lockhaven Hall hates you, Lucy. How could anyone hate you? You must have been imagining things."

"But Bram, it was so real! I would wake up and smell roses, and hear silk skirts rustling, and there was a voice—" Her eyes grew wide and frightened at the memory.

He pulled her against his chest, hugging her tightly. "You were dreaming, then. That's all. Only dreaming. From now on I am going to make certain that you have happy dreams." He leaned his cheek against her black hair. "Do you know where I was, love, before I saw you at The Theatre? I was in Barkers Lane."

"Oh, Bram, no! I wish you hadn't gone there; it's such a wretched place."

"It is wretched," he agreed. "But it wasn't until I looked down that street that I truly understood what I'd lost when you left me. I thought, God in heaven, what spirit, what strength there was in you, to rise out of there as bright and shining as a star."

"I don't want you to pity me, Bram, for where I came from."

"It didn't make me pity you, Lucy. It only made me love you more."

Lucy put her hand to his heart. "What you are doing for Elizabeth—taking those letters in and out of Chartley, copying them for Sir Francis—it is very dangerous, isn't it? Babington would kill you if he ever found out what you are up to."

"What he and Mary are trying to do is far more dangerous, love. They want to turn back time, back to when the power and privilege in this country was concentrated in the hands of a few rich families who wrung all the wealth they could out of the people and the land. Families that kept a whole nation of people like you ground under their heels through the forces of ignorance and poverty. Do you know why they hate Elizabeth?"

Lucy shook her head slowly, seeing blue fire flare in his eyes as he spoke. "Because she recognizes the worth of a genius like Walter Raleigh and knights him even though his father was a nobody," he told her. Because she gives posts and favors to a man like young Francis Bacon simply out of delight in his mind. Walsingham—his grandfather was a shoemaker. Cecil's father kept an inn in Lincolnshire. Babington and his ilk, these rich, petty men with nothing to distinguish them but the pedigrees tacked to their names— they see which way the wind is blowing. They look at the future, and they see their power crumbling beneath their feet like their rotting old castles. They look at the future, and there's no place in it for them. And they're terrified, Lucy. They're terrified of you and all the men and women like you whom Elizabeth is setting free."

"Cecil's father was an innkeeper?" Lucy echoed in disbelief.

"The finest one in Staffordshire, he's proud to say."

"And you believe so much in what Elizabeth is doing that you are willing to die for it?"

"Die for it *and* live by it," he told her. "So I'll ask you again, in person this time: Lucy Jones, will you marry me?"

"Well . . . that depends," said Lucy.

"On what?"

"On how much influence you have with the queen. Do you think you can persuade her to give James Burbage's troupe a chance to perform here at Whitehall?"

"Tarlton's already delivered an invitation to him to appear, on St. Swithin's Day," he told her, grinning.

"Really? Oh, Bram, that was kind of you!"

"I figured it was the least I could do, considering that he would be losing his star attraction—the Rose of Shoreditch." He shook his head in wonder. "I never dreamed, though, that I'd be taking you home with me."

And then his arms were around her, and he held her as though he would never in his life let her go. Lucy began to cry again, and he kissed the tears from her eyes. "God, I have missed you," he whispered. Then there was no sound in the room but their two hearts beating, no words except the breathless wonder of rediscovery as their mouths and their hands touched and explored with mounting urgency—until the queen of England coughed discreetly, looking in through the door.

"You owe me ten pounds, Francis," she said crisply, and then addressed Bram: "He said it would take you at least an hour to talk her into marrying you after pulling that nasty trick; I said only half."

"Your majesty, were you eavesdropping?" Bram demanded. "Why, I've a seven-year-old daughter with better manners than you."

"Oh, Bram! How are Minnie and Stacy?" Lucy cried. "I have wondered about them so often!"

"Of course I was eavesdropping," Elizabeth admitted cheerfully. "How else would we know who had won? Now, about the wedding. I thought we'd have it here, in the chapel at Westminster Abbey. Cecil can give Lucy away, and—"

"They've been utterly impossible," Bram said, answering Lucy's question. "Minnie won't take her baths, and Stacy keeps telling me to go to hell. And—"

"I have already got the cook planning the wedding supper. I thought roast quail and venison, and—"

"On his birthday Stacy wouldn't touch the cake Cook made. And he threw all the presents I bought for him into the goose pond. And—"

"Then I thought since you are supposed to be in the Tower anyway, Bram, you and Lucy might use the royal apartments there for your honeymoon. And—"

"Both growing like weeds. And—"

"Then in a few months, when the whole incident has been forgotten, you can both go home," the queen finished triumphantly, and paused for breath. Not until then did she notice Cecil and Walsingham were laughing uproariously. "What is it?" she demanded of them. "What is so amusing?"

"Oh, Bess!" Cecil wiped his eyes on his sleeve. "They haven't heard a single word you said!"

"They haven't—Bram Carlyle, are you ignoring your sovereign?"

He looked at her blankly. "I beg your pardon?"

"Oh, Bram," Lucy said, "can we leave right away, please?"

"I'm afraid, Bess," Walsingham said, chuckling, "you won't get to plan this wedding after all."

The queen's black eyes had turned suddenly wistful. "Do you know, I had four stepmothers while I was growing up, and not one of them ever gave a cat's damn about me." Then she shrugged off her memories and glared at Bram. "Go along home, then, if you must, but mind you tell that son and daughter of yours how lucky I said they are to be getting Lucy."

He bowed, kissing her ring. "I'll tell them. But I think they already know. Francis, what can you do about getting me out of the Tower?"

The queen's secretary of state shrugged. "Say you bought your way free of the charges against you, I suppose. Everyone already thinks that sort of thing goes on all the time. You'll have to stay clear of court for a few months." He winked at Lucy. "But you were probably planning on that anyway."

Lucy blushed and curtsied to the queen. "I'm ever so

grateful to you, your majesty, for giving James Burbage and his players another chance. They're really very good."

"We shall see," said the queen. "I will give them a chance. After that, they rise or fall on their own merits."

"Do you want to stop and say goodbye to them, Lucy, before we leave London?" Bram asked.

She laughed. "Not if you are thinking of leaving any time within the next week. With the queen's invitation under their belts, James and Toby and all the rest of them will be stone drunk for at least that long. No, I'll write from Derbyshire—and send them a wedding invitation, too."

"They are respectable characters, aren't they, these players of yours?" the queen asked Lucy rather worriedly. "There have been some rumors—"

"Perfectly respectable, your majesty," Lucy assured her, then added beneath her breath, "When they're sober, that is."

"Bram." Walsingham shook hands with him gravely. "You'll have to be more careful than ever now, with Lucy at Lockhaven Hall. Babington mustn't see her."

"Don't worry. I'll look after her. And Babington won't be in any hurry to be seen at my house after the show I put on here last night. He'll be on his guard, too." His arm tightened around Lucy's waist. "I'd say that takes care of everything except how we're to leave London. I've got Bellerophon, but could any of you be so kind as to lend Lucy a coach?"

Not ten yards outside the city gates of London, the carriage in which Lucy was riding came to an abrupt halt. She peered out the window and saw Bram hitch Bellerophon to the rear staves. "Do you know the way to Derbyshire, my good man?" he called to the driver.

"Aye, sir."

"Well, drive there, if you will, and keep going no matter what you hear."

"Aye, sir."

Bram opened the door. "Oh—and you might do your best to avoid any ruts."

"Aye, sir," the grinning driver said.

Giggling, Lucy sank back against the pillowed seat. "I thought gentlemen didn't ride in coaches."

"The rules of etiquette were made to be broken," Bram told her gravely, and kicked shut the door. Then he whistled between his teeth, seeing the plush padded benches, the rugs and pillows strewn over the carriage floor. "The queen certainly travels in style. What is in there, pray tell?" He nodded to a huge wicker basket.

"Elizabeth was kind enough to pack us a supper. She thought we might be hungry. Are you?"

"I am starved for you," he said, and fell on her savagely.

"How long a ride is it to Lockhaven Hall?" she whispered as he yanked open her bodice strings.

"Fifteen hours."

"You'll be taking your time, then."

"The hell I will."

He stripped off her gown with indecent haste, then stared at the rough hose and boots and drawers she wore beneath it. "My God. Do you realize I'm about to make love to someone that everybody in Shoreditch thinks is a boy?"

Lucy reached up self-consciously to touch her close-cropped curls. "I know I must look dreadful."

He pulled her hands away and kissed a cowlicky curl by her ear. "You couldn't look dreadful if you tried." He put his hand to her breast, and her flesh quivered at his touch. "Christ have mercy," he murmured, catching his breath.

Lucy unbuttoned his doublet and shirt and pulled them down over his shoulders, her fingertips tracing the muscles of his arms and chest. "You are beautiful," she told him. "I thought that the day you took off your shirt there at the goose pond, and I still think so. The most beautiful man I have ever seen."

"Have you been looking at a lot of naked men since you came back to London?" he asked, arching a brow.

"In the dressing rooms, every day. But they didn't make me feel the way you do."

"How do I make you feel?"

She leaned toward him, rubbing her breasts against his

chest, her mouth seeking his. "On fire," she whispered.
"You make me feel all on fire."

He pulled her onto the floor of the coach, tucking pillows around and beneath her, and tugged off her stockings
and boots and drawers. She reached for his belt to un-
buckle it and shivered as her hand brushed his manhood,
already swollen and hard. He kicked off his shoes, yanked
off his hose and breeches, and she smiled as she saw that
thick rod of love, running her fingers over its pulsing veins,
its smooth swollen head. He groaned and kissed her
breasts, sucked the pink nipples hungrily.

Lucy began to sigh, quick breathless sighs to match the
quickening of her heartbeat. "Oh, Christ," Bram muttered, "oh, Lucy. You will drive me mad—"

"I can't help it," she whispered. "It is what I feel."
His hand slipped between her thighs; his fingers found the
hard bud of her desire and lingered there, and she buried
her face against his chest, stifling the cry of delight that
rose in her throat.

He pushed her back on the pillows, staring down at her,
his blue eyes dark and watchful. "Am I pleasing you,
Lucy?"

"You are. Oh, God, you are!"

He took his thick shaft in his hand and rubbed it back
and forth over her belly, up across her taut breasts. "And
this, does this please you?"

"Yes," she whispered, arching at his touch.

He straddled her then, his mouth at her ear as he parted
her thighs. "And this—" He thrust into her, quick and
hard. "And this." He drove again, deeper, and withdrew,
and she caught his buttocks, clinging to him, pulling him
into her, refusing to let go.

"Oh, Bram—"

"Lucy. This, does this please you?"

"Bram, Bram. Yes," she whispered, and then shouted
it as the white fire rippled through her in great spreading
waves while he raised her up and plunged her down with
him, as they moved together, as the rhythm of the horses'
hooves, the rumbling wheels, his groans, and her cries all
merged into one.

"Lucy," he panted, "oh, Lucy. Oh, love." Her warm

sheath tightened around him; he sank into her to the hilt over and over again, and then Lucy was aware of nothing but the bright, blinding heat that overwhelmed her as his seed exploded, as they came together in a fierce, shuddering blaze of ecstasy.

Slowly the fire subsided, faded to a glow. Lucy opened her eyes and saw he was still kneeling above her, panting, his chest heaving, his skin bathed in a faint sheen of sweat. "Did you hear me?" she asked.

"I heard you," he said, and grinned.

"If there's still any doubt in your mind, I'd be willing to do it again."

"Oh, we will, Lucy. We will."

They kissed and caressed through Hertford and Bedford and Northampton, while the carriage rolled on and night fell and the moon rose high up in the sky. It was a magical ride, filled with tenderness and warmth, measured in heartbeats and whispers, spaced by fingertips. They ate the queen's cooks' roasted quails while they both lay naked; they drank wine and spilled wine and licked the red drops from each other's mouths. They laughed at nothing; they talked of everything. They made love. They made plans. And they fell asleep at last, somewhere near Leicestershire, sated with everything but their hopes and their dreams.

When day came they dressed each other reluctantly, then undressed and made love once more, slowly, passionately, before Bram called out directions to Lockhaven Hall. As the carriage rolled up the drive, Lucy had to bite her lip to hold back her tears. "What is it?" Bram asked, his arm tight around her. "What's wrong?"

"Nothing's wrong. It is just that I am so happy to be—"

"Home," he finished for her, and she nodded happily.

The carriage stopped before the front doors just as Jeeves appeared on the stairs. "Good day, milord," he said as Bram jumped down.

"So it is, Jeeves!" He reached back into the carriage for Lucy. "See who has come back to us!"

"Good to see you again, Mistress Jones," said Jeeves, not batting an eye.

"Thank you, Jeeves. It is fine to see you again, too."
Lucy giggled as Bram pulled her past him into the armory
and whispered, "Doesn't anything ever surprise him?"

"Poor Jeeves. He's the only man I've ever met who is
completely lacking in imagination," Bram whispered
back, then shouted up the stairs to the nursery: "Minnie!
Stacy! I'm home!"

Minnie's small voice floated back down: "So what?"

"You see what it has been like around here without
you?" Bram asked wryly, then shouted again: "Would
you two come down here, please?"

"Go to hell," Stacy called back sullenly.

Lucy went to the foot of the staircase. "Stacy Carlyle,
is that any way to speak to your father?"

"Lucy?" He appeared at the top of the stairs, his blue
eyes wide in disbelief. "Lucy!" He flew toward her at a
dead run, yelling to his sister: "Minnie, come quick! It's
Lucy! Lucy's come home!"

"Oof!" Lucy laughed as he rushed into her arms.
"Look at you, look at how you've grown!"

"Look at you! What happened to your hair?"

"It's a long story," she said. "But I'll tell you all about
it just as soon as I've kissed Minnie. Where is she, anyway?"

Bram touched her arm, nodding toward the top of the
staircase. Minnie stood there with Reggie clasped in her
arms, her small face stamped with uncertainty.

"Hello, pet," Lucy said softly. "I've missed you terribly. Did you miss me?" The girl nodded, biting her lip.
"Then won't you please come down here and give me a
kiss?" The golden curls tossed, shaking no. "Oh, pet,
whatever is the matter?"

Minnie clung to the kitten. "You will only go away
again."

"No, she won't," Bram told her. "Not ever again."

"But how do you *know*?" Minnie wailed.

"Because Lucy's marrying me."

"Marrying you? Really?" She came down one step.
Lucy nodded. "Really."

"Marry like in forever?" she asked, and came down
two more steps.

"Forever and ever," Lucy said.

"Damn," Minnie breathed. "Stacy, we did it!"

"*You* did it?" Bram echoed, laughing as she ran all the way down the stairs into Lucy's arms.

"Even if you did," Lucy said sternly, kissing Minnie's nose, "you owe tuppence to the Treasury."

Part IV

Chapter 19

Lucy stood in the armory and surveyed her mustered troops, cool and calm as a veteran general preparing for battle. "Ready?" she asked, glancing up from the list she held.

"Yes, sir," Minnie and Stacy chorused, snapping to attention. Jem giggled; Cook looked dour. "Quite ready," said Jeeves, ever unflustered. Bram crossed his arms over his chest and grinned.

"Very well, then." Lucy read out the first item from the list. "Wedding supper."

"Everything's done but the pies, 'n' they're bakin'," Cook told her.

"You're a wonder, Cook, truly." Lucy checked that off. "Tables laid?"

"For forty," Jeeves confirmed.

"Thank you. Flowers?"

"Aye, Miss Lucy. For ye 'n' Miss Minnie both," said Jem, bobbing a curtsy.

"And in the chapel?"

"We took care of that," Stacy assured her.

"And in here, I see." Lucy smiled, surveying the garlands of greenery draped over the weapons that lined the walls and the wildflowers tucked into their great-great-grandfather's steel visor. "Very nice indeed. Where was I? Ah, yes, the musicians. They are coming from Harten House with Margery. So, all that leaves is the priest and the wine. Who had the priest and the wine?" Nobody said anything. Lucy looked down at the list. "I seem to see the initials B.C. next to those items. Now who could that be?"

"Oh, damn," Bram said faintly.

"Tuppence!" Minnie and Stacy both cried, breaking ranks to wrestle him down to the armory floor and tickle his ribs. "The Treasury is growing by leaps and bounds ever since Father had to start paying, isn't it?" Minnie asked Lucy as she sat on Bram's stomach.

"It certainly is. Darling, you didn't really forget the priest, did you?"

"Of course I didn't. He'll be here."

"And the wine?" Stacy demanded.

"All right, maybe I did forget the—oof!" He rolled over, curling into a ball, as they fell on him again. "Back, savages, back!"

Lucy giggled and went to his aid, pulling the children off him. "Upstairs, you two, and take your baths and get dressed. Everyone else is dismissed, thank you very much. Except, Lord Carlyle, for you."

"Uh-oh, Father," the children teased, skipping off upstairs. "You are in for it now!"

"You didn't really think I would forget the priest, did you?" Bram asked Lucy, getting up from the floor.

"Knowing how absentminded you are? Of course I did." She stood on tiptoe to give him a kiss. "It's most unlike you to forget the wine, though."

"I've been far too intoxicated by you these past weeks to even think about drinking," he told her, returning the kiss. "Mmm. Let's go to bed," he suggested, and licked her ear. "We must have an hour or so until the guests arrive."

"No," Lucy said firmly.

"Come on," he coaxed, pulling her toward the portrait gallery. "I'll be ever so quick."

"Bram, I haven't gotten dressed, yet, or done my hair—"

"How long can that take?" he asked, running his fingers through her cropped curls. "It's shorter then mine."

"One more jest about my hair and I will call off this marriage," she threatened, just as the bell at the front gate jangled. "Oh, Lord, who can that be already?" She peeked out the armory window, then started in surprise as she saw the rider Johnny was letting in through the gate. "Why, it's James, James Burbage! I know I sent an invitation to The Theatre, but I never dreamed he would come!'' She ran out to the drive to greet him, throwing her arms around him and kissing his leathery cheek.

''Hello, Lucy.'' He returned her kiss, then pumped Bram's hand. ''Good to finally meet you, Lord Carlyle.''

''Bram. Please.''

''All right, then, Bram.'' Burbage looked up at Lockhaven Hall and blinked. ''Nice little place you've got here.''

Lucy laughed, taking his arm and leading him toward the house. ''I can't wait to hear how your performance for the queen went,'' she exclaimed. ''You must tell me all about it.''

''Oh, we can save all that for later.''

''I want to hear now,'' she insisted. ''And where is Toby? Why didn't he come with you?''

''Well, he's awfully busy back in London.''

''Then the performance for her majesty must have gone well. Have you got a patron?''

''No . . . no, we haven't got a patron yet.''

Beneath his offhanded voice Lucy heard a note of grief that he could not conceal; she looked at him curiously. ''Something is wrong, isn't it?''

''No, no,'' he insisted gruffly. ''What could be wrong?''

''Something has happened, hasn't it? Is it Toby? Is he sick?''

''Toby is fine.''

''James Burbage, you are not so good an actor as all that,'' Lucy told him accusingly. ''There is something wrong, and I want to know what it is.''

''Come on, now, lass, this is your wedding day. You shouldn't be concerning yourself with—''

''Dammit, James, if you or Toby is in trouble, I want to know!'' Lucy cried. ''If you don't tell me, I will only think it is something worse than it is.''

Burbage sighed, pulling off his hat and rubbing his eyes. ''I was going to tell you, Lucy. Only not today. You ought to be celebrating, making merry.''

''It can't be so bad as all that, can it?'' Bram asked.

''It is pretty bad.'' Burbage stared at the armory floor. ''Toby's in prison. The Fleet.''

"Jesus in heaven!" Lucy whispered.

Bram put his arm around her, holding her tightly. "What for?" he asked quietly.

"Forcible sodomy. Rape," the old actor said.

"Forcible—" Lucy stared at him in disbelief. "But that's insane! Toby would never force anyone to—"

"Of course he wouldn't," Burbage said wearily. "It's that damned bastard Dalton's doing. He swore we'd never play for the queen, and by God, he kept his vow. Two days before St. Swithin's they came and took Toby away."

"But who accused him?" Lucy cried.

"Tom Shoemaker."

"Tom! Why, that lying little—"

"Oh, lass, you can't blame the boy. I'd had to let him go, and he was bitter about it. And I'm sure Dalton paid him more gold than he'd ever hoped to see in his life. No, Dalton's the cause of it. He got it pumped right up into a huge bloody scandal, with the clergy preaching against us at Blackfriars and Paul's Cross—calling The Theatre, *my* theater, a den of iniquity. Anyway, the city closed us down. Dalton pushed the trial through. Toby's tried and convicted and sentenced to hang on the third of August." He shook his head. "And to think we almost made it to Whitehall, Toby and me, after all those years."

"God, poor Toby! Bram, we have got to do something right away!"

He was already heading toward his study. "I'll write to Walsingham and the queen immediately. Jeeves!"

"Yes, milord?" the butler asked from the door to the banquet hall.

"Would you please tell Jem's Johnny to be ready to post to London in a quarter hour?"

"Yes, milord," said Jeeves, going out to the drive.

"Lord Carlyle—Bram." Burbage's face was red. "I didn't mean—for Christ's sake, it's your wedding day."

"And we're delighted you're here to share in the happy occasion," Bram said easily. "But we'll take care of Toby first. Lucy, love, unless you are planning on marrying me in that apron and smock, you had better get dressed." He blew her a kiss and hurried away.

"Drat," Burbage muttered. "I've gone and spoiled everything for you. I never should have come."

"If you hadn't come to us, I'd be furious with you. Have you seen Toby? How is he?"

"No one's been allowed to see him." He balled up his fists. "This is all my fault, Lucy. If I hadn't been so greedy for a patron—"

"What's done is done," she told him quietly. "What matters now is to get this mess straightened out, get Toby out of the Fleet and back on the stage."

Burbage shook his head. "Even if we do get The Theatre reopened, Toby's days as a player are finished. A scandal like this doesn't ever die away. It sticks to a man. Toby won't be able to show himself anywhere in Shoreditch, much less on a stage." His eyes were hollow and sad. "He's poured his whole life into the The Theatre, Lucy. I think he'd rather be hanged than never work in it again."

Lucy feared he might be right. "We'll cross that bridge when we come to it," she said stoutly, then turned as she heard footsteps coming from the nursery.

"Lucy, Lucy, how do I look?" Minnie cried, rushing down the stairs with Stacy close behind her.

"You both look like angels. I don't suppose by some miracle either of you remembered to wash behind your ears?"

"Jem made us," Stacy told her, grimacing, and then looked up at Burbage. "Who's this?"

"This is Master Burbage whom I've told you about, from The Theatre in London. James, this is Minnie and Stacy."

"How do you do?" Minnie piped. "I can do a handstand; Lucy taught me. Do you want to see?"

"Not in that dress, Minnie." Lucy rushed to catch her before she could demonstrate. "Why don't you two show Master Burbage where he can wash up, and find him a cup of ale? I really must get dressed. James, don't worry. Bram will take care of everything."

"Say," said Stacy, "have you got any places for actors in your troupe, sir?"

"Well, not just at the moment, Stacy, but—"

"James," Lucy said warningly.

"You never can tell," he went on, ignoring her blithely. "Can you do a handstand, too?"

Lucy shook her fist at him; he winked over the children's blond heads, and she sighed and went up the stairs.

" 'N' just where in hell have ye been?" Jem demanded as Lucy entered her old bedchamber at last.

"Don't scold, Jem; we had an emergency." Lucy stripped off her apron and smock and climbed into the tub that the maid had ready for her, washing hastily.

"Aye, 'n' I'll wager I can guess what it was, too," Jem said with a sly, knowing laugh. "Somethin' the master couldn't wait till tonight for, knowin' ye two."

"Well, your guess would be wrong," Lucy said archly, and then giggled, toweling off her hair. "Though I'll admit he did try."

Jem held up the bodice and sleeves of Lucy's wedding gown for her, and buttoned them up while Lucy put on her emerald eardrops. Then Jem gathered up the great bundle of skirts and settled them gingerly over Lucy's head. "Can't believe ye finished this here gown in less'n a fortnight—specially considerin' how ye 'n' the master have been carryin' on," the maid said as she fastened the waistband. "Why, Mistress Olive had twelve French dressmakers workin' on her weddin' gown for—" She stopped, clapping her hand over her mouth. "Saints preserve us, I'm sorry!"

"For what, Jem?"

The maid's dark eyes were wide. "Why they say 'tis terrible luck to mention a dead wife's name on the second bride's weddin' day."

"Oh, Jem, please, no more talk like that. The next thing you know you'll have me seeing ghosts again."

The maid dropped her voice to a whisper. "Ye ain't seen her, then, since ye came back?"

"I never did see her," Lucy said patiently, "because there never was anything to see. And I never would have thought I saw anything if I hadn't listened to your foolish chatter. There's no such thing as ghosts."

"If ye says so," said Jem, but she plainly wasn't convinced.

Lucy studied her reflection in the dressing room mirror that Bram had replaced. The gown had turned out even better than she'd imagined, if she said so herself. The overskirts were of the sheerest crimson lawn, with an underbodice and petticoats of bloodred satin. "Well, what do you think?"

"Oh, 'tis a gorgeous gown, if ye don't believe what they say about red bein' unlucky for brides."

"Bram likes me in red." Lucy turned to the side to admire her handiwork, the tight-nipped waist and full skirts and tapering sleeves. "Just think, Jem, if he hadn't thrown his brandy glass at the mirror that night, I wouldn't be standing here today."

"Maybe. But ye know what they say about weddin' 'n' hangin' both goin' by destiny."

"You're just full of cheerful thoughts today, aren't you, Jem?" But the maid's words actually gave Lucy encouragement. After all, it surely had been destiny that brought her and Bram together. And Toby Mifflin's destiny couldn't be to hang.

"I'm sorry, Miss Lucy. I reckon I'm just not used to seein' everybody in this house be so happy," Jem told her, fluffing out the red underskirts of Lucy's gown. "It makes me nervy. I keep thinkin' of what they say about the calm comin' before the storm."

"Well, they also say a broken mirror brings bad luck," Lucy told her, "and that just proves how wrong they can be. Lord, more early guests," she said, hearing the gate bell jangle. "Would you go see if Cook needs any help? I'd better go find out who's here."

Jeeves was just ushering the countess of Sutherland and Gordon and a band of musicians into the armory as Lucy came down the stairs. "Good Lord, you look lovely," the frail old woman said, kissing Lucy's cheek. "I made Gordon bring me early so you and I could have a moment alone."

"What am I, invisible?" Gordon grumbled, and kissed Lucy, too. "Congratulations! No, good luck. Which is it, Grandmama, that you say to the bride?"

"You say, 'Where is Bram, and does he need help doing something?' " Margery told him briskly.

"Ah. Where is Bram, and does he need help doing something?"

Lucy giggled. "To tell you the truth, I don't know where he is. Jeeves, would you please take the musicians into the chapel? And do you know where Bram is?"

"The wine cellars, Mistress Jones."

"Well, I'm off to the wine cellars, then," Gordon announced, and went.

Margery beamed at his back. "Such a dutiful boy. Now." She trained her keen gaze on Lucy. "Are you happy?"

"Very."

"No last-minute qualms?"

"Not a one."

The countess sniffed. "Hell, we may as well bring Gordon back if that's as interesting as it's going to get!" She peered more closely at Lucy's hair. "Is that the fashion now in London?"

"Not exactly," Lucy admitted.

"Pity. I like it. And I adore your dress. My, how gay Bram's great-grandfather looks, too, with hollyhocks stuck in his helmet. Minnie's and Stacy's handiwork, I'll wager. Where are the little darlings?"

Lucy looked helplessly at the butler as he returned from installing the musicians. "Jeeves, do you—"

"With the actor gentleman, Mistress Jones, in the receiving room."

"Bless you, Jeeves; I don't know what we'd have done without you today. Did Johnny get off to London with those letters?"

"Yes, Mistress Jones. Half an hour ago."

"Wonderful! Thank you, Jeeves." And again the bell at the front gate rang. "Jeeves, could you—"

"Certainly. Right away." He bustled outside.

"Do you mind?" Margery asked, pulling a hollyhock from the suit of armor and tucking it behind her ear. "I love hollyhocks; my mother used to plant them every year in front of our shop."

Lucy blinked. "I beg your pardon?"

The countess laughed. "That's right; I never did get a chance to tell you my little secret. Oh, it's not really a secret, mind you. It's just that I'm so old everyone who might remember it is dead. I grew up in London, too—Millwall, not Shoreditch. My father had a bakery down at the docks.''

''A bakery? In Millwall?'' Lucy echoed incredulously. That part of the city was even rougher than Shoreditch.

''Mmm. He used to make the most delicious hot cross buns at Eastertide. I swear, I can taste them still.'' And she smacked her lips.

''But how did you—''

''Become a countess? Married an earl, of course, though he wasn't an earl then. Oh, my dear, it made a terrible scandal when we eloped. Albert's family wouldn't speak to him for twenty years, not until his father died and he became the earl—and even then they wouldn't speak to me or have me to call. And of course Albert was banned from court until Elizabeth took the throne.''

''You must both have been very brave,'' Lucy said softly.

''Well, we had each other, and we were in love. Oh, my, we were in love.'' The old woman smiled at her memories. ''Of course, it won't be nearly so difficult for you and Bram, though there always will be dreadful snobs like that Moncrief woman. But you take my advice, Lucy Jones—don't run away from them. No, my dear, you must stand right up to such people and look them straight in the eye and say pooh. Because the world is changing. Queen Bess is making it change, and you and Bram and Cecil and Walsingham and me, we're all helping.'' She reached up and primped at the sleeves of Lucy's gown. ''So stand tall when you marry your lord today, do you hear me? That's all I wanted to say.'' Then she winked. ''By the by, what's this about an actor being here?''

''Oh, that's James Burbage. An old friend from Shoreditch.''

The countess rubbed her hands together. ''My, I can tell already this is going to be a wedding the likes of which this old house has never seen.''

And so it was. None of the bright lights of the kingdom were there, but then they hadn't been invited. Cecil and Walsingham naturally couldn't attend, not with Bram supposedly in the queen's bad graces, but the tenant farmers and their wives did come. The ceremony was held in the family chapel. Stacy stood as groomsman for Bram, and Minnie attended Lucy, and neither of the children giggled or fussed; if anything they looked more grave than their elders as they witnessed the culmination of what they insisted they'd known would happen all along.

Bram's blue eyes were dark as midnight as he promised to love and honor and cherish Lucy for all time; Lucy's eyes swam with tears of joy and pride as she took her vows. Then he slipped a golden ring set with a shining emerald onto her finger and kissed her at such length that Stacy nudged him and hissed in a whisper that carried straight to the back of the church, "Dinner will get cold!" And the laughter of the guests drowned out the musicians' playing as Bram and Lucy left the chapel as man and wife and led the procession to the banquet hall.

There was much shuffling about in the huge room as everyone found a place to sit at the long tables bedecked with silver and candles and flowers. Jeeves poured the wine, and Bram stood up in his place and raised his glass. "A toast," he proposed. "To Lucy!"

"To Lucy!" Minnie seconded, lifting her goblet so enthusiastically that wine went flying all over the tablecloth. Everyone laughed, and Lucy hugged her, and then they all raised their glasses while Lucy blushed becomingly.

Cook had truly outdone herself for the occasion. There was roast beef and pudding and poached salmon and salads of radish and cucumber; there were chicken pies and ham-and-onion cobblers and fruit compote and six kinds of cheese. When the final course of wine cakes and sweetmeats had been served, Lucy called Cook into the banquet hall to take a curtsy, and James Burbage stood up and applauded her thunderously, then proposed to her on the spot. Cook cackled and warned him he'd best beware lest she take him up on the offer, until Lucy told her what Burbage did for a living; then she threatened to run him off the property with her rolling pin.

"Back to the receiving room," Minnie proposed the instant she'd finished her cake, to a loud general groan.

"Sweetheart," Bram told her, "none of us can move."

"But Stacy and I have a surprise for you," she coaxed, tugging at his sleeve.

"What surprise?"

"If I tell you, it won't be a surprise! Just please come."

"Ladies and gentlemen," Bram announced gravely, getting to his feet, "there will be brandy—and a surprise—in the receiving room."

The children led the way there, followed by James Burbage, who borrowed a fiddle from one of the musicians. "Do you know what this is about?" Bram asked Lucy, settling her into a chair next to the countess, and she shrugged her shoulders.

"I haven't the foggiest idea."

Stacy and Minnie waited in the front of the room, with Minnie hopping up and down in anticipation, while Jeeves handed round glasses of brandy. When everyone had been served, Stacy nudged his sister, and she took a deep breath. "Ahem. Just to show how happy we are that Lucy's gotten married to Father and us, Stacy and me—"

"And I," Stacy hissed.

"I said you and me!"

"Aye, but it's you and I!" Minnie looked at him as though he were daft, and he muttered "Oh, never mind" while a chuckle ran through the audience.

"Anyway," Minnie went on, still eyeing him askance, "we thought we would show how happy we were by singing a song."

"Why, how perfectly charming," the countess of Sutherland declared.

"And," Stacy put in, "since this is in honor of Lucy, we thought we would sing the very first song she ever taught us."

"Hear, hear," said Burbage, raising up his fiddle with a gleam of laughter in his eyes. Lucy beamed encouragement at the children. The first song she'd ever taught them—why, she couldn't even remember now what that might be; she'd taught them so many . . .

"Ready, sir?" Minnie whispered to Burbage, and he nodded, choking back laughter, and bowed a long note.

"Oh, no!" Lucy gasped as it all came back to her in a rush. The first song—on the carriage ride from London to

Lockhaven Hall! "Minnie, Stacy, don't!" She waved at them frantically, but they were watching Burbage and beaming like golden-haired angels; then they burst into song, clear and loud as could be:

Now Barry the blacksmith's a fine piece of man;
His hammer strikes sparks 'twixt the anvil and pan;
And fathers can't stand him, but oh, daughters can,
When Barry goes bum-di-do.

"Do you know," Gordon Sutherland whispered, "I don't think I've ever heard this song before."

"Oh, Gordon!" His grandmother was doubled over with laughter. "I have, but it's been a mighty long time!"

"James Burbage, you stop playing this instant!" Lucy cried, but he only winked and plunged into the chorus, with the children singing on lustily:

When Barry goes bum-di-do,
When Barry goes bum-di-dee—

"What's 'bum-di-do'?" Bram leaned over to ask Lucy, but she had buried her face in her hands as Minnie and Stacy sailed into the second verse:

Barry set his cap for the tailor's fair daughter,
Her jugs round as milk cans, her eyes like blue water.
But Tess wouldn't have him, for no one had taught her
About going bum-di-do.

"*Oh,*" said Gordon, as it dawned on him what the song was about.

"Quite so!" said the countess, tears of hilarity streaming down her cheeks.

"You taught them this?" Bram asked Lucy incredulously. She moaned and sank down lower in her chair.

"Lucy, my dear, you didn't teach them *all* of it, did you?" the countess asked, and then dissolved into giggles again.

The rest of the guests at first looked on in baffled silence as Minnie and Stacy cheerfully spouted the racy lyrics; then a few of the men began to laugh, and the laughter spread and then swelled to a roar. The children, thrilled by the enthusiasm of their audience, shouted the words even more loudly. "Everybody sing!" Stacy cried the next time the chorus came round. The countess promptly chimed in, and then the farmers did, too.

"God," Lucy moaned, "I'd forgotten how long this song is."

"Not so long as Barry's hammer," the countess declared, joining the children in the final verse:

> *His hammer was long and his hammer was wide;*
> *It whacked and it thwacked and it drove deep inside,*
> *While Tess lay beneath him and joyously cried,*
> *"So that's going bum-di-do!"*

The applause at the end of the song was deafening. Minnie and Stacy even clapped for themselves, so delighted were they by the success of their performance, and curtsied and bowed again and again. Lucy shook her fist at Burbage as he handed the fiddle back to its proper owner, grinning devilishly. "Hoo, if that didn't take me back," the countess of Sutherland exclaimed, still wiping away tears of mirth. "Did you teach them any more of those, Lucy? How about 'Roll Rory Home in a Barrel' or 'How the French Sailor Caught the Clap'?"

"Grandmama!" said Gordon.

Margery slapped his knee and held her arms out to Minnie and Stacy. "Come here, pets, and give us a kiss. You have made an old woman's day."

"*Have* you taught them any more of them?" Bram asked Lucy, one black brow arched. "When you told me you sang them to sleep, I had no idea."

After that the party went on gaily, if a bit more staidly. There was dancing and drinking, and Burbage put on a pantomime, and Minnie showed how Reggie could jump through a hoop, and a splendid time was had by all. The hour grew late; Minnie finally fell asleep curled in Lucy's lap. "We'd best be going, Gordon," Margery said, "or I'll wind up like that, too." And she scowled at the still merry guests. "Don't know what's the matter with these people, keeping newlyweds from their bed."

But soon the rest of the company began to trickle home. Burbage turned down Bram and Lucy's offer to spend the night; he said that so long as he was back in the provinces he might as well pay a visit to a certain widow he knew in Derby. "But thanks for the hospitality," he told them, winking, and then said more seriously, "And thanks most of all for what you've done for Toby."

"If I haven't heard from Walsingham in a week," Bram said, "I'll ride to London myself to talk to him."

"Here's hoping it won't come to that," the old player said, and kissed Lucy goodbye. "Lose an actor, gain a son," he shouted over his shoulder as he rode out of the yard a bit lopsidedly.

When all the guests had gone Lucy carried Minnie up to bed, and Bram took Stacy. "I don't think I've ever been up this late." The boy yawned as Bram tucked him under the covers. "Did you like our surprise?"

"Very much indeed. But will you promise me, Stacy, not to sing that song anywhere else except in this house?"

"Why not?"

"I'll tell you later."

"Later when?"

"In about four years." Bram kissed his forehead. "Good night." Then he grabbed Lucy's hand and pulled her downstairs. "Come on. I feel like going bum-di-do."

Jeeves was pottering around in the receiving room, cleaning up debris from the evening's entertainment. "For heaven's sake, Jeeves," Lucy told him, "leave that till morning and get some sleep."

"Yes, Mistress Jones."

"It is Lady Carlyle now," Bram reminded him with a grin. Then he squinted up at the painting on the ceiling. "You know, I think I will have that painted over. Remind me, will you, Lucy?"

"Oh, Bram, you can't!"

"Why not?"

"Why, because it's art."

"Doesn't it give you a strange feeling? As though it were watching us?"

Lucy laughed. "And you thought I was being fanciful about that ghost. It's only a painting."

"Well—if you're sure it doesn't bother you—" He scooped her up in his arms. "Do you know what else I think?"

"No. What?"

"That it is highly inappropriate to call this the monk's walk anymore," he said, and carried her off to his bed.

They undressed each other slowly, with leisurely pleasure, brandy and rich food and exhaustion having taken the sharp edge from their passion. But when they lay naked together and Bram pulled Lucy into his arms, she forgot her tiredness in the excitement of his caresses. "I love you, wife," he whispered, and then laughed at the sound of that. "God, it is a fine old word, isn't it, *wife*?"

"I like *husband* better," she told him, lying atop him, her hands caught in the curling black hair on his chest.

"No, *husband*'s not as good. You can husband cattle or crops; you can husband a household. But—" He kissed her as she leaned over him. "You can only wife a wife." Lucy inched higher, arching her back, and he caught her breast in his mouth, sucking at the rosy nipple until it grew hard to his touch. "God, what was the matter with those people in London?" he murmured, shaking his head. "Were they all blind to think you were a boy?"

"I wish I were a boy."

"You what? Why?"

She smiled slyly and slid down over his belly and loins. "So I would know why you shudder and moan when I do this," she told him, and put her mouth to his manhood, tracing the round head.

"Oh, God, Lucy." He laughed while she moved her mouth on that long, hard rod, her hand wrapped around it. She felt his body tense beneath her, heard his breath quicken; then he caught her shoulders and rolled her over, kneeling atop her. "My turn."

He kissed her mouth, still warm with the taste of him, and then trailed his tongue down over her breasts, across her ribs to her navel and then lower still, his fingers parting her thighs while he sought the bud of her desire. Lucy moaned with pleasure as his hot tongue darted into her, scorching her like a bright flame. Just when she thought she could bear the ecstasy of his explorations no longer he brought his head up and straddled her, driving into her with his manhood. She clung to him, crying his name over and over again as he thrust into her, driving his hard shaft deep into her slick, warm sheath again and again. Faster he moved and faster, until they were moving together as one, one body, one flesh.

"Now, love, now!" he urged her on.

"Yes, love, yes!" Lucy panted, and they were riding a great high shimmering wave of love. Lucy cried out again and again as it swelled even higher, and at its very crest felt his seed explode within her as he called her name.

"Oh, wife," he said when he could speak again. "Wife, wife, wife, wife!" He rolled onto his back, a huge smile on his face. Lucy laughed and curled up against him, tracing the smile with her fingertip.

"Wouldn't it be wonderful," she whispered dreamily, "if we have made a baby tonight?"

His body went rigid beside her; the smile vanished, and he sat up abruptly on the edge of the bed with his back to her. "What is it, Bram?" she asked, her cheek against the nape of his neck. "What did I say?"

"I can't give you babies, Lucy. Christ, I thought you knew that." He covered his face with his hands.

"Bram, you can't be certain of that. Why, you can't even be certain that Minnie and Stacy aren't yours."

"She told me they weren't."

"She could have been lying! God knows she lied about how you make love."

"Aye, so you tell me," he said shortly.

Lucy scrambled around on the bed so she could see his face, pulling away his hands. "What is that supposed to mean?"

"You were a player, weren't you?" he muttered. "Perhaps you are a player still."

"Bram Carlyle, how dare you say such a thing!"

"Oh, God, Lucy. I'm sorry." He pushed back his hair. "It's just that—I saw her that night. I know she wasn't lying. And now I can't help thinking—it was wrong for me to marry you. You deserve a family of your own."

"I *have* a family of my own. I have you and Minnie and Stacy—"

"You know what I mean."

"No, I don't. I honestly don't. Do you think I could love you any less if you don't get me with child?"

"Maybe not now. Not in the beginning," he said quietly. "But as the years go by, as we grow old—dammit, Lucy, yes! I'm afraid you'll feel cheated. I'm afraid you will leave me." He looked at her then. "And God, if you did, I couldn't live. It would be—as though someone had put out the sun, taken away the air that I breathe."

"Oh, Bram." Lucy put her arms around his shoulders, holding him tightly. "Margery told me today about what happened when she and Albert were married, how hard it was for them, with his family and friends refusing to speak to him, and their being banned from court for so many years. And I felt sorry for her; I told her so. But she doesn't feel sorry for herself; she doesn't feel cheated. She just smiled and said, 'We had each other. And we were in love.' " She pressed a kiss to the nape of his neck. "And I thought then and there, all I will ever want in this world is to grow old and smile as she did and say the same about you and me."

He caught her hand over his shoulder and kissed the palm. "I don't deserve you, Lucy," he whispered hoarsely.

"Maybe not, but you're stuck with me."

He laughed and grabbed her, pulling her into his lap in a somersault. "Thank God I am," he told her, his blue eyes shining. "Thank God you ended up on my doorstep that night, Lucy Jones."

"Lucy Carlyle," she corrected him, and then squealed as he tumbled her down on the bed in a flurry of cool linen and hot kisses that landed on her eyes, her throat, her breasts. She caught her breath, her arms twining around his neck, as his manhood thrust inside her, eager and hard.

"My wife," he said, arching above her, his eyes ablaze. "Mine forever."

"Forever," she told him, opening herself to him. And then the fire took hold within them; nothing mattered but the raging need burning inside them, engulfing them, and they surrendered to its wild fury and let it devour and consume them. They came together like two white-hot stars colliding in the deep, vast infinity of space, crying out to each other, shuddering, exploding. And then they slept, limbs and hearts and hands entangled, in the cool, quiet light of the dawning new day.

Chapter 20

"Now," said Lucy, putting down the ruler she'd been using to draw a staff. "The important thing to remember is that music is all based on mathematics. The notes are like numbers. And all you have to know to read the notes is how many spaces to skip in between."

"Don't you think this would be easier if you showed us on the virginals?" Stacy asked, frowning down at the parchment Lucy was demonstrating on.

"We can't use the virginals, sweetheart. No one but your father is allowed down in the music room."

"But it would be easier," the boy insisted.

"Oh, Stacy, do hush," Minnie told him. "I want to learn to play the fiddle like Master Burbage did. Besides, it makes sense to me. Lucy, go on."

"You start with all the notes in the scale, all in a row." Lucy sang them as she drew them onto the staff. "C, D, E, F, G, A, B, C."

"If it's mathematical, who don't the notes have numbers for names instead of letters?" Stacy wanted to know. "And why are there only seven notes before they start repeating themselves? And why—"

"Stacy, if you don't shut up we will never get anywhere," Minnie said crossly.

"Please don't tell your brother to shut up," Lucy chided her. "There's nothing wrong with asking questions; that's how one learns. You could use numbers instead of letters if you wanted to, Stacy. Why don't you pick a song?"

" 'Barry,' " he suggested promptly.

"All right, 'Barry.' We'll start on the C; that is this line here. Then it goes up to a G. 'When Bar—' " she sang.

319

"You see? There are four notes up from the C. C, D, E, F, G. 'When Bar—' and then back down two notes to an E. 'When Barry' . . . and then down two more, back to the C." She sang the first line of the chorus, pointing to the notes she had drawn on the staff.

"I get it," Minnie cried in delight. "It's easy, isn't it, Stacy? It is all just a matter of how many notes you skip in between."

"No, it is not easy," he said angrily. "It doesn't make any damned sense to me."

"Tuppence to the—" Minnie started to say, but Lucy hushed her.

"Stacy, pet, different things come easy for different people," she told him. "You are very good at languages and words, and Minnie is very good with numbers. You may have to work a little harder than she does at this, but that doesn't mean you can't learn it. And it wouldn't be very brave to give up so soon. Don't you remember how much trouble I had when you first tried to teach me to read?"

He nodded grudgingly. "But I still say it would be easier to learn on the virginals."

Lucy sighed, thinking of the instrument sitting in the music room, waiting for the proof that would convince Queen Elizabeth of her cousin Mary's scheming. "Someday," she told the boy. "Someday."

"Milord wishes to see you in his study, madam."

Lucy looked up and saw Jeeves's plain round face in the doorway to the nursery. "He must have heard from Sir Francis at last. Minnie, why don't you try to copy out the next line to the song for me? Stacy, you help her. I will be back just as soon as I can." She ran past Jeeves and down through the house to the monk's walk, already calling "It's locked!" before she even reached the door.

"Minx," said Bram, kissing her as he opened it to her. "Mmm. How long have we been married?"

"One week. Why, are you tired of me already?"

"I couldn't tire of you in a million years." He started to kiss her again, but she twisted away from him. "Damn that actor's training of yours; you are slippery as a greased pig."

"There's a fine thing to be calling your wife." She stuck out her tongue at him and danced toward his desk. "Did you hear from Sir Francis? What does he write about Toby?"

"I still haven't heard from him," he told her, frowning. "I can't understand it; it's not like him to ignore a request as urgent as that."

"Well, then you must go to London to see him. August third—that is only a few days from now. Bram, we can't let Toby hang."

"I know that, Lucy. But I have to go to Chartley, to see Mary." He held up a sheet of parchment. "Another letter from Babington; I found it in the music room this morning. He'll be expecting an answer back."

She looked at him, wide-eyed. "Oh, no, Bram. Do you have to go?"

"I'm afraid so. Saving the kingdom and all that."

"It's nothing to jest about! I wish—" She stopped, and he tilted her chin up to him.

"What, love?"

"I almost wish you were going off to see a lover. I will worry about you so."

"I will like that, having someone to worry about me," he said quietly.

Lucy felt tears welling up in her eyes; she turned from him and forced her voice to be cheery and bright. "Well, what does Anthony Babington have to say to Queen Mary?"

"The usual nonsense. His letters to her never seem to say much of anything at all."

"Well, neither do hers to him," Lucy pointed out. "Does he like dirty songs as much as she does?"

"No. He never writes about songs. Only Mary does that."

Lucy wrinkled her nose. "Where do you think she would hear a song like 'When Barry Goes Bum-Di-Do,' anyway?"

"From the servants at Chartley, I suppose."

"What is she like, Bram, the queen of Scots? Is she as beautiful as they say?"

"Not at all. You heard what I told Elizabeth. She is old

and blotchy and fat.'' He tickled her ribs. ''Why, are you jealous of her?''

''Perhaps. A bit. She is taking you away from me on our honeymoon.''

''Not for long,'' he promised. ''I'll leave this with her and get home as soon as I can. Even so, it could be a week. Walsingham likes me to hang about, keep my ear to the ground.''

''But a week will be too late for Toby!'' Lucy nibbled her lip.

''I know that, love. But Mary might get suspicious if I change my habits suddenly. Why don't you have Johnny drive you to London? If you leave tomorrow morning you could be there by midnight. Oh, damn, you may have trouble getting into Whitehall at that hour. Here.'' He searched through the papers on his desk. ''I have a diplomat's pass somewhere that Walsingham gave me in case of an emergency. It will get you right past the guards.''

Lucy couldn't help laughing as she watched him paw through all those stacks of paper. ''Honestly, Bram, this place is as bad as my pawnshop used to be. I don't see how you can think in such a muddle.''

''For your information, I know exactly where every single thing in this room is,'' he told her, and then frowned at a paper in his hand. ''How did that get here?''

Lucy rolled her eyes toward heaven. ''He knows exactly—hah!'' She glanced at the sheet as he laid it down. ''Is that my lute letter?''

''Aye. I thought I gave that to Walsingham. Well, it doesn't matter. Where in hell is that pass?''

Lucy glimpsed an official-looking seal as he pushed stacks of papers about. ''Is this it?''

''Ah—so it is. Just go round to the west gate and show them this; they will let you right in.'' He folded it in half and tucked it into her bodice, taking the opportunity to kiss both of her breasts. ''Mmm. Damn. I don't want to go.''

''Then don't,'' Lucy whispered, holding his head tight against her breasts.

He pulled away with a sigh. ''I've got to. Someday—''

"Aye, I know. Someday. Promise me you'll be careful?"

"Cross my heart and hope to die." He gave her a long, loving kiss; as he let her go at last, she looked into his sky-blue eyes and saw they were shadowed with darkness. "Lucy. Would you—" He stopped.

"Would I what?"

He shook his head. "Nothing. A foolish question."

"Well, ask me anyway."

He hesitated, then said softly, "Would you love me whatever I do?"

"That *is* a foolish question," she agreed. "Of course I would."

"Good," he said. "I'm glad. As for you, be careful going to London, do you hear me?"

"Don't worry about me. I'll be in Johnny's hands."

He kissed her again. "You had better not be in anyone's hands except mine!" Then he put his arm around her, picked up Babington's letter, and led her out of the study, locking the door. "Jeeves!" he shouted down the monk's walk.

"Yes, milord?"

"Have Johnny saddle Bellerophon, please."

"Very good, milord."

"But if you are going to London to see the queen," Minnie said plaintively, "why can't we go with you, and take Reggie too? Then it would be just like in the nursery rhyme."

"I promise I will take you and Reggie next time, pet," Lucy told her. "But this is a special trip, to help a special friend, and there isn't much time." She shivered, hearing the wind batter against the shutters as she tucked the girl into her cot. "I'm afraid we may have a storm."

"We wouldn't be any trouble at all," Minnie insisted. "I would put Reggie in a big basket with a lid, and we'd be ever so quiet, and—"

"Minnie." Lucy leaned over and kissed her forehead. "I am sorry. But sometimes no means no."

"But—"

"Good night, Minnie," Lucy said firmly, and put out

the candle. Then she went to her desk in the nursery; she
wanted to write a note of thanks to Margery for the countess's wedding gift—a beautiful, brand-new feather mattress that had arrived the day before. While she was at it,
she thought she might as well include the music to "When
Barry Goes Bum-Di-Do" that she and Minnie had finished
copying out.

"Dear Margery," she wrote at the head of a sheet of
parchment, and then tried to decide what to say.

"Oh, it's ye, Miss Lucy." That was Jem peeking in
through the doorway. "I thought I'd caught Master Stacy
up readin' after his bedtime again. Shall I shut them windows for ye, then?"

"I'll do it, Jem, before I leave."

"Mind ye don't forget. It sounds like wild wolves howl-
in' out there. Ye know, they do say the dead walk abroad
on that sort of wind."

"Thank you kindly, Jem, for that information; I'm sure
it will help me sleep more soundly," Lucy told her wryly.

"Ooh, I forgot Lord Carlyle is gone. It's an awful shame
he had to go off so soon after the weddin', ain't it?"

"Yes, Jem," said Lucy, licking her quill and staring at
the blank page in front of her.

"That were a lovely weddin', weren't it, Miss Lucy?"

"Yes, Jem." *Dear Margery* . . . Lucy was still so new
at writing letters, and she wanted this one to be especially
good.

"Don't ye never tell Cook," the maid whispered con-
spiratorially, "but I swiped one of her pies that night."

"Did you, Jem."

"Aye, that I did. 'N' me 'n' Johnny ate the whole thing
ourselves after everybody was gone." She giggled. "We
both got terrible bellyaches from it."

"That's nice, Jem." *Dear Margery* . . .

"Well—don't ye forget to fasten up them shutters, Miss
Lucy."

"I won't. Good night, Jem."

Lucy dipped her pen and began to write carefully, as
neatly as she could. "I really would hate for you to think
that Bram and I are spending all of our time in bed, but—"
Thunder snapped right outside the window, so sudden and

loud that the quill went skittering out of control, right across the page. "Oh, damn," Lucy said. Then she laughed. The spattered ink had blotted out almost all the words she had written, so that the first line now read, "Dear Margery, I hate you."

Well, I surely can't send that! she thought bemusedly, crumpling up the page and tossing it toward the fireplace. It really wasn't such a good start anyway. She ought to say something about the sheet of music she was enclosing. It was odd, she mused, picking up that page, how Minnie's mind seemed to work so much like her own did. And Toby . . . poor Toby. What was it he had said about why he liked music? It is as much a matter of what you skip as of what you write . . .

As much a matter of what you skip as of what you write. Like the ruined letter to Margery. Spaces. Spaces between notes, spaces between words—With the music for "When Barry Goes Bum-Di-Do" in her hand, Lucy got up and retrieved the crumpled paper she'd tossed across the room. How had the first sentence in the lute letter begun? *If you hadn't written, I never would have* . . . Start on a C, skip four. I. Then two. Have. I have—how the devil did the rest of that letter go? Still carrying the music, she ran down the stairs shouting for Jeeves.

"Yes, madam?" he asked, coming in from the receiving room.

"Thank heavens you're still awake, Jeeves. Could you please unlock Bram's study for me? There is something in there I must see."

"Certainly, madam." He padded ahead of her down the monk's walk and took a key from the ring at his belt, unlocking the latch. "Will there be anything else, madam?"

"You might light me a candle, Jeeves, thank you."

He did so, setting it on Bram's desk. "Anything else, madam?" Lucy shook her head, already pawing through the unbelievable clutter. "Very good, madam. Good night."

"Good night, Jeeves." Glory, what a mess! Where could that letter be? She'd seen it only that afternoon. She pushed aside piles of all sorts of other correspondence, pages from account books, bits of paper with quotations from people she had never heard of—Lord, there was the Christmas list from last year that the children had made out; didn't he ever throw anything away?

Finally she found it, stuffed between a page of numbers—added up incorrectly, she noted with a single glance—and a calendar from three years past. She seized the letter eagerly, laid the sheet of music down beside it, and used Bram's quill to scratch out all the words that fell between the notes. When she had finished, she stared down at the message that she had revealed:

Dear Anthony,
    I have considered my plan and think it to be workable the date should be Lammas Day of next year my cousin's annual procession to Westminster will provide the perfect opportunity France and the Pope stand ready with arms and men to assure crowns transfer confirm details in your reply.

My God, Lucy realized, that's it!

The songs were the key; it was some kind of code. Lammas Day—good Lord, that was August first, only two days away! It was a bloody good thing she was going to London in the morning: she'd have more than just Toby to tell Walsingham and the queen about. It would be proof, the proof that Queen Elizabeth had been demanding, if those letters Bram had given to Sir Francis all worked out to say something like this!

Wind whistled down the monk's walk, swirling the papers on the desk like dry autumn leaves, making the candle flicker. Lucy shielded the flame with her hand, then lifted her head as she caught the smell of roses, attar of roses, cloying and sweet.

"Who's there?" she called, and heard silk skirts rustle. "Who are you?"

The whispered answer was the same as before: "You know who I am."

As quietly as she could Lucy picked up the candle and tiptoed to the doorway, then darted out into the monk's walk, looking in either direction. At the far end where it opened onto the receiving room, she saw the merest glimpse of something pale and diaphanous floating on the air. She ran after it, raising her candle aloft as she reached the arch.

The frolicking figures painted on the wall gazed down at her; Lady Carlyle's cool blue eyes followed her as she walked to the center of the marble floor, her footsteps unnaturally loud. She turned in a slow circle, sending the light from her candle into every corner of the room, but there was no one there. Then from the portrait gallery she heard laughter, high-pitched and eerie, and that same silvery rustle of skirts.

"Come out and show yourself!" she cried into the shadowy gallery, straining to see all the way to its end. Was there something at the entrance to the armory, some shape, bulky and dim? Thunder rolled; lightning flared green and cold in the armory windows, and in its momentary glare she saw the figure of a woman, pale-haired, in a long, pale gown. Then the lightning was gone, and the gallery went dark again.

But the woman had been there; Lucy was sure this time. She hadn't been sleeping. She wasn't dreaming. The scent of roses was stronger than ever as she moved cautiously beneath the dark paintings of Bram's ancestors, guarding the candle flame. At the entrance to the armory she stopped, her head cocked, listening, but she heard nothing. Just by the front door hung the bell that would summon the servants. She took a step toward it, felt the air move above her head, and darted back just as one of the battleaxes crossed above the doorway came thudding to the floor with a resounding crash, missing her by mere inches.

"Jesus!" Lucy cried, dropping the candle in fright. In the sudden darkness silk rustled wildly, not far away. Lucy lunged toward the sound, and this time her fingers did not close on air but on cloth.

"Got you, damn you!" she cried, holding on tightly, but the silk tore away in her hands with a wrenching rip, and she heard the woman scramble away from her, heading for the stairs. At least I know now she isn't a ghost, Lucy thought grimly as she followed the sound, the silk still clutched in her hand. Up the stairs Lucy ran, determined to catch her once and for all.

Past the nursery they flew, down the pitch-black corridor by Lucy's bedchamber, and above the thud of her own footfalls and those of the woman she chased, above the bustling silk, Lucy could still hear high, wild laughter. She nearly caught her quarry at the turn to the old wing, but this time those smooth silk skirts slipped right out of her hands. One after another they careened blindly around the corner, bumping into the wall. Lucy heard the sound of a latch dropping open, and the squeak of hinges, and then soft, thudding footsteps heading away from her, running down.

The stairway to the music room! Lucy ducked low to enter the hatch door and ran down the stairs after the elusive trickster, plunging deeper into the darkness, circling around and around. She heard the swift footsteps ahead of her pause and then resume, and just in time she remembered the trick stair. She slowed her pace until she felt the high step beneath her shoes; then she ran even faster than before, one hand on either wall to guide her. Then the staircase ended, and she burst out into the music room, into darkness that was silent except for her own panting breaths and the mad pounding of her heart.

"Who are you? Where are you?" she cried, and then screamed as someone leaped at her from behind, clutching at her throat. She ducked down and slipped away, but the hands came lunging toward her again. She fought them off frantically, high crazed laughter ringing in her ears; she caught hold of the woman's hair and yanked at it as hard as she could; just like the silk, it tore away in her fist.

"Jesus," she screamed, feeling its weight, as though the woman's scalp had torn away with the hair. She flung it from her, heard a sharp crack of thunder, and then screamed again as lightning flashed through the room, as she saw her tormentor at long last, as she recognized Jeeves's plain round face above the frothy green silk of Olive Carlyle's wedding gown.

"I didn't want to kill you," he said, sounding quite calm. "I only wanted to frighten you away. But you wouldn't go. You didn't listen." Then he laughed, high-pitched and eerie and thin. Lucy realized something even stranger than the sight of him in that woman's gown: in all the time she had been at Lockhaven Hall, she had never heard the butler laugh.

Thunder shattered the skies, and again lightning crackled, long jagged streaks showing through an open section in the stone wall that led to the cliff. Lucy saw the mophead he had worn for a wig lying on the floor. "Why?" she asked, backing away from him as the room went dark again. "Why do you have to kill me?"

"If you'd been somebody—a nobleman's daughter like the others—I might have borne that," he hissed. "But you're no one, are you? Nobody! A Shoreditch shopgirl. And you think you can take her place!"

"Jeeves," Lucy said desperately, "I'm not trying to take anybody's place."

"I tried to tell you! I tried to make you go away! But you married him. You think you are Lady Carlyle, but you're not. You're not worthy. You want to change things; you want to paint her out so she can't see you! But she does see you. So long as I am here, she is here."

Stay calm, Lucy told herself sternly. Reason with him. Play for time. "I'll go away now, Jeeves, how will that be? Just don't hurt me, don't hurt anyone else, and I'll leave tonight." She could go to Hucknall, fetch the sheriff—

"Too late!" he screamed. "It's too late now! Don't you see what you've done? You've desecrated this place. Her place. You've taught her children those disgusting songs. You've brought your friends here, your disgusting friends— thieves and sodomites, players, filthy trash just like you—"

Lucy shivered as something Jem had said to her that night in the nursery came back into her mind: *Me 'n' Johnny ate the whole thing ourselves after everybody was gone . . .* "My God," she whispered. "You never sent Johnny to London with those letters, did you?"

"Why should I? To save one of your perverted friends from the hanging he was born to?"

"Oh, Jeeves, you don't know what you've done!"

"I know exactly what I've done. I've rid the world of

someone who wasn't worthy to walk where she walked. And now I am going to rid it of another one.''

Lucy dodged away as he rushed toward her in the darkness, then cried out in pain as she banged into the virginals. He found her by the sound, grabbing her by the hair and slamming her head down onto the keys in a resounding chord. God, why did I never notice that he was so strong? Lucy thought frantically, struggling to get away. Why did I never notice anything about him at all?

His hands closed on her throat, choking her breath away; again and again he shoved her head back onto the keyboard. Lucy clawed at his eyes, felt flesh tear beneath her nails, but he did not let go. She brought her knee up, trying to find his groin in the tangle of Lady Carlyle's skirts, but he only laughed his macabre laugh and pushed her down onto the keys in a wild cacophony of sound.

Lightning flashed in the entranceway, igniting his fanatical eyes. In a final wild burst of strength Lucy butted her forehead straight against his with a sharp crack. His grip on her faltered and she scrambled away, heading for the spot where she thought she'd find the passage to the cliff. For an instant the fresh scent of green things and rain overwhelmed the sickly smell of roses; then he shoved her from behind. A great scintillating streak of white fire split the clouds right before Lucy's eyes; she teetered on the brink of the cliff, grabbing at air, and swung herself back. She heard him rush toward her again; catching an outcrop of rock in her fingertips, she ducked down low to one side. He hit the opening in the wall running hard, with nothing to stop him, and sailed straight past Lucy, hurtling over the side of the cliff. ''Not—worthy!'' she heard him scream, loud and long, as he plummeted toward the ravine far below.

''God in heaven,'' Lucy whispered, staring into the blackness, the rain beating at her face and clothes. Trembling, shaken, she crawled back into the music room on her hands and knees. ''Steady, Lucy, girl,'' she told herself, groping her way toward the virginals. Hadn't she seen a candle there? ''You've got to pull yourself together, get to London before Lammas Day. You've got to save Toby. You've got to warn the queen.'' Her hand closed on the brass of a candlestick. Good. Now where the devil was a tinderbox?

"Looking for this?" came a smooth, cool voice from just behind her. Lucy whirled around and saw a spark flare in the darkness.

"Who in 'ell is there?" she cried, lapsing into Londonese in her stark terror.

"You ought to know; you summoned me." Tinder flared into flame, and she saw the thin, bony face of Anthony Babington, circled by the ermine lining of his black cape. "And you must be the new Lady Carlyle. Charmed, I'm sure." He took the candelabra from her and lit the candles one by one, holding them close to her. "But we've met before, haven't we, Lady Carlyle?"

Lucy turned her face from him, shielding it with her hand. "I came to your house," she whispered, "once, for a ball—"

"Aye, I recall that now. But I've the strangest feeling I have seen you somewhere else, too." He put his palm to her chin, yanking her toward him. "Someplace where you weren't dressed in silk; where you dropped your h's as you did just then . . . You're a Londoner, aren't you? Claudia told me that. A commoner. You used to have a shop." And Lucy, flinching, saw the sheer incredulity in his eyes as the memory clicked into place. "Lady Carlyle?" he said. "*You* are Lady Carlyle? Oh, dear me. We do have trouble." And then he brought the candlestick crashing down against the side of her head.

Chapter 21

A blast of thunder roused Lucy from her torpor. Minnie will be afraid, she thought. I must go to the nursery. She tried to sit up, but a hard, throbbing pain shot through her head. The thunder cracked again; as its echo subsided she heard Anthony Babington's smooth, hissing courtier's voice: "Well shot, your lordship."

And then another voice, also silky smooth: "You took a fool's risk, Babington, bringing her here."

She opened her eyes cautiously and saw a canopy of leafy green trees above her head with bright sunlight streaming down, dappling the forest floor around her. If there was sunlight, though, how could there also be thunder? She turned her head slightly, seeking the source of the noise, and saw Babington in his black cape standing next to another man who had his back to her, a man with silvery hair who held a long brown musket in his hands, pointing it into the woods.

"But you see the implications, your lordship," Babington said nervously.

"Oh, quite," said the man with the gun, and shot it off again. Lucy heard the high, dying scream of some bird as it was hit, a thrashing of wings in leaves.

"Very well shot, your lordship. Shall I retrieve it for you?" Babington asked.

"There's no need. It was small game. Just like the girl."

"But what shall we do with her?"

"Why, we will take her to see the queen."

Lucy closed her eyes, a cleansing tide of relief coursing through her. That was what she wanted; that was what she had to do—see the queen. Everything was going to be all

332

right after all. She surrendered to the sweet warmth of the morning sun on her face, and again she slept.

"We are going to get the spanking to end all spankings," Stacy said with awe in his voice.

"No, we won't. You'll see," Minnie told him, holding tight to the wicker basket in which Reggie lay. "Lucy didn't take us only because she thought we would be a bother. But we can't be a bother, can we, if we get to London all on our own?"

"I still say we are going to catch hell," her brother whispered as they crept through the trees toward Hucknall.

"Tuppence," Minnie said. "Though there's no sense in taking it from the Treasury, I guess, to pay it back in. How much have we got, did you say?"

"Almost eight pounds."

"That ought to be plenty, don't you think?"

"I don't know. I've never tried to hire a cart before. Look here, Minnie, don't you think we ought to have told somebody what we are doing?"

"They would only have tried to stop us," she told him impatiently. "If Lucy hadn't already been gone when we woke up, I would have asked her again if we could go with her. But nobody else there would understand."

"We are going to get spanked so hard," Stacy said glumly, "that we will never be able to sit down again."

"Oh, don't be such a spoilsport, Stacy! It's perfect, don't you see? You get your grand adventure, and I get to take Reggie to see the queen. We both get what we were saving the money in the Treasury for."

"We are going to—"

"Oh, shut up. I mean, please shut up," Minnie told him, and skipped ahead through the forest, clutching the basket, humming "Pussycat, pussycat, where have you been?"

Lucy stirred, feeling something warm and wet glide across her cheek. "Bram, stop that!" she said, and giggled as his tongue lapped at her again. She raised her hand to push him away. How long and smooth his hair felt. He let out a strange little yelp; she opened her eyes—

And found herself staring at a very small, very furry black terrier who was just getting ready to lick her face again.

Lucy blinked to clear her hazy vision; then she did see Bram crouching over her, dressed only in his breeches, shaking his head. "Oh, Bram, thank God!" She sighed. "Am I in London? Where is the queen?"

"You damned little fool," he muttered, getting to his feet.

"Bram, listen to me. You must tell Sir Francis—the proof is in those letters from Mary, only there's a secret. You have to read them with the music, the music from the songs! I don't know what it is they are going to do, but it will be on Lammas Day; the queen is going to be in some sort of procession. And—"

"That has always been your problem, Lucy," he told her softly. "You are too bloody clever for your own good." Lucy shivered, hearing the chill in his voice, seeing the cold calculation in his blue eyes.

"Bram?" she whispered uncertainly as the terrier licked her. Then she heard a woman's voice, her English accented and stiff:

"Chou-Chou!" she said sharply. "Get away from that trash."

The dog bounded away from Lucy toward a high canopied bed hung with velvet drapes, gathered his tiny legs, and leaped up atop it. Half a dozen more of the small terriers were lined up on its edge, peering curiously at Lucy as she lay on the floor. From atop the bed a woman rose, auburn-haired, black-eyed, no longer young but still lovely. She scooped up Chou-Chou with one long white arm and draped the other over Bram's shoulders with negligent grace. "And to think, *chéri*," she purred, her fingers catching in the curls on Bram's chest, "that for my sake you would wed such a creature. It is above and beyond duty's call, *non*?"

Bram turned his head and kissed the woman as she clung to him, a slow kiss, openmouthed and lazy, his hand sliding over the bodice of the sheer nightdress she wore. "Mary. Don't you know I would do anything for you?"

Mary. Lucy pushed herself up on her elbows, staring at the woman's thin mouth, her snowy skin, her auburn hair and languid black eyes. The resemblance to Elizabeth was unmistakable but somehow skewed, as though the queen of England's image were reflected in a mirror of shadows, refracted through a prism of smoked glass. Mary, queen of Scots, and Bram. Together. Half naked. Kissing . . . "No," Lucy whispered in disbelief.

Bram smiled, cupping Mary's breast in his hand through the filmy gown, and it was the queen who answered Lucy, throwing back her head and moaning her pleasure as he rubbed her flesh: "Ah, yes, *chéri,* yes!"

Bram was only acting, Lucy told herself firmly. He was spying on Mary, that was all. But what in God's name was he doing in bed with her? Why had he told her the queen of the Scots was ugly and fat? They seemed so cozy together in that room—old lovers, old friends. She remembered how she once thought Bram went to visit a lover when he left Lockhaven Hall. *There is no other woman,* he'd told her. *There never could be.* Had he been acting then? She looked to him for some sign of reassurance, a secret gesture, anything, but he just went on fondling the queen.

"Your majesty." Another voice, male, impatient. "There's no time for that now."

"Always time for this, yes, Chou-Chou?" the queen cooed, nuzzling the terrier's nose and then Bram's neck. "Always there is time for this."

Bram laughed as she lapped at him with her tongue. "Lord Moncrief is right, my sweet. We must talk of other matters now."

"What other matters?" she asked petulantly, sitting back on the bed, gathering the terriers into her lap.

"This trash, as you called her," came the male voice at Lucy's back, and a sharp boot dug into her ribs. She turned her head and stifled a scream as she saw looming over her a man with a harsh, cruel face—a face with eyes so pale they were nearly colorless, and a long nose hooked like a hawk's crooked beak. Lord Moncrief—Claudia's father? And Joe Reilly's killer. He was glaring at Bram. "I think Carlyle is a traitor to our cause. I don't trust him."

The queen raised the floppy ear of one of the terriers and whispered, "Do you hear that, *ma petite*? Lord Moncrief is jealous of our lover!" Her black gaze slanted toward Bram. "Are you a traitor, *chéri*? Are you going to betray us?"

Bram seized her hand and kissed her fingers one by one. "Never, my heart."

"If he is faithful to your cause, Mary," Moncrief challenged the queen, "then why did he marry this common little slut?"

"The better question, Moncrief, is why you let her escape that night in Shoreditch," Bram said coolly.

Beneath his great hooked nose Moncrief's lips drew back over his teeth. "Don't try to lay this at my feet, Carlyle. You're the one who took her into your home. You're the one who mistook her for my daughter. My daughter." He turned that death's-mask face on Lucy. "I'll strip the stinking flesh from your bones myself, bitch, for having the audacity to claim you were my Claudia."

Lucy shuddered and turned back to Bram. Surely he would not carry the role he played so far as to let Moncrief kill her! But he seemed not a bit alarmed by the nobleman's threats; he sat on the edge of the bed, patting one of the dogs that climbed onto his thigh. "I explained all of this to Babington months ago," he told Moncrief casually. "When I found that the wench was a commoner, I realized that marrying her would be the perfect ploy to keep Elizabeth and her ministers from suspecting how much I despised them and all their kind." That was clever, Lucy thought. A clever lie . . .

"But once you found that letter from Mary—once you realized she could have told anyone what she knew about Babington and me—" Moncrief said impatiently.

Bram interrupted him. "It simply became even more vital that I find her and wed her. That I tidy up the mess you left behind."

Another fine lie, Lucy thought. How easily they came to him! "But why marry her?" Moncrief demanded. "Why not just kill her?"

"Mary. Mary." Bram twined his fingers through the queen's long auburn hair. "Where do you find such unimaginative men? That show I put on for Elizabeth and Cecil and Walsingham was pure genius, Moncrief. Those fools think it was glorious, romantic, my saving the wench from The Theatre, carrying her off in triumph the way I did. They saw the happy ending unfold right before their eyes. Nothing in the world could ever make them doubt me now."

"Artemis." Mary was rubbing the belly of one of the dogs. "I do not see what you worry about. No one knows it was you to whom Babington passed my letters."

"He does," Moncrief snapped, jerking his head toward Bram. "And all because that idiot Babington brought this bitch to me."

Mary wagged a finger at him. "Ah, ah, chéri. For once Anthony was wise. He knew he could not come here to Chartley himself; the soldiers who guard me know who he is. But no one suspects the mighty Lord Moncrief when you bring her here and say she is a spy for me."

"I thought we had agreed, Mary—the one imperative to your plan is that no one except you should know it is I who is going to assassinate Elizabeth."

"And so no one does," Mary told him complacently, "except those of us in this room. What, chéri, do you make such the long face about?"

"He knows," Moncrief said, glowering at Bram again. "And I don't trust him."

"Ah." Mary kissed the moist nose of Chou-Chou. "There is a simple enough way to test him if you are afraid. He killed one wife; let us see if he will kill another. Bram, what do you say?"

Lucy stared wide-eyed at her husband. His lies had been good; they had nearly convinced her that he was on Mary's side. But what would he do now?

What he did was to kiss the queen of Scots. "Very well, my pet. If you like."

Moncrief flipped a dagger toward him. "Use this."

Bram caught it, stuck it into his belt, and shook his head. "No, thank you. I've refined my methods since murdering Olive."

Lucy couldn't help herself. "But you didn't murder Olive!" she blurted, frightened and confused.

He shrugged and smiled. "Oh, but I did. I choked the life from her while she begged me for mercy. Of course I killed her. And now, poor, clever, curious Lucy, I am going to kill you, too." He reached into his doublet and pulled out a small glass vial.

"What is that?" Mary asked, her black eyes alight.

"Poison, my sweet. Aconite. I keep it with me in case of emergencies."

"Aconite? Never heard of it," Moncrief said sharply.

"Perhaps you know it by its common name—monkshood. I should call it that, I suppose. A common name for a common wench's death." He took out his brandy flask and emptied the vial into it, his hands perfectly steady as he poured.

Sweet God in heaven. He isn't acting, Lucy realized in horror. He really is on Mary's side. He came toward her with the flask, and there was no trace at all of love's fire in his cold blue gaze.

"Wait," Moncrief ordered him. "Prove it's poison."

Bram turned back to him, grinning, and extended the flask. "Help yourself."

"Not me, you idiot!" the white-haired lord snapped. "Give it to one of those bloody dogs."

"Poison one of my dogs?" the queen cried, aghast, and gathered the whole brood of them into her arms. "Never! Chou-Chou, Magrit, Jacques, Pierre, *mes pauvres petits*, do you hear what this cruel man wants to do?"

Bram laughed. "Don't worry, Moncrief. You'll see soon enough how it works—quick and quiet and clean."

Lucy scrambled to her feet as he turned back to her, his big hand curled around the flask. Her eyes darted frantically around the queen's room. One doorway, and Moncrief stood in front of that with his musket. There were two windows, though, behind the bed, both wide open in the summer heat.

Mary stretched languidly across her satin sheets. "There is no way out. If there were, do you think I would still be here? Go on, Bram, I want to see her die."

"Even if you do kill me," Lucy told Bram bravely, "it's

too late for you to kill the queen. As soon as I realized how to read those letters, I sent word to Walsingham in London.''

''Did you? How did you send it?''

''I—I wrote a letter. I sent it with Jem's Johnny.''

''Before or after you killed Jeeves?''

''Before!'' Lucy cried, knowing he could see through her. Christ, that she were so good a liar as he!

''Really?'' He arched a black brow. ''Then why did you say to yourself in the music room that you had to get to London to warn Elizabeth? You see, Lucy, Babington was there. He heard you. And he told Lord Moncrief.''

Lucy stole another glance at those tantalizing windows. Mary was right, she saw, her heart sinking. The castle yards were at least fifty feet down from the sills. And the wide bailey wall was a dozen yards away from the window, straight out and another ten feet down. Too far to jump. Too far to reach. Unless . . .

Unless. She looked at the long velvet hangings that draped the queen's canopied bed, then forced her gaze back to Bram. ''You are mad, all of you. You will never succeed.''

''But we will,'' purred the queen of the Scots, caressing her lapful of dogs. ''Lord Moncrief has been most diligent in recruiting support for me among the French and the Spanish, and with the Pope. Everything is in motion. All the wheels, as they say, are ready to turn. We wait only for Elizabeth's death.''

''The English people will never stomach a murderous whore as their queen!'' Lucy spat.

Mary's black eyes, so much like her cousin's, flashed fire. ''The nobility will welcome me with open arms. They know I come to restore order, the natural, God-given order that their bastard queen has destroyed. And if by the people you mean ignorant rabble such as yourself, they will support me, too, when they see how Elizabeth is struck down—as though by the very hand of God.'' Then she smiled at Lucy, an evil, cunning smile. ''It is a pity you will not live to see *my* England. But then, there would be no place in it for you except in the gutter.''

''Well said, Mary, my sweet.'' Bram grinned, advancing on Lucy. She sidled away from the window, watching his hands as he held the poisoned flask. As he closed in on her, she darted forward and snatched the dagger Moncrief had thrown to him from his belt.

"Stay back!" she warned, flourishing it at him.

"Why prolong the inevitable?" he asked, and grabbed for the dagger. Lucy deftly eluded him, stuck the dagger between her teeth, and ran for the window as fast as she could. She grabbed hold of the bed drapes, leaped over the sill, and let fly.

"Stop her!" Moncrief cried as she sailed out into the light. Twisting in the air, she saw Bram lunge for the curtain, but he was too late; she had already let go and dropped down onto the bailey wall.

"The spy!" Moncrief roared from the window. "The spy is escaping!" Lucy glanced back and ducked as she saw him point the musket straight at her head. She raced along the wall toward the nearest stairway down to the inner yard, the stolen knife hidden in her skirts. Two armed guards rushed toward her; she screamed and pointed back toward the bailey wall.

"It's the spy!" she shrieked. "Up there! The spy is escaping!" They cursed and gripped their pikestaffs, hurrying past her. Lucy darted toward the postern gate; already half a dozen soldiers were hauling at the giant wheel that would lower the bars. As the huge pointed iron spikes rumbled toward the ground, Lucy dropped to her stomach on the cobblestones and just barely squeezed beneath them before they landed with a deafening clank.

She jumped to her feet and tore off into the woods that surrounded the castle, Moncrief's voice ringing in her ears: "Open that gate! Raise the bloody damned gate!" But the postern was easier to let down than to haul up again.

Lucy kept on running, only one thought in her mind: she had to get to London to see the queen. She flew through the woods, her heart pounding, ignoring the brambles and underbrush that tore at her hair and gown.

The trees gave way suddenly to a wheatfield, a great wide swath of bright gold that gleamed in the slanting rays of the afternoon sun. She paused on its edge, shielding her eyes with her hand. All the way on the opposite side of the field was a farmer, a big burly fellow in a wide-brimmed hat, cursing impatiently as he struggled to hitch up a heavy-hooved gray horse to his plow.

Lucy hunched low and ran through the rippling wheat, popping up just behind him, holding her knife to his throat. He froze, the rope he'd been struggling with falling from his hands. "I've got no money," he said hoarsely, the sharp blade tickling his chin.

"I don't want your money," Lucy told him in a low voice.

"Wh-what do ye want, then?"

"I need your horse."

"Take her and be done with it!" the frightened man cried.

"I can't ride. I need you, too. I need you to take me to London Town."

"London—Jesus, are you mad? 'Tis a two-day ride!"

"I need you to get me there by tomorrow morning."

"Ye are mad," the man said, turning his head to see who was making this impossible demand. When he saw Lucy he burst out laughing. "God's bodikin, 'tis naught but a lass! Get on home to ye mama, girl, and leave a working man to do his job."

Lucy looked him straight in the eye and jabbed the knifepoint into his neck, just below his ear. "I've killed before," she said softly. "And I'll kill again, in a minute, if you don't do just as I say. We are getting on that horse together. And you are taking me to London. Do you understand?"

Something in her small, strained face and steady green gaze convinced him that she meant what she said, for he moved toward the plowhorse slowly, with Lucy right behind him, holding the knife to his throat. "All right, then, lass, all right. I'll do like ye tells me." He put his boot to the stirrup, ready to swing up; then suddenly he whirled around, swinging his fist toward her instead. Lucy ducked the blow and sprang back at him with the dagger hard against his heart.

"One more such trick and you are a dead man," she told him, her expression not changing. He got onto the horse without another word, Lucy leaping up behind him. She grabbed his straw hat and jammed it down over her head, leaning her cheek against his broad back, and threw her arm around his shoulders like any maid on a country outing with her man—only this maid's hand still clenched a knife. "Ride," she said.

"Old Nan here," the man said nervously, "I don't know as how she'll get all the way to London."

"She'll get there," Lucy said as the gray horse clopped off over the fields. "And we'll get there, too."

"Bungler!" cried the queen of Scots, and slapped Artemis Moncrief's cheek. "Idiot bungler, what do you *mean* you can't find her? How could she get away?"

"Mary," Bram said soothingly, "the soldiers will find her. She can't have gotten far."

"She will go to London!" Mary raged. "She will ruin my plan!"

He put his hands on her shoulders and shook her gently. "Hush. Nothing will be ruined. She is one small wench who is two hundred miles from London. There is nothing she can do now to stop you."

Mary's black eyes narrowed. "She could tell someone."

"Come, come, Mary," Moncrief said impatiently. "Who would believe her? Anyone she tried to tell her story to would only think her mad."

The queen turned away from them on her bed, scratching Chou-Chou behind the ears. "Perhaps we should postpone the attempt."

"What," Moncrief demanded, "and wait and plan for another three years? Do you want to stay here that long?"

"Better that than to lose my head."

"Mary. Listen to me," Bram said suddenly. "I have a plan. It is perfect. I have a horse that can get me to London in less than twelve hours. There is no way in hell anyone else could get there that fast. I will go to London, and I will stick to Elizabeth like a thorn. If by some miracle that bloody little peasant-wife of mine should get to London, I'll know before she gets to Walsingham or the queen. And I'll give Elizabeth"—he pulled the brandy flask out again—"a good drink of this."

Mary chewed her lip, her hand running over the backs

of her dogs, one after another. "It is not my plan," she objected. "It will not look like the hand of God."

"But at least she'll be dead! And you'll be free, Mary. Think of it. Free."

"I would not wait for years again," the queen acknowledged, and tossed her head coquettishly. "I do not get younger, *n'est-ce pas*?"

"You are as beautiful now as on the first day I saw you," Bram told her softly, and then kissed her hungrily. She giggled and pushed him back, frowning.

"I do not like to think of your mouth touching hers. Of you making love to her. It makes my stomach sick."

He stroked her breast. "What do you think it did to me?"

She looked up at Artemis Moncrief. "Well. What do you say, *chéri*? Do you like this plan of his?"

Moncrief's pale eyes glittered. "So help me God, Carlyle, if you betray me—"

"If the queen is not in that procession tomorrow," Bram said steadily, "you will know she is already dead."

Moncrief yanked open the door to the queen's chambers. "All right, then. Go."

"One more kiss, Bram?" Mary begged prettily, and he obliged her. "And one for Magrit and Jacques and Mignon and Chou-Chou—"

Moncrief dragged Bram away from the bed. "Just get the hell to London. Just do your job."

"Not a job. A pleasure," Bram told him, and blew Mary a kiss from the door. *"Au revoir, chérie."*

The queen of Scots raised up Chou-Chou's front paw. "Wave bye-bye, *ma petite*, to your Papa Bram."

"Can't this horse go any faster?" Lucy asked impatiently.

"Look, lady," snapped the put-upon farmer, "if ye wanted a racehorse I wish to hell ye'd stolen one of them instead of my Nan! And even she'd go one hell of a lot faster if ye'd let me stick to the road instead of riding through these damned woods!"

"We can't go on the road," she told him regretfully.

Bram would have sent soldiers after her—she might even encounter him or Moncrief.

The moon in the sky was sliced so perfectly in half that it reminded her of the one James Burbage stuck up in The Theatre to show it was night—a painted moon, pure fantasy, illusion. He would have approved of Bram's ability as a player, she thought bitterly. Christ, anyone who could have played the true lover and husband so well while he actually despised her would have taken Shoreditch by storm.

Rich, treacherous noblemen—well, she couldn't say no one had warned her. She thought of the way she'd seen her husband last—fondling the traitor queen, bandying words with Joe Reilly's murderer—and she leaned over Nan's withers, retching into a ditch.

The farmer reined in. ''Lady,'' he said, his gruff voice almost gentle. ''Lady, listen. Ye ain't in no fit condition for traveling. Nan's tired. I'm tired. What do you say we just end this right 'ere?''

Lucy sat up again in the saddle, the knife rock-steady against his throat, ignoring the pounding in her head where Babington had smashed it, ignoring her aching ribs that Lord Moncrief had kicked, ignoring as best as she could the grim, terrible emptiness filling her heart. ''Keep riding,'' she said. ''We'll make it. We have to.'' Because the moon shining up above her wasn't painted; it was real. The queen in the procession tomorrow, that would be real, too. And if the queen of Scots had her way, Elizabeth wouldn't be rising from the dead to take any bows when the day was through.

Chapter 22

London.

Shaking with exhaustion, Lucy saw the Holborn Gate to the city rise up before her, the sea of rooftops that stretched beyond it, and whispered a small prayer. "What time is it?" she asked the soldiers on duty at the break in the wall.

" 'Alf past nine, mum."

Half past nine . . . "And the queen—she will be in a procession today. Do you know what time that will be?"

"Aye, mum," the soldier told her. "At noon."

Lucy realized with shock that she'd made it. Jesus, she had done it! Success drove all her weariness and aching muscles straight out of her head. "You've been wonderful!" she told the farmer still seated in the saddle in front of her. "Nan's been wonderful! Everything is wonderful!" And she hugged him.

He turned to look at her. "Ye're mad, lady, do ye know that?"

Lucy only laughed. "I suppose I am."

"Mum," said the guard, "are ye comin' or goin'? There's other people waitin' to get in the city, ye know."

"Do you want to come in with me?" she asked her traveling companion. "There'll be a reward in it for you, I'm sure of it."

"Where are ye goin'?" he asked suspiciously.

"To Whitehall."

"Whitehall. Where the queen lives."

"Aye," Lucy said happily.

"If it's all the same with ye, lady, I'll just leave ye here."

"Suit yourself," Lucy told him, and slipped down from the saddle, stumbling as her feet touched the ground for the first time in more than sixteen hours. "Jesus, I'm stiff!"

She glanced back up at the farmer and saw he was holding a whispered conversation with the soldier who'd stopped them, casting sidelong looks at her and tapping his forehead meaningfully. "Mum," said the guard, "would ye mind just comin' with me for a little—"

Lucy dodged through the gates and in seconds had vanished in the maze of the city's streets.

They were already growing crowded with men and women and children on their way to see the procession, she supposed, for they were wearing holiday clothes and smiles. Lucy joined the stream of people going south through the city; before long she could see the broad brown expanse of the Thames in the distance, and Whitehall's peaked roofs, and the twin towers of Westminster Abbey. She began to push her way through the mob, ignoring the glares and curses shouted out in her wake.

By the time she reached Charing Cross the narrow streets were well nigh impassable; it seemed that everyone in the world must be heading for Whitehall, all moving at a slow, ambling Sunday-stroll gait. "Excuse me," Lucy murmured as she tried to dart through the crowds. "Pardon me, please. Excuse me!"

"Wot's yer 'urry, there, luv?" a jolly fat man called to her. "There won't be nothin' to see for another two hours."

"I have to get through to Whitehall—"

"Where in 'ell d'ye think we're goin'?" a woman in a white bonnet sniffed. "Jesus, some people just think they're better 'n other people, don't they? Some people just can't take their time."

But somehow Lucy finally managed to fight through to the Whitehall wall and then to a high iron gate shut tight and guarded by her majesty's green-and-white liveried guards. Lucy stuck her hand through the bars and gestured frantically to one of them. "I've got to see the queen," she cried.

"Aye, ye 'n' everyone else in the city," the man said, and started back to his post.

"No, I mean I really have to see her," Lucy said desperately. "If you'll just tell her that I am here. Lucy Jo—Lucy Carlyle. Lady Carlyle."

"Right, 'n' I'm the duke of Buckingham. Move along, wench, move along."

"Wait!" Lucy had suddenly remembered the pass Bram gave her to get into the palace. God, did she still have it? She unlaced her bodice strings.

"That might get ye in," the guard told her, leering as she unveiled her petticoat.

"Oh, do be quiet," Lucy snapped, searching for the paper, finally finding it. She thrust it toward him through the bars. "Here, do you see this? It's a diplomatic pass; you've got to let me in."

He took the document, squinted at it, turned it over, turned it back again. "Diplomat's pass, eh? Ye'll 'ave to take that round to the west gate."

"The west gate?" Lucy groaned as the press of the crowd thrust her against the bars. "Can't you let me in here?"

"Sorry, mum. Them's the rules," he said stolidly.

"Well—what gate is this?"

"East gate, mum. Ye'll 'ave to go all the way round."

He started back to his post again.

"Let me talk to your captain, please!" Lucy pleaded.

He shrugged, his back to her. "Sorry, mum. 'E's gettin' ready for the queen's parade."

"Oh!" Lucy cried in frustration, and kicked the gate so hard that the iron bars rang.

"'Ey!" The guard whirled around, his pike lowered at her. "Any more of that 'n' I'll run ye through, pass or no bleedin' pass."

Lucy sighed and let the stream of the crowd swallow her up again.

"I don't think we have moved ten feet in the past hour," Stacy said glumly from the back of a wagon piled high with hay.

His sister, sitting beside the driver on the seat, stopped

singing "When Barry Goes Bum-Di-Do" long enough to say, "Do stop grumbling, Stacy, please! We are on an adventure."

"It is also hot as bloody hell."

"Just because we are on an adventure doesn't mean you have to keep talking like a pirate. Don't you think it's been splendid so far—making up that story for the innkeeper about being orphans so he'd let us stay for the night, eating anything we wanted, finding a ride to the city, and now all these people?" Minnie swept an arm out as though she would embrace the masses of Londoners packed in around them. "Think of it, Stacy—they've all come to see the queen just like us."

The cart driver who had brought them on the second leg of their journey, all the way from Warwick, tilted back his cap, grimacing at the crowds. "Yer brother's right, little lady. We ain't movin'. If I'd 'ave knowed this was goin' on in London today, I'd never even 'ave left 'ome. Ye'd likely do better just walkin'."

"Do you think so?" Minnie considered the throng. "Well, maybe you're right. Thank you very much; it's been ever so much fun singing with you. Goodbye!" She caught up her basket and hopped down from the seat.

"Minnie!" Stacy scrambled down after her. "Wait!" He barely caught her before she was swept into the ocean of arms and legs and feet.

"Is this the way to see the queen?" she asked a cheery woman bustling along beside them.

"Right enough, sweet'eart. Just follow the crowd. Say, wot's that ye've got in yer basket?"

"My cat," Minnie told her. "I've brought her to see the queen, too."

"I see," said the woman, her eyes twinkling. "Good luck to ye!" And then the momentum of the multitude carried her away.

"This was the stupidest idea you have *ever* had," Stacy muttered as a passing peasant mashed his toes. "We'll never even catch a glimpse of the queen in this mess."

"Yes, we will," Minnie said blithely. "Just you wait and see." She had to trot to keep up with the pace of the much longer legs around her as they reached the esplanade along the bank of the Thames. She yanked at the jacket of a passing youth. "Can you tell me, please, where the queen is going to be?"

"Whitehall to Westminster," he called over his shoulder.

"Whitehall to Westminster—" Minnie scrambled up atop a stone wall to see over the heads of the crowd. "Why, Stacy, look! We are nearly at Westminster now." She leaped down from the wall, holding tight to the basket, and eagerly pushed on.

"Minnie," Stacy wailed. "We'll get trampled to death."

"Just stick with me," she called back to him, blazing a trail toward the Abbey lawn.

The crowd there was already lined up at least fifty bodies deep. "Minnie, this isn't very sporting," Stacy hissed, clinging to her skirts as she threaded her way right between a very tall man's legs. "These people all got here before us."

"They can see over us, can't they?" She squirmed through a small break in the wall of backs. "Excuse me, please. Could we get past you, please? I have brought my cat to see the queen." The group of apprentices blocking her path turned, looked down at her, and then grinning, moved aside.

"Her cat," Stacy mumbled apologetically, following his sister. "For God's sake, Minnie, you're embarrassing me."

"It's working, isn't it?" she asked, and then sighed with happiness as she saw the line of soldiers stationed along the route of the procession to keep the way clear. "You see there?" She ducked under the entwined hands of two sweethearts. "We've made it! We're here!"

Stacy, stumbling up beside her, saw it was true. To their left were the huge brass doors of the Abbey, and to the right, between the long rows of craning heads, stretched the cobblestone road that led to Whitehall at its far end. "So we made it," he said with a groan, rubbing his trodupon toes. "What do we do now?"

"Now," said Minnie, plunking down her basket to stake

her spot right in front of the throng, staring toward White-hall with rapt blue eyes, "now we wait to see the queen!"

"It's a diplomatic pass," Lucy shouted through the west gate at the guard stationed there, flapping the paper in his face.

"I can see that, mum," he shouted back at her above the excited buzz of the Londoners packed tight behind her. "But it's made out for a man, not for a lady."

"It is made out to my husband. I am Lady Carlyle."

"Aye, so ye says, mum, but ye've got no proof of it, 'ave ye?"

"Please," Lucy cried, "if you'll just ask the queen. Or ask Sir Francis Walsingham. Or Cecil—do you know who he is?"

"I ain't stupid, mum!"

"Of course you're not," Lucy said resignedly. "Would you please, please, *please* just go and tell one of them I am here?"

To her utter amazement, the guard bobbed his head. "All right, mum." He marched off; Lucy sagged against the gate, unable to believe she had managed that much. The bells of Westminster chimed out half past ten. Still plenty of time, she assured herself. There's still plenty of time . . .

Equally amazing, the guard was back within minutes, and he was smiling. "Sorry, mum," he apologized, un-locking the gate. "Sir Francis said to show ye right in. Come along this way."

He led her into the palace, down the opulent corridors, past the grand Presence Chamber where Lucy sang—or didn't sing, rather—on her last visit here. Then they went down the flagstone walk to the door Bram had pulled her through once before; the guard knocked, and Lucy felt faint with relief as she heard Walsingham's gruff voice call, "Come in!"

"Sorry again, mum," the soldier said.

"It doesn't matter now," Lucy told him, smiling as she opened the door. She took one look into the room and swayed on her feet. "Oh dear God!" she cried.

Walsingham and Cecil were sitting at the table with

lizabeth, but the queen was slumped in a chair with her
ead lolling back and her eyes closed. There was one more
gure seated there as well: Bram. And by his elbow was
brandy flask.

"You bastard!" Lucy sprang at her husband. "You
cheming son of a bitch, you didn't even wait for the pro-
ession!" She remembered the dagger in her skirts and
ulled it out.

"Lucy, don't!" Walsingham cried, grabbing her wrist.

"He's killed her! He's killed her!" Lucy sobbed, trying
o wrestle free.

"Wife." Bram looked up at her, smiling, his voice
ounding oddly thick. "Sweet . . . brave wife. You made
. . . all the way here."

"He hasn't killed her, Lucy!" Cecil said sharply. "Let
o of the knife."

"He poisoned her! You don't understand; he's in league
ith Mary! I saw him at Chartley," she cried. "He was
n bed with the queen of Scots!"

"Not quite in bed," Bram said with that strange, silly
mile. "You got there, Lucy . . . just in time. My guard-
an . . . angel."

"Lucy," said Walsingham, finally wrestling the knife
rom her, "I think you had better sit down."

"I think you had better arrest him! He has killed the
ueen! He even told me the kind of poison—monkshood,
e called it."

"Laudanum," Cecil corrected her briskly. "She isn't
ead, Lucy. She's asleep. She'll be up and about—and
ikely in a rage—in about four hours."

"But—" Lucy looked again at Bram and saw how enor-
nous the pupils of his blue eyes were beneath his heavy
ids. "Asleep . . . why?"

"To stop her . . . from being in the procession." Bram
vagged his head, slumping lower in his chair. "Couldn't
ave that. You . . . did it, Lucy. You saved her. But there
vasn't . . . time."

"Wasn't time for what?" Bram didn't answer; his
reathing was heavy and slow.

"For proof," Cecil told her. "There wasn't enough time
o decipher those letters when Bram got here this morning.

The queen refused to disappoint her public; she was insisting on being in that procession at noon.''

"But didn't Bram tell her about Mary?'' Lucy demanded. "About Moncrief?''

The queen's ministers exchanged glances. Cecil cleared
his throat delicately. "There was the problem, you see, of
just how Bram obtained his information.''

"Elizabeth has always been as jealous as hell of Mary,''
Walsingham said more succinctly. "She'd have clapped
Bram into the Tower for life if she found out he'd tried to
take her cousin to bed. If we'd had time enough to show
her the letters, that would have been one thing. But there
wasn't time, and so he drugged her.''

"Had to drug myself, too,'' Bram said, and chuckled.
"You know she doesn't . . . doesn't like to drink alone.''

Lucy put her hand to her forehead, trying to make sense
of it all. "But what the hell was he doing in bed with
Mary at Chartley?''

Walsingham looked a touch embarrassed. "Actually
that was my idea. I suggested to Bram that since my conventional methods of gathering information didn't seem to
work with Mary, he might be, well, less conventional.''

"And seduce the Queen of the Scots,'' Lucy said
slowly, then grabbed her husband by the collar. "And you
agreed?'' she asked.

He looked up at her with those huge-pupiled eyes, and
though his voice was groggy there was no mistaking the
truthfulness in it. "The hardest thing, Lucy . . . I've ever
done.''

"If it makes any difference to you, Lucy,'' Cecil put
in, "things didn't get as far as it might have appeared.
Bram told us that Moncrief dragged you in just in time.''

Lucy stared down at Bram. "But you would have gone
through with it, wouldn't you have?'' He nodded once,
slowly. "Oh, Bram. Why?''

"For Elizabeth,'' he whispered. "Stubborn, stubborn
woman. But I . . . love her.'' His heavy-lidded eyes
closed. "And I love you, too . . . sweet, brave Lucy.''
And then he began to snore.

Lucy picked up the brandy flask. "Then he wasn't really going to poison me, either.''

"Of course not, my dear," Cecil assured her. "But he d to think on his feet when Moncrief showed up at Chart- y with you in tow. If he hadn't repudiated you, Moncrief ight well have killed you both. And Elizabeth would be ding in that procession today."

Lucy glared at Walsingham. "I cannot believe you would k a man married for only one week to do such a thing!"

"I didn't," he promptly replied. "I asked him years o, soon after Olive's death. Mary took a fancy to him e first time he showed up at Chartley. Wife-killer and sband-killer—she thought they were kindred spirits, I ppose. She'd been trying to seduce him ever since then. ut for some reason he kept giving me one excuse after other why he didn't."

Of course Lucy knew why. She had restored her hus- nd's faith in his masculinity only to have him forced to cide whether to use his newfound power to dally with e queen of Scots. God, she didn't envy him making that cision. She remembered then the peculiar question he d asked her just before he left for Chartley: *Would you ve me whatever I do?* And she had said yes . . .

Still, "I think you both should be thoroughly ashamed yourselves," she told the two men sitting before her.

"I'd have volunteered for the duty myself," Cecil said, s dark-ringed eyes rueful, "but I doubt Mary would have anted me." Then his voice turned grave. "It's a hard ct of life in these times, Lucy, that sometimes the good private men must be sacrificed for the good of the state. he queen is safe, and that has to be the paramount con- deration. I hope you'll find it in your heart to forgive —and more importantly, Bram."

But Lucy already had; she slipped into the empty chair side her sleeping husband, pushing his hair back from s eyes. "What will happen now?"

Walsingham shrugged. "The plot's foiled. Bram told oncrief that if the queen didn't appear in the procession would know she is dead, but it won't take long for him find out differently. He'll flee the country. We'll go rough the letters from Mary and try to convince the een there really was a conspiracy. God knows whether e'll believe us. As William says, when it comes to Mary she has an infinite capacity for deluding herself.'' He pulled at his beard. "We'll have lost Bram as an inside source to Mary, of course. Three bloody years of work right down the drain.''

"But what about Moncrief and Babington?" Lucy cried. "Surely you can arrest them."

"If we can find them," Cecil said glumly. "Of course if they make it out of the country we won't be able to touch them.''

"And Mary? Well, Mary will be back to her old tricks in no time." Walsingham glanced at the sleeping queen. "God help us all, I don't think Bess will ever bring herself to behead that woman. We can only hope we will be this lucky next time.''

Lucy, too, looked at the queen, and saw in surprise that her high-piled red hair had shifted to one side. It was a wig, she realized, that flamboyant coiffure. And that gave her the seed of an idea.

"What if the queen were to appear in today's procession?" she asked slowly. "What if whatever is in those letters from Mary comes true?"

Walsingham snorted. "That would be proof, all right, but the queen would be dead."

"But if it weren't really the queen," Lucy went on. "If it was just someone that everybody thought was the queen. A decoy, a lure—"

"Who'd be lunatic enough to play the target for an assassin?" Cecil asked rhetorically.

"I would," Lucy said.

The queen's ministers stared at her. Cecil was the first to find his tongue. "Absolutely not! Out of the question! Why, we don't even know what Moncrief is planning. Bram didn't dare press him; the bastard was already suspicious enough.''

"But we know it has to take place during the procession," Lucy argued. "And if someone does try to kill me, then the queen will have to believe Mary's plot is real.''

"There's a very good chance someone *would* kill you,'' Walsingham noted.

"That's a chance I'm willing to take." Lucy was remembering a long-ago night in Shoreditch, and Joe Reilly's eyes as he lay dying in the gutter outside her burning shop. ''To get that hawk-nosed bastard Moncrief. I owe him a debt, by God, and I pay my debts.''

''Bram would kill *us*,'' Cecil said rather worriedly.

''This has nothing to do with Bram,'' Lucy told him. ''This has to do with Moncrief and me.''

Walsingham waved his hand toward the queen. ''It's preposterous, Lucy. First off, you don't look anything like her.''

''No, but I know a man who can make me look like her twin. His name is Toby, Toby Mifflin.''

''Where is this genius, pray tell?''

''He's in prison. In the Fleet.''

''I knew I knew that name.'' Cecil banged his fist on the table. ''It's that player fellow, isn't it, whose place Bram took at the virginals. He's been convicted of sodomy, Lucy. He's sentenced to be hanged in two days.''

''He's been convicted falsely, Sir William, I swear it. And he can make me look like the queen. Just send for him and you'll see.''

He frowned. ''You'd be out there on your own, Lucy. Neither Sir Francis nor I could protect you. I still say it's too much of a risk.''

''Sometimes the good of private men,'' Lucy quoted softly, ''must be sacrificed for the good of the state. That goes for women, too.''

Cecil sighed and looked at Walsingham. ''Well?''

''Well, we'll send for this Mifflin character,'' the secretary of state decided. ''But I'm not promising anything.''

Chapter 23

"Oh, God." Bram awoke groaning, clapped his hands to his head, tried to sit up, and then thought better of it. He heard the sound of laughter and opened one eye. "Toby Mifflin?" He stared at the tall, dark-mustachioed man who stood over him. "Christ, I knew the queen would be angry, but I didn't think she'd put me in the Fleet!"

Toby laughed again and pulled him up so he sat with his head propped against the wall. "We're not in the Fleet; we're in Whitehall. I've been given a reprieve temporarily."

"Whitehall . . ." Bram shook his head to clear the fog that engulfed it and looked around him, seeing racks of magnificent robes and gowns stiff with gold and jewels. "Whitehall where?"

"The queen's closets." Toby turned to look out through a small window. "You're a lucky man, Carlyle. That wife of yours is the most remarkable woman I have ever met."

"Lucy." Bram struggled to his feet. "Christ, I've got to talk to her. I've got to explain about Mary." He found the door and grabbed at the latch, but it didn't open.

"They've locked us in," Toby told him.

"Who locked us in?"

"Cecil and Walsingham. Me for my protection, they said, and you for theirs." Toby glanced out the window again. "You must be very proud of Lucy for doing this."

"For doing what?" Bram asked. Through the fog he became aware of music, the thump of drums and the high blare of trumpets, and of a crowd cheering wildly. "What's going on down there?"

"The queen's procession."

Bram elbowed him aside and stared out at the throngs

lining the road to Westminster, the rows of musketeers and halberdiers and dignitaries marching slowly toward the Abbey, and, in their wake, the queen's gilded sedan chair, borne by her honor guard. From that distance he could just make out the golden crown that topped Elizabeth's elaborate red coiffure. "But the queen is asleep," he said in bewilderment.

"Of course she is," said Toby. "That's Lucy down there." And then, as Bram turned horrified blue eyes on him, he swallowed. "My God, man. I thought you knew. She took the queen's place."

All remnants of the laudanum disappeared from Bram's brain. He reared back and flung himself headlong at the closet door, shattering the wood, and then plunged through. "Where are you going?" Toby called after him.

"I don't know! To do something—anything!"

"Can I help?"

Bram glanced briefly back at him, sympathy in his gaze. "If I were you, Toby, I'd get the hell out of here and onto the first ship leaving for the New World." Then he rushed through the antechamber and down the nearest flight of stairs.

Toby eyed the gaping hole to freedom that Bram had made him, then stared at his wrists, at the grim, harsh lines worn into his flesh by the manacles so recently removed. He could walk out of the palace now, just as Bram said. He could begin life anew. A free man . . .

He turned back to the window, looking down into the yards, and saw Bram burst through a doorway. Far down the road to Westminster, the queen's jeweled robes sparkled in the sun.

"Oh, hell," he muttered. "What kind of idiot would leave a play before the last act was finished?" And he settled in, leaning on the windowsill, to watch the drama below him unfold.

In the Whitehall yards Bram stared, dismayed, at the hindguard of the procession. The eager throngs beyond the gates had swarmed in behind the queen's chair, tight-packed as jarred herring, screaming Elizabeth's name. He would never manage to work his way through them to Lucy before the parade was through.

He climbed up a stairway to the outer wall and scanned the route of the procession. Moncrief, it was Moncrief who would try to kill her. But there were a thousand places along the road where he might be hiding; he could be anywhere in that massive crowd. What had Moncrief and Mary said to each other at Chartley? He'd been so concerned for Lucy's safety, so intent on the act he'd been playing, that he could not recall.

Again he surveyed the scene spread out before him. Westminster Bridge. The Embankment. St. Peter's College. St. Margaret's. The Guard House. The Abbey itself . . .

And then he heard in his mind the soft, seductive voice of the queen of Scots: *They will support me, too, when they see how Elizabeth is struck down—as though by the very hand of God* . . .

Moncrief was in Westminster Abbey. He had to be.

Bellerophon. Where the devil had he left Bellerophon? The stables. He dashed down the stairs and ran to them, calling the big black horse's name, and the stallion yanked free of the groom who held him. "Sire, don't ye want yer—" The groom blinked as Bram leaped onto the horse's bare back. "—saddle?" he finished with a squeak. But Bram was holding tight to the stallion's mane, driving him toward the south yard.

"Open the gates!" he roared at the guards as he pounded toward them. They flung them open hurriedly. "Make way, make way!" he bellowed at the scattering of people on the road outside, slowly heading home after having seen the parade. "Look out!" They scrambled out of his path, and he pointed Bellerophon toward the esplanade.

Once there, the way was relatively clear along the riverbank as far as the bridge. If he rode past the Abbey, Bram thought, galloping westward, and doubled back around to the rear, to the Dean's Yard, he might get through. With the drums beating the slow, steady progress of the parade above even the roars of the crowds he thundered across the grass, keeping one eye on the queen's glittering chair.

As he'd hoped, the Dean's Yard and the square behind it were nearly deserted. He leaped from the horse by the entrance to the cloisters and pounded on its doors. No one answered; he moved back a few paces and slammed his shoulder into the iron-framed wood; it buckled, but held. He was just about to slam into it again when a cross-looking priest threw it open. "No private devotions today! Don't you know the queen is coming?" he cried, shaking his fist. Bram grabbed him by the throat and shook him.

"I'm coming in. Now stand aside."

The priest stepped back. Bram leaped over the low wall of the cloister garden and ran through it, scattering honeybees and butterflies. Even in that secluded spot he could hear the thumping drums. Across the garden was another wooden door; he threw the bar up and yanked it open to confront a whole roomful of priests on their knees in prayer. "Sorry," he said, and ducked out again.

The next door he tried led to the sanctuary, blocked off from the nave by the huge carved panels that marked the choir. He ran through it quickly, searching behind the screens and the great marble pillars, but there was no one hiding among its ornate architecture. He hadn't expected there to be. Wherever Moncrief was, he was sure it had to be someplace with a view of the parade as it approached the Abbey. That left the nave or the towers.

He entered the empty, echoing nave, scanning the magnificent vaulted ceiling, the statues of saints that lined the walls. At the far end, by the doors to the porch, he saw a solitary priest just preparing to unlock the doors. Bram ran toward him, his footsteps impossibly loud in the vast arching church, and the priest whirled around. "How did you get in here?" he demanded.

"Never mind how I got in. Is someone else in here, a man, an old man with silver hair?"

"There's no one else in here," the priest said indignantly. "We've cleared the whole place for the queen."

"Think, man!" Bram snapped, grabbing him by the shoulders. "An old man. Silver hair. With a big hooked nose."

"Oh, like a bird's beak?"

"Yes! For God's sake, where is he?"

"He's long gone now."

"What do you mean, he's gone? Where was he?"

"Up there," said the priest, pointing to the west tower. "He came in early this morning with a big sack of stuff. Surveying equipment, he said it was. He needed to have a look at some land he was buying."

"And he left?" Bram demanded incredulously, the drums and the roars of the crowd outside the doors thundering in his head.

"Of course he did," said the priest. "I told him he had to be gone by ten o'clock. He gave me his word as a gentleman that he would."

"He gave you his—God in heaven." Bram dashed for the tower stairs.

"Here she comes!" Minnie cried, standing on tiptoe as the queen's musketeers trooped by and turned aside at the entrance to the Abbey, forming two long lines flanking the doors. "I can see her chair!"

"Where?" Stacy demanded.

"There, behind all those men with the pikes and the flags. I wish they would move." She peeked under the outstretched arm of the guard holding back the crowd. "Lordy, those drums are loud."

"They're not nearly so loud as those muskets are going to be. Look, they are going to give a salute." Stacy pointed to the musketeers by the doors.

Minnie hopped up and down with excitement as the richly garbed lords advanced on the Abbey; she finally had a clear glimpse of the queen's chair. "You can't see very much of her, can you?" she shouted to Stacy. "Not in that big fancy dress, with the collar sticking up around her face." She looked more closely. "You know, I think she looks a little like Lucy."

Stacy snorted. "She's a million years older than Lucy," he yelled in her ear.

"Why do you think she has her eyes closed.?"

"Probably she's dying of heat. That dress must weigh ten thousand pounds."

"I'm going to let Reggie see now," Minnie declared, unlatching the basket lid.

"You had better not," Stacy warned her. "She'll run away."

"Don't be stupid," said Minnie. "Reggie would never run away from the queen. Reggie loves the queen." She pulled the gray cat from the basket and hugged her close to her chest.

The drums beat a rat-a-tat-tat as the honor guard halted. Sir William Cecil and Sir Francis Walsingham, dripping with sweat in their heavy robes of state, exchanged nervous glances as they split off at the Abbey doors. The captain of the musketeers raised his hand, and a momentary hush fell over the throngs in the street as they waited for the salute from the guns.

"Prepare arms!" the captain barked, so loudly that Bram, only halfway up the tower stairs, heard him and caught his breath. He leaned back his head and roared into the tower, wild and despairing:

"Moncrief!"

"Present arms!" the captain bellowed.

Reggie, spooked by the excitement around her, clawed her way out of Minnie's arms. "I told you!" Stacy cried, hands clapped over his ears.

Lucy, peeking out from beneath her lashes, saw a tiny golden-haired girl dart out from the crowd in pursuit of a sleek gray streak that leaped onto the shoulders of one of the honor guards, flew through the air, and landed, mewling and cowering, admid the queen's white velvet skirts. "Look!" Minnie screeched. "She's under your chair!"

"Fire!"

Astonished, Lucy leaned down to look just as the thunderous guns exploded, then gasped as something hot and bright whizzed through the air just above her head. "Jesus!" she gasped, hearing a splintering sound from the back of the chair. She reached up to straighten her wig, and Walsingham, looking back at her, saw a tiny plume of smoke rise from the midst of her high-piled red hair.

"Reload arms!" shouted the captain of the musketeers.

High in the west tower, Artemis Moncrief was trying frantically to do just that, but before he could ram home the shot and light his matchlock, Bram had reached the top of the stairs.

"Got you, you bastard," he roared, grabbing Moncrief from behind and slamming him against the stone wall.

The musket dropped down the staircase, and the second salute from the guns blasted out below.

The woman in the gilded chair scooped up the gray cat and handed it to one of the soldiers, who laughed and returned it to the little girl with the basket. The honor guard set the queen's chair down right at the Abbey doors. The crowd screamed its joy. The woman stepped down from the chair and walked into the Abbey between the ranks of musketeers and soldiers and nobles, her head held high.

"The queen touched my cat! The queen touched my cat!" Minnie cried in exultation. But Stacy didn't hear her; he was staring at the woman's back as she vanished into the great vaulted nave of Westminster.

"You know, she does look a little like Lucy," he said thoughtfully.

"Let me see," said the queen of England, "if I have this straight. You, Bram Carlyle, had the audacity to put a drug in my wine at breakfast this morning. And you, Lucy, you decided you would take my place in the procession and put on my clothes. And you—" She lowered a finger at Toby. "You came out of prison and made Lucy look so much like me that not even my honor guard noticed anything amiss?" Toby bowed, smiling self-deprecatingly. "And you, William and Francis, you actually agreed to this entire charade?"

"Well," Walsingham began, "Lucy can be very—"

"Silence!" the queen snapped, her black eyes flashing. "How dare you pull such a harebrained stunt behind my back? I ought to have the whole lot of you drawn and quartered!"

"Don't forget Minnie," Stacy said helpfully. "She's the one who let out the cat."

"Don't tattle on your sister, Stacy," Lucy said.

"Bess," Cecil said gently, "the point is, it worked. Bram caught Moncrief red-handed trying to reload that gun. He was trying to kill you."

"So Bram says," Elizabeth declared. "What makes you think I would trust the word of a man who would drug his own queen?"

"Oh, no you don't, Bess," said Walsingham. "Not even you can wiggle out of it this time. You can see for yourself where the musket ball went through your wig and nicked the crown. If this little mischief-maker here"—he nodded toward Minnie—"hadn't let loose her cat, the ball would have gone straight through Lucy's head."

Elizabeth shuddered slightly, her slim fingers tracing the spot on the crown where the bullet had hit. "And you're certain Moncrief was in league with Mary," she said, looking up at Bram as he stood before her with his wife and children.

"Absolutely certain. And I'll wager you a million pounds that when we decipher the rest of those letters, the entire plot will be laid out there."

"But I don't understand," the queen cried impatiently. "If Lucy was so certain that someone was going to try to kill me today, why did she take my place?"

"You wanted proof, Bess," Cecil told her. "And Lucy was willing to die to get that proof for you. It was a miracle that she didn't get killed by that musket ball, but the miracle will be wasted unless you finally admit that Mary wants you dead. Unless you put an end to this right now. Today."

Elizabeth Tudor sat for a moment in silence. Then she crooked a finger at Minnie. "Let us see that cat."

Minnie unlatched the basket and lifted out the bundle of gray fur, setting it in the queen's lap. "Her name's Reggie," she offered. "For you. Elizabeth Regina."

"Hello, puss," said the queen, staring into its unblinking green eyes. "Are you a good mouser?"

"She's the best," Minnie said stoutly. "Only sometimes when she catches one she plays with it too long and it gets away, and then Cook gets cross."

"Silly puss," said the queen. "Why would you do such a thing?" Then she buried her face in the cat's gray fur.

Cecil came forward and laid his hand on her shoulder. "Bess—"

She shook him away, raising her head and letting out her breath in a long sigh. "I know, William. You are right. It is time." She passed the cat back to Minnie. "There will have to be—a trial, I suppose?"

Cecil nodded. "It will be a fair one. In private, as befits her rank and station. You can appoint the members of the commission yourself."

"No," she said wearily. "You do it, William, for me. I couldn't bear to."

Walsingham spoke up, uncharacteristically brusque with an end to the long years of spying on Mary in sight at last. "When she's found guilty—and she will be—there will be a writ of execution to sign. No one else can do that for you."

"We will cross that bridge when we come to it."

"For God's sake, Bess—"

"When we come to it, I say!"

Stacy tugged on his father's sleeve. "Why doesn't she believe that the bad queen wants to hurt her? Lucy told us that about a million years ago."

"I think," said Bram, his blue gaze steady as he looked at Elizabeth, "she does believe it now."

"And do you know what that means?" Lucy asked Stacy, brushing back his blond hair. He shook his head, and she leaned down to whisper to him: "That your father will have a lot more time to play pell-mell."

"Hurray!" he cried, and the queen clapped her hands over her ears.

"Please, young man! I have a raging headache, thanks to your father!"

"You'd have a worse one," Minnie said, and giggled, "if it wasn't for Lucy and him."

"You have a sassy tongue, little miss," said the queen, arching a thin red brow.

"That's Lucy's influence," Bram told her, and grinned.

Elizabeth looked at Toby. "Bram tells me you could have escaped from the palace today, yet you didn't, even though you are under a sentence of death. Why not?"

"Lucy had put her trust in me," he said with quiet dignity.

"You are one of James Burbage's players, are you not?" she asked. "The one charged with raping that boy. Christopher Dalton has been buzzing in my ear for weeks about you and Burbage." Her black eyes were shrewd. "Has he some sort of grudge against you?"

Toby nodded. "I once threw a rouge pot at him. And kicked him. In the behind."

"Odd," said the queen. "I have had that same urge myself at times; he's such a horrid man. Tell me, Master Mifflin, if your case is reopened and you are found innocent, will you go back to the stage?"

"I'm afraid, your majesty, public opinion being what it is, my days as a player are through."

"I know all about public opinion." Elizabeth regarded him thoughtfully. "You've shown today that you can make a young woman into an old one, Master Mifflin. Could you also do the opposite, do you think?"

"Why?" asked Toby. "Does your majesty know someone who is getting old?"

The queen chuckled at the gallant reply. "I do. And because of her friends, it seems she will be growing even older still. Would you consider accepting a post with me, Master Mifflin, as my chief dresser? At, say, a hundred pounds a year?"

"That would depend entirely, your majesty, on whether I could hope to see my good friend James Burbage performing here at court in the near future."

"Master Mifflin." The queen arched her brow again. "Are you blackmailing me?"

He bowed. "Yes, your majesty."

She laughed outright. "I like this player fellow, Lucy!"

Lucy smiled at Toby. "So do I."

"Very well, then," Elizabeth said briskly. "I shall give Burbage and his troupe one more chance. But after that, they will succeed or fail on their own abilities."

"In that case," said Toby, "I look forward to a long and fruitful term of employment with your majesty."

A page bobbed in the doorway. "The Lady Claudia Moncrief, baroness of Tatworth, requests an audience, your majesty," he announced.

"Baroness of Tatworth?" the queen echoed, glancing at Walsingham. "You didn't tell me Bram had murdered Lord Moncrief."

"He didn't. Moncrief's in the Tower," her minister informed her.

"Lady Moncrief seems a bit precipitous in her assumption of her father's title,'' Elizabeth said thoughtfully, and nodded to the page. ''Very well, show her in.''

Claudia Moncrief sashayed into the Presence Chamber trailing yards of rustling silver satin behind her, her ears and wrists and throat laden with jewels. ''Bad Christmas pudding,'' Lucy heard Toby mutter at her back, and bit off a smile. Not sparing a glance for anyone else in the room, she went straight to the queen's throne and curtsied deeply.

''Father,'' Stacy whispered, ''how does she make that gown stay up over her—'' Bram clapped a hand over his son's mouth, his bemused blue gaze meeting Lucy's above the boy's head.

''Your majesty, I came here just as soon as I heard,'' Claudia gushed, ''and I just want to assure you that I had absolutely no idea of what Daddy was up to! I think it's just shocking, and if you ask me he has got exactly what he deserves.''

''What exactly is it that you've heard your father has got, Mistress Moncrief?'' the queen inquired.

''It's Lady Moncrief now, Your Highness,'' Claudia corrected her. ''I did just manage to pop in at Daddy's solicitor's office on the way here, and by the greatest stroke of fortune he was in. He assured me that despite the—well, the *unpleasant,* shall we say, circumstances of Daddy's death, he doesn't foresee any complications in transferring the title, so I've just gone ahead and assumed it. Anyway, that's neither here nor there. The reason for my call is to inquire about the taxes.''

''The taxes,'' said the queen.

Claudia nodded. ''Yes, you see, the solicitor tells me the inheritance tax is nearly ten percent of the estate, which I think is perfectly outrageous! His advice was that I ask you for a deferral, which I'm sure your majesty will be happy to grant. I mean—'' She sighed, dabbing at her eyes with a white silk kerchief. ''We are both in the same unhappy situation now, aren't we? Just helpless women alone in a world of wolves.''

''Dear Mistress Moncrief.'' The queen reached out and patted her gloved hand. ''I do regret having to be the one o inform you of this sad fact. But I'm afraid your father sn't dead."

Claudia jerked back her hand. "Not dead? But that's mpossible! I was informed he was apprehended in the very act of attempting to take your majesty's life."

"So they tell me," said the queen.

"And that he was taken to the Tower."

"They tell me that, too."

Claudia blinked. "Well, naturally I assumed you would have had him done away with by now. After all, a dangerous enemy of the state—"

"Unlike your father and his friends," the queen said dryly, "I am not in the habit of doing away with my enemies in such a manner. I prefer to have them tried and found guilty first."

"Tried—and found guilty?" Claudia said in some alarm. "How long will that take?"

"Francis?" The queen appealed to Walsingham.

"A month at least, I should say."

"A month." Claudia tapped her toes. "Oh, dear."

"Of course, that's just for the treason trial," Walsingham added. "After that will come the process for forfeiture of the estate."

"The *what*?" Claudia screeched.

"The forfeiture of the estate," he repeated patiently. "A convicted traitor forfeits all his goods and properties to the crown. Did your solicitor neglect to mention that?"

"But—but—but—" Claudia sputtered, and then stamped her dainty foot. "Oh, Daddy, damn you!"

"Is she mad at her father because he isn't dead?" Minnie whispered to Lucy.

"I'm afraid she is."

"Well, that isn't very nice, is it?" Minnie said, shaking her head.

"But what will I be left with?" Claudia wailed.

"Well," Walsingham told her, "you will have the title. And of course that very distinguished pedigree. Eight dukes, twenty earls and thirty barons—is it thirty barons?"

"Fifty, I think," Lucy said.

Claudia whirled on her. "This is all your fault, you

conniving bitch! If you hadn't gone to Bram's house impersonating me, I'd be married to him now instead of you!''

"Oh, no, Claudia," Bram told her, his arm tight around his wife. "I'm afraid there was never a ghost's chance of that."

The blonde's pale eyes had narrowed. "I can still marry someone—anyone! I've got scores of suitors."

"Without your father's money, my dear," said the queen, "I frankly cannot imagine why any man would want to marry such a spoiled shrew as you. So let me offer you a bit of advice—from one helpless woman to another in a world of wolves, you understand. Take up a profession."

"A profession!" Claudia cried, scandalized.

"Aye. I can think of one—a very old one—that would suit you well. Now get out of here. It makes me sick to look at you."

"Ooh!" Fuming, Claudia spun on her heel and stalked toward the door. "I'll get back at you, all of you! Just see if I don't!"

"That was a threat," Walsingham declared, starting after her. "I'd better have her followed."

"Oh, Francis," said the queen as even the children burst out laughing. "Give it a rest, won't you, just till the end of the day?"

Epilogue

Lucy opened her eyes to find Bram sitting up in bed eside her, looking down at her, running his hand over er hair. She smiled up at him. "What are you doing?"

"Watching you," he whispered. "Loving you."

"Don't you grow tired of that after so many mornngs?"

"I could never grow tired of you."

He leaned down to kiss her, his mouth warm and hunry. Lucy stretched up her arms, pulling him down to her, hivering in anticipation as the kiss lengthened, as she felt is tongue thrust into her mouth, savoring the taste of her, xploring eagerly. He put his hands to her breasts and ased her nipples with his fingertips, and Lucy sighed /ith pleasure, arching against him in their warm nest of uilts and blankets. "Nor I of you," she told him, her ngers wrapping around his manhood, hard and ready and ot.

He bent his head to her breasts, kissing first one and en the other, and though his touch was leisurely, Lucy ould feel the blood that pulsed in his groin, aching for lease. She burrowed beneath the covers and put her outh to him, ran her tongue over him, and then laughed s he yanked her up again, groaning. "Lucy! You know /hat that does to me!"

"Indeed I do," she said, and promptly burrowed down gain. His breathing grew harsh and ragged as she stroked im, softly at first and then more forcefully; he moved his

369

loins beneath her tongue until he groaned and rolled over, pressing her beneath him, his blue eyes ablaze in the cold gray light of dawn.

"Is this what you want?" he asked, arching above her, his manhood brushing her thighs.

"No . . ."

"This?" He barely pushed into her and pulled out again, smiling.

"No!"

"This, then." He drove deep inside her, burying himself in her, and she shuddered and held him there, awed by the force of her need for him.

"Yes," she said, and then her hands tightened on his hips as they began to move together in a rhythm that was older than memory and yet new every time. The fire caught hold of them, swept them away with its power, until they came together in a single hot blaze of glory, crying out their love for each other in passion's sweet song.

"Oh." Bram sighed and collapsed atop her as the flames slowly subsided. "That is the only way to begin a new day."

"That and breakfast," Lucy agreed, and wriggled out from beneath him to ring for Jem.

"I swear, all you ever think of anymore is food," Bram grumbled. "I don't know what's gotten into you."

"Really," said Lucy. "I can't imagine. Good morning, Jem."

"Morning, Miss Lucy. Morning, sir," said the dark-eyed maid, carrying in a huge footed tray and plopping it down on the bed. "There's letters come from London. One for each of you."

Bram picked up his and glanced at the seal. "From Walsingham. I can only hope I know what this is. Although, considering how the queen is still dawdling—" He ripped it open, glanced at the contents, and shook his head. "Well, I'll be damned. Elizabeth finally did it, three months after the trial. The queen of Scots was beheaded yesterday at Fotheringay."

"Poor woman," Lucy murmured, and crossed herself.

"Poor woman?" Bram frowned. "You and I both went through those letters, Lucy. There is no doubt whatsoever she planned every detail of that plot to murder the queen. Not to mention that she did away with at least one husband and heaven knows how many lovers. She got no more than she deserved, just like Babington and Moncrief.''

''I know. But it is sad when anyone dies,'' Lucy said wistfully. ''And she did love those dogs.''

''Oh, I suppose you feel sorry for Jeeves, too.''

She shivered. ''You have to feel sorry for someone as mad as he was, Bram—holding everything inside himself that way, worshipping Olive for so many years even after she was dead.''

''If ye asks me,'' said Jem, ''he got just what he deserved, too.''

''I don't suppose your opinion on that subject has anything to do with the fact that Johnny's the butler now, would it?'' Bram asked her, one black brow raised.

She giggled. ''Took away his last excuse not to marry me, didn't it? Well, it all ended well, didn't it?'' And she skipped out the door.

''What was that about liking dogs?'' Bram asked Lucy curiously.

''Something Toby once said. Speaking of which, that's who my letter is from.'' She sliced it open neatly with the knife she'd been using to butter a muffin and started to read. ''Oh, Bram, guess what!'' she said through a mouthful of crumbs. ''James has got himself a patron at last, and who should it be but the earl of Leicester himself!''

Bram whistled, kissing jam from her chin. ''Very impressive indeed. It sounds like his troubles are over.''

''Mmm. Not quite. He and his son Dick are having an enormous fight about a fellow Dick has found who wants to write plays. He's from the country, Toby says. Lord, what a strange name he has—here, how would you say that?''

Bram eyed the word she pointed to. ''Just the way it looks—Shakespeare, I guess. Why are Dick and James fighting about him?''

She consulted the letter again. ''James says he doesn't care nearly enough about blood and gore.''

''And Dick?''

''Dick says this is the fellow who is finally going to

hold the mirror up to the world. Well, I rather doubt it, with a queer name like that. Though you never can tell. Guess what else Toby writes?''

''I give up.''

''You give up entirely too easily,'' said Lucy, and snatched a piece of bacon from him. ''Claudia Moncrief has got betrothed.''

''No! To whom?''

''To a very rich London wine merchant.'' Her green eyes danced. ''By the name of Smith. Master John Smith.''

''A commoner?'' Bram shook his head. ''Honestly, I don't know what is happening in England these days.''

''Disgraceful, isn't it?'' Lucy agreed. ''The old aristocracy is just going to hell in a handbasket.''

''That's tuppence,'' said Bram, and kissed her. ''But it can't get there fast enough for me. Jesus!'' He started, spilling soft-boiled egg all over the blankets, as a loud pounding begin in the room over their heads. ''What the hell is that?''

Lucy held up a finger for him to wait until she swallowed her mouthful. ''Johnny,'' she said finally. ''Putting up a scaffold for the painters.''

''I thought the painters were done,'' Bram said in bewiderment. ''What was there to paint except the ceiling in the receiving room?''

''Stacy is moving into that bedchamber,'' said Lucy, pointing above them, ''and Minnie is going to take my old room.''

''Well, what the devil's the matter with their rooms off the nursery?''

''Nothing,'' Lucy said, ''except that the nursery is going to be awfully noisy.'' She reached for another muffin, and Bram shook his head.

''How can you eat so much, Lucy Carlyle? And why is it going to be noisy in the nursery?''

''Guess,'' she said, devouring the muffin.

''Guess which?''

''Guess both.'' He looked at her blankly. ''Oh, honestly, Bram! Why would it be noisy in a nursery?''

''I'm sure I don't know, unless there was a baby there.''

"Very good, Bram!" she told him, and kissed his cheek. "Would you please pass the jam?"

"Certainly," he said, and then stopped with the jar poised in mid-air. "What did you say?"

"I asked you to pass me the jam."

"No, before that."

"I said, very good. You got the answer to both questions at once—why I'm eating so much and why it will be noisy in the nursery. Because there is going to be a baby."

He dropped the jam jar to the floor. "Oh, Lucy. Oh my God. A baby—are you sure?"

"I went to the midwife in Hucknall yesterday."

"And is she sure?"

"She is. And if you ask me if I'm sure it is yours, Bram Carlyle, I swear I will never speak to you again."

He was still staring at her, his blue eyes wide, afraid to believe. "But—how could that happen?"

"The same way it's been happening ever since Adam and Eve," she said softly, tracing his mouth with her fingertip.

"My God," he said again. "Do you know what this means?"

"I do. That Olive was lying about everything on the night she died. Everything," she repeated, and kissed him. "Are you happy?"

"Happy? I'm—oh, Lucy." Tears streamed down his cheeks, and he buried his face in her hair. "I love you so much!" Then he raised his head. "When, love? When?"

"In June." She watched him try to count backward on his fingers, get muddled, and start again, and she laughed. "Not quite five more months. So I'm four months along."

"Four months—Jesus, why did you wait so long to tell me?" he demanded indignantly.

"I thought surely you would guess by now."

"I didn't think it was possible," he admitted. "What made you so certain it was?"

"The way Stacy scowls when he's angry. How Minnie crinkles her nose when she laughs, just the way you do." She took his hand and laid in on her heart. "The fact that Olive lied about the way you make love."

"Five months—that's hardly any time to wait at all!"

He ran his hand over her belly, his eyes wide with wonder. "What do you think it will be—a boy or a girl?"

"It hardly matters. We already have one of each."

He frowned. "We will have to tell Minnie and Stacy soon, won't we? Do you think they will be upset? After all, they've had everything all to themselves for so long."

"Oh, I don't think so." Lucy pulled a slip of paper from the table beside the bed and handed it to him. "Here."

"What's this?" He unfolded it and stared at the words written there: "Lucy" and "Jim."

"They had a hard time deciding, they told me, but those are their final choices for names."

"When did they give you this?" he asked in amazement.

"On our wedding night."

"And you never said a word to me?"

"I was waiting."

"For what?"

"Proof," she said, her green eyes gleaming wickedly. "You can be just as hard to convince as Elizabeth, you know."

He laughed and pulled her into his arms, knocking over the whole breakfast tray, sending muffins and eggs and butter and milk sailing all over the bed. "You can tell the children Jim is fine if it's a boy, but they will have to pick another name if it's a girl," he whispered.

"And why is that?" she asked, giggling as she brushed crumbs from his chest.

"Because there can only be one Lucy Carlyle in all the world," he said, and made love to her all over again.

Author's Note

The question of what to do about Mary, queen of Scots, plagued Elizabeth I of England through much of her long reign. Though the Elizabethan Age brought unprecedented peace and prosperity to the English people, it was also a time of tremendous social upheaval, as the emerging middle class began to make its power felt. This was a time of religious confusion as well. Elizabeth's father, Henry the Eighth, had effected the break of the Church of England with Rome less than fifty years before. Mary was a Catholic, and many of her supporters were motivated by a sincere desire to see England returned to the papal fold.

Elizabeth's chief ministers, William Cecil and Francis Walsingham, argued with her for years that her throne would never be secure as long as Mary lived. But the queen equivocated for nearly two decades while she continued to give Mary shelter in England, partly because of her horror at the notion of beheading another queen (who also happened to be her cousin) and partly because of her natural aversion to the axe, sharpened by what memories she had of the execution of her mother, Anne Boleyn, by Henry the Eighth.

In desperation, Walsingham finally resorted to stratagem. He planted one of his secret agents as the courier who carried Mary's letters out of Chartley Castle to a young Catholic nobleman named Anthony Babington. The coded letters were secreted in false-bottomed kegs of ale. When the attempt on Elizabeth's life detailed in the letters failed and the plot was revealed through deciphering of the code, Elizabeth was at last convinced to bring Mary to trial. She was convicted of conspiring to cause Elizabeth's death; the evidence was irrefutable, and in Mary's own handwriting.

Still Elizabeth could not bring herself to sign her cousin's death warrant; more than three months were to pass before Mary was at last beheaded at Fotheringay Castle, on the eighth of February, 1587. Her execution was one of the prime factors that set the stage for the launching of the Spanish Armada, the defeat of which in 1588 was the greatest triumph of Elizabeth's reign.

Speaking of the stage, the playhouse built by James Burbage in Shoreditch in 1575 was the first in the City of London; thus it was referred to as *The* Theatre. Though Burbage was famous in his time, his son Dick was to become even more renowned for his portrayals of the heroes and villains in the plays of one William Shakespeare, a player and playwright in his company. James Burbage died in 1597. In 1599, after the failure of a lawsuit against the landlord who held the lease for the land on which The Theatre was built, Dick and his brother Cuthbert pulled down the old Shoreditch playhouse and moved the materials across the Thames to erect The Globe, where many of Shakespeare's plays were to premiere.

Despite her cavalier attitude toward husbands and lovers—the details of her marital escapades given in this book are true—the queen of Scots was inordinately fond of her terriers. A story, probably apocryphal, relates how, on the scaffold after her beheading, one of the tiny dogs scurried out of the voluminous sleeve of her red gown, where it had been hiding in order to stay by its mistress right to the bitter end.

CATHERINE FITZGERALD

CATHERINE FITZGERALD comes from a family of teachers (both parents and two sisters) who let her come to Christmas dinner even though she became a writer instead. Last spring she visited England for the first time; in a London antique shop she met a young woman named Lucy whose cocky Cockney charm inspired her to create the heroine of this book. FitzGerald and her husband live in south Philadelphia in a turn of the century barbershop-turned-house; its huge windows a home to their collection of tropical plants.

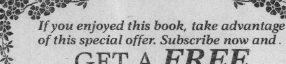

If you enjoyed this book, take advantage of this special offer. Subscribe now and . . .

GET A *FREE* HISTORICAL ROMANCE

——— NO OBLIGATION (a $3.95 value) ———

Each month the editors of True Value will select the four best historical romance novels from America's leading publishers. Preview them in your home Free for 10 days. And we'll send you a FREE book as our introductory gift. No obligation. If for any reason you decide not to keep them, just return them and owe nothing. But if you like them you'll pay *just* $3.50 each and save at least $.45 each off the cover price. (Your savings are a minimum of $1.80 a month.) There is no shipping and handling or other hidden charges. There are no minimum number of books to buy and you may cancel at any time.

send in the coupon below